"ALIANOR—"

She had to say something, tell him to stop, get free of him. Get away. Her mind knew all this but her body seemed to have its own notions. Appalled, she felt herself press yet closer to him as her arms went around his lean waist.

Her head fell back. He made a sound deep in his throat and took her mouth with his. Whereas when he had kissed her in the cottage she had felt his gentleness and above all, his control, this was different. The touch and taste of him engulfed her. Passion, so lightly held in check, ignited like a spark thrown on drought-parched ground. She moaned, clinging to him. Reason dissolved as though it had never been. . . .

Veil
of ❧
Secrets

Maura Seger

A TOPAZ BOOK

TOPAZ
Published by the Penguin Group
Penguin Books USA Inc., 375 Hudson Street,
New York, New York 10014, U.S.A.
Penguin Books Ltd, 27 Wrights Lane,
London W8 5TZ, England
Penguin Books Australia Ltd, Ringwood,
Victoria, Australia
Penguin Books Canada Ltd, 10 Alcorn Avenue,
Toronto, Ontario, Canada M4V 3B2
Penguin Books (N.Z.) Ltd, 182-190 Wairau Road,
Auckland 10, New Zealand

Penguin Books Ltd, Registered Offices:
Harmondsworth, Middlesex, England

First published by Topaz, an imprint of Dutton Signet,
a division of Penguin Books USA Inc.

First Printing, February, 1996
10 9 8 7 6 5 4 3 2 1

 REGISTERED TRADEMARK—MARCA REGISTRADA

Printed in the United States of America

For Katie and Matthew
who always remind me
to leave room for wonder

Chapter 1

They woke to the mist. Conan was up first, unlatching the shutter of the casement window in the room where he had slept poorly and too little. Opening, the shutter creaked. The sound startled the thrushes nesting in the ivy that twined up the old stone walls of the abbey guest house. There was a ruffling of wings and a few irate peeps, little enough against the stillness.

Jesu, it was quiet. The world lay muffled in the fog drifting between sturdy-trunked yew and alder trees, over fields still sered with winter's bracken, along the streams where not days before ice had clung in stubborn chunks, and through the pathways connecting one building of the cloister to another.

It was barely dawn but the day held the promise of warmth, hence the fog. Conan frowned. It would likely linger long. He had the mud to contend with already—that great sucking thing that appeared over all of England at the first hint of winter's end, creeping its way into every nook and cranny. The horses had hard going as it was. The fog would make them anxious, and the journey longer.

He turned back to the room. His squire, young William Blakeston, was still asleep, lying curled on his side with a hand tucked under his chin, the very picture of innocence. Conan kicked him.

It was not a hard kick, just enough to send William leaping off the rush mat, wide-eyed and uncertain. "What—where? Oh, it's you, my lord." He stifled a yawn. "Up already?"

"It's past light," Conan told him. "I'll wager every other squire's been up for hours, polishing armor, caring for the horses." He cast the youth a baleful glance. "Mayhap even arranging his master's breakfast."

"I doubt it," William said, hopping on one foot and then the other as he got into his boots. "I'm like to be the only squire here."

"I meant in the land, dolt. Did you learn nothing at court?"

William's grin deepened. He was the son of Conan's oldest friend, sent to acquire a bit of polish and perhaps even learn a thing or two. At the rate he was going, it wouldn't take long.

"Aye, I learned that a lass with a certain look in her eye will meet me round the back of the stables after vespers. And I learned what to do when she does. Is that what you had in mind?"

Conan sighed. Not for the first time he recalled his duty to marry and sire an heir, a responsibility of ever more pressing significance given the recent expanse of his holdings. The notion of fatherhood could be quelling, at least in so far as he was experiencing it with young William. No wonder Philip Blakeston had leapt at the chance to foster the boy out.

"Not precisely," Conan said. Relenting, he added, "But it's a beginning. Now about that breakfast—"

"Right away," William assured him and thrust open the door. He went pounding down the corridor in a welter of coltish legs, oversize feet, and earnest intentions.

In his absence, Conan dressed, which was to say he put on his own boots and the cloak he had removed the night before, then considered whether or not to shave. The water left in a crockery bowl on a wooden stand was freezing cold. He could call for hot water but that would take time and he was anxious to be back on the road.

Peering in the circle of polished bronze that hung above the basin, he decided he could shave tomorrow. This was not court where certain graces were expected, some of them absurd. He would never, for instance, submit to the curling iron to tame the thick mane of his ebony hair. Rather he would submit to the rack first. This distance from the rarefied air of Westminster Palace, a man could go about looking rough and ready without incurring frowns from the lovely ladies clustered like so many butterflies around the throne.

He smiled at the thought. The ladies of the court could be called butterflies only if nature had taken to crafting those delicate creatures of purest steel. As for the throne— Suffice to say it had not been quite the same since Richard Coeur de Lion had paused barely long enough to say a paternoster at his father's tomb and get himself crowned before departing on Crusade, leaving his beloved mother, the formidable Eleanor, as regent.

Ruler, rather, for she was that in every way that mattered. Woe betide the man who forgot it. Conan did not. He was here, in this fog-drenched abbey miles from the court and his own lands, because Eleanor had bid him there. Or more correctly to Glastonbury, still some distance farther.

He was not a man inclined to dawdle but the knowledge that the Queen awaited news of his progress "most eagerly," as she had said at their final meeting, was more than enough to urge him on.

He went out of the room, his tread ringing on the stone floor worn down by generations of monks, and found William eating breakfast in the refectory. His squire gulped a last mouthful and began hastily flinging bread, cheese, and a flagon of ale into a basket. "I was just coming, Lord."

Conan grunted. The boy was growing, his hunger was constant. Let him eat. As for himself, it was a very long time since he'd been ruled by his appetites. "Never mind, I'll have it here."

William nodded, looking relieved. "Abbot Frey asked if you'd be coming to mass first."

Conan sat down on one of the long benches. "Not today," he said and sank his firm, white teeth into the honey-sweetened bread. He'd yet to find a monastery with bad food and this was no exception. As he ate methodically and without notice except for that first confirming taste, his men began filtering in. There were twelve in all, four of them hardened knights who had been in his service for years, the remainder equally veteran men-at-arms.

One of the knights, Raymond de Langford, approached him. "We go, Lord?"

Conan nodded. "But eat first. I intend to reach Glastonbury before dark."

Raymond made no comment but gestured to the others who made short work of the meal. Abbot Frey could not afford to offend so august a personage as the Baron of Wyndham but neither did he strain to lay an overly generous table. The men were just finishing up, having left scarcely a crumb, when the plump priest bustled in.

"Ah, there you are, my lord," he said, frowning. "I had thought to see you at church."

Conan stood. He was a very large man, well over six feet with the broad shoulders and long, tapered torso of a natural warrior. Added to this formidable aspect were his features, hard-boned, the skin pulled taut, a fitting frame for the unnaturally light blue eyes that looked out at the world with keen intelligence and determination touched by a weariness that was in its own way more frightening than all the rest. A dark man, some called him, dark of hair, dark of mien. Dark, too, of spirit.

His rising was no mark of respect. That he reserved for a very few. It was instead a deliberate act of intimidation. Looming over the abbot, he said, "Did you? And why was that?" His voice was soft, it carried only a little distance in the big room lushly hung with tapestries and fragrant with the scent of new rushes. Yet his men caught his mood and smiled to themselves.

Frey did not. The abbot's jowls bobbed as he swallowed hastily. "I only thought . . . it is customary to take the sacrament especially when journeying."

Conan shrugged. "I do not fear the road. Only a fool would challenge us."

Around him now, preparing to leave, his men nodded. They were all handpicked, the cream of those who had returned with him from Acre and Richard's bloody assault on the Holy Land. Highly disciplined, utterly loyal, they nonetheless did not mind a bit of amusement at the fat priest's expense.

"Only a fool challenges God," Frey declared. He pulled himself up to his full dignity and glared at Conan. But the challenge was fleeting. Barely did he attempt it than some inner voice must have whispered caution.

Deflated, he gathered his richly embroidered robes about him. "As you will, my lord. Good day to you."

Raymond de Langford chuckled. "Forswear, Lord, why do you bother with a sword when all you have to do is look at a man?"

"Fashion?" Conan suggested and took a last swallow of his ale.

They went out into the mist, through the cobbled courtyard with the horses' hooves ringing sharply in the stillness, chickens squawking underneath, children giggling wide-eyed behind their hands, and several rosy-cheeked women waving fondly. Conan never inquired where his men spent their nights so long as they were sharp-witted come morning.

Beyond the abbey's walls, silence descended. There was no sound except the creak of leather cinches on the horses, the jangle of spurs, and the occasional snort of a horse made nervous by the fog. They moved double file with Conan at the head. The road was little more than a wagon-span wide. Horse and man alike sank into mud. It was everywhere, soaking through chausses and braies, flying up to splatter tunics and cloaks, thick, oozing muck, the gift of spring. Conan was resigned to it. The mist worried him more. He could see scarcely more than a few yards in front. Anything or anyone might be lurking behind the ghostly trunks of trees and in the white-shrouded dells along the riverbanks.

He reminded himself that England was at peace or what passed for it in a flawed world. Distracted by the Crusades, shadowed by the memory of a civil war little more than a generation before, the barons stayed to their fires and their hunt, and refrained from making war against each other. They were as tamed stallions bridled with the silk-sheathed steel of the court, their reins held in the most capable hands of Eleanor, she of long experience persuading powerful men to her will.

Conan smiled at the thought. He supposed he was no different from the others although the Queen paid him the compliment of claiming otherwise. She had taken to summoning him late at night to a game of chess. Seated at the small, inlaid table she had carried back from her own Crusade so many years before, she had let it be known that she found his pragmatism refreshing. Devotion wearied her, too many men—and women—had pledged it over too many years. Faith merely made her suspicious. She thought it a convenience behind which all manner of sin could be excused.

And so she had sent him to Glastonbury for no good reason that he could discern but which he was certain must exist. A monk was dead. Hardly a rare occurrence and one scarcely meriting the attention of a baron. He did not for a moment imagine that was all there was to it. Wondering what else might lie behind Eleanor's interest kept his own well occupied as slow mile upon mile dissolved into the mist behind them.

They stopped once for a few scant moments so that the men might relieve themselves, then started up again. Now Raymond de Langford rode beside Conan.

"Shouldn't be much farther," the knight said.

Conan nodded. "If we haven't taken a wrong turn. It's easy enough to do in this cursed weather."

"The men are anxious. They thought the fog would lift by now."

"It clings like this sometimes. They know that."

But in fact the mist was thicker than any Conan had ever seen. Far from fading with the growing day, it seemed to worsen.

"We may have to stop," Raymond said.

Conan shook his head. "The road is clear enough here. We have only to follow it."

The knight was far too well schooled to protest but Conan knew what he was thinking. It was easy enough for the baron to press on, he who seemed unburdened by the dreads that could weigh down ordinary men. For the others it wasn't so simple. The fog might be a sign of . . . anything. God's displeasure, evil spirits, trouble ahead.

Conan smiled faintly. How eager the Church had been to send her sons to the Crusades. Smite the infidel, recover the holy places, and solve the problem of too many armed men with too little to do, all at once. Oh, and gather treasure for the pope who lived as a prince among princes while claiming to be far more.

How unfortunate that there should have been this unexpected side effect of knowledge, rescued from forgotten graves, brought back to lands where the names of Aristotle and Plato had not been heard in centuries, but where, hearing them again, men began to question all manner of things, including their own fears.

Conan's horse shied beneath him. He put out a soothing hand to calm the stallion. "Easy," he murmured, then stopped suddenly, listening.

"Did you hear that?"

Raymond frowned. "Hear what?"

"I thought—" Conan broke off, listening again. His senses strained through the enveloping stillness, past the fretful movements of the horses and men, the drip of water from the hedges, the scurry of a small ground animal. Past all that to find again the sound he had heard.

"That," he said, "listen. There are voices."

Raymond tried but shook his head. He grinned. "I always said you had cat's ears."

For a moment the two men were locked in memory, a moonless night above Acre and the blood-smell of the assassin sent to kill them both, betrayed by a too deep breath or the faintest footfall. Or perhaps merely by the instinct Conan had for cheating death.

The voices grew, sounding at this distance like the faint rumbling of a drum beating against the stillness. Conan stopped, listened.

"I hear it now," Raymond said. "We must be nearing Glastonbury."

"It isn't market day," Conan said.

"Then what—?"

They moved forward to where the road began to widen. Out of the mist a cluster of daub and wattle huts emerged on either side of the road. A hide covering hung over one door twitched at their passing. They did not pause, but moved more quickly, anxious to reach their destination.

And still the noise grew. Voices were raised in an uneasy mixture of anger and exaltation. Conan pressed his heels into the stallion's sides and urged him on. They emerged onto the ground below a sharply rising hill. There were a good number of buildings, many made of stone, arranged along three or four narrow streets. People were hurrying along them, converging on a square at the center of the town.

The crowd parted for Conan and his men, then flowed around and behind them, making an impromptu escort. In the square, Conan drew rein. He looked around, seeking an explanation.

And got it. Two black-cowled monks had hold of a woman. They were trying to drag her up the hill toward the abbey. Some in the crowd were urging them on but most were blocking their way and protesting angrily.

"What is this?" Conan demanded. His voice, deep and strong, roared above the throng. Instantly everyone froze. Except for the woman, who raised her head just then and looked directly at him.

Her face was a pale oval framed by the sides of her sky-blue hood. He could see a wisp of hair touched by fire. She was richly dressed, the fabric of her cloak among the finest he had ever seen and touched at the hem by discreet embroidery. She appeared young, not more than twenty-two or -three. And quite breathtakingly beautiful.

He frowned. What was she? Faithless wife? Town whore, if a highly paid one? Neither seemed to fit. There was a sense about her of quiet self-possession. Despite the obvious intent of the priest, she showed no fear.

He urged his horse nearer. The great stallion pawed the ground not inches from where she stood. Gazing down into eyes green as a summer dell, he said, "Who are you?"

Chapter 2

Everyone began answering at once—the crowd, the priests, everyone except the woman herself. She stood silent, looking at him. Out of the tumult of shouted words, faces pressing close, arms flailing, Conan caught only snatches.

"Witch . . ."

"Healer . . ."

"Alianor the lady . . ."

"The lake . . ."

"The abbot orders . . . !"

This last was from one of the monks who still had hold of the woman. He was a big, burly man, looking better suited to the plow than the altar. His face had reddened with his exertions and he looked suitably concerned by the consequence of the lord who had interrupted them. Still, he stood his ground. "The abbot . . ."

"Which abbot?" Conan demanded, turning to him. He sought quickly in his mind for a name. "Du Sully?"

"Aye, Lord. He suspects the woman of complicity in Brother Bertrand's death. He wants her brought to him for questioning."

"I see . . ." Conan said slowly. He ignored the continued imprecations of the crowd and addressed the woman directly. "I asked you who you are."

Beneath the blue cloak he saw her shoulders

straighten. She faced him directly and without fear. Her voice was soft, melodious, tinged with sadness. "My name is Alianor."

Alianor? Nothing more. No family connection, no place to which she belonged. No husband?

He smiled slightly, pleased despite himself by her courage. Or perhaps by her beauty, for in all truth it flamed like a living thing among the grim visages of the monks and the ordinary people of the town.

"Alianor of Glastonbury then?" he asked, employing that tone of utmost courtesy he used sometimes at court when he particularly wanted something.

The corners of her mouth twitched. What a lovely mouth it was, full and soft, the color of the summer's first roses still many weeks away. He found himself wondering how it would taste.

"They call me Alianor of the Lake," she said, and he rightly took that to mean the townspeople. The crowd had calmed somewhat as they watched the dark, powerful warlord atop his mighty horse conversing with the woman they had sought to save. They pressed closer, not wanting to miss anything. It was a story to be told and retold around the early spring fire, each gesture amplified and every word embroidered.

"Which lake?" he asked.

She gestured vaguely toward the eastern reaches of the town where the River Brue ran. "It is more of a marsh really."

"And that is where you live?"

"I do although I come to town for my work."

"And that would be—"

She hesitated. He could see her choosing her words with care. Finally, she replied, "I have some small skill at healing."

With this, the red-faced monk could bear no more. "She is a witch," he exclaimed, "having dealings with the devil. You imperil your immortal soul by conversing with her. She must be taken to the abbot." He began attempting to drag her off again.

Conan's sword left its sheath so silently there was no warning of its coming. It flashed through the mist-draped air to rest, the point pressed lightly to the monk's throat. "Release her."

The man gave a strangled scream and backed away. Alianor—Alianor of the Lake—stepped free. She looked at Conan quizzically. Above the shouts of the people, he saw her shape the words "Thank you."

"You are welcome," he said gravely and returned the sword to his scabbard. Around him, his men relaxed, if only slightly. They had been prepared to support their lord in anything he chose to do—kill the monk, sack the town, whatever. But all things considered, they preferred not to have to.

Freed from the imminent threat of death, the monk regained a fragment of his courage. Clutching his throat, he said, "You cannot do this. The abbot's orders were clear."

"I will speak with your abbot," Conan said. He could see the townspeople grinning at one another, heads bobbing. Whatever else Du Sully might be, he was not popular. "But later. My men and I are weary. Show us to your guest house that we may refresh ourselves."

Something like satisfaction flitted across the man's face. "There is no such place, not since the great fire seven years ago. What was the guest house has been consecrated to the Lord's service until we can complete the rebuilding."

He spoke as a man embarked on a vast and holy enterprise. As well he might, Conan thought. Richard's Crusade was draining the country of its wealth. There was little coin left over for the rebuilding of an obscure abbey.

"An inn then," he said.

Immediately those nearest in the crowd responded. "The Badger," a gray-haired man cried as a dozen others nodded their approval. "Master Brightersea sets a fine table, he does," a young boy said. He made so bold as to touch Conan's leg. "That way, Lord. I'll show you if you will."

A nod of assent was all that was needed. Even as William scowled at the lad's presumption the crowd was opening a path for them in the direction of the inn. Conan glanced around, intending to tell Mistress Alianor to come along so that he could speak with her at greater length.

But the woman was gone, vanishing into the mist as though she had been no more than a dream.

"Not bad," Raymond said. He wiped the back of his hand across his mouth and sighed with contentment. Conan's men had taken over the main room of the inn. They were sprawled at their leisure on the benches, quaffing ale and looking forward to supper.

Master Brightersea had gone to see to it. Shouts and a great clanking of pots could be heard from the cooking shed out back. The boy who had led them to the inn had remained. He hugged a corner near the door, watchful. Younger than William by a season or two, a few inches smaller, well fed enough by the look of him, and neatly dressed. Conan caught his eye, raised a hand summoning him.

The boy glanced around, as though thinking the signal was meant for someone else. Seeing that it wasn't, he came reluctantly.

"Lord?"

"What is your name?"

"Dermod, sir."

"And who are you, Dermod?"

"I'm an apprentice clerk, milord. I work for the merchant, Master Longueford."

Conan nodded. "Do you like being a clerk, Dermod?"

"It suits me well enough, sir. I like the reading and the figuring."

William snorted. He hovered nearby, the better to overhear. Conan cast him a chiding glance. "So you read and understand numbers as well. Good for you. Was your father a clerk?"

Dermod hesitated. "I don't know, sir."

"I see— How did you come to serve this Master Longueford?"

"The Lady Alianor secured the post for me, sir." Pride crept back into the boy's voice. "She told the master I'd be best for it."

"And he believed her?"

"Oh, yes, sir, of course he did. Hadn't she cured him of the ague only the year before? No one doubts Lady Alianor." He paused a moment, gathering courage, and plunged on. "That's why it's so unbelievable what the abbot's trying to do. How dare he claim she had anything to do with Brother Bertrand's death? She was only trying to help the old man."

"Help him?"

"Aye, he was desperately ill and in terrible pain. She did her best but he was beyond even her skill."

"You have great faith in her."

"I would trust her with my life," Dermod said with all the fervency of youth. Tears shone in his eyes. He blinked them back. "She is the kindest lady in the world."

She was certainly capable of inspiring great loyalty,

Conan thought. "Lady Alianor," he repeated. "How comes she by that name?"

Dermod looked momentarily confused. "She is the Lady."

"Of the Lake?"

"That's right. There's always been one."

Raymond's eyebrows went up. "Fascinating how they still hold to the old ways out here in the west country."

"Isn't it," Conan murmured. Yet something was not right. There were still cunny women aplenty throughout England but they tended to be old and toothless, and to keep to the shadows. They did not go about garbed in rich cloaks with the light of battle in their eyes.

"I would like to speak with her further," he said, careful not to afright the lad. "Where might she be found?"

"Why at the lake, of course, but that won't do you any good."

Jesu grant him patience. "And why not?"

"Because no one can cross the lake without the lady's help, that's why. You'll have to wait until she comes into town again." Kindly, the boy added, "That shouldn't be too long. She comes almost every day."

"Lord—?" Raymond began.

Conan knew what he was about to say. Only give the word and the baron's men would make short work of this lake nonsense. The lady would be brought to his lordship's pleasure, here in the tavern, in the street, wherever he willed it.

"Not yet," Conan said. He had no wish to stir up the townspeople again unnecessarily. Something was afoot here, something that went far beyond the death—murder or otherwise—of a single priest. Something that explained why Queen Eleanor had sent her most trusted baron across the width of England to Glastonbury of the burnt abbey and the beautiful witchy woman.

"I believe I could do with some fresh air before supper," Conan said. He rose.

Instantly his men clambered to their feet. He waved them down again. "I hardly think I need an escort just to view the neighborhood."

They subsided gratefully, all but Raymond, who remained on his feet. "I think I should go with you, Lord. It will be dark soon."

"I prefer to go alone." Conan turned toward the door. Over his shoulder, he said, "Don't wait supper on me. This may take a while."

"If you're not back by nightfall—"

"Go to bed. For God's sake, Raymond, what do you think there is to fear?"

His old comrade-in-arms looked uncertain. "I don't know, sir, but the woman—"

"The lady."

"Aye, that business." He bent his head close to Conan, murmuring, "What if the abbot's right?"

"And she's a witch? Well, then, I assume I will have a most interesting time of it."

Raymond's mouth tightened. "Nothing to joke about, if you ask me."

"Oh, I don't know. The odd thing is I'm finding it amusing."

"Always said you had a strange sense of humor."

"That's true, you always did."

Conan gave the other man a cheerful pounding on the back. William held his cloak. He secured it at the throat and went out into the gathering dusk.

Beyond the inn, the town had quieted. Families were at their cooking fires. He caught the scent of searing meat rising above the usual odors of wood smoke and mud. Pigs rooted in the backyard pens. A woman hummed at her task. Someone laughed—a child by the sound of it—in sheerest merriment.

The fog still clung. He walked round the corner of Master Brightersea's stables and reclaimed his horse. "Sorry, old boy," he murmured as he tossed the saddle on again. "But we've one or two more things to do this day before either of us sleeps."

The stallion nickered softly. They rode out through the narrow rows of houses almost touching at their upper floors, across a small stone bridge that spanned the river on the far side of town, and toward the distant, mist-wreathed marsh.

Chapter 3

Alianor crouched beside the water. Her heart no longer hammered against the cage of her ribs and her breathing had returned to normal. From that, she snatched a few remnants of pride.

Sweet Lord, he had startled her, seeming to appear out of nowhere as he did on that great warhorse, brandishing his sword, putting it at the very throat of poor Brother Raspin. She shook her head, still astounded. Even so, she shouldn't have been, not entirely. Some of what had happened was predictable.

She had always known the risk. Too much healing, too well done, always aroused the suspicion of the Church. Where she saw light, dour-faced men like Abbot Du Sully saw darkness. Where she sought to help, they sought to control.

It was all so unnecessary. She used to ask Matilda to explain why the Church and men were as they were but all Matilda ever said was to keep faith with one's self and bear all things with grace. Certainly, Matilda had done that. When she closed her eyes for the last time five years before, she left the legacy of a life well lived, filled with healing and love.

Alianor missed her still. She wished Matilda was waiting for her right now on the island so that she could tell her all about the dark man on the horse, what he had said and done. They could speculate together over who he might be and, if need be, devise a defense against him.

But Matilda was gone, although there were times when her spirit still lingered among the old hawthorns and wild roses that grew all around the house she and Alianor had shared for so many years.

Alianor could not remember a time before the island. She had known it as a small girl, clambering brown-legged and laughing over the rocks at the water's edge, spying on the larks at their nest building, collecting the plants Matilda taught her to recognize and use. The island had been her life except for the visits into town. At first, those had been very few. As Alianor grew older, Matilda took her with her on her rounds to birth babies and succor the sick, to shop and visit friends, until the town, too, became an ordinary part of life. But the island was home, the source of her strength and her only true comfort.

Cautiously she rose from among the reeds at the edge of the lake. As she had told the dark lord, it was really more of a marsh, fed by hidden streams and underground rivers that came all the way from the sea. Birds normally found along the coast could also be seen there—black-winged gulls, snowy egrets, tall, proud herons. Thick vines hung from the ancient trees. Moss and lichens clung to every rock. Fat bass and trout glinted silver beneath the blue-green water. They came in profusion to this place where no one except Alianor ever fished.

So, too, no one else ever gathered the wild herbs and flowers that grew everywhere around the lake. No one hunted the birds or other animals. Some had become so tame that even now, as she peered through the mist, a doe peered back, watching her from only a few yards away.

Alianor smiled. She judged the moment to be right.

Lifting the hem of her cloak around her ankles, she stepped out onto the water.

Conan went very still. He reined the stallion in and stared in the same direction he had just looked. For a moment he could have sworn—

A flash of light blue appeared among the mist out on the lake. In a heart's beat, the mist parted, just enough for him to catch sight of Alianor.

Alianor. Lady of the Lake. Walking across the surface of the water.

Deep within his soul, in a hidden place he had not heard from in a very long time, something stirred. A hint of dread, a flash of awe-filled fear. Du Sully's accusation, Raymond's worry, Eleanor's mystery, all flowed back with force to make his stomach suddenly feel hollow.

He took a deep breath and shook himself. There had to be an explanation. Most likely, the water was very shallow.

But when he dismounted, tying his horse to a nearby tree, and tried the depth for himself, he quickly sank up to his knees. The ground beneath the lake appeared to slope downward steeply. No one could cross it except by swimming or with a boat.

Alianor had walked across.

She was gone, vanished into the mist, but he was still certain of what he had seen. Slowly he began to walk around the edge of the water until he came to the spot he judged she had begun. Looking carefully, he found a place where the soft, wet dirt bore the imprint of a slender woman's boot.

Again, he tried the water. Again, he sank. Again, the flicker of superstition rose within him. If he had stopped the arrest of a true witch ... if she genuinely had dealings with the devil ... if—

Enough. He silenced his wayward thoughts and considered what to do. He could call to Alianor, tell her he wanted to come over. She must have a boat, however else she was wont to travel.

Or he could return to the village and find a boat there. Except Dermod had said no one ventured out on the lake without the lady's permission. He suspected he would find the townspeople reluctant to assist him.

Or he could cross as Alianor had done.

He walked back to the spot where she had stood, turned, and looked out over the water. The mist was too thick for him to see much, but there, just beyond the edge of the shore, he thought he spied the faintest ripple.

Yes, there it was again. He bent down beside the water and reached out a hand. Immediately beneath the surface, his fingers encountered rock. He straightened and took a step. His foot came down neatly a scant inch or so beneath the surface.

He brought both feet to stand on the rock and looked again. There appeared to be another ripple not far in front. Bearing in mind that he might be about to get a dunking, Conan stepped. His foot passed through the water and instantly encountered rock.

A smile touched his mouth. He looked again, stepped, and found himself just sliding off the edge of yet another stone. Catching his balance, he took a breath and continued. The mist surrounded him. He could no longer see the shore he had left and no island was visible. He had to take it on faith that such a place existed and would in due time emerge. Alone, wreathed in silence with only wit and trust to guide him, he sought his next step.

Alianor sighed with pleasure as she opened the door of the small house. The familiar scents of drying herbs greeted her, mingling with the aromas of fresh rushes, beeswax, and the fragrant lavender soap that was her dearest indulgence.

It was a house uniquely feminine. No shields hung from the walls, no pikes or swords stood close at hand. All was order and light, delicacy interwoven with strength. Yet still very much of this world.

From her perch beside the window, Mirabelle rose, stretching languidly. The cat, a large orange tabby, yawned.

"I'm late, I know," Alianor said. She hung her cloak on a peg and shut the door behind her. Going over to the embers of the peat fire, she poked them back to life. When she had thrown a few extra pieces of turf on the fire, she sought her pantry. Mirabelle followed, brushing against her legs in the way cats have.

"Go away with you," Alianor said, laughing. "It's only fish you're after."

Mirabelle yawned again, not attempting to deny it. She sat down and began to wash a paw as though the whole matter was of no concern to her. But she was watching keenly as Alianor took a piece of dried trout from a basket and cut it into tiny morsels. With a bound, the cat leapt onto the wooden table and began making short work of her meal.

"Glutton," Alianor said affectionately. She wiped her hands off and went to check the bread she had left baking in the brick oven behind the chimney. It was overdone, her stay in town having taken far longer than she'd expected. With a sigh, she tossed it outside for the animals to find.

At least the soup she had left in a kettle over the low fire needed only a few stirs before it looked edible. She'd make bread again tomorrow and hopefully this time be home to see it out of the oven on time.

Fortunately, she wasn't very hungry. The events in

town had robbed her appetite. She could be sitting right now in the abbot's prison, waiting trial for murder—or witchcraft. She might yet be unless she found some way to soothe the situation.

With a sigh, she decided it would be better to eat later. In the meantime she had work to do. The new ointment she was trying for skin disorders seemed to be effective. She needed a larger supply.

Pushing up her sleeves, she took a seat at the wooden stool in front of her worktable. On a clear day, natural light flowed through the windows just above it. But with the mist so thick, she lit several of the wicks floating in bowls of oil.

Mirabelle, her meal finished, took up her position on the windowsill, the better to observe the activities. She licked the last traces of fish from her mouth delicately as Alianor began to crush clay in a mortar. The consistency of the clay was important. It had to be ground as fine as possible or the ointment would not adhere.

Concentrating, she was only distantly aware of the muted sounds coming from the trees beyond the house. They were so much a part of her life that she did not attend them. Even the sudden reverberation of water splashing only brought her head up slightly. She assumed a branch had broken off into the lake.

Not until the splash was followed by a hearty curse did she realize that she was no longer alone.

Disbelief flowed through her. She could not remember a time when anyone had come to the island without her foreknowledge and permission. Yet if the stream of invective puncturing the misty silence was any indication, that was exactly what had happened.

Quickly she stood up and made for the door. Behind her, Mirabelle arched her back and hissed. The sun wreathed in cloud was sliding away to the west when Alianor stepped out of her house. She could barely see a few yards away. The trees she knew as well as her own hand were invisible. The shore had vanished.

She grabbed the torch kept ready in a recess beside the door and struck tinder to it. Instantly the pitch-soaked tip flared. Brandishing the torch, both light and weapon, she called through the swirling fog. "Who's there?"

No answer came except the crashing of what sounded like something very large through the underbrush and yet another muttered curse. She took a breath, considering her alternatives. The man—for that he clearly was—was angry but that didn't mean he was necessarily dangerous. She should wait, do nothing, until he had a chance to explain himself.

Yet for all her reasoning, fear curled through her as she saw the large, dark shape taking form through the gloom, coming steadily toward her.

Conan looked up. He was soaking wet, he'd tripped twice in the damn vines that seemed to curl everywhere, and he'd managed to bash his head on a low tree limb. The fog that had been his downfall, causing him to slip off the rocks, still surrounded him. He could see nothing, hear nothing, except—

Wait, what was that, above the sound of the water lapping against the rocks and the whisper of air in branches just coming into bud? A voice?

"Who's there?"

Ah, a voice indeed, and a woman's at that. He turned in the direction. Through the enveloping mist, he caught a flicker of fire. Instinctively his right hand went to the hilt of his sword. A moment later he emerged from the thicket into what appeared to be a clearing. Just ahead, he could make out a house. And standing before it—

His throat tightened. He was looking at an apparition, floating like a slim white candle tipped by fire.

Even as he felt the hollow place within him open again, reason reasserted itself. "Mistress Alianor?"

"Sir—?"

The doubt in her voice made him feel obscurely better. He came closer. At a distance of only a few yards, he could see that she had put off the blue cloak. She wore a pure white tunic, long-sleeved and with a modest neckline but closely fitted to a figure that was merely exquisite. Her head was uncovered, revealing a blaze of hair almost as bright as the torch she held.

"I am Conan," he said, "Baron of Wyndham. We met in town."

Her eyes were wide as the deep pools of a desert oasis. She took a step nearer, appeared to think better of it, and stopped. "How did you come here?"

"The same way you did except I slipped toward the end and had to swim for it." He sounded as disgruntled as he felt but his mood brightened when he saw her shock.

"You couldn't have."

"Why not?" He came nearer, pleased that she did not try to retreat but held her ground, watching him with the close attention he would give a dangerous animal.

"No one ever has."

He grimaced and wrung the water from his cloak. It did little good. Water sloshed in his boots, matted his tunic and chausses, and dripped off his hair onto his nose.

"More fool them," he said. When she continued to look at him in disbelief, he added, "I saw you."

"Saw me—?"

"Crossing the water. That rock bridge, footpath, whatever, is ingenious."

Alianor cleared her throat. She lowered the torch a notch. "How did you find it?"

"I looked, of course, after I saw you."

"You didn't assume my crossing as I did was ... magical?"

Not for the world would he admit that the thought had occurred to him, if only for an instant. "No, I didn't. Should I have?"

"No, but most people would have."

"Then I suppose that means I'm different. I'm also drenched. Would it be possible for me to dry off before we continue our conversation?"

The request, presented with sardonic courtesy, made her hesitate. For reasons he did not care to examine, it suddenly mattered that she accept his presence of her own will.

Her head tilted slightly to one side. Firelight danced in the red-gold glow of her hair. Tendrils of pitch-dark smoke rose from the torch, staining the enveloping mist.

When she turned, the graceful flow of her skirt revealed long, slender legs. He was sufficiently distracted by them not to notice her extinguish the torch in a nearby pile of sand and replace it in the bracket beside the door.

She folded her hands gracefully, took a breath, and looked at him. "Come in."

Chapter 4

The door lintel was low enough that Conan had to bend his head to keep from hitting it. He straightened just inside the cottage and took a long look around.

It was a woman's place. That much was evident at first glance. Indeed, with the exception of a few solars he had been in, he could not remember a place more clearly stamped with the personality of a woman.

No weapons were in view. No war banners were proudly displayed. No hunting dogs trawled underfoot. There were no bloody joints of meat to be sniffed, no barrels of ale ready to hand. In short, none of the trappings of a man's world, which was to say the world in general.

This was someplace altogether different, this misty isle to which he had come a clumsy and not especially welcomed stranger.

So be it. He was not without experience with women. From whore to queen, he had known and appreciated many. How different could the beguiling Alianor be?

"You're very muddy," she said and frowned with housewifey intent.

Of course he was muddy. He'd fallen in the damn lake. "I'm also soaked," he said, ever helpful, and then on a whim of mischief, "You have a blanket, I presume?" He began to unfasten the leather belt around his waist.

She did not so much as blink, this infuriating creature of the mist. "Of course. I'll hang your clothes by the fire. Will you have a bit of soup while they dry?"

Turning back not being an option, he looked around for some place he might disrobe with a modicum of privacy. A cat rose suddenly from beside the hearth, wiggled her whiskers, and looked at him with wry amusement.

"Yours?" he asked, gesturing at the feline.

"Mirabelle. Here's your blanket."

It was the first rose-colored blanket he'd ever seen and so soft it might have been spun from petals.

He hesitated. She saw and smiled much as the cat had done. Her green eyes flashed in the firelight. "The small room is that way."

Conan went, bending low again beneath rafters hung with drying herbs. The small room was just that, a second chamber much smaller than the main part of the cottage and, he guessed, somewhat older. A single window looked out toward a twilight-gray garden. There were pegs on the walls and a small table that contained a bowl of fragrant herbs, several soft lengths of toweling, and a basket with balls of soap.

He stepped forward only to stop when he realized that a good part of the floor was taken up by a stone-lined depression large enough to hold a good-sized person. It took him a moment to realize what he was seeing and then he only did so because he recognized the contrivance from similar ones he had observed—and used—in the Holy Land.

Here in this rustic cottage in the back of beyond was a luxury rare even in the most luxurious residences of the nobility—a bath. And not of the tin variety that had to be hauled up castle steps and laboriously filled by relays of servants before being used by a shivering aristocrat, his pale nudity adorned by goose bumps. Rather one always available and filled—how?

Conan bent and carefully removed the plug in the side of the stone basin. Immediately hot water with a slightly mineral aroma began to flow in. He replaced the plug but looked at the tub a moment longer, thinking of the hot spring that must flow directly beneath. Such places were wreathed in legend and lore far older than the word of Christ himself. Was it mere coincidence that Alianor's cottage was built on such a site?

The temptation to try the tub for himself was great but he contented himself with stripping off his muddied garments. With the blanket secured around his waist, he returned to the main room. His hostess was at her fire, stirring the fragrant contents of a pot.

She looked up, saw him, and—did he imagine it?—reddened slightly. In the shadows it was hard to tell. Drying her hands on the apron tied around her slim waist, she said, "Give me the clothes. I'll hang them up for you."

He watched her do so, enjoying the grace of her movements and not at all displeased that his semi-nakedness had shaken her composure, if only a small amount. Sangfroid of the sort he sensed in Alianor was rare in a woman. Where it existed at all, it tended to be earned over a long life spent in the bearing and raising of many sons. As far as he was concerned, that was how it should remain. In a woman of Alianor's youth and beauty, such self-possession hinted at a certain dismissiveness toward the proper consequence of men.

"Thank you," he said gravely when she had finished hanging his clothes.

Ladling soup into bowls, she replied, "Not at all. It is I who must thank you. If you hadn't interceded in town today, I fear I would be the abbot's guest rather than you mine, and that under rather different circumstances."

Since she had raised the subject herself—more or less—Conan felt no compunction about pursuing it. "How did the priest die, that you are suspected in his death?"

Alianor handed him a bowl of soup. It smelled of chicken, herbs, and various other things he couldn't quite identify. Belatedly, he realized that he was ravenously hungry.

"Brother Bertrand was poisoned," she said and offered him a spoon.

He was by far the most compelling man she had ever seen. Glancing at him through the veil of her lashes, Alianor marveled that so much beauty could have been bestowed on one individual. She almost smiled at the thought, for surely Conan himself would have scoffed at it. Yet beautiful he was with that symmetry of features and perfection of body the ancient Greeks had so struggled to capture.

She knew about them as she knew of so much else from the stories Matilda had told her, handed down through uncounted generations of women, and, too, from newer stories brought by travelers who had seen such marvels with their own eyes.

Yet for all that he was more than marble shaped by a vision of physical perfection. There was a powerful spirit here, grounded in keen intelligence and a will so strong she could not quite quell a tiny spurt of fear when she thought of what it would mean to challenge him.

Even as she was doing now, spurred on by the wicked bent for mischief that had been with her since earliest childhood. *Asking for trouble,* Matilda had called it and warned where it might lead. Brother Bertrand's death was serious—and tragic—business. She had no call to make anything else of it.

"At least, I believe he was poisoned," she amended. "I can't be sure. He was very elderly and it's possible there was another cause. However, his symptoms do support the idea of poison."

"I see," Conan said slowly. "And Du Sully thinks you administered this poison?"

"So it seems."

"What reason would you have had?"

She turned back to the fire to fill her own bowl. "None. Brother Bertrand was a good man, devout in his beliefs but genuinely kind. I did everything I could for him. Unfortunately, it wasn't enough."

"You know a great deal about medicines then?"

"I'm not sure anyone knows a great deal. Much remains to be discovered."

"Even so, you are skilled in the use of herbs?"

"I have some knowledge," she admitted.

"It isn't unheard of for a healer to ease the suffering of a patient who is going to die anyway."

Alianor sat down on a stool facing the one Conan occupied. Her hands were steady around the bowl despite the shock she felt at his frankness. Worse was the realization that she cared what this man thought of her and not merely because of the protection he had offered. Other, deeper forces were at work. "Are you suggesting I hastened Brother Bertrand's death?"

"I'm simply trying to understand what Du Sully may be thinking. There are drugs given to ease pain that with the slightest miscalculation will bring death instead."

"Do you know of such things or are you merely repeating rumors you've heard?"

"Henbane, for one. Foxglove, for another, and there are more."

She stared at him, her thoughts in confusion. Men did not know of such things. Cautiously, so cautiously, she asked, "You have been taught?"

"Not really. I learned a thing or two from my mother. Enough at least to understand that women with such skills are not necessarily in league with the devil."

"Du Sully believes otherwise." Even as she spoke, she wondered at the broadness of his mind, so rare among men of power and authority who tended to see the world along much more rigid lines. She had been right to think him intelligent.

"Your mother, the baroness—?"

She had heard the whispers in the town after he sent Brother Raspin packing. Baron of Wyndham. Confidant of the King. Warrior and Crusader rising to ever greater power fueled by his own ruthless will.

"My father was landed," he said, "but not a baron. The King made me that."

But what had made him willing to consider that witchcraft might not be the explanation for every woman with a bit of skill and knowledge? Curiosity about him surged within her. She forced it back.

"Congratulations. As to the rest, you are right, there are drugs that can kill as well as heal but I administered none of them to Brother Bertrand. Besides, he had symptoms of poisoning when I was first called to his side."

"And they were?"

"Pain in the lower regions, vomiting, lassitude. Toward the end, the slightest touch was enough to raise bruises on him. He was bleeding internally."

"But you say there could have been some cause other than poisoning?"

Alianor shrugged. "Could have been. As I said, he was elderly. At first, I considered a possible putrefication. That can happen sometimes without any outwardly cause. But as he worsened, I came to suspect poisoning. Lacking study of the body after death, there is no way to truly determine what killed him."

Conan frowned. "Study? You don't mean what the heathens do—?"

She had slipped, saying that. For a moment she had allowed herself to forget who and what he was. A small note of exasperation crept into her voice. "Yes, I do. By refusing to study the human body, we throw away the best chance we have of understanding it better."

"You don't consider such practices desecration?"

"No more so than what happens on the average battlefield. More soup?"

He looked at her for what seemed like a long time. She refused to flinch. He was a man of patience, this big, battle-hardened warrior sitting all but naked in her cottage. And he knew how to use silence.

"Thank you," he said finally.

She took it as a small victory and smiled. "The bread was overbaked but there is cider and cheese."

He accepted both. She noted that his manners were excellent. He had been well schooled. The mother, again? Or had other feminine influences affected him along the way?

"Your lady wife must worry about you so far from home," she said.

He took a long swallow of cider and answered at his leisure. "I have no wife."

"Forgive me. I assumed most men of your age and position were wed."

Perhaps she had died. That might account for the remorseless hardness she sensed in him.

"I have never had time to marry," he said, disabusing her of that notion.

"Too busy fighting?"

"Among other things. If we might return to Brother Bertrand, can you think of anyone who would want to kill him?"

He had a stubborn interest in the monk. That was gratifying in a way for she would have truly liked the murderer brought to justice, or what passed for it in the England of this day. Yet it seemed out of place in a warlord who was—presumably—just passing through.

"Why did you come here?" she asked, realizing that she might have wondered sooner.

"Let's take my question first. Who were his enemies?"

"He had none."

"Clearly he did if he was murdered."

It was a valid point. "You could be right," she conceded, "but it's hard to imagine. He was a good man."

"Devout in his beliefs, you said, *but* genuinely kind. Why not *and* genuinely kind?"

Alianor weighed her words before speaking, not always an easy task for her but a necessary one when confronted by the Baron of Wyndham. That much she had learned already.

"In my experience, devoutness is seen too often as an end in itself."

"Rather than as a means to good works?"

"Yes. Brother Bertrand truly cared about the poor. He treated them with dignity and through his quiet example he encouraged the more fortunate to share. He was never hypocritical or self-righteous. As far as I could see, he genuinely lived his faith."

"How did he and Du Sully get along?"

"Perhaps it would be better to ask the abbot that. Besides, it's my turn to have a question answered. Why have you come here?"

Something moved behind his eyes. He set his food

aside and stood—tall, broad, heavily muscled, a half-naked, overwhelmingly male presence. His hair, dark as midnight, fell to his shoulders. His skin was bronzed by firelight. A smile curved the hard corners of his mouth.

"Why to meet you, of course," he said and held out a hand in a gesture that was both invitation and command.

Chapter 5

Alianor stood, but warily. She did not take his hand. After a moment he let it drop but his eyes never left hers.

"It will be dark soon," she said. "I believe your clothes are dry enough."

"I'm not sure I can find my way back across the lake."

He could see the hesitation in her. She wanted him gone, wanted her island to herself again. But she was also a woman of innate courtesy and—he thought—honor.

"I will guide you," she said at last and went to get her cloak.

Conan dressed again in the small room. He took a final look around at the gracious appointments, even pausing to sniff several of the small soaps. They smelled of a warm summer day. He imagined the scent on Alianor's skin and felt his body harden.

With a wry shake of his head, he emerged to find her waiting for him. Outside, it was almost night. The mist had all but evaporated. A full moon was rising, casting a ribbon of silver from sky to earth.

"This way," Alianor said. She left the torch beside the door. In the bright light of the moon, it wasn't needed.

Conan followed. A narrow path led from the cottage to the shore of the lake.

"Is this the way I came?" he asked.

Alianor's voice was hushed in the stillness. "No. Although we're fairly far inland, this lake is affected by the tides. Right now, the stone bridge isn't usable. We have to go another way."

They reached the water's edge. Except for the ripple of tiny waves against the shore and the far-off cry of an owl, it was very quiet. Where the tide had filled a small pool, a curragh bobbed.

Alianor lifted her skirts, giving him a glimpse of trim ankles and slender calves, and stepped into the pool. She easily maneuvered the hide-covered boat toward the deeper water of the lake.

"I think you should get in first," she said.

He did so, gingerly. The vessel rocked wildly under his weight but he found his balance quickly enough. Alianor followed and took a seat behind him. With a start, he realized that she intended to row.

"I'll do that."

She looked surprised by the offer. "Thank you but it isn't necessary. I do this all the time."

"Nonetheless, give me the oars." Without waiting for her compliance, which he doubted would have been forthcoming anyway, he took them from her and slid them into the locks beside him. With long, powerful strokes, he rowed them out onto the lake.

Alianor sat very still. He could feel her looking at him. By moonlight, her face was a pale oval surrounded by dark fire.

"Is this chivalry?" she asked.

His laughter rang against the breathless quiet of the lake. "You make it sound terrible. I thought women approved of chivalry. Men like myself are supposed to be spending our days strumming the lute and composing romantic ballads, aren't we?"

The notion wrung a smile from her. He counted it a victory.

"I don't much see you strumming."

"It's not a great strength of mine," he acknowledged, "but what's wrong with chivalry?"

"It's a mime play. Oh, the motions are there all right but it's just trickery."

"I disagree. Do you honestly believe that Eleanor would be regent of England right now if she hadn't spent her life so successfully promoting the idea that men should defer to women?"

Alianor scoffed. "Richard left her as regent because she's the only person he can trust. Give him credit, he's smart enough to know that at least."

Conan rested the oars. He let the curragh drift a little as he considered what she had just said. Fair Alianor lived on a mysterious island hidden away in the back of nowhere yet she seemed unusually well informed about the larger world.

Resuming rowing, he asked, "How do you know so much about royal affairs?"

"Everyone talks. You hear this and that."

He supposed that was possible. She went into the town a great deal. There was nothing especially interesting about Glastonbury but it got its share of travelers passing through—merchants, peddlers, priests, students, the occasional playing troupe. They would be bound to air their views in the tavern and the street.

And yet she had spoken of Richard almost with familiarity as though his bold, brash—and not especially bright—nature was well known to her. Hinted, too, at his deepest fear that the family of ravenous eaglets spawned by great Henry and his Eleanor would ultimately turn on itself in a frenzy of self-destruction.

But that was impossible. She could not really know of such things.

The boat bumped lightly against the opposite shore of the lake, jarring him from his uneasy thoughts. He got out swiftly and was helping her do the same when a sudden sound brought him upright, hand on his sword.

"Lord," Raymond said as he emerged from the shadows of the trees. His tone was filled with relief. "We found your mount but there was no sign of you."

Conan scowled but he couldn't really muster anger. It was his liegeman's duty to concern himself with the safety of his lord.

Even so, he said, "I thought I told you and the others to remain at the inn?"

Another of his knights appeared, holding the reins of Conan's stallion. Both men looked at Alianor, then quickly looked away.

"Your pardon, Lord," Raymond said. "But in a strange place and uncertain as we were of your whereabouts, we thought—"

Conan raised a hand, forestalling him. "Enough." He turned to Alianor and spoke softly. "Can you get back all right?"

He half expected a tart reply, something about her being well accustomed to managing for herself. But instead she merely nodded. She even allowed him to assist her back into the curragh. He gave her a push-off and watched until she had vanished into the deep shadows at the center of the lake. The suddenness of their parting left him dissatisfied, as though something should have been said—or done—that had not been. He disliked how swiftly she could go from him.

Raymond looked at him cautiously. "All is well, Lord?"

"Yes, of course." He took the reins and mounted in

a smooth motion that belied his frustration. His body ached, not with the weariness of the road but with quite a different sort of discomfort. Witch or not, Mistress Alianor seemed able to transform him back into the randy young man he had been a decade before. He could not say that he enjoyed revisiting that particular aspect of his youth.

By the time he and his men reached the inn, the townspeople were all abed. A few dim lights—the odd candle or banked fire—shone behind shuttered windows, but otherwise there was no life to be seen.

"Different from London," Raymond murmured.

Conan grunted in assent. They drew rein at the stables behind the inn and dismounted. Conan could have left his own mount to be cared for by the knights but the thought never occurred to him. He had tried over the course of his life to refrain from becoming too attached to any particular horse. After losing a favorite gelding in a battle when he was sixteen, he had steeled his heart and tried to see the animals as mere transportation. But he was only partly successful. His stallion, called Gray, should have been reserved for war but he had an unusually congenial temperament and Conan enjoyed his company.

For that reason, and because of the simple sense of duty so long ago imbued in him, he saw to the animal's needs himself. When all three horses were brushed, fed, and watered, the men were free at last to seek their own rest.

"There is food, Lord," Raymond said. "The innkeeper produced a fair joint and we kept some aside for you."

"Thank you, but I ate with Mistress Alianor."

Raymond nodded. He looked inclined to inquire what that had been like—and perhaps other things—but had far too much sense to do so.

A room had been prepared for Conan at the top of the stairs. It was a simple chamber lacking the private chimney that had become fashionable but warmed all the same by a copper brazier well stocked with glowing embers. There was even water that had been hot not too long ago and was still pleasantly warm.

He stripped off his clothes and, standing naked on the rushes, washed himself, all the while thinking of how good it would feel to loll in Mistress Alianor's mineral bath—with her for company, of course. It was big enough to hold two given a little careful maneuvering.

Amused by his own stubborn lust, he intended to put aside such thoughts as he lay down on the narrow bed. As these things went, it was comfortable with a straw-filled mattress, a bolster filled with down, and a wool blanket. He had slept on far worse in his time without noticing. But now he found himself thinking of that petal-soft rose blanket Alianor had given him and wondering if it covered her when she slept.

He sighed, folding his arms behind his head, and stared up at the rough-hewn roof. It was the way of the world that a man of his position did not lack for women. He accepted that, even as modesty prevented him from acknowledging that his own appearance and manner had a great deal to do with his popularity among the fair sex. He satisfied his needs as a matter of course and without concern for the teachings of the Church, which he regarded as unrealistic. Had the Almighty not wanted man to lust after women, presumably He could have designed him differently.

All that taken into account, he was thinking far too much about Mistress Alianor. Yes, she was beautiful. Yes, her mystery sparked his interest in a way that women generally did not. But he had come to Glastonbury at the behest of his Queen. He had a mission to fulfill—whatever it might really be—and once it was done, he would return to London, to the court, to all the tumult of the world that was his own.

Having clarified all that to his satisfaction, he settled himself more comfortably in the expectation of sleep.

It did not come.

He, who had slept soundly on the eve of battles that had other men wide-eyed with fear, could not still the wayward course of his thoughts or the vividness of his imagination. He saw Alianor, standing straight and slim in the pure white tunic, holding the torch aloft. Saw her again unflinching when he began to strip, daring his masculine superiority. Alianor bending to fill a bowl with fragrant soup, tilting her head slightly to one side as she spoke of Brother Bertrand, disputing him for the oars.

She was a woman of strength and pride who put him in mind of his own mother—although his mother was by far a gentler creature—and most particularly of Eleanor. Alianor and Eleanor. They were entwined in his mind, linked somehow. The one so aged and revered, yet still with the great beauty that had made so many hapless men her slaves. And Alianor, young, on the verge of her life, perhaps not yet realizing the extent of her powers.

Yet surely they had nothing in common beyond that similarity of their names. He opened his eyes suddenly, hardly aware that he had been dozing. Eleanor and Alianor. It was the same name, the first in the anglicized version, the second of the older form. But the same nonetheless.

Coincidence, nothing more. One was a queen and ruler, a woman of legendary proportions whose arena was politics and war, the fate of nations. The other remained hidden away in a mist-wreathed island, content—wasn't she?—to do good works.

Eleanor and Alianor. What linked them? Except for himself, of course, sent by Eleanor, finding Alianor.

Coincidence.

The word tumbled through his mind. At length, he slept and in that realm of dreams heard laughter and saw—ever before him, just tantalizingly out of reach—the flash of fire-bright hair.

Someone was banging on his door. Conan woke slowly. Accustomed to being instantly alert, he felt groggy and out of sorts.

"Who's there?"

His tone should have been enough to discourage any but the heartiest. William must have inherited his father's steely mettle for he persevered.

"The abbot wishes to see you, milord. He's sent a message."

Grumbling, Conan rose. His young squire inched the door open and peered at him warily. He held a basin from which steam rose. "I've brought water, Lord."

Such evidence of William's industry provoked a look of surprise from Conan. He stretched, yawned, scratched reflectively. "What prompts this sudden devotion to your duties?"

"Lord?" The pose of wide-eyed innocence held for perhaps a heartbeat, no more. William shrugged, looking embarrassed. "It's an hour past dawn. You never sleep this late and with your visit to the island yesterday, I was worried—"

"Thought I might have turned into a toad or something similar in my sleep?"

William grinned, more his old self. "Well, maybe not a toad but the lady could have put a sleep on you. Remember that masque we saw the players do in Aquitaine? The one about the princess sleeping for a hundred years?"

Conan dunked his head in the water. The sting of it made him feel better.

"Frippery," he said as he dried his face. Damned if he'd shave for Du Sully.

"Queen Eleanor liked it."

True enough. Eleanor liked all such things. She was patroness to uncounted players and mimes, musicians and troubadours, acrobats, jugglers, jesters, and even the occasional bard, wandering down from the Welsh hills or out of Ireland, to declaim on ancient glories. The Church muttered against such things but Eleanor ignored that. She went her own way.

"Would it be possible to find a clean cotte?" Conan inquired.

With a flourish, William produced one. He even managed to conjure fresh braies and a sherte of finely woven wool.

Conan dressed silently. His clothing was of the finest in material and tailoring but plainer than most men of his class. That was how he preferred it. The neckline of his cotte was only modestly embroidered. Beneath it, the silk sherte was barely visible. He drew on leather boots polished to a high gloss and was done.

Except for the short dagger girdled around his waist. He didn't think Du Sully merited his sword.

Raymond awaited him at the bottom of the stairs. He gestured to two sour-faced monks lurking by the door to the inn.

"He sent an escort."

Conan shook his head, amused. He ignored the monks and helped himself to breakfast. The bread was sweet with a flaky crust. There was cheese and small smoked fish. Master Brightersea himself appeared with a flacon of cider.

"I hope everything is satisfactory, my lord."

"Perfectly."

The innkeeper beamed a smile, looked immensely relieved. Conan set his goblet down, wiped his mouth, and went out into the sunlight and the day.

Raymond followed. The rest were scattered between the inn's main room and the stables. They could be assembled in a moment should the need arise.

The street was busy. Several women walking by paused to look at him, then speeded up. Safely past, they bent their heads together, whispering. One, more daring than the others, stole a quick glance back and smiled.

A boy slouched along, urging several sheep in front of him. He gazed at Conan as he might a being from the netherworld and slapped his stick against the sheep's rumps to urge them on.

The air smelled of wood smoke and the usual effluvia of human habitation. They rounded a corner and saw, on the hill rising above them, the abbey. Or what was left of it.

"Must have been rather grand before that fire," Raymond said.

Conan nodded. The hill was flattish at the top, almost as though a giant hand had come along and swiped part of it off. There was ample space for a large building but all that was left was one modest wing.

"Any idea how it happened?" he asked.

"Master Brightersea said the abbey was struck by lightning nigh on seven years ago now."

"And what did the townspeople think of that?"

"Master Brightersea was far too discreet to say," Raymond replied. "However, I'd wager the abbot isn't loved. Efforts to fund the rebuilding have met with scant response from the locals."

"They're already bled white for Richard and the Crusade. Tax them further to rebuild an abbey they don't seem to miss for an abbot they dislike and there's likely to be rebellion."

Raymond nodded. "These be crown lands, are they not?"

They were climbing the hill. Conan paused to look back toward the town. Smoke rose in leisurely wreaths from several dozen chimneys. For all the harshness of royal taxes, Glastonbury looked to be a prosperous enough place. Seen from on high, as it were, that was clearer than before. It was also unusual in this time and place, in an England racked by changing dynasties and rapacious overlords.

"They are," he said as they resumed walking again. The monks trailed behind, still sour-faced, holding their long brown robes up out of the mud.

"An old Saxon family held them for time uncounted," Conan continued. "They passed to the crown with King William."

The Conqueror had parceled out no more of his war plunder to his followers than he'd absolutely had to. Much had been kept for himself and his heirs. In that, as in so many other things, he had shown unusual foresight. Few of those who came after him inherited even a portion of his talents.

"Eleanor said nothing about rebuilding the abbey," Conan said. He spoke almost to himself, musing over what the Queen had left out. These were, to all intents, her lands. In Aquitaine, she ruled generously, ever ready to help out as needed. Did Glastonbury benefit from the same kindness, and if so, why was the abbey neglected?

He had questions but no answers. Perhaps Du Sully could provide some.

The one remaining structure of the abbey appeared to have been a comfortable guest house. It was a long, narrow building, the wood on one side still showing signs of charring. A monk opened a side door and stood aside to admit them.

Du Sully awaited them in a small chamber adjacent to the improvised chapel. He sat behind a massive table in a chair that might have better suited a king.

He did not rise as they entered but merely frowned and continued reading the parchment in front of him for several moments, as though he were still alone.

Raymond glared. He looked to Conan for direction. Du Sully continued reading.

Conan walked forward, across the flagstone to stand before the table. Raymond followed.

Du Sully read.

Conan lifted one corner of the table. Raymond lifted the other. Together, they flipped it over and dropped it, crashing, onto the floor.

"God in heaven!" Du Sully jerked backward with great force. His chair rocked, teetering on two legs, almost rebalanced but could not quite. It, too, crashed. Splinters of wood shot in all directions. The abbot landed on his back, arms and legs flailing, red-faced with disbelief.

Gasping for breath, he scrambled to his feet and came at Conan. "How dare you! You . . . you infidel! My God, I'll—"

Some instinct for survival, not quite missing from the good abbot, sprang to action belatedly. He stopped, his eyes suddenly focused on the position of Conan's right hand, atop his dagger hilt.

Chest heaving, he looked from one man to the other. Raymond did not engage in such niceties as daggers. Nor did he wait. His sword was already drawn, ready to taste blood.

"Lord?" Raymond asked, calmly but with a certain note of eagerness.

His meaning could not have been clearer. The merest

word or gesture on Conan's part and the abbot would die.

"Hold," Conan said. He took his own hand from the dagger and glanced at the half-dozen monks who were gathered at the chamber door, watching with horrified fascination. The flick of his attention was enough to scatter them. Only one lingered, a young man, well built, with the gleam of intelligence in his eyes. Then he, too, withdrew but not before Conan thought he glimpsed a sardonic smile.

"There seems to have been an accident with your furnishings," he said, as though calling to the abbot's attention a circumstance he would not have noticed for himself. "No matter. I'm sure your men can put it to rights after we've left. Now what was it you wanted to see me about?"

Du Sully seemed to still be having trouble breathing. He was a thin man with a pale, austere face that might have been handsome had it been animated by something other than resentment. With an effort, he dragged his chair upright but did not make the mistake of sitting again in Conan's presence. Instead, he leaned against it.

"Your soul," Du Sully said and straightened his thin shoulders. "If you have a care for it, you will bend your pride." He stared at Conan with malicious satisfaction. "You stand in mortal peril, my fine lord, and only I can save you."

Chapter 6

"I don't think there's anything more to worry about," Alianor said. She replaced the baby's swaddling clothes gently and handed him to his mother. "His breathing has cleared and there's no sign of fever now. Just keep him warm and make sure he's getting his milk."

She rose and fastened her cloak on. "If he should stop nursing again, don't delay sending for me but I really think the worst is over."

The child's mother, a brewer named Eustacia, nodded gratefully. "Thank you, milady. I truly feared to lose him."

Alianor gave her a reassuring smile that masked her own sense of relief. Little Brandon had suffered an inflammation of the chest at barely eight weeks of life that might have killed him. But he was a sturdy baby and the treatment Alianor tried had worked.

Why certain molds gathered from the wood near Avalon and carefully dissolved in a tincture, then fed to the baby several times a day in a false teat of goatskin should drive out sickness was a mystery. Sometimes it failed to work, if the patient was too weak or if Alianor was called too late. But more often than not, the gifts of the wood brought healing and for that Alianor was truly grateful.

Eustacia hugged her baby to her and smiled through

her own tired but victorious tears. "I'll send round a tun of my best, milady, if that's all right."

"Your best is very good indeed. I would appreciate it."

In fact, Alianor rarely drank ale but she understood the importance to Eustacia of payment for her services. These were a proud people. They did not like to take charity. Besides, Eustacia was the best brewer for miles around. One way or another, the ale would not go to waste.

"Thank you again, milady. I don't know what I would have done without you." Eustacia walked with her to the door of the simple but comfortable house set near the center of town. As they stood outside together, she glanced up the hill toward the abbey.

"Damn them," Eustacia said suddenly. Her fatigue and relief left her bitterness unmasked. "My babe would have died if it was up to them and they telling me it's the will of God. What kind of God is it lets an innocent child die when there's medicine that will cure him?"

Alianor placed a hand gently on the woman's shoulder. Eustacia was in her thirties. Brandon was her fifth child, all born alive and healthy. Her husband, Rufus, worked their portion of the common lands. He was away in the fields now, helping with the spring plantings, or he undoubtedly would have been at her side. And sharing her anger.

"Never mind that now," Alianor counseled. Eustacia might forget the power of the Church but Alianor never did. She had been too well schooled in its realities. "Brandon's going to be fine. That's what counts."

"Aye," Eustacia agreed. Still, she continued looking up the hill. "But they'd better not come round to me again asking for my hard-earned coin to rebuild their precious abbey. I'll give them the side of a scythe, I will."

She dropped a kiss on Brandon's sleepy head and sighed wearily. "Forgive me, milady. I'm tired beyond words but that's no excuse to keep you. I know there are others who need your care."

"Call for me if anything worries you," Alianor said. She was confident Eustacia would do so. Brandon was fortunate in his mother. Sadly, the same could not be said of all children.

Her next stop, one she was looking forward to, took her down a lane to a pretty house situated near enough to the center of town for convenience but sufficiently separate to allow for more space and air. It was two stories of daub and wattle with a stone chimney rising along the outer wall, the whole possessing a trim air of comfort. There was a garden in the back being readied for planting and a large expanse in front where several children were at play.

They saw Alianor as she approached and ran to greet her. A little girl of about six reached her first and threw her arms around Alianor's legs.

"Alia, come see, Pookah had puppies."

Half a dozen other children clustered around, all vying with one another to tell her about the great event.

"Puppies?" Alianor exclaimed. "My heavens, what a wonder. When did it happen?" She allowed herself to be tugged along toward the stable behind the garden.

"Last night."

"Very late!"

"We found them this morning!"

"There are five. Two are black—"

"One has brown spots and—"

"The others are tan and white. They're all beautiful."

"I'm sure they are," Alianor said. "And I imagine Pookah's very pleased with herself."

Indeed, the dog had an air of calm achievement, ready to accept the congratulations that were her due. It was difficult to reconcile the sleek, well-fed animal with the half-starved, mangy creature Alianor had rescued from the trap the previous year. Pookah was one of a dozen animals who shared the house and stables with as many children.

The exact number varied but since inheriting the property from a grateful patient five years before, Alianor had seen the population—both human and animal—grow steadily. She was beginning to think of building an addition to the house. Several of the townspeople had offered to help her pay for it.

But that was for later. At the moment she had five handsome puppies to admire before spending an hour with the children and the kindly couple who looked after them. As always, the house was immaculately clean despite the normal disorder that accompanied a large group of happy children. All the children but the very smallest had their chores to do. They also had slates for learning their numbers and letters, musical instruments, and an assortment of toys, everything from dearly loved dolls to hoops and tops, even a chess set carved by Glastonbury's wheelwright.

As she was leaving, Mistress Philomena called her aside for a private word. Like her husband, Edward, Mistress Philomena was gentry, thrown on hard times by the confiscation of land to pay royal taxes. The couple counted themselves lucky to have found Alianor, while she regarded them as a godsend for both were ideally suited to the care of children.

"There's a lass on a farm out toward Cadbury coming near her time," Mistress Philomena said. "She approached me to ask if we would take in the babe."

"She can't keep it herself?"

"She's staying with cousins. Came to escape the shame of the neighbors finding out, I suppose. She means to return home after the birth."

Alianor sighed. It was an old story but one that grew no easier with retelling. "The father?"

"There's the rub. She didn't want to say but finally she let the truth drop. He's a priest." Mistress Philomena spoke with resigned acceptance.

"I see. Will he pay for the child's keeping?" In fact, they would take the babe under any circumstances. But Alianor had a standing policy of encouraging fathers to pay. This wouldn't be the first priest she had dealt with.

"The lass says her family will see to it."

"Tell her it's best if she stays to nurse the baby until it's at least three months old. If she doesn't want to live with her cousins, she can come here. If she insists on going sooner, we'll have a problem."

The two women looked at each other. They had seen other babies through the crisis of being denied their mother's milk, but it wasn't pleasant.

"I'll talk to her," Mistress Philomena promised. On a brighter note, she added, "Dermod stopped by earlier to see the pups. What a fine lad he's becoming."

Alianor nodded. The lad now apprenticed to Master Longueford would always hold a special place in her heart. He had been the first child she took in, a wee scrap of a boy not even two years old, his mother dead, his father unknown. And the abbot—

She frowned at the thought. In other parts of England, even in these hard times, abbeys and convents were the place for unwanted children. But not in Glastonbury. Even before the fire, Du Sully had refused, as he put it, to harbor bastards. He would see them starve on his doorstep before he raised a finger to help.

Alianor took her leave, walking back toward the village. She was thoughtful as she went. The problem with Du Sully remained. Once Conan, Baron of Wyndham, left, the abbot would be free to proceed against her. She had to expect him to at least try, and plan accordingly.

But how? What exactly could she do to protect herself from the charge of witchcraft?

Despite the warmth of the day, Alianor shivered. If Du Sully had his way, she would die. There was nothing to be gained by trying to hide from that hideous truth. He would kill her for being a woman, for not being subservient, for having knowledge forbidden by his Church. Those were her crimes and in his eyes they merited a brutal death.

He would burn her. She had heard the stories of women meeting that fate in other parts of England, in Scotland, and across the Channel. The numbers were unknown, the custom fairly new. But it was spreading rapidly. Already, there were probably thousands dead. Would she be added to their number?

She took a deep breath, steeling herself. In her final days Matilda had spoken of this matter. Her foster mother, a revered healer in her own right, had seen better than Alianor what was coming.

The Church of the Savior, He who came to teach men to live in peace, has not learned that lesson well. Too many who lead it are determined to stamp out the old ways once and for all. They fear and despise us. The day may come when you will have to protect yourself.

They had talked of how to do that. More correctly, Matilda had talked while Alianor listened, however unwillingly. She hadn't wanted to know such things, had resisted hearing them. But in the end, Matilda had won. The knowledge was handed down, in precise detail, the weapon ready to be used if it were ever needed.

Please God, it wouldn't be.

A shadow fell across her path. She glanced up. The afternoon sun fell over ebony hair, softening the hard planes of a face she had not seen before the previous day yet seemed to know as well as her own. Her breath caught.

Conan stood, tall and proud, a massive and utterly masculine presence to shatter her self-possession. For just a moment she was a confused young girl, startled by the sudden awareness of her womanhood. Reason reasserted itself, with some difficulty. She found a smile.

"Good day, my lord."

"And good day to you, Mistress Alianor. Will you walk with me?"

"To where?"

"Anywhere. We need to talk."

He sounded grave. Alianor did not have to puzzle over the cause. "You have been to see the abbot."

"And heard his tale. Who was Matilda?"

Alianor started, the mention of her foster mother unexpected. "He told you of her?"

"He said she was a witch and that you are another. To begin with, he claims she burned the abbey down the night she died."

"Oh, God—"

"So I thought perhaps you would like to tell me your side of it."

Bile rose in Alianor's throat. She was suddenly fiercely angry—against Du Sully spewing his poison, against all men who listened to such lies, against the handsome Baron of Wyndham who stood in judgment of her and in whose hands her life might lie.

"Why?" she demanded. "Why should you care what

I have to say? What has any of this to do with you? Why are you even here?"

"I was sent to investigate Brother Bertrand's death."

Her eyes widened. Whatever she might have imagined, this wasn't it. "You were—"

"The Queen wishes to know how he died."

"Queen Eleanor?" This was madness. What could the Queen Regent, ruling from London, possibly know—or care—about the death of a single monk?

But when she began to ask as much, Conan raised a hand, forestalling her. "I have no idea what lies behind Eleanor's orders. But I assure you, I will carry them out to the letter nonetheless. I—and my men—are in Glastonbury until the mystery of Brother Bertrand's death is laid to rest once and for all."

"You told Du Sully this?"

Conan smiled faintly. "I did."

"And his reaction?"

"He was—surprised."

Alianor almost laughed. It was a nervous reaction completely out of keeping with the circumstances but she could not help thinking how the abbot must have felt. To come under royal scrutiny was not a fate most people sought. Eleanor's dispatching of a baron, no less, to the far reaches of western England to investigate the death of a mere monk raised all sorts of questions, not the least regarding the Queen's true motives.

"After he calmed a bit," Conan continued, "he told me about Matilda and went on to detail his claim that you, too, are a witch."

They had come to the banks of a small creek that ran outside the village. "I'm thirsty," Alianor said. Her head was throbbing and her throat felt parched but she saw no reason to mention that. "Would you mind if we sit awhile?"

"Not at all," Conan replied. He stood aside to let

her precede him, then startled her by removing his cloak and laying it on the ground for her to sit on.

"That isn't necessary," she protested.

"Humor me."

Drinking water from her cupped hand, Alianor considered that he was a man used to being humored. The habit of command wore on him lightly.

"Matilda was my foster mother," Alianor said when the worst of her thirst was slaked. "She raised me on the island. She was a great healer and taught me everything I know."

"Did she die the night the abbey burned?"

"Yes, she did. She had been ill for several weeks. We both knew she was fading. Nothing we tried helped and in the end she wanted to go." Alianor wrapped her arms around herself, hardly aware that she did so. She was back in that night seven years before, the storm raging no more wildly than her own grief.

"The weather worsened in late afternoon. By evening, it was blowing a gale. The lightning and thunder were among the worst I'd ever seen. A large oak tree not far from our cottage was hit. You can still see the remains of it."

"And the abbey itself was struck?"

"The abbey was the tallest building in this area, especially being up on a hill as it was. Everyone knows lightning is drawn to the heights. It was only a coincidence that it happened the same time Matilda died."

"Du Sully believes it was her evil spirit striking out at the Church she hated even as she departed to burn in eternal hell."

Alianor's fists clenched. She blinked against the sting of tears. "Matilda was the kindest person I have ever met. If there is a heaven, she is there."

"Even so, the point is that Du Sully genuinely believes this and the rest of what he says. He's truly convinced himself that he's discovered a servant of the devil practically on his own doorstep, and that it is his righteous duty to call you to justice."

"You mean to kill me."

"I think he may envision that," Conan admitted. "Although theoretically the Church recognizes the possibility of forgiveness and redemption."

Alianor stared at him incredulously. "What are you saying? That I should crawl to that sick, depraved man, confess to being a witch, and beg forgiveness? Do you seriously believe I would do such a thing?"

"When the alternative is the stake, I would imagine people would do a great many things. But we're getting ahead of ourselves. The abbot makes quite a few charges against you but the crux of them is Brother Bertrand's death. If he can make the murder charge stick, you will have a serious problem. The assizes judge is due here in one month. Du Sully intends to bring the case to him."

"Then I have nothing to fear. The law grants me a trial by my peers. No one in this town believes I killed Brother Bertrand."

"Du Sully means to ask that you be bound over for ecclesiastical judgment."

"He can't do that! I am not a nun. Only people in holy orders can be brought before Church courts."

"The Church is trying to establish a precedent for treating witchcraft as a special instance requiring holy intervention."

Her stomach twisted. This was worse than anything she—or Matilda—had ever envisioned. In the back of her mind had always been the comforting knowledge that the late, great King Henry had established in England a rule of law unlike any seen before. It rested on the concept of justice as something distinct from rank or wealth or any other measure of influence. Certainly, the spirit was sometimes violated but the ideal remained, a shining goal for which all men could strive.

She had depended on that.

"Do you think the Church will win?"

Her voice was very faint. Conan had to lean closer to hear her. He was silent for a moment before replying. "If the Church teaches us anything, it is the value of ruthlessness and tenacity. However, it may be that this is the wrong time and place to try to establish the precedent. On the surface at least, the case against you appears weak."

"*Is* weak," Alianor corrected. "It doesn't just appear that way. It is."

"Du Sully is not without friends. He has influence at court."

"Are you one of those friends? Is that why you were sent?"

They stared at one another, there in the sun-dappled glen with the soft murmur of water at their feet and the gentle lowing of cattle in the distance.

Conan sighed. He looked like a man who wished himself just about anywhere else. "I was told to investigate Brother Bertrand's death, nothing more. Eleanor never mentioned Du Sully, or you, or any of this."

"Why do you call her Eleanor?"

His brows drew together. "What?"

"Everyone else calls her the Queen, or Queen Eleanor, or Her Royal Highness. You call her Queen, too, some of the time, but more often you refer to her as Eleanor. I wondered why, that's all."

"I mean the Queen, of course."

"I'm not suggesting that you're disrespectful. You speak of her with a certain degree of familiarity and, I might say, affection."

"But she is the Queen and you're quite right, I should call her such."

"You misunderstand me," Alianor said. She began to rise. Her thirst was no better but water would not slake it. "I did not mean to correct you. It just struck me as unusual. You must know her well."

Conan also stood. She was struck, not for the first time, by how tall he was and how muscular. He looked like a man honed by the harshness of life, like steel tempered in fire.

"I wouldn't assume anyone knows the Queen well."

"But you like her."

"Yes, truth be told, I do."

"Enough to come here, to the back of nowhere, in search of the truth about a humble monk's death, without complaint?"

Conan smiled. "Oh, I complained. I just didn't do it to Eleanor's—the Queen's—face."

"Is she really so august?"

He thought for a moment. They reached the road again. Slowly he nodded. "Yes, she is. She is very old now but she still possesses enormous strength of will. I truly believe she could accomplish anything she set out to achieve."

"Surely that is a rare quality in a woman."

He raised an eyebrow. "Did I say that?"

"No, I was just curious if you could be tempted into agreeing with it."

"Actually, I've known quite a few strong-willed women. They tend to be more interesting than the other sort."

"The weak-willed?"

"No, the kind that pretend they aren't strong-willed, the ones who prefer to work through guile and deceit. Then there are the clingers, imposing a sense of obligation on all whose path they cross. I don't like that sort, either."

"You've made a study of the different types of women then?" Alianor asked.

Conan walked along beside her, his hands clasped behind his back. His presence was oddly reassuring, for all that she had no idea if she could trust him or not.

"Actually," he said, "I've spent most of my life making war. I've grown rather tired of it."

She stopped, looking up at him. The sun caressed her face, strengthening her. "You're in a war here, Baron. Between truth and lies, good and evil. Which side will you pick, I wonder." It was more challenge than question.

His eyes darkened. "Du Sully says you threaten my immortal soul."

"Do you believe him?"

"Frankly, the only thing you threaten at the moment is my peace of mind. But I'll let you know, mistress." He inclined his head gravely, as he might to Eleanor, the Queen. "Good day."

She watched him go, walking down the road, his stride smooth and lithe. He was a powerful man, in body but even more so in spirit. She suspected he would not rest until his mission was accomplished and the truth stood revealed, all the truth, stripped bare of mystery.

That made him a threat. To her and to far more.

The day may come, Matilda had said.

Alianor closed her eyes, shutting out the road, the day, the lingering image of Conan, Baron of Wyndham. But she could not shut out truth. It remained, a hard core of fire like the living sun, burning at the center of her being.

Chapter 7

His peace of mind. Oh, yes, he'd spoken honestly enough right then when he confessed to her how easily she affected him. But that had to change. He had a job to do and the beauty of a woman did not alter that.

Truth again. It was more than beauty. She had courage and intelligence, qualities he admired in anyone, man or woman. And then there was the mystery surrounding her, Alianor of the Lake, like a figure out of ancient myth.

Conan stopped suddenly in the midst of crossing the small bridge back into town. A fragment of their conversation echoed through his mind.

Matilda was my foster mother. He had presumed she was daughter to the woman who raised her but that seemed not to be the case. Who then had borne fair Alianor? What had sent her to the mist-draped island?

Eleanor would know. That conviction sprang full blown in his mind, allowing for not the smallest shred of doubt. The Queen knew. Her interest would be Alianor, not Brother Bertrand. But who was she that the Queen would even be aware of her existence, far less care that she stood accused of murder?

And of witchcraft.

He must not forget that. This was no mere charge of homicide, the kind that could be settled by the payment of a blood fine set according to the dead man's standing in the community. This crime involved the Church—and the stake.

Eleanor had sent him to find the truth about a woman accused of being a witch. What truth did Eleanor anticipate? Did she even allow for the possibility of witchcraft or did she dismiss that as the fabrication of a Church she held in ill-disguised contempt?

He had a sudden flashing image—the Queen's hand, blue-veined now with age, but still slim and graceful, rings gleaming as she moved a piece on the chessboard. *Checkmate,* and a smile while outside the wind whispered around Westminster Palace and the night guard called the watch.

"I know your mother," Eleanor had said when he first became acquainted with her, a young man in Richard's train, full of his manhood, at home on the battlefield, ill at ease in the scented chambers of royal women.

"I fostered her, years ago in Aquitaine."

As Eleanor had fostered many young women, as Conan himself now fostered William. It was the custom. Children sent from their parents' home learned the ways of the world and made valuable friendships that could last a lifetime.

Odd how he had forgotten until just then that Eleanor fostered his mother. As Matilda fostered Alianor.

It was a ridiculous comparison. He could not equate the Queen of England, former Queen of France, Duchess of Normandy and Aquitaine and all her other titles, with a cunny woman of the back country.

What then was her tie to Alianor?

Eleanor was capable of a great many things but not even she could have borne a child at the age she would have had to do in order to be Alianor's mother. Even presuming that the Queen would cuckold her husband, and manage to conceal her pregnancy from the world, nature rendered it impossible.

What about the royal daughters then? There had been five in all, two by Eleanor's first husband, Louis of France, and the other three by King Henry. He couldn't remember when exactly each had been born but he supposed the two French princesses and perhaps the eldest daughter by Henry would have been of an age to bear Alianor. All were regarded as great marriage prizes and as such were both fiercely protected and constantly in the public eye. It was inconceivable that any one of them could have borne a child in secret.

As though on cue, his stomach rumbled, reminding him that he had other needs besides resolving puzzles that seemed to lead only to blank walls. The meeting with Du Sully had soured his appetite but now it seemed to be returning. He met Raymond as he was walking back toward the inn.

"Did you find Mistress Alianor, my lord?"

"Yes. She denies everything, of course."

"Including the part about the abbey burning the night her mother died?"

"Foster mother and no, she doesn't deny that. She says it was a coincidence."

"Well, I suppose it could be."

"You hear things that I don't. What do the townspeople say of her?"

"That she's the very soul of kindness," Raymond said. "Most of what people give her for her healing goes to support a group of orphaned children she cares for. That's the kind of thing the Church here ought to be doing but isn't."

"She makes Du Sully look bad."

"Begging your pardon, my lord, but he does that

well enough for himself. If that man cares about one thing besides his own comforts, I'm the rear end of a horse."

"So you've found no one in the town who will credit the notion that she killed Brother Bertrand?" Conan asked.

"Not a one. They're all very protective of her. If the abbot does mean to try her for witchcraft, there's going to be hell to pay here."

Conan nodded slowly. He stopped just outside the inn and looked up and down the road. Everything appeared calm, ordinary, predictable—the very picture of normal life. But there was an undercurrent to this place, something he couldn't quite get his hand on, as though what he was seeing was like that mime play Alianor had talked about, full of motions that were no more than trickery.

"Lord?"

Raymond was beside him, looking worried.

"Nothing, just thinking. For all that the abbey burned, Glastonbury seems to do well for itself."

"It does that, doesn't it?"

Indeed, several prosperous-looking plowmen were enjoying a brief respite from the spring planting under Master Brightersea's roof. They looked up as Conan entered, nodded respectfully, and withdrew to a back room.

"I wonder how many plowmen are drinking good ale in England this spring," Conan said thoughtfully. He sat down with his men around the large plank table. Their host appeared almost at once, shooing along several young women with pitchers of wine and beer, trays of fresh bread and cheese, and a platter of young chickens freshly roasted in broth and fennel.

"I hope this will be satisfactory, my lord," Master

Brightersea said after he had cast a professional eye down the table and found nothing to correct.

Conan could see why. The meal just set before them was simple but wholesome and perfectly prepared. Throw in a few more courses, add a couple of minstrels, and it could have been served at court without shame.

"It's fine," he said and, at the innkeeper's pleased urging, accepted several slices of fowl. When they had been served, and were again alone, Conan ate sparingly. His men were more enthusiastic and did better justice to the meal. Raymond noticed his preoccupation and put down the knife he'd been using to spear choice bits of meat.

"Is something wrong, my lord?"

"No, not wrong, just—" He broke off, thinking. Abruptly he said, "That boy who showed us here yesterday, his name is Dermod, isn't it?"

"That's right, my lord. He's clerk to the merchant, Master Longueford."

"When you've finished eating, see if you can find him for me. I want to talk with him."

Raymond rose at once, hand on his sword hilt, the light of purpose in his eyes.

Conan smiled. "Easy now, I don't want the lad terrified. He won't be any good to me if he is. Just tell him—"

"Begging your pardon, my lord." From the other side of the table, William spoke. "Sir Raymond's going to scare young Dermod no matter what he says or does. How about I fetch him?"

"You think you can do it more tenderly?" Conan inquired, amused.

"I don't know about that, my lord, but I can get him here with some thought in his head other than impending doom."

Raymond shrugged. "Will's got a point, my lord. It might be better if he went."

"Off with you then but I don't want the lad coming with his eyes popping out of his head, understand?"

Will swore that he did, grabbed his cloak, and was gone. Conan sat back, sipped his ale, and stared into the fire. He didn't have to wait long.

"My lord?" Dermod stood very straight, shoulders back, eyes watchful. His manner was composed but there was a hint of tension in the set of his mouth. He appeared to have thrown on a clean tunic hastily. There were ink stains on his hands.

"Sit down," Conan said in what he hoped was a friendly manner. He wanted to put the boy at ease. "Have a mug of cider. It's quite good."

Dermod sat, but slowly. He kept his gaze on Conan. Will splashed cider into a mug, handed it to him. He gave the boy a reassuring grin.

"Thank you, my lord." Dermod took the mug but did not drink. He continued staring at Conan.

"It's I who should thank you," Conan said, "for recommending such a fine inn. We've been made very comfortable."

"I'm glad to hear that, my lord."

"Yes, well, I thought you might be able to give us some further assistance." Deliberately Conan paused and drank. Dermod raised his mug and did the same.

"You're a man of business," Conan said when he had set the mug back down, "being apprenticed to Master Longueford. We've been noticing how prosperous Glastonbury is and thought perhaps you could help us understand how that came to be."

If there was a boy on earth who wouldn't be flattered by such a request from a man of Conan's stature, Dermod wasn't it. He nodded gravely, man-to-man as it were, understanding the seriousness of this matter of business and willing enough to tell what he knew of it.

"Do you remember, my lord, the sickness that came to the sheep five years ago?"

"I do," Conan said, frowning slightly. "No one knows for sure but half the flock in England may have died."

"That's right. But the sheep here in Glastonbury remained healthy. We lost nary a one. When the wool was brought to market, it fetched two, even three times what had been the going rate."

"Because there was such a shortage?" Conan asked.

"That's right." Dermod looked pleased that he had grasped the concept. "Not two years after that, the drought came."

"We all remember that," Raymond said. There had been droughts in the past often enough but few as bad. England had lain scorched from one end to the other.

"We're very fortunate here because our fields are laced by a system of canals dug who knows how many years ago. Even though no one remembers who started them, people here have always maintained the canals, removing silt and the like. When the drought came, the canals were opened and we were able to water our crops. Again, when they were taken to market, they brought high prices."

"It sounds as though Glastonbury has been unusually fortunate," Conan said.

"Aye, we have, my lord. There's no denying that."

Raymond bit off a hunk of chicken, chewed, and swallowed before he spoke. "You'd think such wealth would bring the tax collector."

"We pay taxes," Dermod said at once.

"I'm sure you do," Conan replied. But not as many as they might. It seemed Glastonbury was favored not merely by nature but also by those who set the revenue rates.

And that meant the crown.

Eleanor again.

Conan stretched out his long legs, folded his hands over his chest, and continued. "That was luck with the sheep. Does anyone have any idea why they didn't become ill?"

"Some folk say it's because Mistress Alianor made everyone pick the feed grain earlier that year. She said a rot would set in if we didn't and she was right. Sheep fed tainted grain will seize up the way they ended up doing all over England."

Conan had heard the theory before, in the highest counsels of government where the sheep blight had been discussed with real concern but little understanding.

"How fortunate that Mistress Alianor was able to predict that the grain would bring sickness," he murmured.

"She's a true wisewoman," Dermod said proudly. "We're blessed to have her."

Conan sent the boy away a few minutes later, having thanked him for his help. When he was gone, Raymond waited until the men had taken themselves off to find some activity. Only William remained, hunched by the fire, trying to look inconspicuous so he wouldn't be dismissed.

"What did you think of all that?" Conan asked the knight.

"The canals sound interesting. We saw something like them in the Holy Land, didn't we?"

"We did, and keeping them maintained so long only speaks of hard work. What about the sheep?"

"That's stickier, isn't it? How would she know the grain would be tainted?"

"I can't imagine," Conan admitted. "But I'm not willing to say it's witchcraft."

"Du Sully would."

"I'm sure he's got a list an arm long he's saving for the trial. Brother Bertrand's death may be the first charge but it won't be the last."

"Then the lady may really be in trouble," Raymond said. He sounded regretful.

Conan didn't answer. Instead, he stood up, pulled his cloak off the bench, and went out. At the stables, he saddled Gray himself. He needed a good hard ride to clear his mind.

"Do you want company?" Raymond asked, having followed him as always.

"Not this time. Find the men something to do. They're looking restless."

"Overdue for drill, I'd say."

Conan grinned. "I'll leave them in your capable hands." He touched his heels to the stallion's sides. The countryside beckoned and with it that luxury of luxuries, so rarely experienced in a life of hard work and duty—a few hours to himself. He intended to use them well.

So intent was she on the small clump of sweet cicely she had discovered growing in the shade of an oak tree, Alianor did not hear the faint footfall. She was gathering the early blooming white flowers, thinking of how the sweet unripe seeds would help ease the taste of the more unpleasant medicines she made, when she suddenly realized that she was not alone. Turning, she found herself face-to-face with a young man. He was about her own age, perhaps a year or two less, well built with broad features and roughly cut brown hair. He wore an unbleached wool tunic of the kind common among field-workers. Something about him was familiar.

She looked more closely. "Jeremy . . . ?"

He nodded but did not smile. "That's right, mistress. I wasn't sure you'd know me."

But she did, remembering the boy she had glimpsed from time to time as she trailed after Matilda. He and his family had lived on the outskirts of the village, working on a small piece of land and hiring out to the larger property owners when they could. His father had died—how long ago now? Ten years perhaps or more. His mother had taken them to live with her brother in the next parish.

"What brings you back here, Jeremy?" she asked, although she knew at least part of the answer already. It was nothing good. The tension in him and the way he had approached her, secretively, all spoke of a man anxious to conceal his presence—and his purpose.

"A friend of mine needs your help, mistress. He's been injured."

"How?"

Jeremy hesitated a fraction. "He had a fall. It's fair serious, mistress. Please come."

Alianor did not hesitate. Although she was certain there was something highly irregular in Jeremy's sudden reappearance—and in the quick glance he gave to be sure no one else was around—it did not occur to her for a moment to refuse her help. No Lady of the Lake ever had or would.

Jeremy knew the forest paths as well as Alianor herself. They walked a mile, perhaps slightly more, reaching ever deeper into the marshy places where few ever went.

At length, they came to a small clearing where a rough shelter had been built. Half a dozen men were seated around a small fire. Another lay on the ground covered by a blanket.

The men stood at Alianor's approach. They stared at her, as though hardly believing she was there.

"I told you she'd come," Jeremy said, not without pride. He led her to the man lying unconscious beside the fire.

Alianor knelt down beside him. He was in his thirties, with short red-blond hair and features that would have been handsome had he been in better health. As it was, they were painfully drawn, evidencing the agony he felt even in unconsciousness. His skin was gray and hot to the touch.

She moved the blanket down slightly, observing the contorted left arm. His tunic was finely made, speaking of wealth, but torn in several places. Through the rents, she glimpsed deep bruises.

"He fell, you said."

"Aye, mistress."

Alianor stood, looking around at all the men. "I can do nothing for him."

A chorus of angry exclamations and denials burst out. She raised a hand. "Unless you tell me the truth. No fall caused these injuries. What really happened?"

The men glanced at one another. No one spoke. Alianor shrugged. She turned to go. "Your choice."

"Wait."

One of the men, a big, hard-muscled sort, stepped forward. He scowled at her, then gazed more gently at the man on the ground. With a deep sigh, he yielded.

"Jeremy swears we can trust you but by God, he'd better be right. Godwin was taken in for questioning a fortnight ago in Bath. He told them nothing but by the time they let him go, they'd done that." His hands clenched with pained fury.

Several thoughts whirled through Alianor's mind.

Bath was fifty miles north. To bring their friend that far—to her—suggested the full extent of their desperation. It also indicated they were very determined and perhaps not without allies to help them along their way. Certainly, they weren't the ordinary landless outlaws she would have thought them. This was something far more serious.

For more than a century, since the coming of William the Conqueror, the Normans had bestrode the land of England. Yet in all that time, through all those generations, the instinct to rebellion had never died completely. It still stirred from time to time, most often in the west country where the ancient Saxon line had been strongest and was still well remembered.

"I see—" she said cautiously, wondering if she really did. What—exactly—were their intentions? How many were they? These eight, counting Godwin and Jeremy, and who else? Had they come to Glastonbury only because Jeremy remembered her and thought she would help, or did they have some other purpose?

Not that any of it mattered, at least not then. She had a patient to care for.

"If I am to treat him, I will need to fetch supplies." She took a breath, knowing what she risked, yet knowing also who she was and had pledged to be. "It would be best if we could move him to the island."

The men looked startled. The big one spoke for them all. "That is kind of you, mistress." He sounded surprised and thoughtful, as though considering that what Jeremy had told him might be true after all. "But it would be too great a danger to you. Best we keep him here."

Alianor agreed but reluctantly. She was thinking of

the time it would take her to reach the island, gather what she needed, and return.

"I'll be back as quickly as possible," she said. "In the meantime, keep him quiet and put cool wet cloths behind his neck and on his wrists."

They promised to do so. When Alianor left the clearing, they were fetching water from a nearby stream and tearing an old tunic into strips.

She was out of breath and hurrying as fast as she could when she reached the narrow road that ran beside the river. It had the advantage of skirting the town. She was hoping to reach the island without being seen. The tide was right. She wouldn't need the curragh to cross.

She was within steps of the water's edge when a sudden sound among the trees drew her up short. Before she turned, before she saw, she knew that luck had failed her.

"In a hurry, mistress?" Conan asked. He sat astride the gray, simply dressed yet resplendent all the same, looking as though he didn't have a care in the world. But his eyes never left her and she knew she would be hard-pressed to hide anything from him.

"I need to get these in water," she said and indicated the sweet cicely still bundled in her overskirt.

"Surely there's plenty of that about?"

"I mean in pots, so that the roots will live. If you'll excuse me—"

Every moment was precious. Godwin could die while she stood there chatting with his lordship.

"Would you like some help?"

Conan, Baron of Wyndham, dirtying his hands to plant cuttings? Were there no limits to the man?

"No, thank you," she replied and was proud of how

steady her voice sounded, at least to her own ears. "Mirabelle is waiting to be fed. I really must—"

"I thought cats fended for themselves?"

"Not that one. She's spoiled. Good day, my lord."

He moved the horse aside, if only barely, but sat very still, not withdrawing.

He already knew the secret of the stepping bridge. There was no reason for her not to use it in front of him. She knew that and yet it was still difficult to step out onto the first stone, knowing he was watching.

Anxious to be beyond his gaze, Alianor went a bit more quickly than she should have. She had crossed the stepping bridge so many times that it didn't occur to her she might misstep. But she did, if only almost, and for a horrible moment thought she would fall. Arms flailing, she managed to right herself and dared a glance back over her shoulder. Conan was laughing. She made a face, let him see it, and went on. Damn the man. He upset her far too easily.

She had to forget him and concentrate on her patient. Long years of training and practice allowed her to do so, but the thought of Conan lingered even as she filled a basket with the necessary supplies.

Mirabelle was asleep in a patch of afternoon sun, looking as though she could survive quite well on her own. Alianor left her and hurried back out. At the edge of the isle, she paused and looked along the opposite shore for Conan. There was no sign of him.

With relief, she crossed the stepping bridge again and started for the clearing. She was almost there when in the distance, back toward town, she heard the sudden tolling of a bell carried on the wind.

The sound was so faint that she couldn't be sure her ears weren't tricking her. It must be later than she'd realized for the monks to be tolling terce. But surely the bells sounded different, not the rhythm for terce at all.

The wind blew again and the sound vanished. She went on.

Chapter 8

"My lord!"

Turning in the saddle, pulling up on the reins to calm Gray, Conan saw Sir Raymond running toward him. The knight held one hand on his sword hilt to keep it from jangling against his leg. He was slightly out of breath when he reached his master.

The abbey bell was ringing.

"My lord, there's been another death."

"Who?" The single word, reverberating in the woodland quiet, sent a score of rooks into the sky. Gray shied again, as though he knew.

"Brother Raspin." Raymond stopped, caught his breath, looked up at Conan with grave intent. "That monk you spoke with yesterday."

"When I put my sword to his throat rather than let him arrest Mistress Alianor?"

"That was him. He's dead."

"So you said. He wasn't a young man—"

"Young enough and in the full flush of health, to hear Du Sully tell it."

"Why am I not surprised?"

"Also the abbot apparently regarded him as he might his own son. He feels the loss most profoundly."

"It tears at him?"

"Rends him deeply."

"Surely he will find consolation in his faith."

"I gather he'd find the sight of Mistress Alianor burning at a stake far better relief."

Conan bit back an exclamation of disgust. It was all so maddeningly predictable, so tawdry and stupid. What was the point?

"On what grounds does he accuse her?"

"Brother Raspin's attempt to arrest her, of course. He claims that was all the motive she needed to take the devil's vengeance."

"Oh, for the love of God—"

"Precisely. He is demanding her arrest. Says he'll go to the sheriff at Bath."

"Find me paper and ink. I will send a message to the sheriff informing him that I have temporary jurisdiction here."

It was a stretch. Eleanor had sent him—so she said—merely to investigate Father Bertrand's death. If he had to, he could make a case that her orders put him in charge of all investigation and indictment. But a good lawyer could make a hash of it.

He hoped the sheriff of Bath was not of that profession.

At the inn, he gave Gray over to William and went inside to write. The task came easily to him, his mother having insisted that he learn to wield a pen as well as he did a sword. He could also read—in four languages.

His ability had embarrassed him when he was younger but no more. Eleanor had made such skill in men even of the highest standing acceptable. He thanked her for it.

By the time he finished and handed the small packet over to one of his knights for delivery, he could hear the hue and cry outside the tavern door. Master

Brightersea bustled into the main room, waving his arms at his serving girls as he urged them to pull the shutters closed over the windows.

"Merely a precaution, my lord," he said. "Nothing more, I assure you. But there's talk of arresting Mistress Alianor again and the people are riled."

More than that, by the sound of it. Conan heard angry shouts, the thud of stout poles, calls for torches.

Would they burn an abbey already burnt? Bring the wrath of God—and presumably of the crown—down upon them when everyone else in England seemed to have the sense to cringe before both?

Interesting people, these good folk of Glastonbury.

He rose, pushed the table away from him, and went out into the street.

It was crowded with men, women, and children, seemingly the whole population of the town. All streaming as of one accord toward the hill.

Those closest, seeing him, hesitated but only for a moment. They pressed on, intent.

William was at his side, his young face hard. Without a word, the squire handed over the sword Conan had not bothered to put on earlier. He buckled it around his taut waist as his men gathered around him, quiet, purposeful, waiting his word.

Together, in a wedge, they shoved through the townspeople to reach the rise before most of the crowd. There Conan took his stand. He did not draw his sword, nor did he order his men to do so. He merely waited, blocking the path, as the townspeople bunched up in front of him.

When their angry shouts had quieted to mutterings, he spoke.

"I saw Mistress Alianor a short time ago. She has not been arrested, nor will any plans to arrest her be carried out. At least not until this matter is fully and fairly investigated. If you act rashly, you will make the situation far worse—for her and for yourselves. Return to your homes and your fields."

The crowd stirred. For a moment it appeared that they would obey. Certainly, Conan expected them to do so. Townspeople tended to be somewhat less subservient than the peasantry, but even they had the habit of obedience to those society deemed their betters.

He was, therefore, surprised when a square-shouldered man stepped forward from the milling mass of people, removed his cloth cap, and addressed him directly.

"We have your word then, Lord?"

Raymond growled deep in his throat. He did not take a step but swayed slightly as though tethered, and none too firmly at that.

"My word?" Conan repeated mildly.

"Aye, Lord. Begging your pardon, but you're unknown to us. Some say you're just passing through. Others think you're here because the abbot's unhappy with us. And then there're those that say the Queen sent you. But no one really knows."

"You want me to explain myself?" The idea was outrageous. If a man of his own rank demanded such a thing of him, Conan would be within his rights to challenge him. For this man, this peasant, to stand cap in hand and look him squarely in the eye, requiring his word, was unprecedented.

It spoke of matters far more ominous than mere murder. Or even the burning of a witch.

Conan took a breath, willing himself to calm. Never mind that what he sniffed now in the wood-scented air of Glastonbury was the sharp bite of rebellion.

Rebellion against crown and country.

Against the established order of the Plantagenet dynasty.

Against everything he knew, was part of, and was honor bound to protect with his life.

Never mind all that just now. This was a time to bide his patience and learn all he could.

"I mean you no offense, sir," the man said. "And whatever this may look like, I want no trouble. But the abbot's determined to blame our Mistress Alianor for everything. That isn't right."

"Lord—?" Raymond murmured through gritted teeth. There was a wealth of meaning in that single word. Would such behavior be tolerated? Could it be?

"England is a land under law," Conan said, reminding himself as well as them. Though he spoke quietly, his voice carried to the farthest reaches of the crowd. They were hushed now, listening to him.

"Good King Henry saw to that. In his name and at his bidding, the law was set down for all men to know. Courts were established and brought to every corner of this land. Can any of you deny this?"

No one spoke but here and there, he saw heads shake. Two years in his grave, Henry's name still had the power to compel.

"Now his son Richard rules, and he upholds the achievements of his father. So, too, does Henry's Queen Eleanor, who holds this land safe for her son. Can any of you deny that?"

A few sharp glances passed between some of those in the crowd. There were those who loved Richard, adoring his golden good looks and his brash valor. But others whispered that he did not have his father's strength or wisdom.

As for Eleanor—The aged Queen, holding tight to power through all the upheavals of a life that had it not truly been lived would have been beyond imagining, inspired respect. And fear.

"Then under law you have no need to be here. As I said, this matter will be dealt with fully and fairly."

He waited, wondering if they would challenge him again. If they did, he was fully prepared to use force to quell them. He just hoped he wouldn't have to do so. Not until he had sniffed out this business of rebellion and found the truth of it. That was far more important.

At the fringes, the crowd began to disperse. Slowly, then with growing speed, the people of Glastonbury moved away. Only a few men lingered, including the one who had spoken to him, and one or two women. They looked at each other, speaking glances, and at him. Then they, too, went.

Even as Conan made sure to learn their faces. Rebellions always had leaders. He meant to find them out.

"Extraordinary," Raymond murmured when they were finally alone.

William shook his head in blank disbelief. "Who would have ever thought common folk would act like that?"

"They aren't common," Conan said. "Something very unusual is happening here. It's our business to find out what that may be."

He turned, looking up the hill at the burnt-out remains of the abbey and the guest house beside it.

"Let's start with Du Sully. He's provoked this. I want to know why."

"Because she is a witch!" The abbot spoke so shrilly that droplets of spit sprayed from his mouth. His face was red, his hands clenched. He eyed Conan with bald contempt.

"I told you so! I said it plain but you wouldn't believe me! You had to have it your own way and now Brother Raspin is dead. How many more souls must perish before she is brought to her just end?"

"I want to see the body," Conan said. He refused to reply to the rest.

Du Sully stared at him, as though not hearing, so enveloped was he in his own mad rage. There was a movement toward the back of the room. A young monk, the same man Conan had glimpsed on his previous visit, glided forward.

His hands were folded in the sleeves of his brown robe. He had black hair neatly cut, smooth-shaven cheeks, and the sardonic smile Conan remembered.

"I will take you to Brother Raspin, my lord. If Father Abbot gives me leave, of course."

"And you are?" Conan asked.

"Brother Wynn. I have the honor to serve as sacristan."

It was an important post for so young a man, or at least it would have been were the abbey more prosperous. As sacristan, Brother Wynn would be in charge of all properties—land, vestments, crops, tithes, and the like. He would assist the abbot in all matters secular and spiritual.

And he would be in charge of seeing that graves were dug as needed.

"Take him," Du Sully said. He waved a hand in dismissal but still wasn't quite done. "Go, look on him you helped kill. If the witch had been handed over to us yesterday, dear Brother Raspin would still be alive today. How many more, O Lord? How many more deaths before she is stopped?"

Brother Wynn saw the abbot safely to his chair, squeezed his hand in sympathy, and withdrew. Conan followed.

"We have him in the chapel," Brother Wynn said. His robe swished lightly over the flagstone floor. "Or at least what serves us as chapel in these days. It has been properly consecrated."

"I'm sure it has," Conan murmured. He stepped inside a moderately sized chamber that looked as though it had been assembled from several small rooms. A plain wooden cross hung at one end where an altar had been set up. On a table in front of it lay the mortal remains of Brother Raspin. Tall white candles stood at the four corners of the makeshift bier. Several monks were in prayer. They looked up as Conan entered with their sacristan, but quickly returned to their meditations.

"There isn't a mark on him," Brother Wynn murmured. His tone held the appropriate hint of awed sorrow.

"He was healthy?" Conan asked. He withdrew the embroidered white cloth that lay over the body and stared at the man's face. He had seen it only once before but Brother Raspin was as Conan remembered him—a big, burly man better suited to the plow than the altar.

"Blessed by health," Brother Wynn said. "I don't think he ever knew a sick day. He even had all his teeth."

"Where was he found?"

"In the garden he tended just behind this building. He didn't appear for prime. Several of the brothers tried to rouse him but he was already dead."

"You saw him earlier?"

Brother Wynn nodded. "At lauds and we broke fast together. He was perfectly well."

"Yet within a few hours he was dead."

"Without a mark on him."

"So you say. I want the body stripped."

Wynn's head jerked. He stared at Conan. "That is desecration."

"A woman's life may hang in the balance. Take him elsewhere if you like, but I will see for myself this markless body."

The monks, hearing, murmured among themselves. Wynn hesitated. But either he knew better than to refuse Conan or he didn't really think the order as outrageous as he pretended.

A few minutes later, as he stared at the body of the dead man, Conan thought he understood why. Beside him, Brother Wynn bore the look of satisfied righteousness. Raspin had led a hard life with much physical labor. Over his years, he had collected several scars and many calluses to show for it.

But he bore no fresh mark that could possibly have caused his death.

"No one heard him cry out?" Conan asked when the dead man was covered again and carried back to the chapel.

Brother Wynn shook his head. "There were brothers close enough, in the kitchen and elsewhere, that they could have heard. He made no sound. He simply died."

"Death is never simple. Something killed this man, either a fault internal to his body or an external measure inflicted on him."

"If such a fault existed, surely it would have made itself known in some manner. Weakness, for instance, dizziness or lassitude? Brother Raspin experienced none of these. He was hale and hearty to the very end."

Conan did not reply. He was thinking. Among the very many aspects of monastic life that had never appealed to him was its extreme orderliness. Everything was done at an appointed time in an appointed way. There was no margin for spontaneity.

"You saw him at breakfast?"

"Of course, the whole community eats together."

"Thank you for your time, Brother Wynn."

The sudden dismissal left the sacristan surprised but he did not object. He remained in the chapel as Conan walked out. Raymond and the others were sitting on their haunches near the door.

"Let's go round to the kitchens. I want to find out what they do with any food they have left over."

"My lord?" Raymond asked.

"Brother Raspin appeared well at breakfast but was dead within a few hours. Monks aren't supposed to eat between meals. If he was poisoned, it was probably administered then."

"And if any of the food is left—" Raymond began.

"It may be possible to discover what was used."

But when they spoke with the small, stoop-backed monk in charge of the kitchens, they were told that there was nothing left.

"We have little, Lord," the elderly man said when he had recovered sufficiently from his shock at addressing so august a personage. "The people hereabouts are ungenerous. My brothers eat every scrap and thank God for it."

"There aren't even a few crumbs for the birds?" Conan asked.

"Alas, not."

" 'Tis a fine thing," Raymond muttered when they had left and were walking down the path back into town. "An abbey that can't even afford to feed a few starlings."

"Or won't. So much for that idea. I think I'd best find Mistress Alianor."

"Before the abbot does?" Raymond asked.

Grimly Conan nodded. "And before anyone else dies."

Chapter 9

Godwin murmured something, sighed, and was quiet again. Watching him, Alianor felt a small spurt of hope. He was still very sick but his fever was down and he was definitely resting more comfortably.

She straightened from beside his pallet and rubbed the back of her neck absently. It hurt but except for the automatic gesture, she hardly noticed. All her attention was still focused on her patient.

"How is he, mistress?"

The big man who had spoken for the others had the creased brow of a worried child. His name was Harald and he seemed to be second-in-command.

"Better but it will be some days yet before we know for sure. His left arm is broken. I have placed it in a splint so that it will heal straight. As for the fever and the rest, that is the result of his ill treatment and should pass with proper care. I just can't promise it."

"It's enough that you try, mistress. Truly, Jeremy spoke right when he said we must come here."

"I have never turned away any patient. I never will. But you must know it is dangerous to be here."

Harald shrugged. He seemed accustomed to the idea of danger. Nearby, the rest of the men were seated around the scant fire, eating a hare they'd caught and roasted. They had offered her food but Alianor had no

appetite. She rarely did when she worked. It was as
though all the life force within her was directed to the
task of healing.

"There's danger everywhere. It's the wise man who
knows what to do about it. Godwin here, he's got a
good head on his shoulders."

"When he's conscious."

"Aye, there's that. Will you come back, mistress?"

Alianor nodded. "Tomorrow. In the meantime, give
him the medicine as I've told you and make sure he
drinks. Only water, mind, and that boiled first."

Harald grinned as though he found the notion foolish but he wasn't about to gainsay her. Not with young
Jeremy swearing she could move heaven and earth, and
not with Godwin looking better already. That much
she could count on.

He sombered as he said, "As to payment—"

"Don't worry about it."

"Wouldn't be fair—"

"If you can manage it someday, that will be fine. But
there's no need for it to be on your mind just now."

"I never met a healer who didn't want to be paid. Of
course, come to think of it, I never met any kind of
healer 'cept a barber or two and an old cunny woman
my mother knew. She wasn't like you, though."

He reddened a bit as he spoke and directed his gaze
at the dirt. Alianor took the opportunity to go. She
spoke quietly with Jeremy for a few moments, urging
him to be careful, and had a final look at her patient
before heading off into the woods. It was getting on
for twilight before she turned off onto the path leading
to the island.

The tide was in, covering the stepping bridge, but
she had a curragh left on the near side. Getting into it,
she poled herself across. As she secured the small vessel
and started up toward her cottage, she breathed a sigh

of relief. The island had always been a sanctuary to her but she never appreciated it so much as she did on a day like this when she had to fight for a patient's life.

Thinking of a nice warm cup of cider, Mirabelle in her lap as she drank it, then a long hot soak to soothe the tension of the day, she opened the cottage door and stepped inside.

One foot over the threshold, she stopped. The smile of anticipation that a moment before had lifted the corners of her mouth vanished. No sight or sound alerted her but she knew beyond question that something was wrong.

"Who's there?"

He rose from the shadows near the dying fire, standing tall and broad, an alien presence shattering her safety.

Mirabelle hissed.

"Mistress." His voice was low, utterly male. Vaguely mocking.

And with an underthread of anger.

"My lord—?"

Twice he had come to her this way, by surprise and uninvited. The first time had been bad enough. But to come to her sanctuary, her home, and find him already in possession. That was not to be borne.

"Do you feel so free then," she demanded, stalking into the cottage and jerking off her cloak in a great whirl of fabric. "So free to march into my home without a by-your-leave? Manners may no longer be the fashion at court, my lord, but they still matter here."

"Do they?"

His quiet was ominous. She hesitated a bare moment. But good sense, which she usually possessed in abundance, was lacking just then.

"I am tired. I do not wish for company."

"Let me reassure you, mistress. I have not come for your hospitality."

He stepped away from the shadows, a commanding, intimidating presence who made her breath catch. Yet he looked as weary as she felt.

"Brother Raspin is dead."

She gaped at him. Indelicate as it was, her mouth fell open and she stared. He looked serious enough but what he said made no sense. How could Brother Raspin possibly be dead? There would have been some warning. Wouldn't there?

"What happened? A fight? What? He seemed in perfect health."

"Did you treat him?"

"No, of course not. He would never have resorted to me. Well, perhaps if he'd known he was dying and was desperate enough, but not otherwise." She was babbling and couldn't seem to stop. He hadn't answered any of her questions. She knew nothing more except that the monk was dead and Conan was in her cottage, staring at her with those hard, intelligent eyes that seemed to see into her soul.

Not that he could. He was only a man. Better educated than most, perhaps, and with a certain keenness of sensibility. But only a man for all that.

She knew nothing of men.

Not true, she knew a great deal. Many of her patients were men. But she knew them as bodies, and sometimes spirits, that were troubled and needed help. She did not know them in their maleness, in the quintessential way that made them so different from herself.

"How did Brother Raspin die?" She asked more calmly this time because, damn him, he wasn't going to have this all his way.

"That's unclear."

"How so?"

"He was found dead in the garden behind the abbey. According to Du Sully and the sacristan, Brother Wynn, he was in excellent health. No one heard him cry out, there isn't a mark on him. But he is most definitely dead."

"That makes no sense."

She hung the cloak on a peg near the door, hardly noticing, and went to poke the fire. All the while, she was thinking. "There must be something to indicate what happened to him. Was he contorted in any way?"

"No."

"Did his tongue protrude?"

"No."

"Had he soiled himself, vomited?"

"No."

"Was his breath foul?"

"No more so than I would expect." He had learned the trick from a fakir in the Holy Land and had actually stooped to it with Brother Raspin. Not a pleasant memory, to be sure.

She looked at him in surprise, and the faint twinging of respect. "You really did inspect him carefully?"

"Meticulously. I had Wynn strip him."

"That must have gone down well." She quickly doused an irreverent grin.

He shrugged. It made no matter to him what the monks thought. He had a job to do.

"So now you are investigating this death as well."

"That's right. He was seen at breakfast, but did not answer the bell to prime. I met you shortly afterward. You seemed—agitated."

He stepped closer yet and without warning caught her hands. Turning her to him, he ignored her instinctive struggle as though it were no more than the batting of a butterfly's wings. "Where have you been these many hours, Mistress Alianor?"

Tending a wounded outlaw who I suspect may be a good deal more.

No, that wouldn't do at all. Between her and her patients there had always been a bond of silence. She could not break it for any reason.

"In the woods."

"Doing what?"

She tried to wrench her hands away, found the effort useless, and gave up rather than expose her weakness yet further. "Where do you imagine my medicines come from?"

"Du Sully thinks all you have, all you are, comes from the devil."

"For pity's sake, the man's a jackass! If he's had a coherent thought in all his life, it involved nothing more than supper."

For just a moment, she thought he might be inclined to agree with her. But instead he said sternly, "You are speaking of a holy abbot of God's Church who has now suffered the loss of two of his brethren in circumstances he finds suspicious. You would do well to curb your tongue."

Her heart plummeted. It truly did for it felt as though a great, yawning hollow opened up inside her. He had seemed so different from the others but no longer. Now he was only the stern face of authority come to impose itself. To crush anything it did not understand or accept.

"I did not kill Brother Raspin," she said slowly and clearly. He would hear her, by God, even if it meant nothing in the end. He would hear her innocence. "I had no more to do with his death than I did with Brother Bertrand's. I am falsely accused."

"No one has accused you."

"That's nonsense. Abbot Du Sully already has me lashed to the stake."

Though she said the words boldly, she quaked inside. She was only human, after all, no more eager for pain or death than the next sane person. The thought of the stake, of all it meant, filled her with terror. But she would not show it, not to him. He would never have that satisfaction.

"I meant in the legal sense which is what matters here. There is still a month to the assizes court."

"What makes you think he will wait for that?"

Something in his eyes told her she had struck a nerve. "He isn't waiting, is he? He wants to try me now."

"He is looking for help to the sheriff at Bath but I have already sent word that this investigation is mine."

"And is it?"

A faint smile flitted across his mouth. He still held her but his hands on her wrists had gentled a little. "It is now, mistress, for well or ill. Where were you?"

"Gathering medicinal herbs."

"All this time?"

"They cannot be rushed."

"You did not see Brother Raspin since yesterday?"

"Not since your own coming. And that brings up a point."

"What?"

"Loose my wrists and I'll tell you."

"Tell me and I'll consider it."

She debated inwardly but decided to give in to him just this once. Not that she would make a habit of it.

"Mayhap your sword point at his throat so terrified him that his heart failed."

"A day later?"

The possibility certainly did not seem to trouble him in any way. He appeared amused by it.

"That could happen," she said.

"In your professional opinion?"

"Well, it certainly isn't impossible. You'd terrify anyone."

She shouldn't have said that. Definitely shouldn't have.

His smile was wicked. It was really unfair that God should have given any man such looks and that smile to boot.

"Do I terrify you?"

"Of course not." Not more than any primal force of nature would.

"You said anyone."

"I was exaggerating."

"Hmmm, perhaps. Your skin feels cold." As though to confirm that, he rubbed his thumbs over the pulse points of her wrists. She shivered.

"Come closer to the fire." Without waiting for her answer, he sat down on a stool and drew her onto his lap.

"Do not—"

"Hush. Look at the fire. You're cold and you need to warm yourself. That's all."

"Are these court ways, my lord? I do not care for them." Sweet heaven, his thighs were hard beneath her bottom. He felt like finely tempered steel, utterly unyielding.

"Did you kill Brother Raspin?"

Fire. The warmth and comfort of the hearth.

The stake.

"No."

"Did you kill Brother Bertrand?"

"No."

"Anyone?"

"No." Her voice broke. She turned her head into his shoulder and felt the wall around her, so carefully maintained since Matilda's death, crack. "Oh, God, I swear, I have never knowingly harmed anyone."

Tears coursed down her cheeks. She hated them, hated showing her weakness, but she couldn't help herself. Not just then, with this man. He seemed to bring out all that was needy and fearful in her, all that sought comfort in a world that could so often be lonely and bleak.

"Hush," he said again and touched her hair so gently that it was as the brush of a summer wind whispering through willows. "Hush." He cupped the back of her head, turning her to face him. So close, his face did not look so stern. His eyes were really quite beautiful, long-lashed, alive with hidden lights.

The fire cracked. Twilight fled. His tongue tasted the salt of her tears, his mouth touched lightly at the corners of her eyes, along the curve of her cheek. Her lips parted on a sigh that he caught and made his own.

Chapter 10

Conan rose from his pallet beside the fire. He poked at the embers and when they brightened, put another log on. From across the room, yellow eyes watched him. He ignored the cat and gazed at her mistress instead.

Alianor slept on her side facing him. Her hair was a red-gold nimbus half concealing, half revealing her face. One hand was tucked up under her chin, rather like a child. The covers had slipped slightly, revealing the curve of her breasts beneath her tunic.

She had fallen asleep in his arms in front of the fire. He had carried her to the bed, taking due note that it was large enough for two before retiring to his solitary—and chaste—pallet beside the fire.

The situation was wryly amusing, but only to a point. He was tired, stiff in his neck, and sexually frustrated. As for his dreams—he refused to consider those at all.

Why had he kissed her? For pity's sake, was he a green boy to be so turned by a beautiful face and form—and by the eternal mystery of women—that he would be ruled by what he had between his legs rather than between his ears?

She'd returned to the cottage empty-handed.

For all that talk about spending hours in the woods

gathering medicinal herbs, she'd had nothing with her. Not a scrap of green, not a hint of a plant. Nothing.

Did she think him a fool?

Yes, probably she did. Secretly, didn't all women hold that opinion of the august male?

Didn't Eleanor?

She'd sent him on a fool's errand. Oh, not that it wasn't important. Rebellion always was, but most especially with a king not two years in his grave and a son who couldn't seem to stay at home to secure his crown, so busy was he finding new people to kill.

Richard was the fool. Lion-Hearted, they called him. Golden, they said he was. Already, he was the stuff of song and legend.

But a fool for all that.

And for all that he had raised Conan high. He owed the man his loyalty, possibly his life. But he still wouldn't lie for him in the privacy of his own mind.

Besides, Eleanor had encouraged the same damnable clear-sightedness that left him now with no place to practice self-deceit.

Eleanor had sought him out when he was still little more than a boy, though he would have killed the man who suggested it back then. She'd—what, exactly? Befriended him? No, the Queen had no friends. She had servants and enemies.

She had encouraged him. Groomed him. Completed the job his earlier upbringing had begun.

And then she sent him to Glastonbury.

For a dead monk, a witch woman, and a rebellion. Perhaps.

Nothing more?

Jesu, his head ached. He really had to get more rest. He wasn't quite so young anymore and this business drained him.

He should have lain with her. A bit of coaxing, a sweet word or two, and he would have had her.

The problem was afterward and the inconvenience of his conscience.

It was almost dawn. He'd leave in a few minutes, not waking her. Raymond and the others would make assumptions but he almost preferred that to the truth.

All right, not almost. He did prefer it. It would embarrass him if the truth were known, which by itself was a good indication of how badly off he was. He couldn't remember the last time he'd been embarrassed.

She might be guilty.

Sweet Lord, that beautiful woman lying there in the glow of the reviving fire might be—what?

Witch?

He strained his imagination, trying to conjure visions of the devil and his worshipers. He'd seen enough engravings, heard the exhortations of enough priests, he ought to be able to manage it.

He couldn't. Perhaps it was the effect of being able to read. Or traveling. Or knowing Eleanor.

The devil that drifted briefly through his thoughts was a vaguely ridiculous creature, prancing on hairy legs with his horns askew, not at all akin to the very real evil of which men were capable all on their own, with no help at all. Ask Richard. Conan stopped his wayward train of thought abruptly. He'd bring himself to the stake if he went on like that.

As though a baron of England, servant of the Queen, could be burnt. That fate was reserved mostly for women who were old or mad or too bold. Or who owned property others wanted. Or who offended someone with influence. Or who—

He looked away from the bed, angry at himself, wishing to God she'd had some plant in her hands when she returned, however scraggly and unlikely to heal. A weed, anything.

It was daybreak. Barely, true, but he could see a faint rim of gray against the horizon. Mirabelle rose from the bed where she'd been ensconced snug against her mistress, lucky cat. She stretched, yawned hugely, and looked at him.

"I'm going," he said softly, a whisper in the so-female quiet of the cottage.

The cat looked pleased. She leapt down gracefully and strolled toward him. Before he could guess her intent, she rubbed against his legs, first one, then the other, making a thorough job of it.

He laughed, caught himself, and stopped. If only the mistress—

Enough of that.

"You're hungry, I suppose?"

She rewarded his perception with a blink.

"You could catch a bird, hunt down a rat. How does that sound?"

Unappealing, by all appearances. She led him, tail high, to a cupboard snugly built into one wall. He opened it and found a well-stocked pantry, one his mother would have approved.

His nose led him to the dry fish. Crumbling bits, he laid it on a wooden board and set it before her. She deigned to give him a low, rumbling purr before attacking the repast with fierce delicacy.

He bent, stroking her coat, thinking that he rather liked cats. They had a certain dignity.

"Tell your mistress I'm not all bad," he said. "Though in justice, she ought to be able to figure that for herself."

Dried fish was too much competition for a mere human. Ignored, he gathered his cloak around him, took a final glance at Alianor, and cracked open the cottage door.

The day was cool. It smelled vaguely of rain but he could see waning stars above. He had left the small boat he'd borrowed on the far side of the island. No one contested him for the oars as he rowed the short distance to shore.

He rather regretted that. Securing the boat, he walked back toward the town. It was just early enough for the boys to be out, seeing to the flocks. Two of them were herding sheep to the pastures. They glanced at him, wide-eyed, stared at one another, and slapped grimy hands over their mouths.

At least they had some sense, he thought as he went on, feeling the morning damp through his cloak and thinking, for perhaps the thousandth time, what it was to be a fool. Not that they wouldn't speak of it. Coming down the path from the island. At that hour. Alone, horseless, on foot like a common man. Commonly undone.

But they'd be careful how they bandied it about, not from any thought of him but out of respect for Alianor. They'd whisper of spells, perhaps, of him summoned by the lady to do her bidding. An ordinary woman would be lessened by such rumors. Alianor would merely have her luster buffed.

Damn her. Not a sprig of leaves, not a clump of roots.

A woman unlatched the shutters of a small house on the edge of town, threw them open to greet the day, and smiled at it. Until she caught sight of him. Then she, too, gaped and darted quicklike back inside. To wake her husband, no doubt. Tell him of the fine lord trudging up the road like any vain suitor.

He'd have to be stern with these people. If there was rebellion brewing— If? Did he really doubt it? They'd challenged him directly. Something was coming. Eleanor knew it and so did he, if he was honest. The dead monks were only incidental.

He walked on, the morning brightening and the town just beginning to stir. On the hill, he heard the bell for lauds.

Raymond was already up. He stood when Conan entered the main room of the inn. An eyebrow rose, nothing more. His self-control was admirable.

"We missed you at supper, Lord."

Ah, so he couldn't quite resist. Raymond was human after all.

"Not now. Find Will. Set a fire under him if you must. I want hot water, clean clothes, and a decent breakfast. Has the town been quiet?"

"As the grave. They're waking Brother Raspin today."

Conan nodded, glad that something went as he expected. "I thought they'd want to weep and moan over his body awhile yet."

"Brother Wynn sent word. He mentioned that you might want to be there."

"Did you tell him I was lying with the witch?"

"No, should I have?"

"Unfortunately not." Honesty would be the death of him. "All right, I'll go but I need a bath and food first, then paper again."

"There's been nothing from the sheriff."

He smiled, a baring of teeth, nothing more. "This one's to London, my friend. The Queen said she awaited news of our progress most eagerly."

"Have we made any?"

"No, but it doesn't do to keep a queen waiting. Besides, I have a thing or two I want to say to her."

But a short while later, with a platter of Master

Brightersea's best laid out in front of him, he tempered his ill humor to address Eleanor.

"*My Queen,*" he wrote, never mind all the high-sounding titles the scribes so loved. "*A second monk is dead, one Brother Raspin, far younger in years than the other, hearty in manner. The abbot accuses a woman, Alianor by name. He calls her witch and will burn her if he can. I find this place disturbing. The Church is derelict in its service to the people who, in turn, give it little heed. Put plainly, there appears to be no authority except for this Alianor herself. We are one month to the assizes court. How does one disprove witchcraft? I trust Your Majesty is well. Your obedient servant, Conan, Baron of Wyndham.*"

Let her think on that, the aged Queen in her Tower with all the threads of power gathered to her. Let her tell him honestly what she expected him to do.

He folded the vellum, held a tube of wax to a candle flame, set his seal. "The quickest route is by ship from Weston-super-Mare," he said, giving the message to Raymond, who had returned from waking Will, "even if it means finding a captain for hire. I want it in the Queen's hands before this week is out."

The knight nodded. The squire bustled about, complaining to the serving girls that they took too long to heat water for his lordship's bath, sending back the cider to be warmed, generally making a fuss of himself while sneaking glances at Conan. Checking him for toadly signs, no doubt.

When the bath was ready, he dismissed Will. Alone in his chamber, he stripped and stepped into the steaming water. A low groan of contentment escaped him. It felt wonderful, not as good as Mistress Alianor's stream-fed bath would feel, but wonderful all the same.

Bless Master Brightersea, he did not believe in doing

things halfway. The tub was as generous-sized as a man of the innkeeper's dimensions would require. Conan could recline full length in it. He did so, tipping his head back and closing his eyes. The hot water soothed the stiffness from his body even as it sweated the poisons from his mind. His thoughts cleared.

Nothing in her hands. Lies on her lips. Alianor was hiding something. Was it a petty secret, a lover, perhaps? She was a beautiful woman after all. Men would desire her.

Heaven knew he did.

The thought of her, entwined with another, sent a jolt of white-hot rage through him. It came without warning, conjured by the image of her naked limbs clinging to a man not himself. He half sat up in the tub and cursed.

It had to stop. He was on a mission for his Queen. This panting after a woman of the mists did him no honor.

He should hope she had a lover hidden away in the woods. How much better that would be than involvement in murder. Or rebellion.

But try though he did, he could not quite manage such sensibleness. The rage eased but an ache remained that no amount of reason would assuage.

The water cooled. He noticed belatedly and rose, sluicing drops onto the floor. Drying himself with a rough length of cloth, he glanced out the window toward the abbey.

They were waking Brother Raspin. Fine, he'd go. Perhaps he'd actually learn something useful. Between where he stood and the remnants of the abbey, smoke rose from several dozen fires. The prosperous folk of Glastonbury were astir, at their breakfasts and their morning chores. Chattering about—what?

The place was like an onion, he decided, liking the

very ordinariness of the thought. He'd peel its layers away, one by one, as many as he had to until he found whatever was within. Fresh green nub or black rot, he'd find it in either case.

And then, by God, they'd see.

Chapter 11

Her hands shook. Pouring water into a pot to make comfrey tea, Alianor splashed hot liquid all over the worktable and just avoided burning herself.

"Damn!"

Mirabelle roused from her nap in a patch of sunlight and stared at her mistress in reprimand.

Muttering to herself, Alianor mopped up the table, then picked up a broom and began to sweep. She hated loose rushes on the floor and wouldn't have them. Instead, she wove neat rush mats and used those, replacing them as needed. Perhaps she'd do that today. The cottage was tidy enough but it could always use a good cleaning. She'd scrub the cupboards, air her clothes, make a dozen or so pots of ointments. It wasn't too soon to mulch the garden and she should chop more wood.

She would keep very, very busy and perhaps, if she was fortunate, she wouldn't think more than a thousand or so times about what had happened the night before.

And hadn't happened.

When had she last cried? When Matilda died, to be sure, but not since then. And never, ever in front of a man. Sweet heaven, what had come over her?

She'd wept like a babe, clinging to him, and then he'd—

Alianor pressed her lips tight together. She could still feel the touch of Conan's mouth on hers. The memory alone was enough to make her tremble.

Angry at herself, at him, at the whole outrageous circumstance, she put the broom down and drew out fresh clothes from the wooden chest at the foot of the bed. Bathed and changed, with her hair newly washed and braided, she felt somewhat better. At least the day no longer seemed quite so unmanageable, herself quite so strange.

She would go to see Godwin. That done, she would do all the other things she had thought of. Exhausted, she would tumble into bed and sleep without dreams of Conan and his too bold, too complex, too compellingly male presence.

Resolved, she left the cottage and walked across the stepping bridge carrying a basket of supplies. The day was pleasantly warm, the sky almost cloudless. Avoiding the town, she crossed a field and moved deeper into the forest, toward where the outlaws were hiding. Her pace was brisk, there was a no-nonsense air she gathered about her for reassurance. She was, after all, still herself.

Alianor reached the clearing quickly but was startled to find it empty. Surely she hadn't mistaken the direction? She looked around, trying to get her bearings, but was convinced very quickly that she was in the right place. Everything was the same. There was even a small spot of charred earth to show where the men had made their fire.

Her mouth hardened. So, despite her warnings that Godwin's recovery was far from certain, they had chosen to move him. Perhaps they didn't trust her as much as they said they did. Or perhaps they merely thought it prudent. Either way, they had placed her patient's well-being at risk.

Slowly she walked around the edges of the clearing, her eyes on the ground and on the bushes near it. Just west of where the campfire had been she found what she was looking for. The undergrowth was trampled and several branches had been snapped off.

Going carefully, she followed the trail that to her eyes, at least, was clearly marked. It was a skill Matilda had taught her, not for any particular reason but just because she thought it might be useful someday. Besides, it was all part of understanding nature and seeing the smallest detail of how the land around her changed.

About a half mile from their original camp, she found the men. They were resting beside a small creek. Godwin was lying on the ground. He appeared to be conscious.

"Good morning," Alianor said. Emerging from the bushes without warning, she hid a smile.

The men leapt to their feet, reaching for weapons. They stared at her in blank surprise.

"Mistress—" Harald spoke. "How did you—"

"Find you? I followed the very clear trail you were considerate enough to leave. Were you concerned that I wouldn't be able to? No need. A child could have managed it."

The men scowled but no one tried to object. They looked at her with caution, glancing at Jeremy as well, as though weighing the truth of whatever he had told them of her. Undoubtedly, he had failed to mention that she could appear at will and that it was useless to try to hide from her.

"You took a chance," Harald complained. "Coming

out like that. We might have hurt you before we even realized who you were."

Alianor doubted their reflexes were anywhere near so fast but she did not say so. Her point had been made clearly enough. Any sense of safety they allowed themselves was an illusion.

"I am Alianor," she said when she had knelt beside her patient. His color was better though he still appeared to be in pain. "You were gravely injured. I'm relieved to find you improved."

Godwin's eyes were blue and very watchful. Awake, he was a handsome man, stamped with intelligence and the habit of command. There was a certain refinement in his gestures and appearance, despite his circumstances. She surmised he had grown up with some gentility and wondered who he was, exactly.

"They told me of you," he said, "but I wasn't sure I should believe them. How did you really find us?" He had a softly Irish accent, from the west of that island, she thought, but couldn't quite be sure.

"By following the trail you left. Truly, there's no magic to it. Your men shouldn't have moved you. It wasn't worth the risk."

A smile flashed across his pain-weary face. She realized suddenly that he was younger than she'd thought. "Evidently not. So you are a healer."

"I have some skill."

"But not a witch."

Her eyes widened. She drew back slightly. "What makes you say that?"

"I've been in Bath. Indeed, I've enjoyed the hospitality of the sheriff there. It's a bit rough, to be sure, but memorable enough."

Her throat tightened. She had seen the results of that hospitality. "I suppose so." They were talking about her in Bath, saying she was a witch. How much farther would Du Sully's obscenities spread?

"You're Irish." Anything to change the subject. "I've always wanted to visit there."

"Have you? It's a lovely place although less than it used to be since the Normans have granted us their attention. It's thirty years now since your King Henry sent his minions to make Ireland safe for him and his. We haven't benefited from the process."

"Is that why you're here?" Alianor asked. "To return the favor?"

Godwin laughed, winced, and looked at her with heightened interest. "Is that what you think? Henry sent Strongbow—lovely name, that—with warships and men-at-arms. Does this little band look like an invasion?"

She didn't answer directly. Instead, she eased the blanket covering him back and gently checked his injuries. Satisfied that he really was doing better, she sat back on her haunches and regarded him gravely.

"Henry's dead these two years and Richard—"

Godwin grinned. "The Lion-Hearted? What a penchant you Normans have for grand names."

"I don't really think of myself as Norman."

"Why not?"

"The way I was raised, I suppose. My foster mother never referred to such things. She thought them of only passing consequence."

"Maybe in the tide of centuries but for the average man—" He stopped again, catching himself. "Jeremy went on about a lake and you the lady of it. Is that true?"

"Well, I don't actually live in the lake, you understand. I prefer the island that happens to be in the middle of it."

His eyes were thoughtful. "We've places like that in Ireland."

"And ladies of them?" She asked casually but the question was anything but. For years she had longed to know if she was truly not alone. Were there others like her, any at all, as Matilda swore there were?

"A few perhaps, still. I've heard tell of such things. This is good country here for the old ways. So's Ireland."

He had changed the subject adroitly. She changed it back. "But we were speaking of the present. Rebellion has become a habit in England. Most people alive today can't remember a time when there wasn't one sort of upheaval or another going on."

"And who's to blame that Henry couldn't get along with his wife or his sons, or they with him? The Plantagenets are a quarrelsome bunch, a foreign sprig planted in this land and doing it little good that anyone can see."

"You're foreign yourself," she pointed out, not unreasonably, she thought.

He hesitated. The habit of caution was strong in him. But he was a young man and she a beautiful woman. Somewhere deep down inside, past all the calculation and the wariness, he was tempted to impress her.

"Not precisely. My family came from these parts."

"The west country?"

"Aye. They removed to Ireland . . . some years ago. But the tie has never been forgotten."

His name was Norse. His family had gone to Ireland "some years ago." He had ties to the west country strong enough to bring him back in this time of uncertainty with armed followers.

Alianor frowned. Before the Plantagenets, before

William the conqueror, a king had risen out of the west country to take the crown and rule all of England. His name had been Harold Godwinson, scion of a mighty Saxon-Norse house and Earl of Wessex. He had died on that bloody field at Hastings but he had never been forgotten.

There had been rumors—

A handfast wife—concubine, the Normans called her—children, at least one son who survived the savagery of the victors and fled to . . . Ireland. But after all these years, all these generations, surely it could not be.

Quietly, so that only he could hear her, Alianor said, "The Queen's sons may be quarrelsome and lack their father's mettle, but Eleanor herself is strong."

"And old. She's almost seventy, an immense age."

"She is said to wear her years well."

"But wear them all the same." His tone was sharpened by impatience. He did not want to debate her and she could hardly blame him. He was still in pain, exhausted, and in need of rest.

"You should try to sleep," she said, rising from beside him. "I will leave more of the medicine. Unless there is absolute necessity, your men should not move you again for several days."

"I'll tell them that," he promised and laid his head back, closing his eyes.

Alianor assumed he would, but she also had a word with Harald before she left. Whoever these men were, whatever they were about, her single overriding concern was her patient's recovery. She was relieved that Godwin seemed to be healing well but she couldn't help but wonder how exactly his renewed strength would be used.

That was still on her mind as she returned home.

The fairness of the day was disappearing rapidly. Storm clouds were gathering out of the west. She gathered her cloak more closely around her and shivered in the sudden chill.

Chapter 12

Conan was reminded of why he did not attend holy services if he could possibly avoid them. The wake for Brother Raspin had been going on the better part of the day. This consisted mainly of the monks keeping vigil and should have been a peaceful occasion. But Abbot Du Sully had chosen it to deliver a ranting, barely coherent sermon on the virulence of witchcraft and the need to be ever watchful for the devil, who all wise men knew preferred to work through the inherent evil and weakness of women.

Disgusted, Conan was leaving. He had learned nothing of any use except to confirm his opinion that the abbot was at the least incompetent and possibly genuinely mad. Oh, yes, one other thing. The more he saw of the workings of the abbey, the more he began to suspect that it was in fact run by Brother Wynn. Certainly, Du Sully wasn't capable of tending to the day-to-day needs of his brothers in Christ and there seemed no one else likely to contest Wynn for power.

Even now, with a violent storm approaching, he was urging half a dozen of them out to dig Brother Raspin's grave. Standing just outside the door to the abbey, the wind blowing away the cloying smell of incense, Conan observed the sacristan. Brother Wynn's dark brown robe whipped around his lean body. The other monks huddled together but he stood alone, tall, obviously proud, and in command.

Against a sky rapidly darkening, he said, "Nonsense, we're not going to let a bit of rain stop us from preparing our brother's final resting place. Follow me." He strode off across the flat top of the hill in the direction of a small graveyard that lay just behind the ruins of the old abbey.

Conan watched with some amusement. The monks followed, albeit reluctantly. They all carried picks and shovels. Brother Wynn did not. His role appeared to be supervisory.

For no particular reason, Conan decided to watch. Perhaps it was that he didn't want to admit that his visit to the abbey had been a waste. Perhaps he was merely curious.

Or perhaps it was because he knew that once he left, he would have no further excuse to keep from thinking about Alianor.

She haunted him. He had never spent such a night with a woman, never before experienced the need to protect and give simple comfort except perhaps with his mother and sisters. But he had been so much younger then, so far more innocent himself than he was now. It had not occurred to him that he was still capable of such feelings, much less that they could come accompanied by the full, heavy weight of desire.

He did not know what to make of it, it was so far outside the normal stream of his life. So he preferred not to think of it at all. Yet will he nill he, his mind drifted steadily toward Alianor no matter what other course he tried to set it.

Better to watch a grave dug. And a storm come.

The clouds continued to roll in, gray and yellow, black-edged, eating the sky. They mounded up against each other, butting giant thunderheads, and presently it rained.

Not the bit of rain Brother Wynn had anticipated but great, fat plops of rain that fell onto the springtime earth and over the headstones of old graves. Rain that quickly spilled in streams off the early green leaves and in small rivulets along the muddy earth.

Mud rain, back again, just when the world had looked poised to dry out ever so slightly.

Conan sighed. He was close to deciding that he hated rain, necessary though it was, when a streak of lightning cleaved the sky, followed swiftly by a clap of thunder loud enough to rattle death.

The monks had dug down perhaps two feet. They stopped, looked at the sky, and began to climb back up to level earth.

"Continue," Brother Wynn said. "It will grow no easier so might as well be done now."

Conan could see their reluctance from his position several dozen yards away. Slowly, hesitatingly, they resumed their labor.

Almost all the sky was filled now. Only a small rim of clear blue remained to the east as a reminder of the gentler day. Though it was only a little after terce, the light was fading fast. Soon torches would be needed to complete the work.

They were brought, spitting and steaming black smoke as the rain struck them but burning all the same. Several more monks stood about, holding them and getting soaked, as they watched the others dig.

How far down did they intend to put him? Conan wondered. Tradition said six feet but in graveyards so long used that often wasn't practicable. Still, he noticed they'd picked a spot fairly far away from where most of the abbey's late brothers rested. It was near the westernmost edge of the hilltop, looking out away from the town toward the lake and Alianor's island.

Alianor again. Impatient, he kicked the dirt at his feet and watched mud ooze over his boot. Another bolt of lightning ran half the length of the sky. Several monks called out, anxious as they might well be for they were wielding iron shovels and everyone knew iron drew lightning.

Were they also remembering how their abbey had burnt in a storm that probably hadn't been all that different from this one? Did they link the events, dead monks and the abbey's destruction? It would suit Du Sully's intentions for them to do so.

Conan's cloak was good English wool against which water beaded, but even it was becoming sodden. It made no sense to be standing there. He should go back to the inn, have a bowl of Master Brightersea's fine soup, and consider what to do next.

He had just about decided on that course when he heard a shout. It came from the direction of the grave, more correctly from within it. At first, he thought he was mistaken for the earth muffled the sound and the clamor of the storm almost muted out the rest. But then he saw the monks, calling out and gesturing to one another as though gripped by a sudden agitation.

Thunder clapped.

He moved forward. They were peering into the grave, exclaiming to one another and now—what was this? Brother Wynn, still wet but pristine without a speck of dirt upon him, was climbing down into the grave. The torches were brought closer. Monks were on their knees all around the edge of the newly opened earth, watching.

Conan drew closer. He peered over them into the grave. Wynn was there and another monk, crouched over something.

They must have found an old burial. It was a common enough occurrence. Why then all the excitement?

Two of the monks were running back toward the abbey. Conan shoved into the spot they had vacated and yelled to Brother Wynn.

"What is this? What have you found?"

The sacristan looked at him over his shoulder. A bolt of lightning ripped the sky, illuminating his face. He appeared transformed, consumed by excitement.

"More than we could have ever dreamed," he shouted above the wind and pointed to what lay within the grave.

The afterimage of the lightning still seared Conan's eyes, but through it he could just make out what looked like the trunk of a very old tree lying there in the opened earth. It could have meant nothing, except that it had survived, not rotting, suggesting it had been sealed somehow. And then there was the cross laid on top of it, very large and ornately carved in a style he did not recognize.

Brother Wynn brushed his hands over the cross reverently. He wiped rain from his eyes and bent closer. "There's writing on it. I can't make it all out but—"

He looked up again, triumphant, elation in his eyes. "*Rex Arthurius*! That's what it says. It is King Arthur's name engraved here, and by my soul, it is his grave we have found!"

"They've what?" Alianor, rising from the stool beside her worktable, inured now—or almost—to Conan's sudden appearances in her domain, stared at him as though he were daft.

"They think they've found King Arthur's grave," he said. Water dripped from his sodden cloak onto her rush mats. He'd come over in a boat but he might as well have swam. He started to apologize, was distracted by the sight of her in a thin day robe of finest lawn, and forgot what he'd been about to say.

"That's impossible."

"Unlikely, but there's definitely something down there. As I left, they were trying to raise the coffin or whatever it is."

She shook her head in disbelief, went over to the fire, and poked it with sudden fierceness. Belatedly, it seemed to occur to her that she was not dressed for company. Seizing her cloak from a peg near the door, she wrapped it around herself and glared at him.

"Must you disturb me with the mad ramblings of monks? Whatever they've found, it isn't Arthur."

"How can you be so sure? There are legends enough about him in these lands."

"And don't the legends also say that when he died, three queens carried him to Avalon, there to sleep until needed again by his people?"

"You don't believe that."

"We aren't talking of my beliefs. We're talking about those fools at the abbey. What were they doing digging in this weather anyway?"

"Brother Raspin's grave. Remember?"

She did, and paled slightly. "Oh, they were digging his grave and think they've found Arthur's instead. That seems sane to you?"

"I was there. They definitely found something, a tree, a piece of wood, and a cross with Arthur's name carved on it."

"I would wager that there have been at least a hundred Arthurs in this land who had some claim to fame, at least enough to get their name carved onto one thing or another. It means nothing."

A gust of wind, whirling down the chimney, set the fire to dancing. The selfsame wind rattled the shutters and made the old rafters beneath the roof creak. Wrapped in her cloak, her hair falling to her waist, Alianor stared into the flames. Her face was a mask, Conan could not guess her thoughts. But he felt the tension in her and wondered at it.

"What are you afraid of?"

She started, as though torn from thoughts that had held her strongly. "Nothing."

The response was too quick. He did not believe her. "What if it is Arthur? What does it matter? He must have been buried somewhere, after all. Why not here?"

"Why here?" she countered, firelight dancing. The wind rose. He had to strain to hear her. "What makes Glastonbury so special that it would have been honored as the burial site of the great King Arthur?"

He thought he caught a glimpse then, a fleeting hint of what she truly meant. Of what she feared. But he couldn't be sure and his attention was distracted. The wind succeeded in blowing open a shutter. It banged against the outer wall.

They both moved to close it. Their hands brushed. The effect was not unlike a spark of lightning moving through them. Quickly they parted but Conan's gaze lingered on Alianor as she turned away. "I must dress," she said and drew a curtain across the sleeping area of the cottage. Behind it, he could hear her moving around a little, heard the lid of a chest being lifted, put down again. An image of her, naked, the fine-spun gown pooled at her feet, shot through him. He closed his eyes for a moment against the force of raw desire. When he opened them again, Alianor was drawing the curtain aside.

She had dressed simply in a plain dark blue tunic and overcote. Her hair was gathered over her shoulder. She was braiding it as she came toward him.

Quietly, not looking at him, she asked, "Why did

you bring me this news yourself? I would have heard it quickly enough in any case."

He had asked himself that question coming over to the island. Word of the find would be all over Glastonbury by morning. The moment she set foot anywhere near the town, she would have been told.

Why had he come?

"I want to know the truth, if this is Arthur or if it isn't. If the monks are attempting a deception, I want to know that. And if they aren't . . ." If they weren't, it would all be a good deal worse. He thought of the lingering aroma of rebellion he had sniffed and frowned. "Let's just say that the actual discovery of King Arthur's body at this time could have political implications."

Alianor smiled humorlessly. "The King who was and will be?"

"Precisely. England has a king—Richard Plantagenet. It doesn't need another."

"And what makes you think I will know the truth?"

"You know this place better than any other. Certainly better than anyone else I can put a hand on at the moment. If the monks are lying, I trust you to recognize it."

"You honor me, my lord, but the monks will never let me near whatever it is they've found."

Conan turned toward the door. They had delayed long enough.

"They won't have a choice," he said as he plucked the torch from its brace. "I stopped at the inn before coming here. Sir Raymond and the others will have secured the grave by now and be waiting for us."

She looked at him in surprise. "You sent your men onto Church ground? Du Sully will be enraged."

"By the time he figures out what to do about it, I intend to have this matter settled. Come on."

He did not look back to see if she followed. If she did not, he would have to force her and that he did not want to do. Better she made the choice for herself.

A moment later, when he heard the soft sound of a footfall behind him, he felt a small spurt of relief. But it passed quickly enough as his thoughts turned to what might lie in that ancient grave.

And the very real havoc it might wreak in an England where only one old woman stood between the crown and the chaos of rebellion.

Chapter 13

The storm was blowing away to the east when they reached the far shore from the island. A crisp, pleasant breeze remained but nothing more. The world looked washed clean.

Ordinarily Alianor would have enjoyed it. But her thoughts were on the abbey. And on Conan.

He had come to her for help. He believed she would be able to tell him the truth of what the monks had found. What did he know—or guess—about her to bring him to such a conclusion? Especially when she didn't have quite so much faith in herself.

Arthur. The very name conjured power. He had been so many things—king and hero to his people, unifier of a land threatened by enslavement, envisioner of a better world. But the truth of Arthur did not stop there. Unwittingly, perhaps unwillingly, he had been the chosen instrument of powers far beyond his own. In him, the shimmering barrier between realities grew very faint indeed. So much so that in all the generations since his death, he had never been forgotten. Nor even truly assigned to the realm of the past that was his rightful place. He was still, in some sense, a living presence in this land.

Hence her shock at hearing his grave had been found. And her unwillingness to believe it. But she would go and she would see. And she would speak true.

Conan took her hand to help her from the boat. She was almost, if not quite, becoming accustomed to the effect his slightest touch had on her. But then she accepted so much from him. There was a kind of intimacy between them already as though they were lovers of long standing. She could neither explain nor deny it.

Also, he trusted her. He had said so himself and she believed him. What an extraordinary thing that such a man should trust her. Or perhaps not. What, after all, did she really know about Conan, Baron of Wyndham? Except that he came at the Queen's bidding and seemed fond of his mother.

And that he was willing to challenge the Church. That, in itself, was no small thing. A few more men like the baron and all things might be possible.

All right then, to the abbey, and hellfire take any who tried to gainsay her. Conan wanted truth? He would damn well have it.

"Father Abbot is resting," Sir Raymond said. He stood, feet planted apart, hand on his sword hilt, beside the opened grave, the very picture of calm command. His gaze slid to Alianor for the briefest instant. Absolutely nothing registered, not surprise or dismay, not shock or disapproval. He was a thoroughly professional knight and, Alianor suspected, Conan's true friend. "I have allowed no one to touch anything," he finished.

Conan nodded. "Good. Where is Brother Wynn?"

"The sacristan? He went to help make the abbot comfortable. Ah, there he is now."

Alianor turned and saw the young, stern-faced monk coming toward them. She had noted him once or twice around the town but he was relatively new at the abbey and she had paid him little heed. Now he stared at her in disbelief.

"What is *she* doing here?" He spoke to Conan directly, not deigning to address a word to her, yet his eyes never left her. He seemed to fear she might vanish if he did so.

"Mistress Alianor is going to help us determine what it is you've found."

Brother Wynn reddened. For just a moment he forgot himself. Pure fury filled his eyes as he glared at Conan. "That is ridiculous! She is useless in any such regard. Get her out of here."

Conan gestured Raymond to stay where he was. Alianor took note of the small, silent message that passed between them but she doubted Wynn realized how close he had come to the point of a sword.

"She stays," Conan said. He did not raise his voice or look especially concerned. He simply gave the order in the way of a man so accustomed to obedience he does not consider any other possibility.

She almost smiled but restrained herself. Liking him was dangerous. As for desire—

No, she would not think of that, not now. Ignoring Wynn, she stepped closer to the grave and looked inside. Daylight was fading fast but torches had been positioned all around the opening. She could make out the trunk of a tree lying flat against the ground. A cross lay on top of it. She had difficulty telling from this distance but she thought the cross might be made of lead.

"Everything down there needs to be brought up," she said to Conan.

"And taken where?" Wynn demanded. "If you think for one moment that you can remove—"

"The chapel will suit," Conan said. "But with my

men on guard at all times." He turned to Sir Raymond. "We'll need ropes and more light."

They were produced. Several more monks watched from a safe distance but only Brother Wynn remained near—and did not offer to help—as Conan's men brought out the cross, then slowly and laboriously raised the tree trunk from its resting place. As it emerged into the torchlight, clumps of dirt falling back from it into the hole, Alianor allowed herself the faint hope that it would turn out to be nothing more than what it looked like, part of an old tree.

"It was an oak," she said quietly.

Conan had removed his cloak, the better to lend his own strength to the effort. He stood, hair ruffling in the evening breeze, and touched a hand very gently to the wood. "See here, it was cut."

She leaned closer, her shoulder brushing his. Where he indicated, she could make out the thin line that ran all the way around the long side of the tree where it had been sliced in two lengthwise, then carefully placed back together.

After what was laid inside?

"I have heard of this," she said as they walked together with the men carrying the tree trunk into the abbey. The monks hovered, dark presences, their excitement palpable. But when they saw her, they pulled back, shock and titillating fear swamping all else.

"It was done in the old days, a tree, cut down, the trunk split and hollowed out to form a coffin."

"Was it commonplace?" Conan asked.

She shook her head. "It couldn't have been. The oak was considered a sacred tree."

"I must fetch the abbot," Brother Wynn said. "Have the decency to do nothing until he has come."

Conan shrugged. For a moment the monk hesitated, as though to press his case. But caution had the better part and he hurried off, his sandals slapping against the flagstone floor.

"Let's get the rest of the dirt off it," Conan directed. More clumps fell to the ground.

"It's big enough for a large man," William said. The young squire was all eagerness. Alianor sensed none of the reserve in him that she felt from the other men. They were older and battle-hardened. Their obedience was assured. But that didn't mean they had to like this mucking about with coffins that might or might not hold the remains of Britain's most illustrious king. And, some might say, of her greatest dreams.

There was a disturbance at the entrance to the chapel. Du Sully hastened in, hands clasped to his chest, hair disheveled, a look of wildness in his eyes. He did not see Alianor at first but focused on the coffin.

"Praise be! God Almighty has answered our prayers! To think here, in this very place, we find—" He broke off, his gaze shifting suddenly to—

"The witch! What abomination is this? Get her!"

Swiftly, before any monk could be so foolish as to obey, Conan stepped in front of Alianor. He raised an arm, the bulging muscles visible even through the tunic sleeve, and casually swiped it through the air, knocking Du Sully down.

"By God," Conan said, his voice all the more deadly for its iron control, "that's the second time you've needed a reminder of who rules here. Let it happen again and abbot or not, you'll taste my sword."

The monks paled, reeling back, except for Brother Wynn who remained where he was, his expression not quite controlled enough to hide his satisfaction.

"This is holy ground," the sacristan said, almost mildly.

Conan gave him a look that withered. Even Wynn,

strangely confident as he was, had the sense to stand down. He busied himself helping Du Sully up, murmuring reassurances.

"Get it open," Conan said.

"Wait." Alianor stepped forward. Strange how alive her mind was, stirring in all sorts of ways. She was vividly aware of every impression, however slight. The tension in the room was knife-edge sharp, as was the surprise when Conan held up a hand, stopping the men who had been about to do his bidding.

"I think we should try to read what is written on the cross first," she said, speaking softly so that only he could hear her. Belatedly it occurred to her that he was giving her a great deal of leeway. It was only courteous to acknowledge that.

"It says Rex Arturius," Brother Wynn said. "What more do we need to know?"

"The whole of it," she said and bent to the task.

Someone found a small bristle brush, the kind used for currying horses. Another brought a pail of water. Going slowly, careful to do no damage, Alianor cleaned the last fragments of dirt away. When she was done, she stood back a little and examined her handiwork.

The cross was perhaps a foot and a half high and a foot wide. Gray metal gleamed dully in the torchlight. It was elaborately carved with curling spirals leading inward one upon the other. Writing was incised along the arms of the cross. Her eyes flowed over them. Abruptly she turned away.

Conan glanced at her, said nothing, and took her place. He studied the words for several moments. Quietly, in the hushed stillness of the abbey, he read:

"HIC IACET SEPULTUS INCLITUS
REX ARTURIUS IN INSULA AVALONIA"

No one spoke. No one so much as breathed. The knights exchanged puzzled glances as, truth be told, did several of the monks. It was left to Conan to say what the others, those who had their Latin, already knew.

"Here lies buried the renowned King Arthur in the Isle of Avalon."

"I knew it." The voice was Brother Wynn's, the satisfaction fierce.

"But why—?" Du Sully moved closer, stared down at the cross, traced with his fingers the words Conan had just read. His brow creased. Suspicion lit his eyes. "The spelling is wrong and the letters are wrongly shaped. How can this be?"

Alianor released a breath of air. For just a moment, she shared Wynn's satisfaction, albeit for a very different reason. Du Sully never failed to live up—or down—to her expectations. Faced with a discovery of astounding magnitude, he would nitpick it to death.

Let him. Her mind shouted the command. Let him dismiss this miracle as an irrelevancy. In his prideful ignorance, let him cast it out. He deserved nothing more. Indeed, he begged for the treatment he so richly merited.

But Conan did not. He had said he wanted truth. And he trusted her to give it to him.

"It isn't wrong." She spoke softly, almost hoping she would not be heard. But there was no chance of that in this place where the sound of any female voice would be alien in the extreme, the source of all fear and hatred.

Every eye turned on her, some cautious, some filled with malevolence, some coolly neutral—she felt Sir Raymond there—and one other, strong and calming. Conan.

"Why do you say that?" he asked.

She had not realized he was standing so close to her. His nearness offered comfort. She managed a faint smile, hardly aware that she did so. It faded as she looked at Du Sully.

"The writing is different from what you are used to. Some of the words are spelled differently from the way you would spell them. But that doesn't mean they are wrong."

She drew herself up, unconsciously straightening her shoulders. This was the man who called her witch. Who wanted her to burn. And not her alone but any woman who dared to challenge his twisted view of God's creation.

"Different does not mean wrong," she said.

It was useless, she shouldn't even bother. Yet some compulsion forced her on. She looked again at Conan, into the silver fire of his eyes, and found her courage there.

"People change," she said. "The way they live, the words they speak, even the writing they use alters over time. What seems obvious and ordinary to us now, things that we accept without question, will seem very strange someday to those who come after us. The same is true right now. Just because this writing isn't what you're used to doesn't mean that it's wrong."

Du Sully's mouth curled. He waved a hand, dismissing her. "Typical, weak-minded woman. How could she possibly understand? Eve could not comprehend when God told her the tree of knowledge was not hers to eat from and this one is truly her daughter. Still—" He broke off, looking toward the coffin. Disgusted though she was, Alianor watched the play of thoughts across his face. He didn't have the wit—much less the skill—to conceal them. She saw calculation, the greedy weighing of where advantage lay.

In this case, there was no question.

"Still," Du Sully continued, "we have found Arthur's grave. That those who buried him were not as literate as we are can be forgiven. What matters is what this means for the abbey." He turned, raising his arms, and addressed the monks.

"Brothers, this is a glorious day! Truly, we have found the salvation for which we have searched so long in vain. As the burial place of King Arthur, there is no question but that the abbey will be rebuilt. Pilgrims from throughout the realm and beyond will flock to us. We will become rich beyond our dearest hopes—"

He went on but Alianor no longer listened. Her gaze focused on the tree trunk. Was it possible? The message on the cross was clear enough and she was inclined to believe it, for all sorts of reasons. But did that necessarily mean—

"We must open the coffin with all reverence and confirm what is within," Brother Wynn was saying. With an effort, she turned her attention to him. "Then we can begin making plans for reburial. Notice must be sent to the archbishops of Canterbury, Winchester, and York. They will be most gratified to learn what has happened here."

"No notice will be sent anywhere," Conan said. "I will agree to the coffin remaining here only because I don't want to create any curiosity in the town by taking it elsewhere. But—" He raised his voice slightly, assuring that even the monks farthest away would hear him. "Heaven help the man who speaks of this. It is a matter of state, not the Church, and as such it will be brought to the Queen's attention first. Am I understood?"

He looked around slowly, studying each face. "If you fail in this, I promise you that not only will this abbey not be rebuilt, what remains of it will be razed and all of you dispersed to find your livelihoods as best you can. The vengeance of the crown is swift and sure. Make no mistake on that."

Du Sully started to speak but Brother Wynn laid a hand on his arm, forestalling him. "I believe what the baron means is that it is in all our interests that the crown fully appreciate what is happening here. Undoubtedly, King Richard himself will be delighted by this news."

"Undoubtedly," Conan murmured. "Now, with all reverence, let's open this and see what we're dealing with."

It was on the tip of Alianor's tongue to protest but she stopped herself. She had no grounds, save her own fear. Burials were unearthed all the time and usually treated with far less respect than this one was receiving. Still, she could not shake a sense of impending doom as slowly the top of the tree trunk was pried loose.

Four men were required to lift it. When they had done so, and set it carefully on the chapel floor, no one moved. Clearly, there was something inside the hollowed-out trunk of the tree but there was no rush to inspect it.

Finally, Conan stepped forward. Raymond stood beside him. The knight lifted a torch high, illuminating the interior of the coffin.

Alianor held her breath. She had a sudden, flashing vision of the King, rising before them, wearing his armor and his diadem, come to reclaim his realm. But that was absurd. There was nothing except . . .

She moved closer, steeling herself. Death she had seen all too often, bones she had studied when she got the chance. But she had never before seen the remains of a human being long buried.

It was not so terrible after all. Certainly, she had

seen worse. There was a kind of peace about the yellowing bones. She could glimpse little but the skull, turned to one side, set in eternal smile. One side of it appeared crushed as though from a mighty blow. Nearby, something far brighter than bone glinted in torchlight.

"A man," Conan said. He had seen more than she, recognized what it meant.

"How do you know?"

"He wears armor." He pointed. "Here and here, see? Different from ours but it can't be anything else. And the skull is too large to be a woman's. What's that on it?" He, too, leaned closer. His breath brushed her cheek, so alive, so real in the presence of death.

"A crown," he murmured, touching gold.

The monks went wild. There was no containing their jubilation even in this holy place. They bounded up and down, shouting their delight, pounding each other on the back before their abbot called them back to order. Or more correctly, Brother Wynn did although he made it seem as though he spoke for Du Sully. Smiling, he herded them like so many unruly children toward the altar.

"Let us pray, my brothers. Let us give thanks for the great bounty of the Almighty. Father Abbot, if you will—"

Prayers droned. In Du Sully's mouth, the holy words seemed especially defamed. Alianor did her best to screen them out. Ignored, she, Conan, and the others were free to concentrate on the body.

No, she realized, bodies. At the man's feet, crouched there below the remains of what appeared to have been leather boots, she glimpsed a second skull.

"Conan."

She had never used his Christian name before but now she hardly noticed, so great was her shock. This skull was smaller. She could see, still remaining on it, long lengths of what had been blond hair.

"A woman?" she murmured.

"So it seems." His mind made the obvious leap. "Guinevere, perhaps?"

Alianor did not reply. The monks had lit incense. The smell seemed suffocating. She walked away, nearer to the door of the chapel where she could catch the clean scent of evening. Clouds scudded across the sky. A full moon was rising.

She glanced back once, not at Conan but at Brother Wynn instead. Her mouth, normally so soft and generous, set in a hard line. Deliberately, she turned away.

Chapter 14

"Still no sign of her?" Conan asked. He was buckling on his sword belt. William waited beside him, holding his cloak. Gray was already saddled.

"None, my lord. No one in town has seen the lady since yesterday."

"I checked the island myself. She isn't there."

"We can continue searching," Raymond suggested.

Conan hesitated. He was tempted to order it done. Where could Alianor be? He had seen her last when she left the abbey, turning aside the offer of an escort. He had let her go because he needed his men to guard the bodies and because he was convinced no one would dare to harm her.

But in the hours since then, she seemed to have disappeared. The cottage itself was empty. Even Mirabelle was gone.

Damn the woman. He did not want to leave not knowing where she was. But it seemed he had no choice. He had to reach Eleanor by the fastest route possible.

"She will return," he said, willing himself to believe it. "If she does not, send men to search the countryside, but remember, the remains must be watched at all times."

"I understand, my lord. If I might ask once more that you take some of the men with you?"

"They can't be spared. Besides, I'll move faster alone." He took his cloak from William, fastened it, and sprang easily into the saddle. The look on Raymond's face was eloquent. Quietly Conan said, "You worry too much, old friend. If there's danger to be faced, it's going to be right here. I won't tarry."

"As you will, my lord," the knight replied but he looked only slightly reassured.

Not so William, who laid a hand lightly on Conan's leg and looked up at him with the beseeching gaze of youth. "Please, my lord. It's not right that you be going off without a squire. Who will see to your needs?"

Conan forebore from mentioning the many mornings he had let Will sleep, or the times he had seen to it that his young charge was warm enough and properly fed. The youth's pride was at work here.

"It won't be easy, Will, but I'll manage. Right now, I need you here most of all. Watch Sir Raymond's back for him and keep your ears open for any talk around the town. I'll return as soon as I can. I'm counting on you."

The boy nodded, shoulders squared. "As you say, my lord. I won't let you down."

Sparing a thought for what it would mean to have such a son, Conan pressed his heels into Gray's sides. The horse bounded forward. They clattered over the stone bridge and were quickly free of the town.

A surge of guilt spiraled through him. He really did feel free and he should not. He was worried about Alianor and he was on a mission for his Queen. And yet, the solitude of the woods, the power of the horse, the blissfulness of privacy, all combined to put him in an excellent mood.

So good, in fact, that it continued all through the

morning as man and horse followed the River Brue westward until at last they came to Weston-super-Mare. It was a bustling and relatively prosperous seaport with a decent bay coming off the Bristol Channel. Slightly larger than Glastonbury, it was considerably less well kept. His nostrils contracted at the smell of rotting fish as he and Gray approached the docks.

The stallion whinnied with excitement. Unlike most horses, he liked water. It was just as well.

"What do you think, boy," Conan murmured as he bent over in the saddle, stroking the horse's mane. "See anyone who looks likely?"

The stallion tossed his head and pawed the ground with controlled fierceness. Despite the ride of more than thirty miles, he was eager to go. So, too, was Conan.

But first he spent an hour or so observing the traffic along the docks. Men came and went, as did a few women. Most were crew members of the half-dozen sea vessels in dock but there was also the usual assortment of merchants, peddlers, bargemen, whores, and hangers-on. Once or twice a more prosperous individual passed by, a wealthy trader or a captain.

Still, Conan waited. He was looking for a particular sort of individual, a man who appeared both entirely competent and capable of keeping his mouth shut.

He found him just as his patience was running thin. The man was in his mid-thirties, only a few years older than Conan himself. He was cleanly dressed but not luxuriously. His face had the weathered look of one long accustomed to being outdoors. He walked with confidence, greeting a few people he passed but not many. He ignored the women and headed directly for a barque riding at anchor a short distance from where Conan waited.

Gray whinnied softly when Conan tied him to a post beside the gangplank.

"Don't worry, boy," he said softly, "she looks sturdy enough and with a bit of luck you'll be on board before you know it."

An urchin, dirty-faced with a gap-toothed grin, heard him talking to the horse and stared. Conan flipped him a copper penny. "Watch him for me, will you?"

The boy caught the coin in a single leap. He stared at it in wonder. The odds were good he'd never held such a thing in his life.

"Aye, sir," he said breathlessly. "Won't no one get past Davydd, count on that."

In fact, Conan counted more on Gray's own savagery should anyone be foolish enough to approach him with ill intent. But he left the boy going proudly about his task and climbed the gangway.

Several crewmen were busy on deck. They glanced at him as he came aboard, took in the fineness of his sword and the strength of his body, and looked away hastily. He found the captain at the prow, studying what appeared to be a manifest.

"Good day to you, Captain," Conan said.

The man looked up, started to speak, stopped, and looked again, more carefully this time. His eyes narrowed. He rolled the parchment, tucked it into his tunic, and faced Conan.

"Good day, my lord. What could I be doing for you?"

"I require passage for myself—" He nodded toward the dock. "And my horse."

The captain followed the direction of his gaze. He nodded slowly. "I'm bound for Plymouth. If that suits you, you're welcome aboard. The charge is ten pence for you and another two for your horse."

The price was high but not exorbitant. Conan guessed that was about to change. "Plymouth's a charming town but I'm going to London."

The captain rubbed his chin speculatively. "Ah, well, now that's a different matter."

"I thought it might be. Perhaps we could find ourselves a couple of mugs of ale and discuss it."

If he was surprised at being invited to drink with a member of the nobility, the captain didn't show it. He smiled, called an order to one of the seamen, and led the way back onto the dock.

The inn they entered was relatively clean and busy. The captain found them a table near the back. Conan guessed it was his accustomed place for two men seated there, seeing them, stood and took their drinks elsewhere. That they did so quickly and without complaint told him much about the man he had selected.

"I am Diego," the captain said when they were seated. "And since people always seem curious to know, I'm not from these parts. My home is in Galicia but I settled here years ago and like it well enough."

Conan wasn't surprised. There were many such men and not only from Spain. In his travels, he had met men from far beyond the confines of his own lands. There were riders from the windswept steppes of Ruska, strange men with slanted eyes who spoke of vast empires to the east, night-skinned Saracens who claimed to know of immense lands and great trading cities to the south, and even men who whispered of yet more lands, far to the west across the open sea, where it was said a few brave souls had ventured. Through it all, he had grasped the idea that the world was bigger by far than most imagined. Compared to all that, a Spanish sea captain was of only mild interest.

"Wherever you call home," Conan said, "I am concerned only with your ability at sea." He noted that the captain had not asked his own identity, nor did he seem to have any expectation of being told it. That was sensible of him. "I need to reach London quickly."

Diego sat back and regarded him closely. It took no special trick to know what was passing through his mind. Not only London, but with speed.

"I would have to forgo my stop at Plymouth to accommodate you."

"And my horse."

Diego smiled. "Ah, yes, let's not forget the horse."

"I'll need straw bedding for him, very clean, hay and oats, and an ample supply of fresh water."

"And for yourself?"

Conan shrugged. "My own needs are small."

"I see. Very well then—"

They haggled. Conan did it very well, having learned the art at his mother's knee. Bargaining was thought the province of women until a man found himself in need of it. Conan was actually good but so was the captain. They spent a pleasant hour—and two mugs of passably good ale—coming to an arrangement.

"I won't get rich," Diego grumbled good-naturedly when they rose to go.

"Close enough," Conan replied. He squinted in the sunlight just outside the tavern door. "When do we sail?"

"On the evening tide, shortly after sext, but you can come on board whenever you like. I'll send men to see to the straw and the rest."

Conan agreed. More quickly then he would have expected, Gray was settled in the place made for him toward the stern. He seemed reasonably content. The last of the cargo was being loaded. It would be delivered, Diego told him, on the return trip. Meanwhile, it made useful ballast.

The tide would be turning soon. Before it did so,

Conan decided to take a walk around the town. He purchased a few amenities—a round of cheese, some bread, a flacon of wine—and had just finished paying for them when the bells rang for sext.

Returning to the quay, he found Diego preparing to cast off. "The weather is with us, my lord," the captain said as the ropes were hauled in. "We've a fair wind and a calm enough sea."

"I'll hope that lasts," Conan said. He was moving toward the prow, thinking to check on Gray, when Diego called to him.

"By the way, my lord, your squire came on board."

One hand on the rope railing, Conan stopped. "My squire?"

"That's right. He's with your horse."

Conan nodded, covering his surprise. He thanked the captain as his gaze slipped toward the prow. He could see Gray, lightly tethered, bales of straw around him. There was a canvas awning rigged up over the horse to protect him from spray. A shadow moved beneath it.

Conan stepped closer. The rest of the crew was busy at the oars, guiding the barque out into the channel. Softly he called, "Will?"

The shadow moved. He caught a glimpse of flame-touched hair tucked under a cap.

"No, not Will," Alianor said and stepped into the light.

Chapter 15

Conan stared at her in disbelief. He might have been looking at an apparition cast up by too much sun and too little water. Or too much battle, for men were known to be haunted by such things on bloody fields.

And yet, for all that, a part of him knew she was real. Knew it to the very bone and sinew.

And welcomed her.

All the same, he had a position to maintain. "This is madness," he said, anger hard-edging his voice. "What do you think you're doing here?"

There was a flicker behind her eyes, very brief but there all the same. She was just the smallest bit afraid of him. Still, she faced him boldly and without apology.

"The same as you." She even smiled, as though this was the most ordinary thing in the world.

"As me?"

"I want to go to London," she said patiently, all sweet reasonableness. "This seemed the most practical way to go about it."

Practical? She thought dressing up as a boy to stow away on a merchant vessel in these times when a heavily armed warrior such as himself thought twice before journeying alone was *practical*?

"Dare I think the desire for my company had a part

in this?" he asked even as he suspected he knew the answer.

She hesitated. With no more emotion than she might bring to a discussion of smoked herring, she said, "You can if you want to."

Ah, then, so he'd been wrong. He'd expected a flat-out denial, perhaps even a heated one that would have left just the smallest bit of suspicion aglow with hope that she did desire his company. Not that maddeningly accommodating response, that bit of pabulum tossed to male pride.

"I think I'd prefer to assume you mad," he said. Let her swallow that. Deliberately turning his back on her, he looked Gray over, as though inspecting him for any sign of damage from such proximity to a madwoman.

"He's a lovely horse," Alianor said.

Conan grimaced. How could so beautiful a woman so grate his temper? He felt irked along every inch of his skin, as though a thousand tiny pinpricks of fire were dancing within him.

Madness.

"He's a warhorse," he said. "They are never lovely. Has it occurred to you that I can send you back?"

"We've already cast off," she pointed out. "You'd either have to return to dock, thereby losing time, or toss me in the water." Her smile was purely female. "You should know that if I can't get to London this way, I'll simply find another."

The problem was he believed her. She really would trek across the width of England regardless of the danger. If he put her back on land, heaven only knew what would happen to her. As for tossing her into the sea, that did have a certain attraction.

He was about to say so when his attention was distracted by a loud meow. Mirabelle emerged from a pile of straw, yawned, and gave one ear a good scratch.

"You brought her along?"

"I couldn't leave her to fend for herself."

"Cats are supposed to be good at that."

"Well, she isn't. Truly, I'm really sorry to impose on you like this."

"But you will anyway?"

She did look genuinely abashed. "I'm afraid so."

"How did you get here? I rode but so far as I know, you have no horse."

"I walked."

Disbelief compounded disbelief. Walked? Thirty miles through untamed land, following the river as he had and as every brigand with an eye to a quick kill might go? She must have started the previous evening not long after she left the abbey and walked all night. In darkness. Alone.

By God, he'd throttle her.

"To reach London," he said through gritted teeth. "For what reason?"

She was tempted, he could see that. Part of her really wanted to tell him. She struggled briefly. He watched, unwillingly fascinated, as a shutter seemed to slip down over her eyes.

"I can't tell you."

"There's the water—" He said it half humorously, but only half. And what came next held no levity at all. "But then they say a witch will always float."

She said nothing, merely looked at him with those vast green eyes filled with hurt, and turned away. He was left to contemplate the steady rocking of the vessel and his own self-disgust.

The problem on every ship he had ever been on was that there was really nowhere to go. They were just too damn small. Though he found a seat at the farthest point of the bow and pretended great interest in the view, he could think of nothing but Alianor.

He had hurt her. As deftly as though he had spent hours crafting the insult, he had chosen the one word most guaranteed to cause her pain. And just when she'd been beginning to trust him.

If she weren't, she would never have come up with such a harebrained scheme to get herself to London. She had come with him because she believed he would keep her safe. Instead, he acted like a vicious boy who, denied what he most wants, seeks to destroy it.

He'd been no angel growing up but he'd never been like that. Staring at the gray sea, he decided he would give her a bit more time, then try to make amends. Meanwhile, he could try to figure out what she intended to do in London.

Obviously she was going there to see someone or do something, but who and what? So far as he knew, she had never been away from Glastonbury. But then he knew very little about her. Perhaps there were other healers like her in London and she wanted to consult with them. That might be it though if there were many such people, he thought he would know. Unless they kept themselves hidden away, fearing attacks by the Church.

Whatever the reason for her presence, he was determined to have it out of her before they disembarked. It was absolutely inconceivable that he would allow her to go wandering off into London on her own. She would simply have to accept that.

He glanced back toward the stern but could see nothing except Gray, calmly nibbling at a bag of oats. Alianor must have fed him, playing the squire. It was getting on for supper. Several of the crew were preparing what smelled like stew using an area of the deck carefully set aside for that purpose. They had a small fire lit, the wood laid on iron sheeting and surrounded by stone. Pails of water stood ready to douse the flames at the first sign of trouble.

When the food was ready, Conan accepted two bowls. He carried them back toward the stern. With the canvas awning and the bales of hay, there was an area blocked from the crew's view. Alianor was sitting there. Her eyes looked red. She did not acknowledge his presence.

"I'm sorry," he said and held out a bowl to her. When she hesitated, he tried a repentant smile. "At least I'm not handing you food and telling you how some poor monk may have been poisoned at the same time. That put me off my appetite, I'll tell you."

"I didn't notice."

Victory! She was speaking to him again. He breathed a sigh of relief and reached for the wine he'd brought. When it was laid out along with the bread and cheese, he said quietly, "Truly, I am sorry. I would not hurt you."

She took a small bite of bread and chewed it thoroughly before she answered. "I should not care."

The admission elated him but he concealed his response. Once as a boy he had spent two days in a blind, waiting for a hawk to become so confident of him that she would get close enough to be netted. The moment of her capture thrilled him, as did all the thoughts of taming her, and the hunting they would do together. But in the end, he let her go and returned home empty-handed. He never really knew why.

He settled beside her. Breaking the wax seal on the flacon, he handed it to Alianor first. "You still won't tell me about London?" he asked as she took a sip.

She lowered the bottle, cleaned the neck politely, and returned it to him. "I will when we get there." The way she spoke, it was a concession that had to be respected for all that it was reluctantly given.

He had a choice, either continue trying to drag the truth out of her or be content with her promise. He chose the latter, thinking of the lengths a man will go to for a little peace, however temporary.

One of the crewmen began to play a set of small reed pipes stitched together with hemp, a simple instrument carried by many sailors since time immemorial. The sound was light enough but with an undertone of longing for the vanished shores of home. Conan and Alianor settled back to listen.

Night was falling but a full moon had risen out of the sea, pouring silver across the water. Good to his word, Diego kept the barque under sail. If the men grumbled, they didn't let Conan hear. Perhaps they had been told of the generous bonus they would receive once London was reached.

The air was cooling fast. Conan removed the blankets he had tucked into his saddlebag and spread them out on top of some of the straw. Gray nickered softly, settling down for the night.

In her boy's short tunic, her hair still hidden away, Alianor shivered. She had a cloak but it was thin. Weariness etched her face. Thirty miles of walking through the night was too much even for the Lady of the Lake.

"Come and lie down," he said.

She looked at him blankly. He urged her gently over to the blankets. Without protest, she lay down, turned on her side, and was instantly asleep.

Conan sighed. If nothing else, knowing Mistress Alianor was doing wonders for his humility. Twice now she had fallen asleep on him. He covered her snugly against the sea breeze, then lay down beside her. The gentle rocking of the barque should have eased him into dreams but instead he lay awake, staring up at the night sky. The moon was so bright that there were few stars to be seen. He had to content himself with imagining them, tracing the patterns he had learned as a child. He could just make out Andromeda and farther to the north, Cassiopeia. Did Alianor know them? He suspected she did.

A flash of light streaked across the sky, followed by another, then several more. Falling stars, the harbingers of good luck, some said. Others said they bespoke doom. Conan thought them merely beautiful. For the scantest moment, he was tempted to wake Alianor to share the sight. But then he remembered how far she had walked, how tired she was, and instead pulled the blanket more securely around her.

She murmured faintly and drew her knees up closer to her chin. Despite the blanket, she still seemed cold. As well she might be considering the scant clothes she wore, probably gotten from that house she kept for children. He shook his head, thinking of her carelessness. She wouldn't allow anyone else to go journeying so ill-prepared yet she did it to herself without hesitation.

Contemplating her refusal to accept the innate frailty of women, he moved a little closer to her. She really did look cold. There were dark shadows under her eyes and her face was pinched.

He was a man and a warrior. Honor was the foundation of his life.

Besides, he ought to be used to this by now.

With a sigh, he gathered her close. Even in sleep, the warmth of his body brought a soft murmur of contentment from her. At least one of them was satisfied.

Sighing, he resigned himself to yet another long night.

Chapter 16

"Once when I was very small I climbed a tree and slipped. My tunic caught on a limb and I was left dangling perhaps ten feet in the air. I only hung there for a few minutes before Matilda found me and got me down but the time seemed endless. It didn't even feel like real, ordinary time. It stretched out all thick and gooey, featureless like taffy. I thought I'd smother in it."

Breaking off her thoughts, Alianor sighed, sharply enough for Mirabelle to rouse momentarily from her latest nap and blink at her. The cat did not appear sympathetic, but then the sky would fall if she did.

"I should talk to him," Alianor murmured, "instead of to myself." *He* was standing near the prow, chatting with the captain. Something seemed to amuse them. They both laughed.

Sunlight glinted off Conan's ebony hair. He'd shaved that morning, using a stone-hewed knife that made her wince every time she looked, which she had out of the corner of her eye, finding the process oddly fascinating.

She had never seen a man shave before. But then that was just one small item on the very long list of things she didn't know—or had never experienced—involving men.

She had slept in his arms.

Never mind about that. It was part of the night, she didn't have to think of it by day. They both knew, of course, but neither spoke of the matter. Come dark, and cold, and the loneliness of the open sea, she had found herself in his arms. He held her as chastely as he would a child.

Did he think of her that way?

The possibility stung but she dismissed it. She wasn't quite so ignorant that she didn't know he desired her. His self-control was formidable. She wondered what so disciplined a man would be like when the dark heat of passion was upon him and—

With a sharp tug, she reined her wayward thoughts in and stared out over the water. It seemed unchanging, gray-green by day, black by night. So, too, the land they could glimpse altered little. Yet two days at sea they had rounded the southwestern prong of Britain and were sailing in the Channel now between England and Normandy.

She had heard the captain say three more days would see them in London—if the weather held. He hadn't said it to her directly, of course, since he never addressed either a word or a look at her. She wondered if he had guessed that it was no slightly built boy accompanying his lordship to London. If he did, he didn't seem to care.

What could she—should she—say to Conan to explain herself? To explain the whole sorry business?

"Matilda got me down from the tree, I'm not quite sure how. I suppose I've just forgotten but she had ways— Or I thought she did. She said I would understand when I was older. I am now and I do, somewhat, but there's more out there, waiting. I need to walk toward it, embrace it, but I can't seem to take a step—"

Matilda had liked men. She'd spoken of them with true affection, citing the loyalty and courage so many of them showed, the gentleness of which they were capable often under the most terrible circumstances. But she had cautioned Alianor as well, speaking of passion's treacherous path and how very easy it was to slip astride it.

As her mother had.

She shut her eyes for a moment and saw again the whirling red mist she always glimpsed when she thought of that unknown but deeply felt woman in whose body she had grown and whose life had ended soon after her own began.

She had been too weak, her mother had, not for bearing children necessarily but for the harder task to which she had been called. Not chosen, Alianor reminded herself. Her mother had never had a choice. When she'd tried to make one for herself, she'd perished.

The island—and the lake—could be jealous of what they held. They gave up nothing willingly.

A ray of sun struck her face. At its warmth, she opened her eyes. The fancies of her mind seemed to evaporate. She was being foolish. There were always choices.

Conan and the captain were still talking. They seemed to like each other. Conan raised an arm, pointing toward the distant coast. She watched the play of muscles across his back and sighed.

Sweet heaven, he was a beautiful man, hard, ruggedly strong, with a powerful will coupled to that most seductive of all aspects—intelligence. She was in very deep and sinking fast.

Three more days. She could last that long, couldn't she? In fact, she didn't really know for she had never tried. "I should have been a cat," she said, looking at Mirabelle, asleep again or appearing so.

The suggestion apparently did not merit a response.

She was considering currying Gray again, a task she had already performed several times but which he seemed to enjoy, when she realized the barque was slowing. Conan came toward her.

"We are going to stop briefly to take on fresh water," he said. "You can stretch your legs, if you like."

Escape, however brief, was exhilarating. She agreed immediately. The patience she had hoarded through two long days suddenly ran out. She could hardly bear the few minutes needed to run the barque into shore.

They made land within sight of a small cluster of huts. Several people came out to watch but showed no alarm. From their behavior, Alianor gathered this was an ordinary enough event.

"Diego tells me there's a sweet stream nearby," Conan said. "The villagers, if we can call this place that, make their living providing water to passing seamen."

She ignored—as best she could—the steely strength of his arms as he lifted her onto the sand and pretended great interest in the process. "Will it take long?"

"An hour or so. Gray needs a run. Want to come?"

As though to encourage her, the stallion pawed the sand and whinnied.

Say no. Say you need to walk. Say anything so long as it means that you don't go off with him, alone.

"I'd love to."

The advantage of wearing a boy's garb was that she could ride without a sidesaddle. But then so could Conan. He swung up onto the horse in a motion that only hinted at his full strength. Mounted, sitting astride Gray as though man and stallion were one, he reached down a hand to help her up.

She had strength and agility beyond that of most

women but neither was needed. He merely hoisted her up with humiliating ease and settled her in front of him so that her bottom was neatly cradled between his thighs.

She should have walked.

That much was crystal clear to her the instant Gray began to move. Every step the horse took made her rock up and down against Conan in a highly intimate fashion. When she tried to pull herself forward slightly, the saddle blocked her. She was trapped, unable to escape without admitting her predicament.

And that was too embarrassing to contemplate.

Grimly she set her teeth and hoped the flush she could feel darkening her cheeks would be credited to the sun. His chest was like warm, carved stone directly behind her back. She could feel the power in him, held as always in careful check, and wondered where he had learned such control. On what battlefields? In what beds?

Down that twisting road she would not go. Better to concentrate on the beauty of the day, the clarity of the sky, the pleasure of being on dry land however temporarily.

My, wasn't this a lovely place, this southern England, all curving coast and high rugged cliffs except where they broke just enough for the little village of water providers. Gulls circled overhead, calling to one another. She glanced down in time to see a hare dart for thicker cover.

"Where are we going?" she asked and was pleased, not to say surprised, by how steady her voice sounded.

"Diego says there's a small lake this way. I thought you might like to bathe."

"I don't think so." She wasn't tempted for a moment, absolutely not. The idea of a blessed bath after three days of travel didn't draw her at all. Even less appealing was the notion of slipping off her clothes, throwing off all restraint, in the presence of one Conan, Baron of Wyndham.

Perish the very notion.

"I assure you," he said with a hint of laughter, "I'm the soul of discretion."

"I'm sure you are." Couldn't the blasted horse quit lopping up and down so much? Never mind that Gray was unusually surefooted. The dratted animal was far too enthusiastic.

"Why do I think you don't believe me?"

"Oh, it isn't your discretion I doubt. I'm sure that's one of the many virtues the Queen values in you. But I have noticed that men of a certain class—yours, to be specific—apply different rules to different women under different circumstances. Chivalry, in short, seems to be a sometimes thing. Or not at all. Depending on the whim of the man."

Did she imagine it or did he bend his tall head ever so slightly? She thought she felt the brush of his breath against her cheek. Very close, he murmured, "I would have thought I'd proved myself to you by now, Mistress Alianor."

Damn sun, it had her flushing again. All right, he had a point. She had slept—actually slept—in his arms two nights now without consequence. No, three, for she had to count that night at the cottage. Yet, he desired her. She needed no great knowledge of men to be quite certain of that.

"I warrant patience is another of your virtues," she said.

His voice deepened, roughening around the edges. "Only up to a point."

They went on, over the crest of a small hill. Alianor's breath caught. There, laid out before them suddenly, was a small but perfect pool bubbling up from beneath the limestone plateau, the water sparkling in the sun. It was surrounded by a natural screen of poplar and oak trees. If the captain hadn't told Conan where to look, she didn't doubt they would have gone right by, so secluded was it.

He drew rein. Gray stopped at once.

"What are you doing?" Alianor asked as he dismounted.

He brushed a lock of hair from his brow. "Since you decline to bathe, I believe I'll take the opportunity. Also, Gray needs to water and rest. He isn't accustomed to this much exercise."

In point of fact, the stallion looked as though he could go straight into battle but who was she to quibble. Especially when Conan was striding toward the pond, already undoing the laces of his tunic.

"I'll unsaddle Gray," she called but had no idea if he heard her. He had disappeared in among the trees near the water's edge. As she undid the horse's cinches, she could clearly hear the rustle of clothes being discarded.

She shut her eyes for a moment, willing her imagination to think of something, anything, other than what was happening just beyond her sight. A soft, lilting sound filled the air. She looked up, startled.

Conan was whistling. It was an air she dimly recognized though she couldn't put a name to it, light and happy, without a care in the world.

Damn him.

The whistling stopped. There was a splash, then stillness.

She should be hearing something, shouldn't she? But there was nothing, only the whisper of the wind and the far-off cry of gulls. What if he'd slipped, struck his head perhaps? What if at that very moment he was lying facedown in the water drowning—

She lunged forward, past the trees, fear gripping her only to come to a skittering halt on the edge of the pond. Nothing. The water was flat as polished metal.

"C-Conan . . . ?" Her voice caught. She felt a surge of panic rising within her.

Even as he rose from the water, suddenly, without warning, shaking his head vigorously so that diamond droplets flew in all directions. He stood, laughing, hands on his hips, the water licking just below his navel.

"It's wonderful," he said, grinning broadly. "Sure you won't change your mind?"

His shoulders were immensely broad, his chest lean and tapered, burnished skin stretched taut over clearly articulated muscle and sinew. A fine dusting of dark hair arched downward across his flat belly to disappear beneath the water. It was so very easy to imagine the rest of him.

"I'll just see to Gray," she said and turned so quickly she almost stumbled.

In fact, the horse was perfectly capable of seeing to himself. He drank to his satisfaction, then began to graze. Alianor was left to her own devices.

The poplars were fascinating. She couldn't remember ever seeing better specimens. So, too, the oaks. They deserved to be studied with greatest care. Now if she could just keep her gaze on them rather than have it stray toward the pool—

"Could you hand me the soap?" Conan called.

Her head turned reflexively. She jerked it away but not before she glimpsed him floating on his back, the long, hard shape of him just visible beneath the water. He seemed almost—playful.

"The what?"

"Soap. It's in my saddlebag."

The man carried soap around with him. And why not? Grace be to Eleanor, cleanliness had become the fashion. Yet even so Alianor was willing to wager there were few enough warriors in England with soap in their saddlebags.

"All right." She found it readily enough, a round, palm-sized ball unscented except for a crisp, clean smell. Not at all like the perfumed soaps that were her dearest indulgence.

"I'll toss it to you—"

"It's too soft," he cautioned. "Just come a little way in and hand it to me."

"I don't want to get wet."

"You, the woman with a mineral bath in her cottage? I can't believe you mind a little water. But very well, I'll come and get it."

"No!" She felt ridiculous, with good reason. She, a healer for whom the human body held no secrets at least in its outward design, quibbling over nakedness? Well, this man's at any rate. "Wait a moment." Swiftly she removed her sandals and hoisted up the hem of her tunic. Stepping forward, she held out the soap.

His smile broadened. "I'll have to come farther out to reach it."

She grimaced and stepped deeper. The water passed her knees. Still, he didn't seem quite able to reach the soap. "Just a little farther."

At midthigh, she stopped. "You have to be able to reach this."

"Possibly—" He held out a hand. The light in his eyes warned her an instant before his fingers closed around her wrist. She was yanked forward, landing smack up against a bare, wet, rock-hard chest. And various other things.

"Yiiipp!"

"You *can* swim, I assume."

"Like a fish, you—you!"

He let her go, raised a finger in admonishment, and laughed. "Now, Mistress Alianor, what kind of language is that for the Lady of the Lake?"

"Damn appropriate, I'd say. I'm soaked."

"Only to the . . . uh . . . shoulders. But be careful, the bottom here is slippery."

Indeed it was. Extremely. Even as he spoke, it went straight out from under her. She fell backward with a resounding splash and came up sputtering.

"I'm going to get you for this! If it's the last thing—"

"First," he said, "you have to catch me." He dove, cutting the water cleanly, and was suddenly beyond her reach.

But not for long. She was a good swimmer with many years practice. He might be vastly stronger but she was very, very determined. So much so that she was almost upon him before two things dawned on her: He was letting her win; and did she want to?

Too late. The sheer force of her stroke—not to mention his own coming to a sudden halt—hurled her against him. They collided with an audible thud that knocked them both over. Yet for all that, Conan managed to keep his arms around her. Indeed, he seemed to have no difficulty at all doing so. Surfacing, she found herself locked in his embrace, his body hard against hers and his mouth scant inches from her own.

"Alianor—"

She had to say something, tell him to stop, get free of him. Get away. Her mind knew all this but her body seemed to have its own notions. Appalled, she felt herself press yet closer to him as her arms went around his lean waist.

Her head fell back. He made a guttural sound deep in his throat and took her mouth with his. When he had kissed her in the cottage, she had felt his gentleness and, above all, his control. This was different. The touch and taste of him engulfed her. Passion, so lightly held in check, ignited like a spark thrown on drought-parched ground. She moaned, clinging to him. Reason dissolved as though it had never been.

He carried her out of the water and laid her gently on the shore. Coming down on top of her, his weight held mainly on his arms but pressing just lightly enough to let her feel his strength, he kissed her softly, over and over, the corners of her eyes, the slender line of her cheek, her mouth again and again, trailing fire down to the sensitive hollow at the base of her throat until she could bear no more. She could feel her nipples becoming acutely sensitive, feel the molten tension deep within her, the longing building until it would have to find release.

"Conan—" she murmured, her back arching, pleasure rippling through her like shards of light torn from the heart of a storm.

His hands had slipped beneath her tunic. He stroked her breasts, cupping them in callused palms, thumbs brushing over her nipples. His heavily muscled thigh moved possessively between hers. She was vividly conscious of his nakedness. Her own clothes suddenly felt unbearable. When he eased the tunic over her head, she didn't even think to protest.

Cool air touched her heated skin. The grass was soft beneath her back. His hair was rough silk in her hands as he bent his head and suckled her. His hand slipped between her thighs, stroking lightly, over and over. She looked up past the branches of the trees, past the few thin streaks of clouds to the high, empty places where only wind dwelled.

The sun was very bright. Its heat was inside her, expanding outward, dissolving all the barriers of bone and skin, muscle and sinew, until—

A woman's voice cried out once sharply, but the sound faded quickly, vanishing somewhere far behind. Alianor fell into the blazing bowl of the sky.

Chapter 17

When this business for Eleanor was all over, he was going on pilgrimage. Not to any of the easy places—Canterbury, Compostelo. They weren't for him. He'd go back to the Holy Land, steep himself in all the heat and sand he'd hated the first time, and perhaps meet up with Richard again. Coeur de Lion could always use a good fighting man.

What he wouldn't do—ever again so long as it pleased God to let him live—was fall under the spell of a fey girl who tormented his days and made his nights exquisite hell.

What in the name of all the saints and angels had he been thinking of? Nothing, of course. No saint and certainly no angel had prompted him to take Mistress Alianor to the pool, strip naked, coax her to join him, and then proceed—in an exercise of sheer madness—to introduce her to the finer points of sensual pleasure. And furthermore to do it all while—and here was the part that truly confirmed his madness—leaving himself painfully, persistently, inexhaustibly unsatisfied, simply because he refused to take the final, irrevocable step of intercourse.

He deserved it. Any man who would involve himself in so deranged an enterprise deserved all the torments of the damned that were the inevitable result.

Plus she wouldn't speak to him.

Conan sighed and leaned back against the side of the barque. He had the prow to himself. Alianor was forward, talking with an older crewman, the one who doctored the rest. They were exchanging lore. She looked beautiful, of course, even in her boy's clothes. He was more conscious of her beauty than ever now that he knew for certain the perfection that lay beneath the simple homespun.

He had come very close to losing all control.

Even in the privacy of his own mind, the admission was a hard, sharp thing pricking at him. Control was what had raised him high, from the son of a simple knight to the right hand of the Queen. Control had kept him alive on more battlefields than he cared to remember, but could never forget. His ability to rule his own emotions rather than be ruled by them lay at the deepest source of his pride.

Mistress Alianor had managed to change all that. And now she shunned him, refused to meet his gaze, murmured only those responses she absolutely could not avoid, and slept by herself. Gray was their chaperon, the great stallion sleeping with Conan on one side of him and Alianor on the other.

The only humor in the situation, and he had to dig deep to find it, was the realization that there were more than a few men in this world who would pay dearly to know of the mighty Baron of Wyndham's predicament. They would laugh themselves sick over the picture of the King's Scourge, as they had called him in the Holy Land—along with various other, less polite things—struck down by a slip of a girl.

He could have had her so easily. Physically she wasn't the remotest match for his warrior's strength and skill. He could have forced her to his will with utter ease but that was neither here nor there. She wouldn't have fought him, not by the pool and probably not even in her cottage that first night. Afterward, of course, she would have hated him, but she seemed to do that anyway.

No, it was his own damnable conscience that had landed him in this situation. When they got to London he was going to do the sensible thing, find himself a woman, two or three if he had to, and so sate his passion that he would forget there ever had been a Mistress Alianor.

And then he'd sprout wings and fly.

The only comfort, if he could call it that, lay in what he saw off the port side of the barque. Since they'd turned north up the eastern coast of England the landscape had gentled. Sheer white cliffs had given way to rolling woods and farmland. And now the gray of the open water was changing color, taking on the ruddy brown cast of the great tidal estuary where the Thames ran down to meet the sea. Another hour or so would see them in London.

He waited, eking out his patience, until he recognized right up ahead the curve of the land where it opened for the mighty river. The crew, seeing the end of their journey, redoubled their efforts so that the oars flew between air and water, singing the ancient anthem of a voyage almost done.

Conan rose. He made his way forward. Alianor was looking out at the swiftly passing land. She gave no sign that she felt his presence.

"We are almost there," he said.

She nodded. That much at least she gave him.

"And now you must keep your promise."

She half turned, looking at him at last. He ignored the jolt of pleasure he felt at that simple gesture and kept his face carefully expressionless. "Tell me what brings you to London."

"I have told you."

When he did not respond, but merely waited, biding silence, she said, "I told you I had the same reason you did."

"I am going to see the Queen." Surely, she could not have forgotten. Nothing else took him to London.

She faced him fully then. He could see her take a breath—for courage? Even before she spoke, the truth came rushing in at him. Why she had done this, why she was there, all his thoughts about who Alianor of the Lake truly was and why he had been sent to—do what? Protect her? Serve her?

Control her?

The thought was strange, inexplicable, but somehow it fit.

Alianor and Eleanor. Lady of the Lake and Queen.

"So am I," she said and the look in her eyes was so starkly sad that he wondered how to bear it.

There were men who claimed to dislike London. They called it too crowded, but Conan had seen Byzantium and knew what a crowded city really looked like. They said it was dirty, but he had been in Jerusalem. And they called its citizens rebellious, which was true enough but didn't allow for the predictability of their rebellion. If it was bad for business it was bad for London, otherwise they let it be.

Standing at the prow of the barque, he felt the air change from the clean, salt tang of sea to the heavy-laden smell of land. Smoke rose from the huts and forges of settlements clustered here and there wherever the marshy land allowed. Children running along the water waved to them but for the men and women going about their tasks such vessels were too common a sight to merit interest.

The river traffic grew apace. They were soon in the

midst of a steady stream of barges, skiffs, dories, punts, and yet more barques all plying their way up-river on the incoming tide.

"Do you know London?" Conan asked.

Beside him, quiet in her watchfulness, Alianor shrugged. "Somewhat. I haven't been here since I was a child."

He wanted to ask the circumstances of that visit but the stillness in her warned him off. They were approaching the Tower. It rose, a mass of stone almost as broad as it was tall, utterly dominating the landscape. Around it clustered additional, smaller buildings—several chapels, a hall, and beyond them high stone walls dotted with watch towers. Together, they were the most visible and formidable sign of royal power in a city where kings had found it well advised to make their presence known.

"Where do we dock?" Alianor asked.

"Billingsgate."

She looked up, surprised. "I thought we would continue on to the west minster."

"I think it more likely the Queen is here," Conan said and gestured to the fortress slipping past them. He was guessing, of course, but if he knew Eleanor at all—and he believed he did—she would forswear the greater comforts of the palaces at Westminster or Lambeth and keep herself to the Tower. More than all the Plantagenets combined, Eleanor had the greatest nose for trouble.

Billingsgate was a busy place, as evinced by the docking master who came bustling toward them as soon as they made anchor beside an unoccupied pier.

"None of that now," he shouted. "Every place here is reserved. I can't have people just come barging in.

Try Queenshithe, farther down, they'll have room. Or you could—"

Diego stepped onto the dock. He put his head close to the man's and murmured a few words. Conan, busy saddling Gray, spared a moment to note that a purse changed hands, exactly as he had instructed.

The dockmaster stopped in the midst of his tirade, stared hard at Diego and even harder at the barque. For the barest instant Conan allowed their eyes to meet. Instantly the man's demeanor changed. One did not get to be an official on the London docks without a certain discernment.

"My apologies," the dockmaster said just loudly enough to assure that his voice would carry on board. "I didn't realize you had a reservation. By all means, make anchor and stay as long as you like. If there's anything you need, don't hesitate to let me know."

Conan hid a smile. "You see why I like London," he said in an aside to Alianor.

She grimaced. "Because a fat purse never fails to smooth the way?"

"Because its citizens are practical people. Come on, let's go."

He settled up with Diego, thanked him for his speed, and led Gray onto the pier. Alianor followed carrying Mirabelle.

To all appearances, she was his groom and he no more than a nobleman of minor standing. They blended easily with the crowd streaming back and forth between the river and the streets beyond. All around them were peddlers hawking their merchandise from pushcarts and wooden trays hung round their necks, merchants and their servants hurrying back and forth about their tasks, soldiers, and what to Conan made London most enjoyable, musicians, artists, acrobats, and all the like performing on the street for the amusement of passersby and to earn their keep.

Even Alianor, preoccupied though she was, stopped to gawk at a fire-eating magician who appeared to swallow a great plume of flame.

"How—" she murmured, entranced.

"Never mind that now," Conan said and urged her on. They both walked alongside Gray. He preferred not to mount the horse in the teeming streets if he could avoid it but as they approached the Tower, he stopped long enough to swing into the saddle.

"Stay close," he ordered, making no pretense that it was a request. The stallion's hooves rang sharply on the wooden bridge that spanned a dry moat. Ahead, on either side of a raised portcullis, stood guards in full armor, helmeted, with lances in their hands and swords at their sides.

"Your purpose," one growled as the other edged a little closer, ready for any trouble. Conan took due note of their caution. The Tower was normally well protected but not quite to this extent.

"To return this," he said and withdrew from the pouch around his waist a gold ring engraved with the royal insignia, a leopard giving chase. Both guards looked, both stepped back. In an instant they assumed the closed-in expressions of men who have too much sense to be involved with the doings of their betters.

"Pass," said the senior man and promptly gave every appearance of having forgotten their existence.

"Handy thing," Alianor murmured as they passed through the wall and emerged onto the broad, open bailey. Several squadrons of men-at-arms were at drill, tilting at the targets on the quintains, practicing their archery, throwing javelins, wrestling, and here and there engaged in swordplay that had the look of being deadly earnest. Giving them broad breadth were the

Tower servants, hurrying about their duties, and a variety of clergy, townsmen, and hangers-on of unknown purpose, all the usual effluvia of a royal residence.

A breeze just then caught a pennant hanging from the highest turret and snapped it out full length, revealing the royal insignia emblazoned upon it.

"She is here," Alianor said softly and quickened her step.

They left Gray in the stables behind the White Tower. A boy there recognized Conan and made quick to assure him the horse would have the finest care. That was well and good but Alianor preferred to hold on to Mirabelle. If nothing else, the cat was a comfort.

The same should not have been true of Conan who, throwing off the guise of simple nobleman, looked every inch the warrior and liegeman of the Queen. His midnight hair glinted in the late morning sun, his hard face set in lines of command, Alianor struggled not to look at him. Every time she did, the confusion that had been her constant companion these last days swept over her yet again.

And yet she was so very glad to have him there. All the rest she would think about later, as she had thought about it endlessly over and over, but for the moment she was honest enough to admit that his presence gave her courage.

They climbed the high outside staircase of timber that led to the first floor of the Tower. More than a century old already, it remained the largest and most impressive structure in London. Alianor blinked once, twice as her eyes adjusted to the relative dimness of the hall. At first glance, it seemed to her there were a great many soldiers. They stood at intervals around the perimeter of the vast room, watching all who came and went.

"The Queen is being very careful," she murmured.

Conan nodded but said nothing. He took her elbow lightly and steered her toward the farther reaches of the hall. They passed dozens of people, all apparently waiting, who glanced at them with curiosity but made no attempt to stop them. Neither did any of the guards.

He was known, it seemed, if not by the guards on the outer wall, then by these closer to the inner sanctum of the Queen.

"Wait here," he said and disappeared behind a red velvet curtain that partitioned off an unseen space beyond.

She stood, holding Mirabelle, and glanced around at the vast, columned room. There were two huge fireplaces, each large enough to roast a whole boar in, on opposite walls. The ceiling was wooden and vaulted. Instead of rushes on the floor, there were rare carpets in vivid colors and elaborate designs, from the East, she guessed. Shields and war banners hung everywhere, testament to the proud warrior tradition of the Plantagenets. Throughout there was an impression of heavy solidness coupled to vast power.

The curtain fluttered. Conan emerged again and beckoned to her. She followed and found herself in a small antechamber. Copper braziers had been lit against the spring chill. Several pretty young women sat by a window of leaded glass, busy at their needlework. If Conan noticed their glances, he gave no sign of it.

"Through here," he said and opened a wooden door braced by iron. There was another small room beyond. A man sat behind a plain wooden table bare except for several rolls of what looked to be accounts. Well if sedately dressed, he looked at Alianor for a moment before nodding.

"Please wait," he said and disappeared behind yet another curtain.

The air was dank with the smell of the river and the aroma of old stone and mortar. Mirabelle stirred in her arms, wanting to be let down. Alianor hesitated but finally relented. The cat jumped to the floor, tail twitching, but stayed close.

The man reappeared. "You may come in."

They passed beyond the curtain and, it seemed, into another world. Light flooded the chamber beyond, pouring in from high windows set below the ceiling as well as others lower down. The walls were hung with rich tapestries, the floors covered with more rugs. Greenery and wildflowers had been brought in and arranged in ewers, creating the impression of a garden. There were books, wonderful reams of fabric, the scent of perfumes. Somewhere a lute played.

A figure stood in front of the windows. Silhouetted against the light, she seemed done all in black and gray. Until she moved and the colors of her rich robes shimmered boldly.

She was a very old woman. The hair just visible around the edges of her wimple and veil had long since gone gray. Her face was sered by time. And yet she was as beautiful as Alianor remembered. A child's memory, it seemed, could also weather the years and still prove true.

"Your Majesty," Conan said and bowed his head.

The Queen raised a hand, blue-veined, sparkling with gems. "Leave us." Her voice was low, soft, slightly husky, the tone accustomed to command. Certainly, she showed no surprise at their arrival—or anything else.

The lute stopped abruptly. Several people Alianor hadn't even noticed got up and departed with hardly a sound or wasted motion. They were alone.

"Your Majesty," Conan began, "I should explain why I am accompanied by—"

"Never mind," Eleanor said. She stepped a little farther away from the windows. In this, her sixty-ninth year, she stood remarkably erect. Her eyes, large, thick-fringed, and brown, were still her loveliest feature. They appeared to miss nothing. "I have your message. What brings you here so swift upon it?"

Conan hesitated. Alianor's presence—undiscussed, unexplained—clearly discomfited him. But the Queen was waiting for his answer. Briefly he told her. He explained the discovery in the graveyard, the monks' conviction that the bodies were those of Arthur and Guinevere, and his own concern about where such talk would lead. His words were succinct and to the point. He did not exaggerate in the slightest but neither did he withhold any pertinent fact. Eleanor heard him out calmly. When he was done, she seated herself in a high-backed chair next to a small table. Her fingers toyed with an inlaid knife.

"This Brother Wynn, the sacristan, can you tell me more about him?"

"Only that he is young, intelligent, and appears able to control Abbot Du Sully at least to some extent."

"And he found the bodies."

"There were others present."

"Including yourself. How convenient."

Conan looked puzzled. "I was investigating Brother Raspin's death."

"As well you should. So they've found Arthur, have they, and his Guinevere as well? What marvelous news. Every troubadour and mime player will be enraptured."

"I'm sure, but the political implications—"

"Are all too clear." The Queen favored Conan with

a kindly look. "You serve me well." Her gaze shifted to Alianor. "And you, mistress, make a charming boy."

Mirabelle was rubbing against Alianor's legs, wanting to be picked up. She obliged. Over the cat's head, she studied the Queen. "Thank you, Your Majesty."

Conan looked from one to the other. Slowly he said, "You are acquainted with Mistress Alianor, Majesty." It was not a question. "She asked to come and I could hardly refuse her."

Eleanor smiled—a bold, almost flirtatious expression that gave a clear glimpse of the young woman she had been. "I'm sure you couldn't. However, I imagine after such a journey you would value a bit of ease. Come back at supper. We will dine together."

He turned to go, stopped, looked at Alianor. She had not moved.

"We will have partridge, I think," the Queen said. Her smile deepened. "Until then."

He was dismissed.

When the curtain had closed behind him, Eleanor rose. She splashed ruby wine into two goblets and handed one to Alianor. "Would your cat like a bit of cream?"

"Undoubtedly."

"Then I'll send for it. You've grown."

"Fifteen years will do that." Her calmness astounded her. She had never thought to see this woman a second time. Indeed, had told herself she would not want to.

"Has it truly been so long?"

"I think so. Do you know him well?"

"Conan? I've known him all his life. His mother is my foster daughter. This is quite a good wine actually. It's from my father's old vineyards in Aquitaine."

Alianor took a sip. "It is excellent."

"Good. Do sit down."

Alianor hesitated only briefly before obeying. The

Queen took her own seat across from her. They studied each other for a moment.

Eleanor sighed. She drank a little of her wine, then set the goblet aside. "Now, my dear, I want to hear all about what's happening in Glastonbury."

Chapter 18

Dismissed like an errant boy so that those two blasted women could talk. Angrier than he could remember being in a very long time, Conan strode through the great hall and out of the Tower. He needed the company of men—or of whores. He couldn't quite decide which.

The decision was made for him when a piercing yell tore the air right behind him at the same time that steel-hard arms lifted him straight off the ground.

"By God, Conan lad! It's a dragon's age since I saw you. Where've you been hiding?"

"Not far away enough apparently." He broke the grip with a favorite wrestling move. The two men grappled briefly, old friends testing each other's strength for old times' sake. They broke off laughing.

Conan stepped back a pace and looked at the large, heavily muscled man with the shoulder-length blond hair and a roguish grin. He grinned. "I thought you'd be dead by now, Olaf."

"Yah, I could have been but I decided to leave Ruska instead. Crazy people, the Ruskas. Not that I didn't have a fine time with them."

Conan grinned. For Olaf to term anyone crazy was a feat indeed. The two men had met in the Holy Land, fortunately fighting on the same side. Olaf was the second son of a Viking chieftain out to make his own way and doing a damn good job of it.

"What brings you to London?" Conan asked as they walked across the bailey together. Crowded though it was, they had no difficulty. People tended to get out of the way of two extremely large, innately dangerous-looking men armed for battle.

"Oh, this and that," Olaf replied. "I'm glad to meet up with you actually. What are you doing these days?"

"This and that."

Olaf laughed. He and Conan had always enjoyed sparring verbally as much as physically. "And I hear you do it for the Queen."

Conan shrugged noncommittally. He was remembering that Olaf enjoyed the common misapprehension that a man so powerfully built and muscular was lacking in intelligence. In truth, this second son of a chieftain was anything but. He tended to have a better grasp of what was going on around him than just about anyone Conan knew.

"Have you eaten?" Olaf asked when it was clear Conan wasn't going to comment further on the nature of his duties.

"No, I just arrived a short time ago."

"What do you say we go over to Smithfield? There's an inn with decent meat pasties and some of the best ale I've found anywhere. Afterward, we can give the horses a run."

"Sounds good." In fact, it sounded perfect. No women. Just proper food and drink, excellent male companionship, and hard exercise to work off all that energy he had roiling around inside him. Not to mention whatever scheme was simmering in Olaf's ever active mind.

They fetched their mounts from the stables and rode out. Smithfield lay to the north of the city. It was a large, open plain surrounded by trees and ponds. On Saturdays a horse fair was held there that usually drew a good crowd. But the rest of the week it was popular among boys and men seeking a place to practice their fighting skills. Or just find a bit of peace from the womenfolk.

The inn Olaf had mentioned was just beyond the north wall of the city. They left the horses in the capable hands of a young groom and found a table outside. It was a fair day, sunny and pleasant. This part of England at least was having a good spring.

"Been in the city long?" Olaf asked after a buxom serving maid—were there any other kind?—left them a pitcher of nut brown ale and took their orders for food.

"I arrived this morning. You?"

"A sennight now. I hadn't meant to stay that long but the place is—interesting."

"Aye, London's that."

"No, I mean more than usual. I haven't been through here in two, three years. Not since before old Henry died."

"You find the city changed?" So did Conan but he wanted to hear what Olaf had to say.

"I find it unsettled. There's talk, you know."

"There's always talk. That's the principle business of London."

"True but people are uneasy. They were used to Henry whether they liked him or not. Besides, he was good for business. All those laws and that kind of thing made people feel it was safe to drag their money out from wherever they'd hidden it and put it to work. Richard's different."

"No man is a copy of his father."

"Not a copy, no, but this one scarcely seems cut

from the same cloth. He got his sire's temper, that's for sure, but the wits are lacking."

"Richard's intelligent enough. He just has different interests from his father."

"Aye, Henry made law. Richard makes war."

"He truly believes he is chosen by God to free the Holy Land from the infidels."

Olaf quaffed his ale. He wiped the back of his hand across his mouth and belched. "I know some of those infidels. So do you. They're fine people."

"Careful you don't say that in a priest's hearing."

"Is that what you've come to, my friend? Worrying about what a priest thinks?"

"I worry about the peace," Conan said honestly. "England's had little enough of it. With Richard busy elsewhere and Eleanor ruling in his name, we've got a fair chance to keep things going here. Anything that threatens that, I oppose."

Olaf glanced over his shoulder. No one was seated nearby. Quietly he said, "Then you'd better listen to this, my friend."

The two men parted an hour or so later. Conan returned to the Tower deep in thought. He was informed that the Queen was resting and was directed upstairs where quarters were kept for guests.

One day soon, he supposed he would have to establish a residence in London. Most of the greater nobles did and he had certainly moved into their ranks, even if the fact still took some getting used to. His estates were large and contained no fewer than four castles, all more or less pleasant. But he tended to be at court most of the time. It was a mark of his swift rise that he was readily housed there and shown every courtesy.

The room he had been directed to was large and luxuriously furnished. Chimneys had been added to the

Tower after its construction to allow for fireplaces in the more important rooms, including this one. A large bed curtained by embroidered hangings was set off by itself in an alcove. There was a table, actual chairs instead of stools, a clothes press, and on the far side of the chamber a drawn curtain that undoubtedly concealed facilities of a more private nature.

The sound of splashing could be clearly heard from behind the curtain.

Interesting. He hadn't even had an opportunity to request a bath, much less get it occupied. Obviously, the steward had made a mistake directing him to this room. Chivalry required him to withdraw. He should go back downstairs, find out where he was actually supposed to be, and—

"Conan?"

The voice filtering out from behind the curtain was Alianor's. She sounded mildly concerned, as though wanting to make sure it was him and not someone else.

"It's me," he called.

"I'm almost done. Do you know, there's the cleverest thing in here. The tub is set on top of a little drain cut into the floor. The water sluices right out down the side of the building. Oh, there's plenty more. The girls brought extra in case you'd like a bath yourself."

She was talking to him again. Indeed, she seemed almost friendly. He was relieved by that—if a little puzzled—but the thought of a bath overrode all else. It was positively enticing.

Still, he was a courteous man. "Don't rush on my account."

"No, really, I'm done. I just need to find that sheet—"

An image flashed through his mind. Alianor rising naked from the water, her body glistening in the light, trying to find where the serving girls had left the toweling sheet.

"Ah, here it is."

He exhaled sharply and walked away from the curtain, putting the width of the room between him and it. A short time later Alianor emerged. She was no longer wearing her boy clothes but had on a simple, graceful gown in a deep shade of plum girded at the waist by a belt inlaid with gold. Her hair was freshly brushed and hung uncovered down her back. Her smile when she saw him was a little tentative, almost shy.

"I wondered where you'd gone," she said.

"I met a friend. Look, the steward directed me here but he was mistaken so—"

"No, he wasn't. The Tower is very crowded. There are no extra accommodations. We were lucky to get these." She walked over to the table where there was a ewer of cider and a plate of honey cakes. Pouring a goblet, Alianor offered it to him. "Her Majesty wants us to stay until tomorrow. She's looking forward to speaking with you at supper which, incidentally, will be in her chambers, not the hall."

So Eleanor was dining with them—both of them—privately. And she had extended the hospitality of her home to them even if it did stretch to only a single chamber.

"I can sleep in the hall," Conan said. He turned to go but the thought of the bath slowed him. There was always the river, of course, but it couldn't compete with hot, clean water.

"I'm sorry," Alianor said. The words were blurted out. She was blushing.

He hesitated, his hand still on the door latch. "For what?"

"You know . . . for behaving so badly. I'd just as soon forget about it if that's all right with you."

Forget the beauty of her face and form, the incandescence of her passion, the sheer triumphant sense of joy he had felt at bringing her to pleasure? Forget feeling closer to another person than he had ever done in his life?

"All right," he said without conviction.

She smiled again, relieved, and gestured to the curtain. "Don't let the water get cold."

He nodded. "You'll be—"

"Her Majesty suggested I might want to take a look at the supplies in her still room. She has some rare items from the East."

"How thoughtful of her."

"Very."

They stood for what seemed like a long moment looking at one another before Alianor took a cloak from the bottom of the bed and tossed it around her shoulders. He was blocking the door. She had to wait for him to realize it and move aside. Their bodies brushed. Instantly his hardened.

"Enjoy the bath," she said. He caught her smile as she departed.

Despite all that, or perhaps because of it, he found the bath delightful. Sinking into it, he felt the tension of the past week begin at last to ease from him. Off in the distance, he could hear the muted sounds of the castle but they were remote enough to be ignored for the moment. Soon he would be back in the thick of it. A small interlude of peace was exactly what he needed.

Or so he thought until he heard the curtain twitch and realized he was no longer alone.

"The still room wasn't as interesting as I'd hoped," Alianor said. She stood, just inside the alcove, a slight, uncertain smile on her lips. And in her eyes—

"Wasn't it?" He sat up slightly, just so he could get a clear enough look and make sure his mind wasn't playing tricks on him. She had removed the cloak and was wearing only the plain gown that simple as it was managed to cling alluringly to every curve of her body.

The water had cooled, indeed he'd been thinking of getting out, but he suddenly felt swept by blazing heat. Unless he was very much mistaken, Mistress Alianor had come to a decision.

Slowly he stood, giving her plenty of time to change her mind. She didn't move but merely gazed at him as the water sluiced off his body. Her flush deepened but the look in her eyes was balm to a vanity he hadn't really known he possessed.

He crossed the distance to her quickly and took her into his arms, but lightly, carefully, not wanting her to feel in any way trapped or compelled.

"Alianor," he murmured against the fragrant silk of her hair, "are you sure?"

He felt rather than heard her assent.

The bed was wide and welcoming. He laid her on it, withdrawing just long enough to close the shutters and make certain the door was secured. He wanted no interruptions.

She helped him to undo her belt and slip her gown over her head. Beneath it she wore a thin chemise of finest lawn. The contours of her body were clearly visible through it. His throat tightened as he ran his hands down the length of her in a gesture that was blatantly possessive.

"Lovely," he murmured as he slid the fabric down over her shoulders, baring her breasts. They were perfect, high and firm, tipped by nipples the shade of ripened apricots. He groaned deeply, fighting the driving urge to bury himself in her instantly.

His desire was a writhing force within him, threatening to overcome all consideration and control. Had she been anyone else but Alianor that would have been a very real possibility. But this was his Lady of the Lake, proud, strong, in every way a match for himself. He took a deep, shuddering breath and vowed to go slowly.

If she let him. Did she have any idea of the effect her body had moving against his as she was doing? The soft moans that broke from her as he suckled her breasts almost shattered his resolve. And when her hands stroked down the hard line of his back even as her legs opened he feared himself undone.

"Stop," he said roughly and took hold of her wrists, stretching her arms out above her head. Restraining her effortlessly, he touched her womanhood, stroking the hot, soft sweetness there. Her eyes flew open, staring into his. She gasped, small white teeth biting her lower lip. He eased a finger into her and breathed a small sigh of relief to find her fully ready for him.

But she was still small and virgin, and he a man of control and honor. His lungs burned, every inch of his skin was painfully alive, but he clung to his resolve with all the tenacious strength of his warrior's nature. With his hands, his mouth, his body, his entire being, he cherished this beautiful, enticing woman. Time seemed suspended. Even the raging hunger of his own need mattered little beside Alianor and the trust she was placing in him.

When he at last moved to make her his, she welcomed him without restraint. The small instant of resistance faded as though it had never been. Sheathed within her, he waited, giving her time to become accustomed to him. His heart rammed against the wall of his chest and his breath came in gasps, but still he held on, moving with exquisite care, in slow, deep thrusts.

Her eyes flew open, meeting his. She cried out as pleasure crested within her. The undulating rhythm of her womanhood took him. Control shattered. His release was savage, beyond anything he had ever experienced. He poured his life into her and knew nothing more.

Chapter 19

Alianor stirred. She turned over on her side and burrowed a little more deeply into the soft mattress. A small spurt of awareness trembled at the edge of her mind. She was lying up against something very warm and very solid. Mirabelle? No, it couldn't be. It was far too large.

Slowly her eyes opened. At the same time, memory flooded back. The journey, London, the Tower. Her meeting with Eleanor and her decision—boldly taken, not a flicker regretted—to throw off restraint and live for the moment. For who knew when there would be another? Soft shadows of evening filtered through the closed shutters.

Propping herself up on an elbow, she gazed at Conan. He lay on his back, one arm flung out toward her. His thick, black hair was rumpled. A lock drifted over his forehead. His eyes were closed, the lashes casting shadows over his lean cheeks. His mouth was slightly parted. She stared at it, marveling at how much softer it looked asleep than awake. And, too, remembering the feel of it against her skin.

Remembering everything.

A warm flush crept over her from the very tips of her toes right up to her tousled hair. She took a small, shuddering breath and eased the cover down slightly.

She had never really thought much about men's

chests. They were simply there, different from women, lacking breasts, more or less muscular, more or less lean, not particularly interesting. Not until now.

His chest and shoulders were ... beautiful. Truly, that was the only word for such symmetry of form, such grace and power. He appeared as a sculpture might, one done by a master artist. His skin was smooth, vital, taut over clearly articulated muscle and sinew. An arrow of dark hair arched downward bisecting the ribbed walls of his torso, thickening toward his groin.

There was a thin, white scar near his navel. She stared at it as the full realization of what it meant sunk in. There were other scars on his arms, higher up on his chest, but this one—this innocuous-looking thing no more than a few inches long—could have meant his death. Whatever blade had done it—whatever enemy— had been perfectly positioned to gut him. As it was, she suspected he'd been spared by the smallest margin for such wounds could rarely be survived.

Her throat thickened. She had to put her hand to her mouth to hold back a sob. The thought of him dying—

But he hadn't died. He was there, alive, real, and so very close. Cautiously, not wanting to wake him, she brushed her fingers down his chest. Her touch was infinitely light but some awareness of it must have reached him for he stirred. His arms closed around her. He murmured something and nuzzled her breasts. A hair-roughened leg, heavily muscled by years in the saddle and on the battlefield, slipped between hers.

"You're awake." Her voice shook ever so slightly.

He raised his head and smiled. It was really quite unfair that he could smile like that—at once boyishly innocent and devastatingly male. "So are you."

Awake and growing more so by the moment. His hands slid down to cup her buttocks. Gently he urged her closer against him. His manhood was hard, erect, tantalizing.

Shadows gathered in the Tower room. Day had almost faded but night was not yet upon them. With the world poised between light and dark, there was still this small interlude to make their own.

Smoke from pitch torches set in brackets around the walls of the great hall rose to stain the rafters high above. The hall was crowded. Conan recognized several high-ranking nobles, men of the great landed families and others like himself risen to power through their own efforts.

His presence was duly noted by them, but the greater curiosity—and interest—was reserved for Alianor walking at his side. A low murmur followed in their wake. Already word had spread that the Queen would not be in the hall that evening. She was dining privately with guests.

They were shown into the same chamber where they had met with Eleanor before. It was empty save for two attendants setting a small table. They finished quickly and left. A door opened in a side wall, so cleverly concealed that its existence was not immediately evident. Eleanor stepped into the room. She was alone. No ladies in waiting or servants hovered about her, as was usually the case.

Despite the warmth of the evening, she wore a richly embroidered tunic beneath a brocade surcoat trimmed with fur. Her head was almost entirely covered by a wimple and veil that framed the austere beauty of her face. The clothing, and the chill they staved off, seemed the sole concession to her years. Certainly, there was nothing old in the smile she gave them.

"I trust you are rested."

Conan started to cough, stopped himself, and instead bowed low. The gesture gave him time to consider—and decide to reject—the possibility that Eleanor was perfectly well aware of what had gone on between the two of them. The Queen had her spies aplenty but not of the bedchamber variety.

"Thank you, Highness," he said. "Be assured that we are."

"I used to like traveling," Eleanor said as she led them over to the table. "When I was a girl, I was prone to pick up and go at a moment's notice. It didn't matter where. Why when I went with poor Louis on Crusade, the world was scandalized but I had a marvelous time."

"I thought most of your army was destroyed and you yourself shipwrecked," Alianor said mildly.

Conan's head jerked in her direction. It was one thing to accept that she and the Queen were somehow acquainted. It was quite another for Alianor to bait this woman who had bested kings and popes.

"You have to expect some inconvenience on any journey," Eleanor said. "My lord, do pour the wine for us. I thought it more pleasant if we did without servants this evening."

Conan complied. It seemed the safest thing to do under the circumstances. When he had filled the silver goblets set with precious gems, he took his seat.

"The chef tells me partridge with red wine is all the thing these days," Eleanor said, indicating the platter. "I do hope you like it."

"This is delicious," Alianor said, "but have you ever tried a mustard dill sauce?"

"No," Eleanor replied. "I haven't. How is it prepared?"

And so it went, back and forth, mostly between the two women as Conan contented himself with listening. They discussed food and wine, the merits of various troubadours, different techniques for weaving cloth, and whether or not a particular clay from the Somerset region was beneficial to the skin.

It reminded him of conversations he had listened to between his mother and her ladies when he was very small and apt to sit in the solar of a rainy afternoon, amusing himself with his wooden soldiers. But this was subtly different. There was an undercurrent of both familiarity and not quite animosity—that was too strong a word. Wariness, certainly, mainly on Alianor's part and something that seemed very like contrition on Eleanor's.

But that was impossible. She was the Queen and never known for being the least contrite about anything. Hadn't her stubbornness and pride rent a kingdom, set father against sons, and almost brought down a dynasty? And hadn't she then patched up the same and set it on a new and, Conan believed, better course?

Contrite. It didn't fit and yet he could have sworn, as he devoured a quite excellent partridge accompanied by early peas brought no doubt from Eleanor's estates in Poitiers, that the Queen was making an enormous effort to make Alianor like her.

What was this admittedly enticing woman to the Queen of England?

The fire crackled. He poured more wine. Musicians were playing in the hall beyond, amusing those not gifted with the royal presence on this evening. Their tunes filtered through the stone walls and resplendent hangings into the private chamber.

Alianor smiled at something Eleanor had said. Eleanor smiled back and for just an instant, it was there in the eyes, a quicksilver impression gone as quickly as it had appeared, yet unmistakable all the same.

Conan set his knife down. He looked from one to

the other. "You know," he said amiably, "I entertained the notion that Alianor might be Henry's daughter."

Eleanor stiffened as though she had been struck. She stared at him incredulously. "You didn't." On the other side, Alianor made a soft, surprised sound.

Neither had expected this. Good. He could play the civilized male well enough in the scented chambers of clever women but it was just as well they understood the veneer was only that.

"Forgive me, madam, but it seemed logical enough. Hidden away on that island as she has been, yet obviously acquainted with the royal family and of interest to yourself, I had to consider the possibility. Of course, I should have realized that were the late king her father, your interest would not have been quite so— benign, shall we say?"

"You came to that conclusion, did you?" the Queen inquired. She, who for Henry's love of a young mistress, had launched a civil war.

"It seems unlikely. And then I saw just now as the two of you were talking what I suppose I should have seen much earlier. There is a family resemblance."

A splash of wine spilled from Alianor's goblet and spread bloodred across the damask cloth.

"Conan—"

"It's all right, my dear," Eleanor said, reassuring her. "I've played chess with him often enough. He likes the direct gambit from time to time. He thinks it tends to catch his opponents off guard."

Conan leaned back in his chair. He twirled the wine goblet between his fingers. The two women were silent. It made for a nice change.

In his own way, he was drawn to them both. Eleanor was hardly the mothering type—he would never mistake her for that. But she had been teacher and mentor to him. He respected her deeply even as he knew to always be cautious of her. As for Alianor—now that was more complicated. She was beauty, passion, a woman worth slaying dragons for, in the whimsy of the poet.

Together they were—what? Power, certainly, though of different kinds. And by necessity in this land where the crown did not sit firmly on any head, they were also danger.

"He's thinking," Eleanor said. "Henry used to do that. He was good at it."

"And Richard?" Alianor asked.

The Queen shrugged. "Ah, now, that's a different matter."

"What I don't understand," Conan said, "is how you could have concealed it. Royal births are too well attended for duplicity."

Eleanor smiled. She, too, had been known to try the direct gambit. "I was in Angers, at my own court surrounded by my own people. Louis had divorced me the year before and Henry and I had married forthwith. It was always such a chore getting with child by Louis and then I had only girls. Henry was—different. At any rate, he was off seeing to his holdings when I was brought to childbed."

Conan shook his head, perplexed. This was not what he had expected. He had thought one of her daughters had somehow after all, despite the seeming impossibility, borne a secret child. Yet if he understood the Queen correctly, she was telling him that—

"Wait a moment. Your firstborn by Henry was a son. He died when he was—what?—three or four."

"Guillaume," Eleanor said softly and for a moment the memory of grief swept across her face. She suppressed it sternly. "He had a twin."

Alianor reached across the table. She covered the Queen's hand with her own. "Madam, you don't have to do this."

"I know, but as with all things I do, it has a purpose. Tomorrow, I am sending you both back to Glastonbury, back into danger. It is as well that the Baron of Wyndham understands what it is I expect him to protect."

Conan had set his wine down. He was as close to being stunned as he had ever been in his life. She was serious. This extraordinary woman was actually telling him that she had borne a child in secret and kept its existence concealed from the entire world. Or had she?

"The King—?" he asked.

"Never knew. He was delighted to have a son. Nothing else mattered."

And that stung, even after all these years. Oh, she was good at hiding it but Henry's fixation with male offspring still rankled. Did it with every woman? Did they simply pretend otherwise?

He looked quickly at Alianor, thinking of what they had shared and what might result. The possibility riveted him. He almost missed what the Queen said next.

"Her name was Gwyneth. When I knew her to be healthy, I sent her to Matilda for fostering."

"Send a royal child to a cunny woman in the back of nowhere and never reclaim her? Forgive me, Majesty, but that is beyond reason."

"There were reasons," Alianor said. She looked at Eleanor.

The Queen shrugged. "And they are yours to tell when you feel you should. *If* you do."

Conan waited. Alianor looked at him for what seemed like a very long time. At last, she said, "The partridge really are excellent, Your Majesty, but what do you do for salmon? I have a recipe you might enjoy. To begin, the flesh must be smoked, ideally over ash wood, and then—"

She was not going to tell him. She had lain in his

arms, given him her body—and, he thought, her heart—
but she was not going to tell him the truth at the center
of the mystery that was Alianor.

The stab of disappointment that shot through him
was keen as a sword's point. He lifted his goblet and
took a long swallow of the wine. It was, not surprisingly, bitter.

Chapter 20

Heather had claimed the hillsides. In the short time since they had journeyed to London and returned, the full glory of an English spring had arrived in all its unbridled exuberance. Standing at the prow of the royal barque, Alianor gazed out at the changing landscape.

Here and there, amid the fields and pasturage they passed, she could make out sweeps of color that she knew to be primroses and larch sprays. Out of sight, but easily imagined, were the shyer violets, wood anemones, periwinkles, and oxlips nestled among the ferns and ivy in every dell and glen.

Around her cottage, the first bluebells would be in bloom, with a tiny touch of frost still nestled in their bells of a morning. "For the wee folk," Matilda had always said but with a wink to let Alianor know she was funning.

She missed Matilda more than ever now. What she would have given for a chance to talk with her even for a few minutes. In the five days from London, confusion had roiled her mind. She had not wanted to like Eleanor, still wasn't sure she did. But she didn't despise her either. Meeting the Queen again, feeling the aura of her power and conflict, the great sweeping tides of history that engulfed her, she had actually felt sympathy.

And then there was Conan.

She had no regrets for what had passed between them. Her decision taken, she was at peace with it. But that was past. What lay ahead remained unknowable.

She had hurt him. Incredibly, since the notion seemed so unlikely, she could feel the wounded spirit he was at pains to conceal from her. Feel but in no way address. The royal barque, luxurious as it was compared to Diego's vessel, afforded no greater privacy. Indeed, with all the men-at-arms accompanying them, there was even less. That was fortunate in its way. With no time or place to be alone, she and Conan simply avoided one another as best they could.

Her boy clothes were packed away. She traveled as the Lady Alianor. A tent had been set up for her in the prow. It was small but absurdly comfortable. The walls were richly hung silk. Rugs brought from the East covered the decking. She had a bed, a basin, even a lute miraculously discovered in one of the several trunks she had found suddenly accompanying her.

From Eleanor, of course. All sent along without a word. Alianor would have been less than human not to be at least a little enraptured. She spent hours admiring the rich fabrics, some already made up in gowns and surcoats, others waiting for the tailor. There were ointments, perfumes, ivory combs, even an inlaid box that opened to reveal the glint of gold.

"These would have been your mother's." So the note inside the box said, signed only: *"E."*

The note was the first solid acknowledgment of her heritage that she had ever possessed. Before now it had always been words and few enough of those. She read the one-line message over and over until the parchment threatened to tear and she had to lay it carefully aside.

The jewels she left untouched. Perhaps someday she would consider wearing them. Perhaps not.

Weston-super-Mare was as they had left it. The arrival of the Baron of Wyndham with two dozen men-at-arms caused the predictable stir. Children clustered on the quay to watch the unloading of horses and equipment while more than a few adults apparently found it prudent to be elsewhere. Word of their coming would spread on the wind. Before sext, everyone would know of the baron's return and his apparent intent to deal with trouble.

A mare had been brought along for Alianor. She was a well-behaved chestnut with a dainty step, perfectly suited to one who liked horses but had found little opportunity to ride. Alianor told herself not to become too attached. She had no way of keeping the mare and should not consider her to be her own. But she took to calling her Fiona all the same. A horse had to have a name and Fiona seemed to like hers.

She was mounted, Fiona lightly pawing the ground, when Conan rode up to join them. His head was bare but he had a helmet tucked under his arm and armor gleamed beneath his cloak. From his greater height, he looked down at her expressionlessly.

"Are you well, my lady?"

He had addressed very few words to her since leaving London and all in this tone of correct exactitude. That stung but she could hardly blame him.

"I am fine, thank you," she said, exquisitely polite.

He signaled several mounted men attending him. At once, they spread out, surrounding Alianor. "Your guard," he said by way of explanation. "They ride with you at all times."

They were hard-faced men, helmeted, battle swords at their sides, chain mail visible. She felt as though a wall had suddenly sprung up between her and the world.

It was on the tip of her tongue to point out that she had journeyed to Weston-super-Mare alone, with no escort save her own wits, and arrived perfectly fine. But the hard, closed look of Conan's face suggested he would not be swayed. She was now the Lady Alianor and therefore subject to all the protection—and restraint—accorded a woman of her class.

To reach Glastonbury before dark, they had to maintain a steady pace. The men were inured to it. Alianor was not. But she found riding easier than she had expected and even enjoyed it. The view of the world from atop a horse was more pleasant than she'd known.

She would have liked to stop from time to time to admire the wildflowers and perhaps gather a few rarer specimens, but a war party on the march had no time for such things. And she did not delude herself, that was exactly what this was. These men had not come for the pleasure of a country spring, or the excitement of a journey, or any other reason save the expectation of trouble and the willingness—indeed the eagerness—to deal with it.

She suspected each had been personally selected by Conan. They rode with pride behind his banner, a golden hawk in flight against a field of blue. Beneath the hawk, in letters large enough to be seen from a distance, were the words *"HONORIS CAUSA."*

She hadn't seen the banner before. If it had been visible when he rode into Glastonbury that day a fortnight ago in time to stop her from being arrested, it had gone unnoticed. But now she stared at it.

From what he had told her, he was the first of his line of sufficient rank to possess a family crest. He had designed this one then, or had it designed for him. The hawk was interesting. It was a clever, beautiful animal that killed only to survive. As for the motto—

For the sake of honor.

That was certainly clear enough and believable. Conan, Baron of Wyndham, was a man of honor in the noblest sense. It was at once his greatest strength and vulnerability.

From the fold of Alianor's cloak where she rode, Mirabelle meowed. The cat was less averse to travel than most of her species but still managed to convey her disdain for the process.

"Hush," Alianor murmured. "We're almost home."

Dusk was settling over the gently rolling hills and broad marshlands as they entered Glastonbury. Few people were about, the scents rising from cook fires explaining their whereabouts. Conan drew rein in front of the inn.

Master Brightersea appeared at the door, took in what was before him, and hurried out.

"My lord, welcome back. Your presence honors us, and all these men . . ." He eyed the war troupe with mingled avidness and concern. All these mouths to feed, all these bodies in need of a place to sleep, all these horses to board. But, too, all those swords, all those hard stares, all that power but lightly sheathed awaiting the command of the baron for any purpose he might think proper.

"Where is Sir Raymond?" Conan asked.

"At the abbey, my lord." Master Brightersea hesitated. Under normal circumstances, Alianor suspected he would have said nothing more. But two dozen armed men on his doorstep was far from normal.

"I believe Sir Raymond will be glad to see you, my lord," the innkeeper ventured.

Conan raised an eyebrow, nothing more. It was

enough. He turned, spoke to the knight behind him, and made to go.

"Wait." Alianor spoke without thinking. At once, two dozen pairs of male eyes swerved in her direction. She was abruptly aware of having transgressed. So be it. If Conan expected her to turn into a tame, compliant, simpering, doltish noblewoman, he was in for a rude surprise.

"I want to go with you."

If she had announced her intention to strip naked and dance, the general surprise could not have been more evident. Disciplined though they were, several of the men gaped. Only Conan failed to react. With perfect reasonableness, he said, "You are tired from the journey. You need to rest."

Her hands tightened on the reins. How dare he tell her how she felt and what she must do? She hadn't asked for a protector and most certainly would not accept a warden.

"In fact, I am not tired at all, my lord," she said, controlling her temper with an effort. "But I am most anxious to see how things are at the abbey. Pray, let me accompany you."

He did not so much as hesitate. Not for the merest instant did he consider agreeing. Instead, he said, "The abbey is not the best place for you right now." To one of the men accompanying her, he instructed, "Escort the Lady Alianor to her residence." With courtesy grave as her own, he added, "Pray remain there, my lady."

And he was gone. Riding up the cobbled street toward the hill and the abbey above.

Alianor stared after him. She felt a spurt of disbelief. He honestly expected her to obey.

Remarkable.

But then why shouldn't he when there were two

dozen armed men to see to it that she did? A terrible sense of helplessness seized her. Angrily she turned Fiona toward the river road.

He had done the right thing. She was tired, whether she wanted to admit it or not, and he didn't need her to distract him while he assessed the situation at the abbey.

That he took a certain base pleasure in controlling her was neither here nor there.

A faint smile played around the corners of his mouth as he considered the unenviable task he had set his new men. Did she realize how much any self-respecting warrior dreaded being delegated protection of a lady? Did she begin to understand the concern it generated, that a misplaced word or look would be interpreted as disrespect? That the lady would complain to her lord? That she would fuss and bother, leaving the hapless man-at-arms at sea as to what to do with her?

Probably not. But these new men were well chosen. He knew each one's experience and aspirations. He was well satisfied with them. However Alianor felt about it was entirely her affair.

Content with his decision, he spurred Gray up the hill to the abbey. As he approached, the bell was ringing to call the brothers to prayer. Good, that would give him a chance to speak with Sir Raymond undisturbed.

He found the knight seated on a bench in front of the abbey door. He looked weary but at the sound of hoofbeats, he straightened quickly. One glance at Conan was enough to bring a smile to his face.

"My lord, you are back."

Conan slid from the saddle. He walked over to his old friend and comrade-in-arms. Rank forgotten for the moment, the two men embraced. When they stepped apart again, Conan said, "I'm not alone. I've brought a fresh company with me."

Raymond looked relieved. "That's fortunate. The men have been standing watch in relays but I can't deny they're tired."

"Where are the bodies?"

"Still in the chapel." When Conan glanced toward it, the knight said, "I have four men in there at all times, night and day. The monks are permitted to view the remains and pray over them, but they can touch nothing."

"Excellent. Has there been any trouble?"

Raymond hesitated. He was a professional, not given to complaining. Still, it had clearly been a very long eleven days.

"Not precisely trouble, my lord. There are . . . stirrings in the town. I sense the townspeople are very careful what they let us hear. But as we have been here almost all the time at the abbey, it may be I am mistaken. Then there's the abbot—"

"Has he been difficult?" Did a crow fly?

"He is . . . obsessed. I can think of no other word to describe him. Night and day, he works on plans for the new abbey. He sleeps hardly at all and has to be reminded to eat. And yet I must admit that his temper is greatly improved. He seems genuinely happy."

"I'm not sure I can picture that."

"He hasn't spoken to me directly but I gather he has met privately with some of the townspeople to let them know what's been discovered. As you know, the folk here haven't seemed particularly devout but I gather some of the more prosperous have already pledged funds for the reconstruction. That merchant, for instance, the one the boy Dermod works for—"

"Master Longueford?"

"That's right. He's been up here several times. What he saw seems to have caused him to discover a new religious fervor."

"No surprise there," Conan said. He would have preferred to keep the discovery secret but had understood how unlikely that would be. At least Du Sully hadn't tried to trot the whole town through.

"If the abbot gets his wish, Glastonbury will become a major pilgrimage site. Master Longueford and his kind will find their generosity to the Church returned a hundred times over."

Raymond nodded. "If not more. Ah, well, each man's path to God is different."

Conan glanced around at the old building. It required little effort to imagine what was likely to rise in its place. "Have you become a philosopher then?"

"It's hard not to think when you've spent as much time with dead bodies as I've been doing." He hesitated, a bit abashed. "I mean, what if they are Arthur and Guinevere? They loom as giants in the telling of their lives yet there's nothing there but a bit of bone and hair."

"You expected more?" Conan asked softly.

The knight shrugged. "I suppose not. But if every man, even the greatest, can become the pawn of a Du Sully—"

"Remember what the old holy man we met outside Jerusalem told us?"

"Holy man—? Oh, you mean that skinny old fakir who smelled like a camel?"

"That's the one. He said there were people far to the east beyond even Persia who burn their dead. Mayhap Arthur's wishing right about now that he'd lived among them instead."

Raymond laughed. He cast Conan a fond look. "Or that he'd had a proper Viking funeral at least. Now there's how to do it, sail off on a warship all ablaze, spend eternity in the hall of warriors with drinking horns that are never empty and beautiful women who never refuse you."

"Not exactly the Christian heaven," Conan pointed out.

"Ah, well, speaking of women, we never did manage to find Mistress Alianor but that boy, Dermod again, seemed to think there was no reason for concern."

"He was wrong." Conan said darkly. At the mention of Alianor, his good humor fled. He was reminded of her pride and stubbornness, her refusal to trust him fully, and his own remorseless hunger for her.

"Don't say she came to harm?" Raymond said. He was genuinely alarmed.

Conan laid a hand on his shoulder. "Little enough. She accompanied me to London."

The knight's eyes widened. "She what?"

"You heard me. While I arranged to take ship, she crept aboard claiming to be my groom. By the time I discovered her, it was too late."

"Never say! Jesu, she's a bold one. You boxed her ears well, I presume?"

"Uh, no, not exactly, but I did bring her back with me. I sent her off to her island with a good company of men to make sure she stays there. I expect she'll be better behaved."

Raymond grinned. He seemed to find the situation highly amusing. "A man can always hope. Speaking of which, that Brother Wynn was gone for a few days. I was starting to think maybe he'd found himself some other place to be, but it seems his mother was ailing. At any rate, he asked to speak with you when you returned."

"I believe I can stand to postpone that until tomorrow. I'll send some of the new men up to relieve you."

"I'll tell the others. It'll be welcome news."

"Tell them also to enjoy Master Brightersea's best. They've earned it. But the food, not the drink. I want everyone stone sober till we're out of here."

Raymond nodded. "Aye, Lord." The look in his eyes said that time couldn't come soon enough.

Chapter 21

There were men outside the cottage. Oh, not right outside. They were too well trained for that. Having seen her inside, they withdrew a small way and set up camp. She could see their fire from her window, hear the low murmur of their voices.

The intrusion felt unbearable. In her own home, on her own island, she might as well have been imprisoned. And all because of Conan. It was by his will that this was happening. Because he ordered it, her sanctuary was violated, her cherished independence brushed aside.

"Damn him," she murmured under her breath. Mirabelle glanced up, yawned, and went back to washing. From just outside the cottage, Alianor was aware of the soft movements of Fiona, settling down for the night.

They had come across on the horses, the men-at-arms hesitant about swimming the animals across unknown water but convinced when she assured them it was safe. They had a deep reluctance about being parted from their mounts or she suspected they would have ignored her advice purely on principle.

So here they were, all together, and she restless as—what? She could think of nothing to match the anxious, angry state of her spirit. Her unease seemed too big to contain. She paced back and forth, wishing weariness would finally lay her low but it did not. Night crept up out of the west, overhanging the sky until the first stars were visible. She fed Mirabelle and made sure Fiona had everything she needed but her own appetite was missing. Not even a long, hot soak in the mineral bath—normally her favorite indulgence—helped.

Wearing a lawn chemise with a cloak thrown loosely over it, she lit several oil lamps. The evening was cooling rapidly. Seated at her worktable, she drew out a fresh roll of parchment and studied where she had left off on it. Matilda had taught her to read and write while she was still a very young child. She had also impressed in Alianor the importance of keeping good records about the medicines she used and the results they brought.

"In times past," Matilda had said, "it was enough for our knowledge to be kept in memory and repeated one generation to the next. But now, with so few of us remaining, it is vital that our learning exist in some form that can survive us."

And so she kept her records meticulously. Glancing back a little way, she found the notes she had made while treating Brother Bertrand. Each medicine and dosage was carefully set down. She read them over, reassured that she had done nothing—absolutely nothing—that could have brought about his death.

There had been no time to note down her care of Godwin. She hesitated now, debating how to do it. Her records were well hidden but these were troubled times and she had to consider that they might fall into the wrong hands. Finally, she recorded him simply as *Patient* and let it go at that.

She had just finished, and was washing the ink from her fingers, when a sound outside alerted her. One of the men was pouring water onto the fire as the others mounted. She opened the shutters wider, trying to see what was happening.

She could hear conversation, some laughter. The mood of her dour-faced guards suddenly seemed much improved. But why? They couldn't just decide to leave on their own. They would have had to be ordered out by—

Her stomach lurched. She caught a flash of gray against the darkening trees and saw the toss of a stallion's mane.

Moments later the men were gone, making haste for the town, the tavern, for Master Brightersea's hospitality. She was left alone, or almost.

He rode toward her out of the shadows astride Gray. Coming to a stop some little distance from the cottage, he sat rock-still, surveying it. And her, for with the light of the fire and her lamps she had to be clearly visible standing at the window.

Retreat was impossible. Pride would not allow it. He dismounted and led the horse over to where Fiona was sheltered. Alianor heard the mare nicker.

She was out the door in a flash and confronting him. "What is it you think you're doing?"

He gave her a long, steady look that encompassed everything from her disheveled hair to the bare feet peeking out from beneath her cloak. Gravely he said, "Good evening to you, too, my lady. Surely you wouldn't begrudge Gray a bit of oats?"

No, of course she wouldn't. She would never allow an animal to go hungry or thirsty. But there was still a point to be made. "I don't want him troubling Fiona."

Conan frowned. "Who's Fiona?"

"My horse—that is, the mare. She was here first and, well, I just don't want him causing her any trouble."

The frown vanished, replaced by a smile he tried

very much to repress but couldn't quite. "Gray's a good sort. I think he'll mind his manners."

"He'd better," Alianor muttered. She gave the stallion a final suspicious glance before removing herself to the cottage. There she bustled about, quickly tidying her worktable, putting water on to boil, just things she would normally have done for herself and which had nothing at all to do with Conan's sudden appearance. Absolutely nothing.

He ducked his head to enter below the low lintel of the door and looked around cautiously. His helmet was gone and he had removed his armor but she didn't let that fool her for a moment. He had all the appearance of a man girding himself for conflict.

So be it.

"Do you distrust your men so much that you had to come yourself to make sure your orders were carried out?" Alianor asked sweetly.

His eyebrows rose. They were really quite eloquent eyebrows, capable of expressing a whole range of emotion from mild amusement to outright surprise to the stirrings of anger. She was definitely in the latter range at the moment.

"If I did not trust them," he replied, "they would not be in my service. No, I sent them back to the inn to rest and eat. Do you want to know what I found at the abbey or would you prefer that I just leave?" He spoke mildly, as though her choice was of no particular importance to him.

For just a moment she was tempted to match him tit for tat. He was being insufferable. Let him go. She wouldn't care at all.

Except that the temptation was just too great. The temptation to know about circumstances at the abbey, not any other. Not Conan himself, for example, blatantly male presence that he was, filling her cottage with the wild scent of wind and steel.

"You might as well have a bite to eat," she said and poked up the fire.

He sliced the ham. She found a round of cheese. He opened a jug of cider. There was no bread, she'd had no time to bake. But she did manage to toss together a few fern heads and other greens with a vinegar she'd put up the previous summer. All in all, not a bad meal for being spur of the moment.

Certainly, Conan seemed content enough when he sat down to it. He had removed his cloak and was wearing a simple, unadorned tunic that stretched tautly across his powerful chest. Alianor had slipped away briefly to put on a proper gown. It seemed she was always getting dressed or undressed because of him but she wasn't going to think about that just now.

He poured the cider. Outside the wind had begun to blow a little stronger. With the shutters closed and the fire leaping brightly, the cottage was warm and cheerful. It was all so dreadfully comfortable that Alianor could almost have gone without mentioning the abbey. Almost.

"I suppose Du Sully is in his glory," she ventured.

"So it seems. I didn't see him myself. Sir Raymond says he's been spending all his time designing the new abbey."

"The one to rise as a memorial to Arthur and Guinevere?"

"Arthur, at least. Somehow I doubt Guinevere is a favorite of the abbot's."

"Just because she betrayed her husband and took a lover?"

Those eloquent eyebrows twitched. "You don't think that's reason enough for a woman to be condemned?"

"I think it ought to work both ways but doubtless

never will. At any rate, there's no certainty the bodies are Arthur's or his Queen's."

"What about the inscription on the cross? You said yourself that the shaping of the words could indicate that it came from another time."

She chewed a piece of ham and nodded. Odd how her appetite had returned, and so very strongly. "Could but it doesn't necessarily. Even if the cross is real, that doesn't mean that the bodies the monks found are the same as those it was originally buried with."

He sat back in his chair, regarding her. "Do I understand you? You're saying that the cross might have been found by itself, then reburied with two bodies so that they could all then be discovered together?"

Alianor nodded. "It makes sense, doesn't it?"

"Only up to a point. The man's a warrior, I saw that for myself, and he's wearing a gold diadem."

"How many warrior kings do you suppose have lived in this land through all the ages? Did they go to their graves naked?"

Conan looked unconvinced. "Someone would have had to find ancient bodies as well as the cross and then decide on this fraud. It's a stretch."

"But not impossible. Besides, the cross could have been made as it is deliberately in order to look like something not of our time."

"It seems a great deal of trouble to go to just to—"

"Get an abbey rebuilt after seven years of not being able to do so *and* turn it into a major pilgrimage site *and* attract a great deal of wealth in the process. People will go to enormous lengths when there's so much to be gained."

Conan was silent. He appeared deep in thought. Slowly he said, "There may be more to what you say than you know. Do you remember my mentioning that I'd run into an old friend in London?"

Alianor nodded. "The one who told you people were talking."

"Olaf spends probably more time than he should over by Southwark. You don't find anyone of Norman blood there. It's all Angles, Saxons, and Danes who still hold to the old ways. He likes the tales they tell, including the one about King Arthur returning someday to throw off the Norman oppressor, restore the land to its ancient glory, and so on. At any rate, he says suddenly the word going around is that the day of Arthur's return is almost here, that he'll rise in the west and lead a mighty army to restore him to his throne before the year turns."

"It's amazing the things men will say with a mug of ale in their hands."

"Olaf can drink with the best of them but he was sober when he told me this and he swears the men saying it were the same."

There was something more; she could see it in his eyes. Cautiously she asked, "And how, would you tell me, can a man killed in battle—not to mention being dead all these centuries—suddenly walk the earth again?"

"If the tale tellers have it, there's only one way for that to happen."

"And that is?" Sweet heaven, did she have to drag it from him?

"Arthur has to be healed by the person who has waited all this time to do exactly that—the Lady of the Lake."

"Who's she?" It was the only thing Alianor could think of to say and it was weak. Thank heaven, her mouth had always worked even when her mind didn't. Matilda had cautioned that could be a danger but there were times when it served her well.

He smiled. A wholehearted smile of enjoyment. She

wondered if it was the same look he gave Eleanor across the chess table.

"Surely you remember the legend?"

"I have had little time for such things."

"Oh, come now, everyone knows it especially since Geoffrey of Monmouth penned his history."

She grimaced. "If you must call it that."

"You think it in error? Queen Eleanor and even King Henry—who heaven knows had little patience for such things—were delighted by it."

"Because he flattered them shamelessly. Geoffrey would have made an excellent troubadour."

"He called himself an historian. Never mind, there are more voices in this besides his and their tale's worth the telling." He leaned back and his voice took on a soft, soothing tone—as though bent on no more than an evening's entertainment.

"Behold Arthur, King of England, slayer of the invader, conqueror of an empire, brought low by his old enemy, Mordred. Dying, he is carried back to Avalon, wherever that may be. Doctors attend him but he is beyond saving. Bishops prepare for his burial but even as they do so his body vanishes from the bier, carried off into the mist by three queens—his own Guinevere, Morgana the witch, and the Lady of the Lake, that mysterious creature who provided Arthur with his sword, Excalibur, and through it his power."

The wind had increased. It seemed to rattle the walls of the cottage.

"You astound me," Alianor said.

"How so?"

"That you have had time, far less the inclination, to learn such things."

"At Eleanor's court, it is not necessarily a matter of choice."

"Nor in Southwark either, it seems." She reached for

her mug. Perhaps she was tireder than she'd thought—
or too distracted. Her hand struck the handle, knocking the mug and its contents onto the table.

She jumped up, reaching for a cloth. Conan cleared
plates out of the way for her but she could feel his
eyes, knew he was gauging her anxiety as she mopped
up the mess. Putting the best face on it, she smiled.

"Fortunately, there's more cider."

"If you want it."

He was standing very close. She could smell the
crisp, clean scent of wool, leather, and man. Looking
straight ahead, she found herself staring at the hard,
broad contours of his chest.

Sweet heaven, she needed him so much. The days of
abstinence had taken a cruel toll. Desire rose in her—
hot, sweet, undeniable.

Did he reach for her? Did she for him? No matter.
The cider was forgotten. Moments passed. Mirabelle
leapt, a silent shadow, onto the table and settled herself
to enjoy the last bits of ham.

Five days. Five long, excruciating days. More to the
point, five nights. Ample time to remember, to long, to
plumb to the full the deepest void of unsatisfied desire.

His hand shook. He brushed it lightly across her
cheek and saw the tremor that signaled how very per-
ilous his control had become.

Thank God she was no longer a virgin, if he could
cherish so impious a thought. But she was the next
thing to and he knew he had to go carefully when all
he wanted to do was pull up her skirts and plunge into
her sweet, hot passage.

No, not all. He wanted to see her tremble for him,
watch the flow of passion across her beautiful face, feel
it explode deep within her. Slow then, whatever it cost
him.

A bolt of molten pleasure rocked him to the core. Shock followed as he realized her small, soft hand had crept beneath his tunic.

"Please," she whispered, her breath hot against his ear, "it's been so long."

Again she touched him. Again the world rocked.

"Alianor, you need—" His voice was husky, little more than a growl. Speech was almost beyond him. Reason was about to follow.

"You," she said and moved against him, her breasts lightly brushing. Through her gown and his tunic, he could feel the erectness of her nipples. See them, too, by firelight.

He had come victorious through battles where the fighting lasted all day and the ground ran red with blood. He had not merely survived but prospered at a court where deceit was as common as air and treachery dwelt behind every smile. He had fought to preserve honor and decency in a world that seemed to encourage neither.

But never in all his life had he confronted the struggle he did now. All his fine intentions were in danger of dissolving.

She moved back toward the bed, drawing him with her. He smelled the sweet, clean scent of her hair and skin, felt the infinite softness of her touch. Her girdle fell away. She was left with only the gown, drifting about her, little more hindrance than gossamer.

He wound his fingers through that flame-hued hair and took her mouth hard. She met the plunge of his tongue, clinging to him. There was no hesitation in her, only the need to match his own.

So be it.

His hands racked up her skirt, baring her to the waist. Long, silken legs gleamed whitely in the firelight, and between them, the nest of curls shielding her womanhood was already damp to his touch.

He breathed a silent prayer of thanks for her passion and freed himself. Tumbling her across the bed, he came down hard above her. Her hips moved against him.

The violence of their desire overcame them both. Her hand closed around him, guiding him to her. He sheathed himself in a single thrust, then waited through the pace of a heartbeat before beginning to move, hard and fast.

She moaned beneath him, her hips arching, matching him stroke for stroke. A fine sheen of perspiration dewed her skin. She grasped his hips, holding him closer, taking even more of him. The velvety passage of her womanhood tightened, released, tightened again. He groaned, his head falling back, unable to contain the force she unleashed within him. His climax erupted without warning, savage in its intensity, seemingly endless.

Stunned, he slumped against her, hardly believing what had happened. He had never taken a woman like that in all his life. But then he had also never known one so explosively responsive. And she could seem so demure! Well, no, actually she couldn't. He'd never been fooled by the quiet pose she adopted from time to time when she was busy thinking thoughts she didn't want anyone to know. A complex woman then with depths to her he was only too happy to explore.

Indeed, he grinned at the thought and, lifting his head, gazed into her eyes. She smiled back but with a certain smokiness to her glance that sent a small frisson of sensation down his spine.

"I'm so glad you stayed for that bite to eat," she murmured.

"What man could turn down such a courteous invitation?" Oh, good, he could talk. That must mean he was breathing again.

She moved, lithe as air, and before he guessed her intention, had wiggled out from under him. He turned onto his back and watched her quizzically.

"What a shame. My gown appears to have gotten wrinkled."

"I'm terribly sorry about that."

"Oh, no," she assured him, "not at all. But I do so hate to appear disheveled." With a swift, graceful movement she removed the gown and let it drop to her feet. Naked, she walked toward him.

He stared, drinking in the sight of her. From the top of her flame-bright head to the bottom of delicate feet, she was perfection. Her limbs were slender, her waist a deep indentation above the chalice of her hips. Her breasts would fill his hands, the nipples perfectly made for his mouth. She was everything he had ever desired in a woman and more than he had known could exist.

His throat tightened. She stopped at the edge of the bed and touched his tunic lightly. "Are you comfortable in that?"

"No," he said at once, "not at all. I'll just—"

"Let me." Gently, never taking her eyes from his, she undid the laces at his throat, then slid the garment from him. When he was nude, she looked at him with frank admiration that for all its artlessness was exquisitely seductive. Also flattering.

"You are . . . quite magnificent."

To his astonishment, he actually felt slightly embarrassed. He could never remember a woman looking at him so boldly before. The houris he'd enjoyed in the East had confined their compliments to his manhood but he had discounted that as mere trade talk. This was different, astoundingly so.

He reached for her. She caught his hands in hers,

playfully encircling his wrists as though to restrain him. "I learned something today."

"What's that?" Whatever it was, she undoubtedly did it enchantingly and he'd be happy to hear all about it. Just at another time.

"To ride."

His eyes opened a tad wider. "You'd never ridden?"

"Well, very little until today. I discovered that I like it."

"Do you now?"

"Quite a lot."

"I see—" For a man who scant moments before had experienced a climax that had made his very sense of consciousness flicker darkly, he was remarkably, intensely aroused.

"So I was wondering—"

Her cheeks were a most delightful shade of pink. He took her hand, fingers twining in hers, and gently drew her to the bed. "By all means, my lady," he said, the very soul of magnanimity. "I wouldn't dream of denying you the opportunity to refine your skill."

"So understanding—" she murmured as she swung herself over him. Her hand encircled him, squeezing lightly. "And so very accommodating."

He did his best, at great length and repeatedly, until at last sweet, sated Alianor curled against him with a satisfied murmur and drifted into sleep. Moments before he did the same, he gathered her close and pulled the covers over them both.

Night wrapped round the cottage, shutting out the world just a little time more.

Chapter 22

Conan paused directly in front of the abbot's open door. He stared at the man working busily at the table. Was this truly Du Sally? He had the appearance of him right enough but not the manner. The abbot he remembered was a sour, anxious sort riddled with fear, seeing danger everywhere, spitting venom. This man smiled as he worked and even hummed a little tune to himself.

Remarkable what the prospect of wealth and privilege could do.

He cleared his throat. Du Sully glanced up, saw him, and—smiled. "Ah, my lord baron, I had heard you were back. Come in, come in."

Conan advanced into the room with caution. He did not credit such swift changes of character. They shrieked of an unstable mind. Still, it would be ungrateful not to appreciate this smiling fellow, so cheerfully intent upon his task.

"You must see how much has been accomplished already," the abbot said. He actually took Conan's elbow, urging him over to the table. "Here are the drawings for the main portion of the abbey. Of course, a great deal more must be added but I think you can begin to see the general plan."

Conan glanced down at the drawing. It was pen and

ink on vellum, but meticulously rendered with no small skill.

"Did you do this yourself?"

Du Sully nodded. "When I was a boy, drawing was my great love, after God, of course. Since assuming the responsibilities of abbot, I have had little opportunity to pursue that interest. But now—" He smiled again, expansively. "Now I find it all coming back to me."

"I can see that—" Conan said slowly. Incomplete though the drawing was, there was a tremendous amount of detail. Du Sully had sketched every stone, every pillar and column, even the illuminated glass of the windows. Looking at the intricacies of his plans, it was easy to believe what Raymond had claimed, he was a man obsessed.

Yet also far more at peace than he had been before, or at least tending in that direction.

"Magnificent," Conan said and meant it. There was an elegance about the plan in the way it drew the eye upward, making it seem almost as though the building would float on the hill high above the town rather than press down upon it.

Du Sully shot him a quick look, saw that he was sincere, and blinked rapidly. "Thank you. I can't remember when I did work so exhilarating. But tell me, when you informed Her Majesty, what was her reaction?"

Conan thought for a moment. He did not wish to discourage the abbot in any way and yet the truth was that the Queen had said damnably little about the discovery. She seemed interested solely in its political implications.

"She called it marvelous news." Well, she had, however sarcastically.

Du Sully nodded. "I knew she would feel that way. Perhaps she would like to see my plans?" He had the look of an eager boy.

"I'm sure she would," Conan agreed. "However, there is another matter—" When the abbot merely looked at him, puzzled, he went on. "Your concern that two monks have died as a result of witchcraft. Surely, if Glastonbury is to become a major pilgrimage site, the possibility of satanic influences in the area must be put to rest."

Du Sully did not respond. For a moment Conan wondered if he'd heard. Finally, his mouth pursed and he let out a long sigh. "I have a duty to expose evil wherever it is found."

With an effort, Conan suppressed his irritation. He had a perfect opportunity to end this problem for Alianor—and by extension, for himself. He did not intend to waste it.

"True but surely one would have to wonder how Divine Providence would ever allow evil to come to pass in this place sanctified by the grave of the great King Arthur. If there is anywhere in this land that would be immune from such influences, it must be Glastonbury. Don't you agree?"

Du Sully appeared to consider it. At length, he said, "Well, Canterbury, first. I don't think the devil could expect much chance where the martyred Becket lies entombed."

"After that, Glastonbury would enjoy rare protection. Correct?"

"It is possible—"

"I thought as much. Brother Bertrand was a very old man. It was hardly surprising that God called him. As for Brother Raspin, difficult as it is to accept the loss of a man cut down in his prime, it does happen often enough and frequently for no reason we can determine."

"True," Du Sully said slowly. "But not a mark on him—"

"A fever, no doubt, one of the terrible, swift kinds that can descend without warning. How fortunate that the rest of you were spared. But then hardly surprising given the obvious evidence of holy favor."

If he had to go on much longer in this vein, he was going to be ill. Fortunately, Du Sully seemed inclined to accept his reason. And with it the implicit warning he was sure the abbot grasped. Holy Glastonbury, hallowed by the presence of King Arthur, could hardly also be the den of witches. The two were mutually contradictory, not to mention bad for business.

Slowly the abbot nodded. Still staring at Conan, he reached out a hand and drew his plans closer. "I worry that the nave is too narrow."

Conan was careful to conceal his satisfaction. Later, he would find a way to celebrate. He could think of several highly pleasant methods—all involving Alianor—but would not do so just now.

"I thought it elegant," he said, truthfully enough.

Du Sully looked surprised. "Really? Elegant?" He smiled, delighted. "Actually, I thought that myself but I wasn't sure. Tell me though, how do you regard the transept? I could shorten it, just here . . . and here—"

More than an hour passed before Conan was able to extricate himself. He had a sharp pain behind his eyes and the back of his neck felt stiff from bending over drawings, but he was well satisfied with his efforts. The abbot appeared to have put all thought of witchcraft behind him.

Alianor would be safe.

His relief was so profound that it threatened to outweigh all else. Only his deeply imbued sense of duty prevented him from returning to the island immediately. First, he had to see to the needs and readiness of his men.

* * *

Alianor awoke to late morning sunshine, the softest of spring breezes and solitude. Without opening her eyes, she knew that Conan had gone. His absence resonated through the cottage—and through her.

Slowly she rose. Her legs felt unsteady. Vivid recollections of the previous night flooded back. Heat suffused her skin. She dressed in the plainest clothes she had and braided her hair tightly, as though she might similarly contain her thoughts. Thus armored against the world as best she could be, she cracked a shutter open and looked outside.

The guards were back.

Her eyes widened at the sight of them, disbelievingly. Yet there they were, gathered once again around a campfire, talking quietly among themselves as though they never left.

Had she dreamed it all? Conan coming to her, sending the men away, the ecstasy they had shared. All a dream? Tempting though it was to believe, the deeply rooted satisfaction of her body told her she could not. He had actually left her, gone off to do whatever it was he was doing, and set his men to keep her neatly contained.

Truly, he must have a blind spot when it came to simple issues of reasonableness. She had been absent from Glastonbury for almost a fortnight. There were patients to see, not to mention the children she was overdue to visit. Philomena and Edward did a wonderful job looking after them but they were no substitute for Alianor's own attention.

Above all, she could not stay cooped up on this island like some damsel in a tower waiting for her lord to deign to remember her. The notion that she would do so was actually amusing.

Her humor considerably better than it had been the night before, she fed Mirabelle, tended to Fiona, and did a few simple tasks in front of the cottage, making sure all the while that the guards saw her. To them she must appear a woman content with her captivity, too docile to even think of it that way. They had to loathe such duty. In very little time, boredom would creep in and with it lapses in attention. She intended to take full advantage of them.

But not without a certain guilt. She felt sorry for the trouble she was about to cause them. Conan would be angry. However, she had every confidence that he would realize—if only later rather than sooner—his own foolishness in expecting her to meekly accept his will.

Besides, she thought she knew a way to soothe what masculine annoyance resulted.

Smiling at the thought, she bundled up her bag of supplies, threw a cloak over her shoulders, and snuck out the back door.

The tide was just low enough to take the stepping bridge. She crossed over it and headed in toward the village. It was her intention to stop first to see Philomena, Edward, and the children, then make sure no patients needed her care. But just as she neared the house—at the crossroads that led to the village—she encountered Brother Wynn.

"Mistress Alianor," he said, all courtesy. "Good day to you."

"And to you, Brother."

He hesitated as though he wanted speech with her but wasn't quite sure how to go about it—or if he should. "You have not been seen these many days," he said finally.

"I have been in London." Let this upright young man whose aura shone with such intensity digest that.

"London? But—"

"I went with Baron Wyndham to see the Queen."

His Adam's apple bobbed ferociously. A dull stain of color crept over his cheeks. "You jest."

The smile she gave him was dazzling. "No, I don't. Now if you will excuse me—" She started to walk past him but before she could, he lashed out a hand and took hold of her. Startled, she almost dropped her basket. "What are you—"

"Do not mock me. I will not tolerate that."

His grip was hard enough to hurt. Alianor tried to twist loose but without success. With the exception of Brother Raspin when he had tried to drag her up to the abbey, no one had ever treated her in such a way. She was completely unsure how to respond.

Matilda had made certain that she knew something about defending herself physically, contending that it was a skill every young woman should possess. Tempted though she was to use her knowledge, Alianor hesitated. This was a monk, after all, and she had more trouble with them already than she wanted.

Opting for discretion, she said, "I assure you, Brother Wynn, I am not mocking you in any way. Now kindly release me."

He stared at her for a long moment. Slowly his grip eased. She removed her arm quickly. Still, he blocked her way. He seemed about to say something more when they were interrupted.

Philomena came hurrying along the road, her plump face red with her exertions and her wimple slightly askew. "Oh, my lady, thank all the saints! I had despaired of finding you. Mary woke vomiting and several more of the children are ill. I'm terribly afraid they've taken a fever."

Brother Wynn stepped aside. His face suddenly smoothed, like a mask. He nodded gravely. "How unfortunate. Fevers are very common this time of year."

Alianor shot him a piercing look that revealed nothing. It occurred to her that she knew very little about this young monk so lately come to Glastonbury. Du Sully had always been her idea of a fanatic but perhaps he wasn't alone.

"I'm coming, Philomena," she said and made quick to do so. This time, Brother Wynn did not try to stop her. He merely stood there in the road with the scent of blooming chestnut trees on the air. Alianor stole a single backward glance at him before putting all thought of him from her mind.

She and Philomena reached the house a short time later. Mary was lying in the chamber she shared with several other young girls. It was a small room but well furnished with beds and chests, the walls whitewashed and the floors swept clean. The windows were open to admit fresh air. Philomena did not hold with the notion that evil vapors traveled that way, fortunately so, or Alianor would have had to correct her.

"I hear you're feeling poorly," she said as she sat down on the bed beside the child. Mary was barely eight, a small, slender girl who had been at the house for two years. Her mother was dead from a fall, her father unknown. She had a lovely voice and a gift for singing.

Mary nodded shyly. She responded to Alianor's questions readily. It took little time to determine that she—and several other children—had found themselves a crab apple tree. Despite everything they knew about the ill effects of the hard, green fruit, they had dared each other to eat it. The results were predictable.

"She'll be fine," Alianor said when she had finished reassuring the little girl. "They all will be. I ate crab apples myself when I was little and I well remember how ill I felt."

"She could have just told me," Philomena said. She wasn't angry so much as resigned. "But she wanted you to come. I said I wasn't sure I could find you, but she insisted."

That Philomena had yielded to the importuning of a small child reminded Alianor yet again why she had chosen the dear woman and her husband to oversee her household of orphans. That she herself would have been unavailable just the previous day reminded her of how closely wedded she was to Glastonbury and its people. Her life would never be entirely her own, no matter how much she might sometimes long for that. Such was the bargain she had made years ago and which she renewed every day of her life. The same bargain her mother had broken—and died for.

Alianor stayed a little longer at the house. Philomena had made meat pies and insisted she try one. A pleasant hour passed but at length, stomach filled, spirits renewed, she left. The glory of the spring was such that each day brought changes. There were always new plants to be found and gathered. After almost a fortnight gone, she had a great deal of catching up to do. Having said farewell to Philomena, she set off.

Chapter 23

Conan wiped the sweat from his eyes and grinned at the man on the ground in front of him. "Close, old friend, but not quite good enough."

Raymond rose slowly, shaking his head. He brushed dust from his tunic and recovered the sword that had gone spinning out of his hand when Conan brought him down.

"Luck," he said.

Conan laughed. "You think so? Let's try it again then."

They raised their blades, careful not to actually injure one another but serious all the same. Armed drill was far more than an amusement. The knowledge that their lives would rest on it someday—or indeed, any day—concentrated their attention marvelously.

The feint and parry began again. Conan went at it with a will. He had missed this, the companionship of the war party, the company of his fellow males. Alianor . . . *dazzled* him, there was no other word. But he was a warrior for all that, and a leader. A good session of sword and sweat restored the balance of his spirit.

They were done, and washing themselves in a nearby trough, when the church bells began to ring. Conan looked up, puzzled.

"Terce, already?"

Raymond shook his head. "Can't be. It's too soon."

"What then?"

Both men came to the same conclusion simultaneously. Still dripping, they yanked on their tunics and reached for their swords. Raymond barked an order to the men-at-arms even as Conan whistled for Gray.

They were armed and ready for any trouble when Master Brightersea hurried into the yard. His face was ashen and his breathing came in gasps.

"My lord," he said when he saw Conan, "you must come at once. There's been another death."

A crowd was gathering outside Master Longueford's house. They were unnaturally quiet. As Conan came up the narrow street on Gray, followed by his men, they parted to let him through.

The boy, Dermod, stood just within the door. He appeared to have been crying. Conan dismounted, gave the reins to a man-at-arms, and looked around carefully.

The house was far from ostentatious but nonetheless bore the stamp of wealth. It stood two stories high with plaster and timber outer walls and a slate roof topped by a chimney. The windows were small but the ones on the second floor had glass in them. The first floor appeared to have been Master Longueford's place of business. Immediately inside the door was a large work area with several tables, benches, a fireplace, and a large quantity of scrolls neatly arranged on broad shelves. Master Longueford himself sat slumped in a chair at one of the tables. He appeared to be sleeping but for the too sharp slant of his head.

"No one else enters," Conan said over his shoulder to Sir Raymond. The knight nodded. Immediately he took up his post just outside the door.

Beckoning to Dermod, Conan moved into the room. "You found him?" he asked.

The boy nodded. He was clearly waging a terrible struggle to keep from sobbing. Gently Conan said, "It's a good thing if you loved your master. Would that all apprentices could feel the same. But now, for love of him, you must help me."

Dermod stared at him wide-eyed as his words sunk in. He sniffed loudly and wiped his hand across his nose. Self-consciously he said, "I'll do anything, Lord. The master's a fine . . . was a fine man." His mouth trembled. "God strike whoever did this."

"When did you find him?"

"Not a quarter hour ago. A shipment of cloth arrived this morning. He told me to stack it in the storeroom. When I finished, I went to see what I should do next."

"He was like this?"

"Aye, Lord."

"Did you touch him?"

Dermod nodded. "I called his name first, thinking he was just resting. When he didn't move I went closer and put my hand on his shoulder. That's when I realized—"

"All right. Did you touch anything else?"

"No, Lord, nothing. I was . . . scared, I guess. I ran out into the street, trying to get help."

"Has anyone come into the room?"

"No, I don't think so. A couple of people stuck their heads in but when they seen him, they went back out right away."

Conan sighed, relieved as much as he could be under the circumstances. It appeared the room was undisturbed. That was fortunate. Brother Bertrand's death could be understood. Brother Raspin's could be rationalized away. But this third death, of an apparently healthy man, at a time when there was no obvious plague at work in the town— This was a different matter altogether.

"Am I right," he asked, "to think that Master Longueford enjoyed good health?"

Dermod nodded vigorously. "He did, Lord. Course now a couple years back he had the ague but Mistress Alianor cured him of that. Since then I never knew him to have an ill day."

"That's right, you mentioned he took you on at her suggestion after she'd cured him. Do you know if he's had any reason to see her since?"

The boy hesitated. Gently Conan said, "He's dead, lad. There's nothing you can say that will hurt him, but if there's a chance of finding out what happened here, I need to know the truth."

"She came a few times, Lord. But I don't think it was because Master Longueford was sick. His wife died going on for five years and they had no children. He wasn't the sort of man who made friends easily. Mistress Alianor would sit and talk with him, they'd have a cup of comfrey tea together. Sometimes they played draughts."

"Then they were friends?"

"Aye, Lord. I know Master Longueford helped support the children's house but he did it quietlike. He said charity was for the glory of God, not our own."

"A wise man, Master Longueford." But also a very dead one. Conan moved closer, looking at him carefully. There was no mark, no wound, no sign of anything that could possibly have killed him.

There was a sudden commotion outside the door. Voices were raised.

"Let me pass! You have no authority to bar me."

Raymond answered, too low for Conan to hear but he didn't have to. He could see Abbot Du Sully just outside, gesturing angrily.

"It is too late for last rites, Abbot," Conan said. "The man is dead."

"Of course he's dead!" Du Sully tried to squeeze round to get a better look into the room but Conan wouldn't let him. Still, that was scant discouragement. "Not a mark on him, I'll wager! Just like poor Brothers Bertrand and Raspin. She's struck again, by God. The witch has killed again!"

A murmur ran through the assembled townspeople. Faces tightened in anger. Several of the women sneered openly at the abbot and one or two men took a step toward him.

"Enough." Conan held up a hand. He forced Du Sully back out onto the street. Confronting the crowd, he said, "Master Longueford has died. I understand that he was a good man. Respect that and do not dishonor his memory."

No one tried to challenge him openly but the muttering continued. Clearly, the people of Glastonbury were in no mood to listen to their abbot's rantings.

"Master Longueford's house will be secured by my men," Conan said. "A full examination will be made. If he died from any unnatural cause, it will be discovered."

"How?" Du Sully demanded. He drew himself upright and glared at Conan. The excited, happy designer of the new abbey was gone. In his place was once again the venom-filled witch-hunter. "I allowed you to lull me into a false sense of security and now look what's happened. Not merely another death but that of a beloved son of the Church, an avid supporter of our works who had only lately rediscovered the joy of giving to God. Do you think for one moment that it is a coincidence he was taken from us now? This witch knows exactly what she is about and she knows how best to lull weak, susceptible men into her evil ways."

Conan's eyes narrowed. The skin tightened over his high-boned cheeks. A pulse leapt to life in the hollow of his jaw. Watching him, Sir Raymond instinctively took a step back.

"Exactly what are you saying, Abbot?" Conan asked with deceptive calm.

Had Du Sully been entirely in his right mind it would have screamed caution. But he was gone, wallowing in the red haze of madness. He could see nothing except the stake and the fire.

"I am saying you took the witch with you to London. She seduced you, didn't she? What mortal man is proof against the wiles of the devil's minions? You lay with her. She polluted your soul and she will see you damned to hell before she is done."

A gasp went round the crowd, the in-drawn gasp of people who have been pushed too far. A woman holding a babe in her arms stepped forward.

"How dare you?" she screamed at Du Sully. "When my sister died bearing her youngest, you told her husband she had sinned and deserved to perish. When Thomas Ferris's little boy drowned last year, you said it was because his family hadn't contributed enough to your coffers. You are an evil man, you are!"

Flecks of foam appeared at the corners of Du Sully's mouth. "Begone, woman, back to the devil you serve!"

"Nay," a man shouted. "You'll not bring that filth here! By God, you won't! When my father was dying, you played on all his fears, telling him he'd burn through all eternity unless he deeded you our best pasture. He did it and died weeping, knowing he'd betrayed his family!"

"You never raised a hand to help anyone here!"

"You turn away the sick and needy!"

"Mistress Alianor is good and kind. She helps us. Don't you dare try to hurt her!"

This last was from Dermod who suddenly hurled himself against the abbot, weeping and hitting all at

the same time. Conan pulled him off. He scooped the
boy up and held his thin body with gentle firmness.

"Easy, lad, it's all right. As for you— Get back up on
your hill, Abbot. Gather your monks around you and
pray to all the saints that I don't decide to let these
people loose. Right now the only thing that stands between you and their vengeance is my sword."

Fear flickered in the abbot's eyes but it was small beside the fury of his madness. "I carry the full weight of
the Church behind me! I will appeal to Canterbury, to
the pope! I will see you excommunicated!"

Conan laughed, a harsh, cruel sound that carried a
keen appreciation for hypocrisy. "By all means, do
that, Abbot. I'll be in good company. Your pope flings
excommunication about as a laundress does her dirty
wash water. What king hasn't it touched, what prince?
The sword overused is the sword dulled. Now run, Abbot! Pick up your skirts and run back up your hill because, by God, I see less reason by the minute to hold
these people back."

As though to underscore what he said, the crowd
shouted its agreement. Amid the jeers and threats, the
expletives and accusations, Conan caught the dark current of deep flowing rage. These people had been ill-
used by the Church that claimed to represent salvation
and they had a fierce loyalty to Alianor. It was a bad
combination.

For a moment Du Sully looked disposed to argue.
But even in his madness, some instinct for survival remained. Cursing, he pushed his way through the crowd
and was gone.

Conan set Dermod down slowly but kept the boy
near him. William materialized out of the mass of
stone-faced men with their weapons at the ready and
put an arm around the youngster's shoulders. "You're

a good one, you are," he said admiringly. Dermod managed a watery smile.

"Hear me," Conan said. He did not shout but the power of his voice was such that it reached to the farthest edges of the crowd. Or rather the mob, for they were on the verge of being that.

"Master Longueford's death will be investigated. If there is reason to suspect murder, the sheriff will be called in. But no one—not the abbot and not any of you—will take the law into your own hands. Be very sure you understand me on this. I will keep the peace here as I have been charged to do by Her Most Royal Majesty, Eleanor, Queen Regent of England and God pity any who stand against me."

He took hold of the hilt of his sword and withdrew it just enough so that the light struck the dark gleam of steel. "I have wiped more blood from this blade than I care to remember but it has never been English blood. Never. That will not change unless you will it. Stand against the crown and I will lay waste to Glastonbury. I will scourge it as Du Sully and his kind never could. When I am done there will be nothing here but broken stone and shattered hopes. Do you understand me?"

The faces of the crowd had gone very still. Not a man or a woman even seemed to breathe. They stared at him as though looking into the void of death itself.

Good. Let them fear. Let them feel the stomach-churning dread that could be their greatest safeguard. For truly, he had never seen a people closer to disaster and seeming not to know it.

Richard was Eleanor's most favored child. Though he was a man now and a king, she still loved him with all the passion of her strong, proud nature. For him, she had defied her husband, destroyed her marriage, and damn near brought down her dynasty.

It was hardly impossible that she would also destroy the very place upon which she had showered such favor.

"Do not let rebellion come here," Conan said, more softly so that they had to strain to hear him. "It will be your end."

Without waiting for their reaction, he turned and mounted Gray. His men formed up around him. They had the close-faced look of professionals. Not a flicker of emotion showed in them. He hoped that would continue to be the case if worse came to worst.

And it might, for quietly on the wind, not from any one particular voice, he caught a murmur.

"Then do not let the burning come here."

Not a mouth seemed to move. He could not even tell if it was a man or a woman who had spoken. Or something else all together.

He touched his heels to the stallion's sides. There was one thought only in his mind: Alianor.

Chapter 24

The cottage was empty. Late afternoon light cast a cheerful glow over the main room and the bed alcove beyond. It shone across the work-table scarred by long use, the floor covered by rush matting to the fireplace where only a few embers glowed weakly.

Not even Mirabelle was in sight, proof that cats just might be as sensible as some claimed. Only the soft nicker of Fiona—what kind of name was that for a horse?—from just outside suggested the presence of life.

That and the guards who were gathered around their fire, patiently doing their duty.

"She is gone," he said when he had walked over to them. He spoke quietly but the effect was as a thunder clap. The men looked at one another disbelievingly, stumbling to their feet in belated diligence.

"Gone," he repeated and addressed the hapless fellow who was their lieutenant. "I don't suppose you have any idea when she left?"

The man was gray. He tried to answer but couldn't get enough air and had to start over. "Lord, I swear—" That was the extent of his articulateness. Conan couldn't blame him. The man had failed in his sworn duty to his master. It would hardly be unusual for him to be whipped, then turned out to fend for himself as best he could.

For the briefest moment, Conan was tempted. His anger was a cold, hard thing that threatened to take up permanent residence inside him. But then he remembered who he—and the guards—were dealing with.

He had told them merely to take her to her residence and he had indicated that he wanted her to stay there. He'd said nothing about her stubbornness, her refusal to show the proper decorum of a woman, nor most especially had he warned them that this was no ordinary female they were dealing with. No one knew this land better, no one could move over it more easily. And no one seemed more blithely willing to ignore his own authority.

"How could she have gotten off this island?" the lieutenant managed to ask finally. "We found the boat we assumed she used and secured it."

Why hadn't he told them of the stepping bridge? It needed only a handful of words. *There is a way off the island other than a boat.* There, it would have been done. But the bridge was somehow private, not knowledge to be bruited about to all and sundry. He had kept silent, thinking in his male arrogance that she would do what was expected of her and like it.

More fool him.

"Go back to town," he said. "I'll wait here. Sir Raymond is securing the residence of Master Longueford who has died. You will assist him in that."

The lieutenant nodded, overcome by a reprieve he hardly dared think real. He gathered the men with creditable efficiency and shortly had them on their way.

Conan unsaddled Gray. The horse tossed his mane in Fiona's direction. She seemed pleased enough to see him. Good for them. Conan had no illusion that his own reception would be similar. Grimly he settled down to wait.

And wait. An hour passed, judging by the position of the sun. It felt longer. His stomach growled. Belatedly it occurred to him that he'd eaten nothing all day. There was a stone well behind the cottage. He brought up a bucket and drank several ladlefuls. Strawberries were growing in a pot set in the sun. He plucked a few, ate those. Glancing around, he noticed other pots with other plants, most of which he couldn't identify.

More careful examination revealed that a substantial area behind the cottage was given over to an herb garden. It wasn't laid out in the formal beds common to castle gardens, but a garden it was nonetheless. He couldn't be sure but it looked to him as though Alianor was cultivating the plants at the same time she was trying to encourage them to retain much of their wildness.

At the thought, a slight smile played across his mouth. It faded quickly when his keen hearing picked up the sound of footfall. He was back in the cottage, seated at the worktable with his long legs stretched out in front of him, when Alianor entered.

She stopped just within the door and sighed. Coming in, she dispensed with her cloak and went about putting away her basket, poking up the fire, and so on as though his presence caused her no concern at all.

"Is this to be a habit then?" she asked finally.

He shrugged. Never mind that his loins had hardened at the first glimpse of her. He would match her insouciance in kind or be damned.

"I was surprised to find you out."

"You shouldn't have been. I have work to do."

Killing work? He didn't say it, barely let himself even acknowledge the thought. Not for a moment did he believe she had killed Longueford or the others.

That wasn't the issue. This was in very real danger of becoming a matter of law. Evidence would be taken and it would not look very good for her.

"When did you leave here?" he asked.

"A few hours ago. Seriously, Conan, you didn't really expect me to stay?" She came to stand in front of him, looking absurdly young in a simple, saffron-yellow gown, her hair but lightly covered with a gossamer veil.

She smelled of primroses.

"I'd been gone almost a fortnight. There are patients to see, supplies to gather. I have responsibilities."

"So do I," he said and came upright suddenly, straightening to his full height so that he towered a good head over her. "My responsibility is to keep the peace. You aren't helping."

She frowned. "I don't see how I—"

"Were you in the village?"

"Yes ... well, no, not exactly. I went to the children's house. Mary was ill and Philomena needed reassuring. After that, I was in the woods."

"Who saw you?"

"Saw me? What are you talking about?"

"Who can vouch for where you were and what you did?"

"Why should anyone have to—?"

"Master Longueford is dead."

She stared at him. Her eyes widened even as the color fled her cheeks. "What are you saying—?"

"Exactly what you heard." A quiver of guilt stole through him. He could have told her more gently but he had wanted to see her most honest, unprepared reaction. Everything he knew told him she was shocked to the very marrow.

"Dermod found him," he said quietly. "He was dead at his worktable. There isn't a mark on him."

Alianor shook her head. She appeared dazed. "I don't understand. He was in excellent health."

"For a man his age, you mean, and he wasn't young."

"For a man of any age. He was temperate in all his habits, drank sparingly, ate little meat, and despite his work, he was very fit. I saw no sign of any kind of illness in him."

"He'd had the ague."

"Two years ago but he recovered quickly. How could he possibly have just died?"

"I don't know," Conan admitted. "My men are guarding the house. Du Sully's been asking questions but I've put him off. He—"

"No, don't tell me, I can imagine. He blames me."

"Yes, he does and the good people of Glastonbury look ready to tear him limb from limb for it. Do you understand what that could mean?"

Her eyes were wide and dark. "They wouldn't—"

"They were damn well ready to do it a few hours ago. If a Church official should come to harm here, the crown would not be able to protect anyone even remotely responsible. But there's more. The habit of rebellion is insidious. It can start with justified ill feelings against an idiot like Du Sully and carry all the way to the throne."

Her head came up. She stared at him angrily. "That's ridiculous. You have absolutely no grounds for suggesting that anyone here would be disloyal."

"I have what I can see and hear. This place is on the edge and you may be what pushes it over. Now I'll ask you again, who saw you?"

"Philomena, of course, the children. Other than that, I don't think anyone . . . no, wait, I saw Brother Wynn. We spoke briefly."

"What about?"

"He asked me where I'd been. I told him."

One eyebrow rose. It was enough. "You told him you were in London?"

"Yes."

"With me?"

"Yes."

"To do what?"

"See the Queen."

"You thought it was wise to impart all this to him?"

"No," Alianor said angrily, "I didn't. But he was insufferably rude. He grabbed hold of me and acted like a crazy person. Du Sully isn't the only one. He's collecting them."

"He touched you?"

"Didn't I say that? Philomena came along and he let me go but for a moment—Never mind," she said hastily when she saw the look on Conan's face. "The point is I acted impulsively and I'm sorry but I have no patience left for those people. They are supposed to serve God yet they seem to do the opposite."

Conan passed a hand over his eyes wearily. He couldn't really blame her. The urge to throttle the abbot had been very strong in him. Compared to that, her own reaction was mild.

"Wynn must have told Du Sully. Between that and Longueford's death, it seems to have renewed all his interest in hunting witches."

"How unfortunate." Her voice was very small. She turned away quickly but not before he saw the stark terror that moved behind her eyes.

Anger was forgotten. So she had done something stupid and impulsive? If he counted up all the times he'd done the same—This was beautiful, passionate, brave Alianor. Alianor of the dazzlement. The thought provoked a smile but hard on it came the desperate need to banish her fear, shore up her courage, make her believe that everything truly would be all right.

"He will not harm you," Conan said—Queen's man, sworn to justice, but never mind that. His arms closed around her. She held herself very stiffly for an instant, then softened suddenly, all but melting against him. A faint sob tore from her.

"Oh, God, he makes me so afraid. I see myself at the stake with the flames—"

For just an instant, he saw it, too.

"Don't," he said fiercely and stilled her mouth with his own. They moved as one toward the bed. Clothes were tugged and pulled away, giving way before impatient mutterings. Conan yanked off his boots, Alianor slipped off her tunic. They clung to one another. Her skin was hot as his own, smooth as satin. He fell back, carrying her with him, hands tangling in her hair.

She moved above him, her tongue tracing a path down his chest, across his flat abdomen— He gasped, disbelieving. She looked up for just an instant.

"Let me," she whispered and licked him slowly, avidly, with breathtaking delicacy and effect. Pleasure spiraled through him, not the languid mounting of desire but hot coils of need. He bore it as long as he could, determined to allow her whatever freedom she needed. But there came a time—

"Enough," he said. His voice was a low, rasping sound in the gathering shadows of the room. He turned suddenly, tipping her onto her back beneath him. She made a soft murmur of surprise but his iron-hard thigh was already slipping between hers, opening her to him. His hands slid beneath to cup her buttocks. He felt the moist heat of her and bent his head, touching the tip of his tongue to a swollen nipple, taking more, suddenly suckling her deeply at the same moment he thrust within her. The wildness surged, heart pounding, tumultuous, brooking no restraint.

She cried out as her back arched and clung to him,

her nails digging in sharply enough to draw blood. Conan barely felt it. He held her, fighting to contain the fury of his lust, until he felt the long, shuddering spasms of her surrender. His own release followed instantly, soul-shattering in its force.

A long time later—timeless time—he emerged. Raising himself just slightly, he brushed the hair away from her face and gazed down at her. She might have been asleep but for the rapid-fire pounding of her heart and the slight smile that curved her ripe mouth as she felt him looking at her.

She was so beautiful, so wise, and so . . . sweet? No, not sweet. She had a tart tongue and a proud will. But there was true gentleness and affection in her, mingling with all that hot blood-rushing passion, unlike anything he had ever known in the world.

Dazzling.

He sighed and gently tucked an errant curl behind her ear. She caught his hand and pressed her lips to it tenderly. Her eyes opened, smokey gold-green in the aftermath of passion.

"Would that we might stay like this forever," she said, a young girl's artless longing, a woman's eternal dream. "But I know—"

"Hush." He dropped a kiss light as hummingbird's wings, then another, playful things but serious in their intent. "Never mind what you know or think you do. There'll be time for all that."

She shot him a quick, wistful glance from beneath her lashes but said nothing more. He gathered her against him, pulling the covers over them both, and settled back. Slowly he felt the tension slip from her. She eased into sleep.

He did not, but lay looking up at the rafters of the ceiling, blackened by the ages of this island, this place.

Time. Aye, there was the trick. He simply needed to

gain enough of it—moment by moment—then pile it up, a wall against the world and all its madness.

Sleep whispered at the edges of his consciousness. He could feel himself falling into it. But just before he did, a memory emerged—Eleanor in her solar when they met alone just before he left London, holding the note he had sent to her before realizing he would have to go himself.

How does one disprove witchcraft?

"Protect her," the Queen said and tossed the parchment into the fire where it curled, blackening at the edges before abruptly bursting into flames.

Chapter 25

The Queen in her Tower might be the best-guarded individual in all England but Master Longueford—or his mortal remains—came a close second. No fewer than a dozen men stood watch in front and back of his house. Well aware by this time of the fiasco on the island, they were painfully alert.

Conan dismounted and hitched Gray's reins to a post beside the house. He turned to help Alianor down off Fiona. If Sir Raymond was surprised to see her, he gave no sign.

"Anything?" Conan asked the knight.

Sir Raymond shook his head. "No one's stirred along the street, Lord. The townspeople seem to have vanished."

Indeed, it seemed so to Alianor. Glastonbury appeared to have been deserted but that was deceptive. Riding into town, she had noted the quickly closed shutter, the fast-darting shape. The people were watching—and waiting.

"Master Longueford?" Conan asked.

"As you left him, Lord."

"Good, come with us." Together with the knight, they entered the merchant's house and went into the death chamber. Alianor's throat tightened when she beheld her old friend slumped in his chair. He might almost have been asleep.

"Sir Raymond," Conan said, "it is possible that you may be called upon to bear witness in court. I wish you to note that I have asked Mistress Alianor to come here at this time because she is most skilled in the healing arts. I judge her to be best able to try to determine the cause of Master Longueford's death. However, she will not be allowed to alter or conceal anything. Is that clear?"

Slowly the knight nodded. "Yes, Lord, clear."

"Good. Then you will observe all that occurs here and if called upon, you will give a full and truthful accounting of it no matter what person may be injured by you doing so. Is that, too, clear?"

Sir Raymond's face was very still. Alianor could imagine the conflict in him. He was the Baron of Wyndham's sworn liege man. His loyalty to Conan was absolute. Yet here was the baron himself telling him that a higher loyalty—to the truth and the law— had to take precedence.

"Yes, Lord," he said hesitantly. "I understand."

"Good, then we will proceed."

Together, they laid Master Longueford on his worktable and removed his clothing. Alianor felt a moment's hesitation at this violation of her friend's modesty but she had known him to be a stalwart and pragmatic man. Above all, he would want his killer found. She was determined to do it.

"Help me," she whispered as she bent over him. The answer was here somewhere. People did not die for no reason at all.

"He looks as peaceful as Brother Raspin," Conan said.

"No sign of pain," Alianor agreed. "No convulsions. Dermod never heard him call out?"

"No, just as the other monks heard nothing from Brother Raspin. What could account for that?"

"Instantaneous death so that there would be no time to try to summon aid or—"

She opened Master Longueford's mouth slightly and looked inside. "Paralysis could also account for it. There are substances that rob the body of the ability to speak or indeed to make any sound. Death can follow minutes or hours later."

"Neither of these men could possibly have taken hours to die," Conan pointed out.

"Minutes then." She turned Master Longueford's head one way and the other, then studied his arms, particularly the insides. "You realize there is still the possibility that this is simply a coincidence?"

"Do you believe that?"

Sir Raymond was listening intently. He was clearly uncomfortable in his role as witness but determined to fulfill it well.

"No," Alianor admitted, "I don't. I acknowledge that it could be the case but it is highly unlikely. All the same, Master Longueford bears no sign of injury. For example, death can be instantaneous when the neck is broken but his is not."

"Neither was Brother Raspin's."

"Are you sure?"

Conan's face tightened slightly. "I know how to break a man's neck and I know what it looks like when it's done. His wasn't."

"I see— It is also possible to crush the protuberance in front of the throat, thereby preventing the intake of air. But this, too, leaves signs and I find none. Similarly, I find no indication of any sort of bite, from a venomous serpent, for example."

"All of which means—?"

Alianor hesitated. Her conclusions were inescapable yet she hated to voice them. They meant that Du Sully

was right in at least some regard—great evil had come
to Glastonbury.

"Master Longueford and Brother Raspin may have
been poisoned."

Sir Raymond drew his breath sharply. Conan, on the
other hand, showed no sign of surprise. It was clear
that he had come to the same conclusion on his own.

"All right," he said with the air of a man now prepared to get down to business. "What could have done
it?"

Alianor considered what he was asking. If she understood him correctly, he regarded her as some sort of
expert, or at least very knowledgeable on the subject.
That was not entirely wrong but it wasn't fair either.

"The plants and other substances that I use are intended to heal," she explained quietly. "It is true that
some of them, given in the wrong dosage, could cause
death. But not this kind—not death that comes silently
and doesn't leave a trace."

"What about foxglove?"

"You asked me about that when we spoke of
Brother Bertrand's death. You also asked about henbane." She had been struck then by his knowledge,
surprised that he even knew to ask. What was it he
had said about his mother?

"Alone among these three men, Brother Bertrand
was ill when I was called to his side. His symptoms indicate that he may have—*may have* been poisoned. He
also may not have been. If he was, it wasn't by foxglove or henbane. Foxglove would have caused his
heart to beat with unnatural speed until it was so damaged it could beat no more. I was attending him. If
that had happened, I would have known. It did not. As
for henbane, it causes convulsions and usually a rash.
There was no sign of either."

"As there is not here," Conan said thoughtfully.

"Very well, then. Let us assume that we are dealing with a poisoner who has access to a substance that causes his victims to die within minutes, having first robbed them of the ability to call out for help, and that further, having done its work, leaves no outward sign on the body. What could it be?"

Alianor's fists clenched. A terrible sense of dread was growing in her. Whatever she said now, it would reflect poorly on her. She was supposed to be a healer. Why would she have knowledge of substances that could kill?

"Surely," Conan said, "as you have just said, there are substances with healing powers that if given in too great quantity or in the wrong way can result in death?"

He was leading her, suggesting what she could say to both tell the truth and protect herself. She suspected he was doing it innocently enough and was tempted to go along. Only deeply imbued honesty stopped her.

"There are such things," she agreed, "but if they are used wrongly—either by accident or on purpose—they will leave signs. They won't kill silently like this. Only the deadliest substances can do that, things far too dangerous to ever try to use for healing."

"You know of such things?" Sir Raymond asked. Barely was the question out than he looked as though he regretted it. As well he might for Conan scowled at him.

"Why would she? She is a healer."

Alianor put a hand on his arm gently. Truth would out. It might as well do so now. "When I go in search of plants, I need to know as much about what to avoid as what to choose. Otherwise, I could make a terrible mistake. For instance, you found me gathering cicely the other day. It is a very useful plant, but there is another, called fool's cicely, that is deadly. I have to know the difference."

"Could fool's cicely have done this?" Sir Raymond asked. Her honesty emboldened him.

"Possibly, but a huge quantity would have been needed to bring death so quickly. Hemlock is more likely but understand, whatever the exact cause, we would have to be dealing with a poisoner of rare skill. Most poisoning is done clumsily. Anyone with even small ability can detect it."

"But not here," Conan said. "This was done to look like something else entirely."

Alianor nodded. "What could be more terrifying than the idea that any person can die at any moment without the slightest forewarning? What is better guaranteed to rouse people to such terror that they will contenance the most horrible brutalities to try to save themselves?"

"Glastonbury's people will not," Conan said. He spoke with unswerving conviction.

She blinked away tears. "And I thank them for their loyalty even as I fear it could lead them to disaster."

Sir Raymond cleared his throat. He had turned his attention from them—and from Master Longueford—to look past the main window that fronted on the road. Having seen what was out there, he said, "Begging you pardon, my lady, but I've got a feeling it may already be here."

"I fully understand your position, my lord," the stiff-necked young man said. Alianor judged him to be in his early twenties, tall and thin with an air of self-seriousness. His name was Hugh FitzWilliam and he was the sheriff of Bath.

"What happened to Gilbert FitzStephen?" Conan demanded, ignoring the young man's remark. They

were standing in the street outside Master Longueford's house, Conan having refused him entry, the baron's men and the sheriff's faced off against each other.
Alianor thought Conan's had the better of it. Hugh
FitzWilliam's men looked none too happy to be there
and especially not to find themselves confronting seasoned warriors.

"A fall from his horse," FitzWilliam said. "I was
next in line to succeed him as sheriff. Now as to the
matter of jurisdiction—"

"There is no matter," Conan replied. "I was sent
here by the Queen to investigate these deaths. When I
am done, I will report my findings to Her Majesty and
she will decide how to proceed."

"Interesting," FitzWilliam murmured. He had a supercilious smile but it faded when his gaze fell on
Alianor. From atop his horse, which he had so far
failed to dismount, he looked away quickly. "The
Queen charged you with investigating a murder that
has only just occurred?"

"A death," Conan corrected. "You are out of your
depth here, Sheriff. Take your men and head back to
Bath while you still have light."

FitzWilliam frowned. It did not seem to have occurred to him that he would encounter quite so blunt
a dismissal. "I cannot do that."

"Why not?"

"Because I have come at the express request of the
abbot of Glastonbury. He sent a messenger to inform
me that he fears this town has become the focal point
of a great struggle between good and evil. He says he
despairs for the fate of all England unless something is
done immediately."

He drew himself up solemnly, full of the august importance of his task.

Conan muttered an expletive. He kicked a clod of

dirt so hard that it rebounded against FitzWilliam's mailed leg. "Abbot Du Sully is lacking in his wits, Sheriff. You have come at the bidding of a madman and by doing so you place yourself in direct conflict with the crown."

"Not so!" The very idea clearly appalled him. "How can you say such a thing about a respected churchman? He warned me, he said you would—"

Conan had heard enough. He walked over to the horse, which stepped sideways skittishly, lashed a hand out, and hauled FitzWilliam from the saddle. His men instinctively moved toward him but stopped just as quickly as Conan's guards raised their weapons.

"You sniveling cur," Conan said but almost pleasantly, as though FitzWilliam was no more than a mere annoyance. For a moment he held him at arm's length, feet dangling off the ground. Then he dropped him. He landed hard, mud spraying all around and a great deal of it sticking to the red-faced sputtering sheriff of Bath.

"Very well then, you have come at Du Sully's bidding. Now what exactly do you expect to do?"

"I . . . I . . ." Vainly trying to wipe the mud from himself, FitzWilliam stumbled to his feet. He looked at Conan with loathing tempered by a judicious amount of self-preservation.

"I intend to call the assizes court into session immediately," he said. "First, the coroner will be asked to rule on the cause of these deaths."

"Who is the coroner?"

"Uh . . . I am. That is, I was before becoming sheriff but there's been no time to appoint someone else to fill the post so therefore I will continue to carry out the duties of it until it is possible for—"

"Enough," Conan said. "What training do you have in determining the cause of death?"

"Training? I know the law, surely that's enough. Besides, I've yet to see a case where the death didn't result from some cause readily obvious to anyone with the wits God gave him."

"You haven't seen Master Longueford nor did you see Brother Raspin."

FitzWilliam's head swiveled from Conan to Alianor and back again. Along the way, he managed to stare wide-eyed at the baron's men, helmeted, in chain mail, swords drawn.

Still, let it be said for the sheriff of Bath that he knew his duty. "There was a third one."

"Brother Bertrand," Alianor said. FitzWilliam jumped when she spoke, as though he'd heard a thunder clap. He looked at her for a horrified moment before quickly averting his gaze.

She took a deep breath, willing herself to patience, and went on. "His case was different. He was very old and quite ill when he died. Even so, it is possible that he was poisoned just as the other two may have been."

FitzWilliam's color fled. He looked bilious. "P-poisoned?"

Conan sneered. "Du Sully didn't mention that to you, did he? He prattled on about evil designs and witchcraft without ever mentioning that there may be a particularly clever murderer loose here in Glastonbury. Now that you know, tell me all about your expertise in poisoning. No doubt you can enlighten us as to exactly how it was done and by determining that, discover the culprit."

"I know nothing of poisoning," FitzWilliam said. He grabbed hold of the reins of his horse and began to mount but his foot slipped from the stirrup. No surprise given that he was shaking mightily. Yet again, his gaze slipped to Alianor as though drawn without volition. This time it stayed.

"Except that it is the weapon of witches," he whispered and hurriedly crossed himself.

"The man's an idiot," Conan said. They were sitting in the main room of Master Brightersea's inn. Sir Raymond and a guard of the men were still at the house. Others remained at the abbey. William and Dermod were off in a corner talking quietly. A serving maid had brought a mug of ale, some bread and cheese, then wisely vanished.

Conan sloshed ale into his goblet but didn't drink. He was seated on a bench with Alianor across from his. His big, honed body radiated tension. She could not remember ever seeing his temper up like this.

"Du Sully's actually managed to find someone crazier than himself." His disgust was equally evident.

"Whether he is or isn't," Alianor said, "he has to be dealt with. Things can't be allowed to continue this way."

Conan's hand fell to the hilt of his sword. He touched it almost fondly. "I'll deal with him gladly."

"I don't mean like that. It's not a solution. Look, I've been giving this a great deal of thought and I believe I may know what's happening here. We touched on it back at Master Longueford's house."

"By all means, enlighten me."

She ignored the sarcasm, understanding that it stemmed from deepest worry and regretting that she was about to add to that. Quietly she said, "Someone is deliberately killing people in a way that looks like the work of a witch. Whoever is doing it is going to a great deal of trouble to create that impression. I live alone, I'm a woman, and I'm known as a healer. I'm the obvious suspect. The goal here isn't the murders. It's to bring me to trial for witchcraft."

Conan frowned as he listened. He didn't immediately dismiss her assertion but he didn't agree either. "Maybe this person just likes killing and wants to deflect suspicion from himself."

"I thought of that but this killer has a knowledge of poison that could have enabled him to go on murdering undetected for years. By simply arranging for the victims to ingest the poison toward the end of the day, rather than in the middle, he could have made it appear that they died in their sleep. If he stretched out the intervals between killings, maybe even moved around from village to village, deaths would be put down to natural causes. He could have killed dozens, maybe even more, without ever being caught."

"All right," Conan said slowly. "There's a chance what you're saying is correct but then the obvious suspect is Du Sully. You hold the loyalty of the people that he undoubtedly thinks should be his. That you've earned it while he hasn't wouldn't make any difference to him."

"I agree but I don't think the abbot has the knowledge needed to commit these murders. My guess is that he's merely a tool." She took a deep breath and forced herself to give voice to her deepest fear. "If I go to the stake for witchcraft, what happens here?"

Conan didn't hesitate. He answered her flatly. "There will be an uprising."

"Exactly. Now Glastonbury is only one town but there is great unease in this land. A spark thrown on tinder dry ground can ignite a firestorm."

He stood up and walked a little distance away. With his back to her, he stood staring out the window. She made no attempt to interrupt his thoughts. Finally, he returned to the table. "A rebellion has to have a leader to have any chance of success."

A look flashed across her face. She tried her utmost

to repress it but Conan was already too sensitive to her moods. He frowned. "What?"

"Nothing."

"No, there was definitely something. What is it?"

"Just that I agree with you, there has to be a leader."

He studied her for a long moment. Finally, he said, "I suppose I should be reassured that you are such a poor liar."

She reddened. It was desperately unfair that she could hide nothing from this man. She considered trying another denial but the look he gave her quelled any such thought.

"You must understand," she said, "confidentiality lies at the very heart of what I do. People often have to reveal information to me that embarrasses or even possibly endangers them. If they didn't know absolutely that I would never repeat it, they wouldn't come to me at all."

Conan stared at her in disbelief. "Are you seriously telling me that you have learned through a patient of someone you think may be the leader of a planned rebellion?"

Alianor took a deep breath. She let it out slowly. "I'm telling you nothing at all."

"Even though this person may also be plotting to arrange your execution?"

"We can't have this discussion anymore."

The word he hurtled at her reeked of the war camp and the camaraderie of men. It was blunt to the extreme. Worse, he took hold of her with force and shook her soundly.

"*You cannot do this.*"

The fury that came from him in waves was so powerful that she felt almost as though he had struck her. He hadn't but her shock was great, so much so that she came very close to simply giving in. It would have been so easy. Tell him what she knew and it all became his problem. He would accept that willingly, he was trained for it, it was in his blood and his breeding. Take charge, take control, make the decisions, shape the outcome, and everyone else follows along.

So easy.

He took a deep, shuddering breath, fighting for self-control, and stared down at her. What she saw in his eyes stunned her. Conan—Baron of Wyndham, warrior par excellence who had risen to power in a world where strength, savagery, and cunning were merely the minimal requirements for success—looked afraid. Because of her. For her.

Amazing.

"I won't let you do it," he said. "Your life is at risk here. You will tell me everything you know or suspect."

"I cannot."

"You must. You have got to trust me to deal with this situation."

"It isn't a matter of trust."

"Isn't it? Back in London, the Queen virtually admitted that you are her granddaughter but she stopped short of explaining how she could possibly have sent a royal child to be fostered by a cunny woman. She said it was for you to tell me, *if* you ever chose to."

A look of pain flitted across his face. "You haven't. You've lain in my arms, opened your body to me—and, I thought, your heart—but there is still no trust between us. You won't even give me the information that could not only save your own life but prevent this country from sinking into civil war."

He let go of her abruptly and took a step back. With deadly softness he said, "I will not let that happen, Alianor. I will do absolutely anything I have to in order to stop it no matter what the cost."

Her head came up. Through the hot blur of her tears, she faced him squarely. Her voice was rock-steady. "Then you will do the one thing that can stop this now before it goes any further."

"What?"

"Bring me to trial."

Chapter 26

He was no stranger to terror. The gut-wrenching, blood-icing fear that was the antechamber of battle was well known to him. He had passed through it on so many occasions that it was but one more itinerant stopping place in the journey of his life to which he would inevitably return again and again. In his opinion, a man who had seen battle and claimed not to know fear was a fool or a liar. Such a man was also most likely to be left, one more bloodied corpse for the carrion feast.

And yet he had never known fear quite like this.

"Oyez, oyez! All good men and true, this royal court of the assizes now being in session, draw nigh and state your complaint."

Having spoken, Master Brightersea sat down quickly. He had been pressed into service as clerk of the court, Sheriff FitzWilliam not having thought to bring such a man with him.

But then he could hardly have expected to have a court thrown into session with such haste. Indeed, from his position behind one of Master Brightersea's tables, scrubbed and with a fresh white linen cloth tossed over it for propriety's sake, the good sheriff looked just a bit queasy.

Conan might have felt a small flicker of humor at

that but the fear had him in too firm a grip. He could feel nothing but it—and disbelief.

Disbelief that this had come to pass. That Alianor had said what she had, then promptly followed it up with a general announcement to all and sundry that she was ready to answer to any charges anyone cared to bring against her.

There she was now, a little distance from him, standing straight and slim in a simple dark blue gown she had put on during a brief visit to her island. Her expression was composed. Only the tiny beat of a pulse in the corner of her right eye revealed her emotion. He was sure he was the only one who saw it. To all others, she must look calm and utterly confident.

Damn the woman! How could she do this loathsome thing? What could she possibly be thinking of?

No, he knew the answer to that well enough. She was throwing herself in front of the jackals, hoping to prevent not only more murders but also a rebellion. That last part in particular was less likely by the moment. It seemed every resident of Glastonbury from the tenderest babe in arms to the eldest granny was outside Master Brightersea's inn, now an impromptu courtroom.

They were crowded round the door where Conan's men stood post to keep them back, and up against the windows left open to the faint breeze. A low, droning murmur rose from them. They were as confused and dismayed as he was himself but they were also willing to wait. After all, Alianor had asked them to.

"I submit myself," she had said as she addressed them all outside on the street moments before entering the inn, "to justice. I do so with a clear conscience and a confident heart. If I have ever been of service to any of you, I beseech you to do nothing to bring harm upon yourselves or any other."

The hardiest man among them had wiped away tears at that. And, no doubt, steeled his resolve to wreak terrible vengeance if their Lady of the Lake was harmed.

FitzWilliam cleared his throat. He had thrown a deep red velvet cloak over his riding ensemble, no doubt to make himself appear more judicial. It caused him to sweat profusely. Or perhaps the situation itself was to blame.

"This court being in session, we will proceed to hear the complaint brought against the woman known as Alianor by the most reverend abbot, Brother Du Sully."

Temper, Conan cautioned himself. Precisely one minute into the whole damnable exercise and he was ready to throttle the cretinish FitzWilliam.

"Hold."

All eyes riveted to him as Conan took a step forward. He had deliberately donned mail despite the heat. It gleamed dully in the sunlight filtering through the windows.

"The first order of this court," he said, "must be to determine the cause of the deaths of Brother Raspin and Master Longueford."

"We know the cause," Du Sully exclaimed. He pointed a finger at Alianor. "This witch killed them. I avow before this court that she is an agent of Satan and as such must be turned over to Holy Mother Church for redemption and purification."

"How did she kill them?" Conan demanded. He had a brief, tantalizing image of himself rending Du Sully limb from limb but it was gone before he could really enjoy it.

"By cursing them, of course." Du Sully spoke with the exaggerated patience of one attempting to explain a very simple concept to a very backward child. "She conjured evil, doing the bidding of her unclean master, and these fine men were her tragic victims."

"How did she accomplish all this?" Conan demanded. "What were her precise methods, Abbot? You seem to be such an expert on the subject, one might ask how you came by such knowledge."

The crowd stirred, people closest to the room passing along what they were hearing to the others. There was a murmur of satisfaction.

But not from Du Sully. He sputtered angrily. "What are you suggesting, Baron? I am a man of God. I have dedicated my whole life to the service of the most holy. Unlike you, I might add, who should be on his knees at prayer, beseeching the Almighty Lord to forgive you your own sins with this woman."

FitzWilliam's Adam's apple bobbed in agitation. He half rose from his chair. "Now, now, there'll be none of that. If it please your reverence, we will stay to the matter at hand. Baron Wyndham holds the royal writ. He does have the right of question."

The abbot shook his head in disgust. "So speaks the folly of these secular courts. They manage well enough for your average thief needing his hand lopped off, but for truly important matters of evil they are useless."

FitzWilliam frowned. His piety did not extend quite so far as to viewing himself as extraneous. "Whatever your opinion, the law of the land is clear, Reverend Abbot. This court holds jurisdiction. Now, if we might proceed—"

"As I was saying," Conan interjected before Du Sully could reply. "Are there any witnesses to this supposed conjuring? Will anyone come forward and say under oath that he saw it being done?"

"Of course not," the abbot snapped. "The devil's minions work in darkest secret. How else could they accomplish their filthy machinations? But let this witch be put to the question and by God, she'll tell us how it was done."

Conan looked quickly at Alianor. She paled slightly but otherwise showed no reaction to this suggestion that she be tortured.

"I remind this court that King Henry outlawed the use of torture to acquire confessions. Although," he added scathingly, "Mother Church is known to cling to the practice."

FitzWilliam puffed himself up, looking solemn. "The court needs no such reminder. The accusation has been made that the deaths of Brother Raspin and Master Longueford were unnatural. We will consider that matter. Does anyone wish to speak to it?"

"I do." Alianor stepped forward. She ignored Du Sully's hate-filled glare and addressed FitzWilliam directly. "There is not sufficient evidence to be absolutely certain, but I believe it likely that these two men were poisoned."

The sheriff hesitated but addressed her directly. "Why do you believe this?"

Quietly, speaking with calm reason, she told him. Both men were in good health. Neither had complained of any ailments. In both cases, there were others close to hand who could have been summoned at any complaint of illness. No summons had been given. Each man had died suddenly with no time even to call out. Yet each man appeared perfectly at peace, as though death had come so suddenly there hadn't even been time to react.

Before she was done, Du Sully interrupted. "Don't you see what she's doing? If poison was used, she was the one who used it. By explaining all this, by pretending to cooperate, she seeks to divert suspicion from herself."

"Which was it then?" Conan demanded. "Did she conjure them dead or poison them? You can't have it both ways, Abbot."

"What matters how she did it? She acted as a servant of the devil. The exact method is of no account."

FitzWilliam cleared his throat. He still looked green but Conan was beginning to think there might actually be a man in there somewhere.

"Begging your pardon, Reverend Abbot," he said, "but it does matter. This court must have evidence of motive, of opportunity, and of means. Suspicion by itself is not sufficient to convict."

Rather than fume at this, as Conan had half expected, Du Sully merely nodded. He looked pleased, surely a bad sign.

"Very well then," he said. "First, opportunity. It is well known that this woman is admitted everywhere throughout the town. She goes wherever she likes. It would have been but a small thing for her to enter Master Longueford's house."

"But what about the abbey?" FitzWilliam asked.

"Ah, now, that would be more difficult. However, you must remember that few men are as predictable in their routine as monks. We are summoned at regular intervals to pray. Everyone in the town hears the bells and knows what we are about. It would hardly have been difficult for this woman to intrude upon the sanctity of the abbey when she knew she would not be seen."

FitzWilliam nodded thoughtfully. "All right then, as to motive?"

"I have already stated what I believe to be the motive—service to her master, the devil. However, I will enlarge upon it. Brother Raspin was obviously a holy man. He was chosen for his vocation and also because he was involved in my sadly failed attempt to bring the witch to justice sooner. Master Longueford was a worldly man who had only recently returned to the bosom of the Church. He had promised a large endowment to help rebuild the abbey. That was enough to make him the target of the witch's wrath."

FitzWilliam looked to Alianor. "Do you wish to speak to this?"

"Master Longueford was my friend. I would never have harmed him. As for the notion that I stole into the abbey to leave poison someplace where Brother Raspin would happen to find it, that is ludicrous. If I'd wanted to poison the man, I would have made use of the ale he was always slipping down here to get."

Even as Du Sully tried to object, Master Brightersea chimed in. "Now there's truth in that. Brother Raspin liked his tipple."

"Then perhaps that is where she put it," the abbot exclaimed. "Before Almighty God, she surely had the means!"

"You will have to prove that," Conan said quietly. He caught Sir Raymond's eye. The crowd was utterly silent. Not a breath of air stirred.

Du Sully smiled. He looked like a man seeing vindication within his grasp. The hairs on the back of Conan's neck rose.

"By all means. Not an hour since, I visited the witch's cottage. I will not disgust this court by reporting all that we found but look here—"

He drew a small box from beneath his cloak and held it out to the sheriff. "Look inside. See what is there. Then tell me you still question her ability to kill."

FitzWilliam stared at the box as he might at a serpent. He took it gingerly. "What—?"

"Open it!" Du Sully demanded. "Open it and look upon evil!"

Slowly, with utmost reluctance, FitzWilliam lifted

the lid of the box the smallest fraction. He peered inside. "I don't—" He raised the lid farther. A look of puzzlement spread over his face. "There is nothing in here but peas."

Chapter 27

 Conan lunged for the box but FitzWilliam, startled though he was, managed to yank it back.

"He knows!" Du Sully cackled. "Our fine baron knows what these are. You understand their significance, don't you, Wyndham? Did the witch confide it to you? Did she gloat with the suffering of her victims?"

"You sick, twisted—"

"Enough!" FitzWilliam roared above the tumult, then looked surprised when he realized what he'd done. He made haste to interpose himself between Conan and the abbot. Glaring at them both, he said, "This is a royal court of law and by God and King Richard, both of you will respect that! Stand down, Lord Baron, and take your hand off your sword. As for you, Abbot, one more word from you intended to incite riot and I will have you thrown out of here—witch or no witch!"

When neither lightning nor Conan himself proceeded to strike him dead, FitzWilliam drew a breath. He was very pale, but a rather ordinary man who had just done a truly extraordinary thing had a right to be.

"Now then," he said, his voice shaking only a bit, "we will proceed. Reverend Abbot, calmly and clearly explain to me what is in this box."

Torn between anger at the reprimand and eagerness to further his cause the abbot chose cooperation. "First, good Sheriff, you will see that the peas are strung together. They were tied but I have undone the knot. Kindly lift them out carefully so that we may all behold them."

Gingerly FitzWilliam did so. He held up at both ends a string about a foot and a half in length strung with many small peas separated in places by larger ones.

At the sight of them, Du Sully made the sign of the cross. "You are looking at a sacrilege, a mockery of the holy rosary. There are—or more correctly were—five sets of the smaller peas grouped in tens, separated by the larger peas. Were this a true rosary, the small peas would be used for saying the Ave, the larger ones for the paternoster. I removed one of the larger ones and used it to confirm my darkest suspicions."

"Which were?" FitzWilliam prompted.

"That these are the dreaded paternoster pea, deadly poison and the tool of witches. I fed a pea to one of the hogs we raise at the abbey. it died in agony within the hour."

Alianor grimaced. Under her breath, she murmured, "Savage."

Du Sully whirled on her. "What was that, witch?"

"I called you a savage for letting that poor animal die so cruelly."

"The effrontery of this woman that she should claim to care about such things while she reaps victims for her satanic master!"

FitzWilliam raised a hand. "Don't start again, Reverend Abbot. Mistress Alianor, do you deny that this box and its contents came from your cottage?"

Conan took a quick step forward. He had gone white and a nerve twitched in his jaw. His hand was straying back to his sword. "Alianor—"

She stared at him for a long moment, regret burning in her. It took all the courage she possessed to look away.

And to reply to FitzWilliam's question.

"I do not deny it. They belong to me."

Du Sully gave a harsh, ugly sound of triumph even as Conan groaned. Quickly she went on. "They were given to me long ago as a curiosity. I barely remembered that I had them."

FitzWilliam looked doubtful "Do they have any healing purpose?"

"No, they are far too poisonous. It would be unsafe to try to use them under any circumstances."

"I see—but then why would you have them?"

"There is no particular reason. As I said, they were a gift."

"A gift?" the abbot interjected scornfully. "Who would give a decent Christian such a thing? Who would keep it? I tell you, this is the tool of witches. Its presence in her cottage proves that everything she says about using herbs and all the rest only for healing is a lie. She kept poison under her very roof. It was close to hand. How can anyone then believe that she did not poison Brother Raspin and Master Longueford, perhaps Brother Bertrand as well?"

An angry muttering came from the crowd. Conan and the sheriff's men made swift to hold them back from the door but their agitation was growing.

"This is ludicrous," Conan said. He faced Fitz-William. "There is no evidence that these peas were used to kill. Only one is missing and the abbot himself admitted to taking it."

"That is not the point!" Du Sully exclaimed. "Since she had this poison in her possession, it is reasonable to believe there is more, better concealed. If nothing else, the presence of the paternoster peas in this woman's cottage is enough to merit her being turned over to the jurisdiction of the Church."

FitzWilliam hesitated. He stared at the peas. "If it is true they are poison—"

"They are," Du Sully said.

The sheriff looked genuinely distressed. "Mistress Alianor, the fact that you have been found in possession of poison makes it very difficult for me to refuse to give you over to a Church court."

Conan made a sound deep in his throat. Before he could act, Alianor said, "If you do that, I will be tortured and executed." She spoke with quiet dignity. Around the room, men's faces tightened but none could dispute her.

Outside, the people began to shout as those closer to the windows spread word of what was transpiring. Children were crying, their mothers too caught up in their own outrage to even try to quiet them. Conan caught Sir Raymond's eye. Alianor saw the look they exchanged and knew she had very little time left.

"While I remain before this court," she said, loudly enough so that those outside could hear, "I have certain rights. Among them is the right to proclaim my innocence before Almighty God."

Conan frowned. In a moment he would realize the implication of her words and then he—

"I demand to be tried by ordeal."

"*No!*" His fist smashed down against the table so mightily that it leapt up from the floor. All the papers, the candle and whatnots, even the pure white cloth, went slipping and skittering in every direction.

"No man can gainsay me this," Alianor said quickly above Conan's rage and the shocked cries of rejection from the crowd. "I have the right."

FitzWilliam was staring at her in disbelief. He shook

his head as though to clear it. "Mistress, do you truly understand what you say?"

Her heart was racing. It hammered so wildly against her ribs she feared it would burst free. Yet her voice was rock-steady. "I do." She walked toward the sheriff. He could not tear his gaze from her. Her hand rose.

"The Abbot Du Sully has proven to the satisfaction of everyone here that this box contains paternoster peas and that they are deadly. Is that correct?"

"Yes, but—"

"I am without guilt in this matter. Let Almighty God be my judge."

Before anyone could speak or move, she reached into the box. The string was already untied. The merest flick was enough to send the peas free. She seized the largest, four in all, and, before the horrified gaze of Fitz-William, threw them into her mouth.

Sweet heaven, they were dry. Dry as great balls of dust clogging her throat. But she had to get them down, had to swallow them all. Her throat worked. For a horrible moment she thought she would choke. Then painfully, grudgingly, the peas cleared her throat and she felt them no more.

"Oh, my God—!" FitzWilliam cried out. He looked as though he was about to be sick. "She swallowed them! Mercy of heaven, she swallowed all four!"

Pandemonium. Everyone seemed to be screaming and shouting at once. Conan reached her first, taking hold of her shoulders. She could see his mouth moving but couldn't make out what he said. Perhaps it was just as well. A strange sense of numbness was settling over her, separating her from the rest of the world.

Du Sully appeared before her suddenly. For a moment she couldn't hear him either. But his voice was high-pitched, almost shrieking. It penetrated the pleasant fog that seemed to be growing steadily thicker.

"She seeks to take her own life! Rather than face the wrath of Holy Mother Church, she would condemn her soul to eternal damnation!"

"Alianor, is this true?"

Conan. She could hear him now. Dear heaven, he looked so tortured. it broke her heart to see him. Tears filmed her eyes. So great was her emotion that she had difficulty speaking. Each word had to be torn free.

"I am innocent. God knows that and will not let me come to harm."

She thought she managed to sound confident enough but dread filled her all the same. Her knees felt weak. She feared she would collapse and might have done so had not Conan swept her off her feet suddenly and carried her over to a bench. He set her there but stayed beside her, the warmth and strength of his nearness giving her comfort.

People were still shouting, Du Sully among them and there, pushing his way into the room past FitzWilliam's men, Brother Wynn. The young sacristan took one look at the scene and hurried to the abbot's side. He tried to speak quietly to him but Du Sully was beyond hearing. All his attention was focused on Alianor. If he was to be cheated of seeing her burn, he at least intended to enjoy every moment of her death.

FitzWilliam cleared his throat. He still looked horrified but he was beginning to calm a little. "Hold those people back," he ordered. "If they want to do something useful, let them pray."

His suggestion was heard outside. Remarkably, those closest to the door hesitated only a moment before falling to their knees. Word spread. In an instant the entire street in front of Master Brightersea's inn was filled with kneeling people, their hands clasped, praying fervently.

On the bench, Alianor put a hand to her mouth to

hold back a sob. She would not disgrace herself. Matilda had raised her to be a woman of pride and courage. Just now, she needed both desperately.

Conan was still looking at her. He had the bleak expression of a man staring into hopelessness and unable to do anything about it. Her fingers caught his, intertwining.

"Do you not believe in the mercy of God then?"

His voice rasped. "I have yet to see any evidence of it."

She swallowed with difficulty. Her throat felt raw. The effort of swallowing the peas, no doubt. FitzWilliam was staring at her. Out of the corner of his mouth, he addressed Du Sully.

"How long did you say it took the hog to die?"

"An hour."

"She is a slender woman and she swallowed all four of the peas. You wouldn't think it would be much more time—"

"Any moment now you will see the vengeance of the Almighty. I only regret she is allowed to die with so little suffering."

"You said the hog died in agony?"

"Yes, of course, and so will she but it is still too quick. She should have gone to the flames, burned—"

"I'm going to kill him."

Conan spoke flatly. He might have been announcing his attention to take a nap. He started toward the abbot.

Alianor grabbed for him. She hung on for dear life. "Don't! Please, I beg of you, no more trouble. Let's just get through this." She pulled on his tunic until he was forced to bend down. When they were eye to eye, she said, "If you feel anything for me, trust me now. I swear to you the mercy of the Almighty will be evident to all and so will my innocence."

His brow furrowed. She could see his mind considering the shadows of meaning in her words, trying to decipher which were real and which only the longings of his own imagination. Slowly he straightened but his hand continued to hold hers.

Outside in the street, a soft rain began. The drops fell gently over heads bent in prayer.

Chapter 28

The rain worsened. Conan could feel the dampness seeping through the daub and wattle walls of the inn, through his wool cloak and tunic, feel it to the very bone. It felt like the clammy hand of death.

Time had slowed down. He was vividly aware of each passing moment. The room had taken on a sharp clarity he knew would remain with him forever. Breath by breath, heartbeat by heartbeat, the scene etched its way into his soul.

There was FitzWilliam, pale, wide-eyed, still holding that damn box. His gaze would stray to Alianor, be wrenched back, stray again. He had the sick fascination of a man who cannot believe what is unfolding right before him.

And Du Sully—eager, gloating, fairly bursting with anticipation but soured round the edges by the knowledge that it would be too quick, not remotely as satisfying as it could have been.

If ever a man needed killing, it was the mad abbot.

As for the rest—Master Brightersea was red-eyed, stunned, as miserably unhappy a soul as Conan had ever seen. By contrast, Sir Raymond remained the consummate professional despite the strain showing around his eyes, keeping watch on activities in the street. There were none except for the praying. They were doing it out loud now, their voices rising with each passing moment as they beseeched the mercy of God for their beloved Mistress Alianor.

His men, he was glad to see, were blank-faced, eyes averted, too well schooled in their discipline to lose control even under these bizarre circumstances. Fitz-William's men were less certain but even they seemed to be holding themselves in good order, at least for the moment.

And Alianor—

Alianor sat on the bench, her hands folded and her head bent. Her eyes were closed. From time to time, he saw her lips move in prayer. She was the very picture of reverence. Beautiful, devout, sincere, *healthy* reverence. Nothing about her suggested she was ill in any way, much less about to die from lethal poison. Granted, she was a bit pale but he put that down to the circumstances. Her breathing was regular, she did not appear to be in any pain. She was simply—infuriatingly—Alianor.

She coughed suddenly and everyone in the room jumped, including himself. With an apologetic glance, she returned to her prayers.

FitzWilliam leaned closer to Brother Wynn. "How long has it been now, do you think?"

"Half of the hour, maybe more." The sacristan spoke flatly. Alone among all those in the room, he appeared almost disinterested.

Du Sully frowned. "I don't understand. She should be showing signs."

"It must take longer to work on humans," Fitz-William suggested.

"Are you sure she swallowed them?" the abbot demanded, grasping at straws.

"Absolutely. I saw them go down her throat."

"Well, then, there shouldn't be any doubt—" The abbot returned to his watching.

More time passed. The praying outside continued. The rain ended, began again, faded. Rays of sun appeared among the scattering clouds.

"She shows no signs," FitzWilliam said.

Alianor heard that. She lifted her head and looked directly at him. "On the contrary, I show the clearest possible sign of my innocence. I am still alive and unharmed."

"It is a trick!" Du Sully glared at her. "She is deceiving us somehow!"

"You yourself agreed the peas were deadly poison," Conan said.

"And I saw her take them," FitzWilliam averred. "There was no trick."

"There has to be an explanation," the abbot insisted. "No God-fearing man can believe for a moment that this witch could be spared through divine intervention."

"Unless she isn't a witch," FitzWilliam pointed out, not unreasonably Conan thought. There were definitely makings to the man.

"It is not God who aids her," Du Sully insisted. "But the devil himself. He is among us now! We see his power in her survival."

The abbot glanced round from one to the other, gauging what effect this exhortation was having. There wasn't much. The men merely looked puzzled. FitzWilliam spoke for them all.

"The Church has always agreed that trial by ordeal is the means by which God may choose to show His favor and thereby proclaim an accused person's innocence beyond all questioning. There has never been any claim made that the devil is equally able to intervene in the process. Indeed, if there were, what would be the point of the whole thing?"

"There wouldn't be one," Alianor said quietly. She stood up, smoothing her gown, looking so young and serious that Conan had to resist the urge to take her into his arms and carry her away from this loathsome place.

These were not men used to being addressed on such weighty matters by a woman. Yet they stood still and listened to what she said.

"If we say God and the devil are somehow equally able, we fall into heresy. I assume that isn't what the abbot means."

Du Sully, flustered, started to speak but Alianor ignored him and went on. "On the other hand, if we do away with the idea that God will intervene directly in the judging of a human being, then we are left with nothing but our own ability to ferret out the truth through examination of evidence. There would be no reason at all for Church courts. They could be abolished without any loss."

"Exactly as King Henry wanted to do," Conan said.

FitzWilliam eyed the abbot. "And as may yet come to pass. Now, as to the present circumstance, it is evident to all that Mistress Alianor is not poisoned. And yet I myself saw her swallow what must have been a lethal dose. Therefore, I must conclude that this is the hand of God at work."

"It is too soon!" Du Sully exclaimed. His color was high, his fists clenched. "I tell you, she will die! She must!"

The sheriff shook his head. "When, Abbot? In a few minutes, in an hour, sometime later tonight? When? The hog died within an hour. It is that now and more, but she shows no sign of illness at all. If I refuse to recognize the clear and evident handiwork of God, I place my own soul in peril."

"I will absolve you! She must be held. You cannot let this witch go free!"

"I see no witch," FitzWilliam said flatly. "I see a woman wrongly accused, her innocence held forth by God Himself. Does anyone here say otherwise, besides the abbot, of course?"

No man spoke. They stared at Alianor, some openly, some furtively, but all with the dawning glow of fascination of what went beyond feminine beauty into the realm of the supernatural. Was this truly the word of God made flesh before them? Several looked as though they might be about to join the townspeople on their knees.

Brother Wynn took Du Sully's arm. He spoke quietly for the abbot's hearing alone. This time, it appeared his words were attended. The older man slumped slightly, as though some great burning energy had been extinguished within him.

The sacristan gestured to Conan. "We may need some assistance returning to the abbey."

Conan agreed. The mood in the street was such that they would be lucky to reach the abbey unharmed. Half a dozen men were quickly delegated. Master Brightersea scurried about, making his back door available. The abbot departed slowly, too numbed for even a final word, a black, crowlike figure of utmost dejection clinging to Brother Wynn's strong arm.

Barely had the door closed behind them than Fitz-William turned to Alianor. Looking quite pleased with himself, if somewhat dazed, he said, "You are free, mistress. I declare this court adjourned."

From just beyond the windows there was a great indrawing of breath, then silence as though the whole of

Glastonbury—perhaps the whole of nature itself—had just suddenly stopped. It lasted but a moment.

In its wake came a wall of sound bursting over and through the inn, a great outpouring of shouts and cheers as word sped to the far fringes of the crowd.

"*Free!*"

"*Innocent!*"

"*The mercy of God!*"

Jubilation reigned. Before it, the startled men-at-arms were no barrier. The door was breached, then the windows. People were running, climbing, leaping into the inn any way they could.

Conan turned to reach Alianor's side but he was too late. Others were there first. He recognized the burly man who had spoken for the others when they challenged his authority, a woman who had also stood in that crowd, various people he had noticed around the town. They were laughing and crying at the same time, reaching out to Alianor.

Swiftly they lifted her onto the shoulders of the burly man who looked bedazzled by his slight burden. Head high, suffused with pride, he carried her out into the street, into the sea of rejoicing.

Conan made haste to follow. He was certain no harm would be done to her but still deeply concerned. What exactly had happened there in the inn? Had he truly witnessed the hand of God at work? He had spoken true when he told Alianor he had never seen evidence of God's mercy. But perhaps he hadn't known where to look.

His men gathered swiftly around him. Over the tumult, he shouted to Sir Raymond, "Keep her in sight at all times. They've earned their celebration but there's a chance this could incite them to more."

Raymond nodded. He detailed men to fan out through the back lanes of the town, moving swiftly to get ahead of the crowd. Within minutes, it was effectively surrounded although no one seemed to notice. They were far too busy carousing.

Master Brightersea, caught up in the enthusiasm of the moment, had his servants rolling barrels of ale into the street and was busily cracking them open. From every cook shop, bakery, and home, food was appearing. Tables were hauled out and rapidly laden. A fiddler struck up a tune, another followed. Within minutes Glastonbury was in the midst of an all-out festival.

Conan sighed. As profoundly grateful as he was for Alianor's survival—and he still wanted an explanation for that—it looked as though he and his men had a long evening ahead.

"No drinking," he said to Sir Raymond when the two managed to get close enough together through the crowd to exchange a few words. "Tell the men, anyone who takes so much as a drop answers to me. I want clear heads and steady arms."

"Aye, Lord, I'll tell them. You're expecting trouble?"

"I'm expecting these people to get drunk and start talking about how much they hate the abbot. One thing will not lead to another. Understood?"

Sir Raymond nodded. "We'll keep the peace, Lord, but still—"

Conan shot him a quick glance. "Still what?"

The knight looked slightly abashed. "I didn't see it all, I was watching the crowd. But she did take the poison, didn't she?"

"It looked that way to me—and to the sheriff."

"Aye, and he was standing directly in front of her. He had to see. She swallowed them right enough but look at her, she's the picture of health."

Over the heads of the crowd, Conan could see Alianor, sitting on a table, a goblet in her hands, smiling and laughing. No one would have thought she had a care in the world.

"So it appears," he said.

"It's not some kind of slow-acting thing, is it?"

"It wasn't with the hog. No, she's fine enough. But why doubt it, Raymond. You didn't really think she was a witch, did you?"

The knight scoffed. "Course not, but all that business, trial by ordeal, the mercy of God, do you really believe in that?"

"After today, I may not have a choice."

"Aye, true enough. It's an amazing thing all these years, seeing so many people die in battle and from disease, to actually see someone spared. Kind of makes you wonder, if the Almighty could do it this time, why doesn't He make more of a habit of it?"

"Careful, old friend, you'll have the abbot after you."

"Oh, I think he's going to have his hands full with this lot right here." Sir Raymond grinned at the crowd. "They're a happy bunch, aren't they?"

"For the moment. Let's see to it they stay that way."

The two men separated, Sir Raymond moving out to check on the men while Conan pushed closer to Alianor. He did not intend to interfere. These were her people and God knew, she had earned some enjoyment.

God knew. He stumbled over the thought. Did He or didn't He?

Did it matter?

She looked happy and so blessedly healthy. There were poisons with delayed action but he knew about paternoster peas. He'd heard about them in the Holy Land on Crusade. They didn't necessarily kill quickly but they showed their effects quick enough. They could take hours or days to kill but always in agony, never with this smiling, laughing, goblet-in-hand manner of bedazzling Alianor.

When he got her alone—

The mere thought was enough to make his body harden. This time the rising eyebrows were for himself and his own foolishness.

The fiddler struck an even faster beat that carried away the day.

They had lit a bonfire. Townspeople had gathered the wood, the children running back and forth wildly, helping to pile it on until everyone judged it high enough at last and the torch was set. It ignited at once, flaring high against the darkening sky. Staring at it, Conan thought of different flames—with a stake at their center—and took a long, deep breath of the sweet wood smoke.

The festival had been going on for hours. Drink flowed with abandon, more food appeared as if by magic, additional musicians arrived, and a space was cleared for dancing near the bonfire. There was laughter, singing, and a great deal of talk. Conan kept a close ear, drifting here and there, blending with the shadows where he could.

That was easier than he would have thought. The people were swept along by the great event in which they found themselves, possibly the greatest from their point of view that they would ever experience. Almighty God had shown His divine favor upon their dearly loved mistress. All they believed, indeed all they were, was vindicated in that single moment.

And the music played on.

Leaning against a wall, he caught his foot tapping and almost laughed. God, how he wanted to. How he wanted to let loose, roar his own relief and joy, and join in the celebration. But there he was, keeping his distance, keeping watch while she—

Alianor danced, in the circle, around the bonfire, passing hand to hand, flame hair flying, eyes laughing, her slender form the pole star of his eyes. He could not look away. All right, truth be told, he did from time to time but only because his duty compelled it. His gaze was drawn back so inevitably that he hardly realized until he found himself staring at her yet again.

Like a lovelorn swain.

Heaven help him. If there really was a God, if He genuinely cared, if He actually could intervene, then shouldn't there be a remedy for the heart-aching, reason-banishing ailment that had sunk its claws deep into him?

He did not believe in love.

It was an invention of the troubadours and the minstrels, encouraged by women such as Eleanor for their own purposes and amusement.

It did not exist.

Lust existed, that was real. Affection could occur. And between some parents and children, he had seen a bond that was undeniably touching. But romantic love was the stuff of fools, moon-addled nonsense, spun by lute and harp, the resort of men—if they could be called that—who had no calling to the true purposes of life, namely war and politics.

He did not love her.

She was heat in his blood, a throbbing in his loins, and a certain confused recognition that his life was not quite so tidily ordered as he had thought. That was all.

But she did dance well. He was willing enough to give her that. She was all slender grace moving to the music, her feet flying to steps he suspected were very old indeed but which everyone in Glastonbury seemed to know. When they all got going at it, even the youngest, the ground itself seemed to quiver in response.

He caught sight of FitzWilliam, hovering like him on the edge of the crowd, looking relieved yet perplexed. A young woman, blond, cheerful, grabbed his hand. A gaggle of girls near her giggled behind their fingers, as though she'd taken a dare. She dragged him into the circle. He protested at first, but it was feeble. Quick enough, he let himself be carried off.

There would be others. Not his men, to be sure, but the sheriff's own and anyone else who happened to wander into town on this night, drawn by the fire and the music. The rest of the world was still out there somewhere but just now it didn't seem to matter. Even the dark shadow of the abbey, crouched on the hill, hardly counted.

His men were up there, too, still guarding the remains found in the graveyard. Conan spared a thought for them, thinking he'd have to find a suitable reward when this was all said and done. Yes, they were merely carrying out their duty to him but they were good men for all that and they deserved some recognition.

Was Du Sully asleep or was he hovering at his window, gazing down at what must surely appear a pagan spectacle of firelight and music, revelry and song? Or perhaps he was at prayer, on his bony knees before the altar, demanding of his God why the witch had not been struck down.

A man came by, bearing a tray of meat pasties at his shoulder. He paused, catching sight of Conan, and offered him one. "Eat, Lord," he said with a grin, "the night is young. Let's revel while we may." He moved on, leaving Conan to munch on the savory tidbit and contemplate the wisdom of his words.

Sir Raymond appeared. Still watching the crowd, he said, "I've set up a cordon across the road to the abbey. A few men drifted over that way but they moved on when they saw us."

"Good. Anything else?"

"Doesn't seem to be. Plenty of talk but even that's been fading. They're too happy."

"As well they should be." He wasn't feeling too badly himself. The full realization of what had happened was just beginning to sink in. He still had trouble believing it, but there she was, dancing by again. Her cheeks flushed. Hand in hand around the circle, until she was dancing suddenly with FitzWilliam.

The sheriff looked startled, then pleased. He'd had an ale or two, Conan judged, enough so that he wasn't entirely sober. His gaze, settling on Alianor, held more than respectful interest. A great deal more.

Conan moved. He flowed away from the wall and into the crowd. It melted before him. The music faltered and with it the people's pleasure. Those closest, who could see what was happening, stopped and fell silent.

Alianor pushed a lock of flame hair from her eyes and met his steadily. She said nothing, nor did she look in the slightest surprised. FitzWilliam, on the other hand, started guiltily.

"Uh, my lord, there you are. I didn't see you."

Conan didn't reply. He merely held out a hand to Alianor. "It's time you got some rest," he said and took her to him, away out of the circle and the dance, away from the leaping fire, into the quiet of the night that was their own.

Chapter 29

She was going to die. Not the way she'd feared earlier in the day but die all the same. "And then there's that problem with the smile," Matilda had said one night when they stayed up late drinking mead, this when Alianor was sixteen, talking as women did—about men. Well, it wouldn't be her problem. She'd be safely dead. Someone else would have to deal with it.

"*Conan*—" Her back arched, hips lifting to meet him, and she was gone, over the edge, bliss exploding.

Consciousness returned in fragments. She was breathing erratically, heart hammering, skin dewed. He was slumped above her in the aftermath of his own release, his weight so familiar to her now, the strength and power no longer quite so strange.

Her hands stroked down his back. He trembled slightly and raised his head, looking at her. "I'm going to die."

She laughed, still feeling him within her, loving it. "I had the same thought myself."

He rolled free of her, onto his side, and propped an elbow beneath his head. "No, I'm not joking. How is it we manage to survive this?"

"Luck?"

"I'd call it that, all right." His fingertips brushed along the length of her arm. She should have been lost to sensation, burnt out, but his merest touch was enough to make her stir again. He saw and grinned.

"Insatiable, are you?"

"Only where you're concerned." It was the simple truth. She, who had always prided herself on such discipline and self-control, was utterly helpless when it came to this man. What a thing to discover after all these years.

He dropped a light kiss on her upturned mouth. It deepened. She breathed in the touch and scent, the taste and feel of him, and knew a moment of fierce gratitude, for life, for intimacy, for everything that made this possible.

Slowly they parted. His gaze was hooded, thoughtful. He left her, surprisingly, and stood, naked in the shadowy light of the fire. She drank him in with her eyes, unabashedly, savoring every chiseled plane and angle of him. His body was perfectly honed, each muscle and sinew clearly articulated. There was nothing in the least soft or yielding about him. He was the epitome of masculine strength and grace.

Sadness pierced her suddenly for she understood all too well where all that marvelous, stirring beauty came from. He had been bred for battle, trained for it since birth. A great deal of his life had been given over to it. His body was conditioned to survive under harsh, unforgiving circumstances. And it was designed to kill.

But for all that he was tempered by intelligence and perhaps—grace to his mother—gentleness. And it was that, not the warrior's strength, that had him standing there in the shadows of the firelight when a warm and oh, so willing woman waited for him in bed.

"I want to know how you managed it," he said, without warning although she needed none. She had known all along this was coming. He was singularly lacking in the superstition that was so common a part of life it might have been air.

Feigning far less concern than she felt, she settled herself against the pillows and smoothed her hair over her shoulder to braid it. "Managed what?"

He turned, framed by firelight. "Survival. The peas were poisonous."

It wasn't a question but she answered it anyway. "Extremely. Are you entirely lacking in faith then or just uncertain?"

Conan laughed, a startlingly rough and virile sound in so feminine a domain. "Long ago, as I understand it, men prayed to the god of battles. Perhaps he heard. I've seen no sign this one does."

"Mayhap you've been looking in the wrong places. Those paternoster peas really were given to me years ago. I'd almost forgotten I had them until I came back here to change my gown and suddenly remembered."

He frowned, coming closer. "And did what?"

Her shoulders rose and fell. "Left them where they could be found if anyone happened to search. Truthfully, I had little hope anyone would but Du Sully came through after all. I should have had more faith."

"What a singularly inappropriate way to put it. You *wanted* him to find them?"

She nodded. "They were the perfect solution. Most priests have at least heard of paternoster peas and all that nonsense about them being used for the devil's rosaries. I knew there was a good chance he would recognize them as poison."

He came closer still and with his hands clenching into fists at his sides. She took a breath. "Please understand, your own reaction was essential. If you hadn't appeared convinced, and genuinely worried, the abbot would have been suspicious."

"As, I gather, he should have been. Explain."

It was an order from a man accustomed to command. Surely she would have been better advised to begin all this when she was at least up and dressed, not lying naked so very near to his hand? Too late to think about that now.

Hesitantly she said, "Paternoster peas are poisonous—if chewed, which apparently is what that poor hog did. But they have a coating around them which, if it remains intact, prevents the poison from getting out into the body. I knew I would be safe enough provided I swallowed the peas without breaking the coating on any of them. I did and you know the rest."

He stared at her in disbelief. It became very quiet in the cottage. There was no sound but for the fire crackling.

"*Damn you.*" He spoke so softly she could barely hear him. But there was no mistaking the anger swiftly overriding him.

"You risked your life deliberately and you damn near drove me mad. What in hell were you thinking of!"

She drew the covers a little higher over herself, not because she was afraid of him. Not at all. She was merely cold. "I needed to gain some time."

Color stained his high-boned cheeks. His eyes were narrowed to slits of cold fire. "To do what? Continue refusing to tell me who you think is involved with the rebels? Continue risking that this whole damnable business will blow up in our faces in a civil war? Do you have any idea what that will be like? Any idea how many will *die*?"

"Yes," she said quietly, "I have a very good idea. And no, I am not going to tell you what you want to know. I can't."

With the covers held around her, she moved to leave the bed. Her intention was to dress, to put on a little dignity along with her clothes and try to salvage what she could of a situation that had turned lightning fast from joy to anger.

Conan stopped her. His hand, accustomed to the sword, closed hard around her arm. Through gritted teeth, he said, "You will not do this. I will not permit it."

"Let go of me."

He did not. His grip tightened. Steadily, relentlessly, he forced her back toward the bed. A tremor of fear ran through her. She suppressed it and faced him squarely. "Stop this."

His smile was a mere baring of the teeth, a feral look more suited to the battlefield than the bedchamber. "Stop what? You don't trust me anyway. You put me through hell and expect me to come back for more. It's time you learned that I am not your lap dog, my lady. I rule here. I rule *you*."

He shoved her, once, enough to send her sprawling onto the bed. The covers remained in his hand. She lay naked before him. With a gasp she rolled over and tried to get up. He stopped her. The weight she had relished such a short time before was suddenly an intolerable burden. The strength she had cherished was turned against her. Without warning, he had become not lover, but enemy.

Without warning? No, not true. Hadn't she always thought of him that way, if just a little? Since he had come riding into town on his great horse, flashing his sword, even if in her defense, hadn't she seen him as male, warrior, conqueror? The opposite of everything she had been taught was good and valuable? The destroyer of so much that had been and would be still if it weren't for those like him?

Enemy.

He made a low, harsh sound she had never heard

from him before and stretched her arms out over her head. His free hand moved over her with insulting thoroughness, as though asserting his right to touch her in any way he chose.

"Damn you," he said again and shoved his thigh between hers.

She lashed out at him with all her strength. Her foot caught him in the back hard enough to at least startle. He cursed and moved to subdue her but she was frantic now, desperate. If he did this to her, if he did it to them, there would be no recovery from it. All they had shared, all that might have lain ahead, would be shattered in an instant.

She fought then not only to protect herself but in some way to protect him as well, the gentler Conan, the man of music and sunlight, smiles and laughter. Not this dark, angry figure who seemed to believe in nothing and no one.

For all that, one truth undermined her resolve. She had hurt him. For good reason, perhaps. Unavoidably, she could claim. But she had hurt him all the same. Indeed, if she believed him, she had sent him into a kind of hell.

Tears burned her eyes. Her strength was as nothing against his. He forced her back down effortlessly. With humiliating ease, he spread her legs wide and moved between them.

It was going to happen. She was not going to be able to stop him. A sob broke from her. She twisted her head to the side, desperate at least not to have to look at him, to see this raging, brutal creature he had become.

Abruptly he went still. His grip lessened. A great silence, like a hushed winged thing, settled over them. It lasted only moments but it was enough. He pushed himself up off her and was gone.

She began to shiver not so much from the cold as though with a sudden seizure. Dragging the covers back over herself, she huddled in them.

He was dressing, dragging on his clothes with purposeful intent.

"Where are you going?"

He turned to her, tying the laces of his shert at the throat. His face was in shadows. "Away from here."

Away from you. He hadn't said it but he might as well have. The words stung, absurdly under the circumstances.

He retrieved his sword belt from the floor and cinched it around his waist. Still not looking at her, he tossed his cloak over his shoulders. At the door, he paused.

His back to her, softly as though almost to himself, he said, "I have never hurt a woman in my life. Not in the aftermath of battle, not in carelessness, not ever. I swear this."

"I believe you." Her throat was tight with tears. For him, for herself, for them.

"I despise men who do such things."

"You did not—"

His eyes were silver, like the wolf's. "I came very close."

And with that he was gone. For a moment after the door closed, it seemed as though the dark and night were still seeping into the cottage. But that was only an illusion. They were safely shut out by the familiar oak door, iron-banded, set in the familiar wall between the familiar windows.

The fire still crackled cheerfully in the same fireplace that had warmed her since she was a child. Matilda had been so proud of that fireplace, chortling over it. She'd had one of the very first chimneys anywhere thereabouts, built by a grateful stonemason anxious to do a service for the healer who had saved his son. Or was it his daughter? Alianor could no longer remember.

She tried very hard to for a little while but the effort seemed to give her a headache. Although to be fair, the tears slowly trickling down her cheeks might have had something to do with that.

She knelt on the bed and listened to the wind blow around her cottage; heard, too, the whisper of it in the empty places of her heart.

Chapter 30

He had come to the island in fog and now, as he left, the fog was returning. Swimming through it on Gray's broad back, he felt the tendrils of ghost-white mist brush past him like so many mocking spirits.

Jesu, he had turned fanciful. Never in his life would he have had such a thought—until this place and this time. Fog was fog. At worst, it might hide an enemy. At best, it might go away. Just fog.

Yet how merciful it would be if a bit of that swirling mist could enter into his brain and blank out his thoughts. He knew men who went blank-minded through most of their lives and seemed content enough. He wasn't one of them. His mind, ever active, was piercingly alert. His thoughts ached, not in the familiar way of an old hurt but new, throbbing, demanding of attention.

How could he have?

The hood of his cloak was draped over his head, the heavy wool glistening with moisture forming a point just at the center of his brow. Beneath it, his eyes were hard.

Why shouldn't he have? God and all the saints knew she was an infuriating woman. Overly proud, presumptuous, given to self-rule. Not at all the way a woman should be. Surely she deserved punishment for what she'd done to him. He could still see the moment when she swallowed the peas, still feel the soul-grinding horror that would be a part of him for the rest of his life.

But rape? He shied away from the thought but the warrior's honor held strong. Turning back in his mind, he forced himself to confront it.

Rape.

Ugly word for an ugly reality. In the aftermath of his first battle, fighting for Henry against his sons' rebellion, he had heard screams in the street of the town the King's army had taken. Women's screams, terrified with an undercurrent of raging anger that could find no outlet. His instinct had been to go and try to help but knowledge was already there, implanted deep, and besides his father stopped him.

His father—a good and honorable man by any light, infinitely relieved that his son had survived his first blooding—put an arm around his shoulder, stuck a mug of ale in his hand, and spoke quietly. Everyone knew this was the way of things. It was well understood, no secret, no horrible discovery after the fact. The town leaders should have surrendered without a fight, not closed their gates and waited for rescue that didn't come. They shouldn't have been in rebellion against King Henry in the first place. They'd picked the wrong side, made the wrong decisions. What else could they expect?

Thinking about it now as the water sloshed around his boots and the mist drifted through the night, Conan fancied he could still hear the screams.

He shook his head, as though to clear it, and urged Gray up the bank to shore. The world was the world. He certainly wasn't going to change it. But he didn't have to add to the aching and if in the natural course of things, he found a way to prevent just a bit of harm, well, then, he could count his days well spent.

He was angry because she didn't trust him. The bright streak of fairness that lay folded within the many hammerings of his nature like buried steel flexed itself. Why should she? What, precisely, had he done to earn her trust?

Made love to her? Good for him. She was an easy woman to love, physically and in other ways he wasn't going to think about just then.

Saved her from Du Sully? Maybe he'd helped but it seemed as though she'd done most of that herself even to the extent of risking her own life in a terrifying gamble.

Impressed her with his wit and charm? He smiled wryly at the thought. Mayhap when this was all over, he'd slip a purse to one of Eleanor's troubadours, get the fellow to compose a song for fair Alianor.

Quicksilver as a harp's chord, he realized exactly how much he was presuming. How much he longed for. A deep sigh escaped him. Gray heard and pricked his ears. Conan patted the stallion gently. "Easy, boy. Be glad you've four legs instead of two."

It would be dawn soon. He could go back into town, summon men, send them to the island to guard her. He could warn them about the stone bridge, remind them that she also had Fiona, do everything he had to in order to keep her from wandering into danger, yet again.

Keep her penned, captive, under control. The way a woman ought to be.

Or he could give her the trust he wanted her to give to him. He could let her do whatever she thought best and hope to God it worked out in the end.

Barely had the thought flickered than his mind tried to throw it off, rearing almost like Gray would when struck by a particularly troublesome fly. Let her do whatever she liked? Wander off who knew where, into any kind of godforsaken danger? Oh, yes, surely he'd do that and sleep well for the doing.

He had to find another way. A compromise, of sorts, that didn't require him to cast aside the training of a lifetime. It was a dangerous world. Even Alianor would surely admit that. In battle, he had Sir Raymond to watch his back. There was nothing wrong with her having a bit of protection, too.

His eyes darkened. Between rapist and knight errant, there had to be some middle ground where women were concerned. The first chance he got, he was going to find it.

But for the moment— He turned Gray into the shadow of the trees at the edge of the lake and settled down to wait.

She wasn't coming. An hour had passed, perhaps slightly more, and still there was no sign of Alianor. Across the water, through the screen of trees, he could make out a faint light in the cottage window. She was there all right, but was she still awake? Had she, perhaps, fallen asleep in that tumbled bed, in her tears?

The air was damp and almost chill. Gray didn't mind. He'd found ample forage and was at his ease. But for his master, time dragged. What if he was wrong? What if she had no intention of pursuing the matter of the mystery patient?

He sighed again and settled his back more comfortably against a broad-trunked oak. Patience was a hard school for him but one he had returned to over and over. He could honestly say he was getting better at it.

All the same, the sense that this was wasted effort grew in him. There was no reason to presume Alianor would venture out at night. She might be too tired, too distraught, or simply uncertain as to what to do. She was, after all, merely human for all that there were times he caught himself wondering otherwise.

Lady of the Lake. It was the stuff of legend—and fancy. A tale told by the troubadours for the entertainment of their sweet patronesses. A man could enjoy it well enough without ever mistaking tale spinning for truth.

And yet—

He'd known his own moments when it seemed as though the world was no more than a shell, concealing vastly more than it revealed. There were holy men in the East who claimed world upon world existed, all side by side, sometimes shifting one into the other. Who was to say otherwise?

The fog had thickened. He strained to keep alert, knowing he might miss her. The land was familiar to him now, with his eyes shut he could feel the contour of it. But she knew it so much better. If he let himself drift off for even an instant, he could—

What was that? There, at the far edge across the water, a thickening in the mist? A trick of the eye?

No, something white and slender was moving quickly, but it couldn't be Alianor. Even as he watched, it appeared to shrink to less than half its original size. He frowned, bewildered, then abruptly slapped himself on the forehead. She was on Fiona. When the horse went down into the water, naturally the rider on her back appeared to become smaller.

Quickly he mounted Gray, whispering to the stallion of the need for quiet. A small frisson of excitement ran through him. He had been right, after all.

She came across swiftly and mounted the opposite shore without hesitation. In an instant she and Fiona disappeared into the trees.

Conan waited. If he followed too close upon her, she

would sense him for sure. Or Fiona would. Better to wait, counting heartbeats, until he thought her far enough ahead. Only then did he touch his heels to Gray's sides, silently urging him on.

Horse and man alike were experienced trackers. More than once Conan had stalked an enemy, waiting for the best opportunity to strike. This was different. Despite his expectations, he could scarce believe she had actually ventured out alone and at night. In a land where rebellion threatened. In which there might well be someone trying to get her killed.

And women claimed to find men puzzling. Compared to the pale sprite on the dainty horse picking her way across moss-covered rocks and through tiny, burbling springs by moonlight, his own sex was a paragon of clarity and reason. A man would know better.

Or not be quite so desperate.

He willed silence within himself, projecting it outward. Be like the tree, his uncle had told him when he was sent north to be fostered by his mother's brother on the edge of the cold, dark sea. Be like the wind. Find the stillness within yourself and let it grow until it becomes the whole of you

That was impossible. A man's thoughts would always intrude, concerns about the world. But he kept them quiet as he could, letting his breathing become so shallow that his chest scarcely moved. Gray moved on, needing no direction. He had the mare's scent.

They moved away from the town in the direction of a hill that rose to the west. As the lake dissolved in mist behind them, the air cleared. Clouds rode the sky but where they parted Conan could glimpse the full moon. From time to time, as the forest thinned, he caught sight of Alianor. She appeared to ride not on land but on ribbons of molten silver.

Fancifulness, he thought, and let it go at that.

She seemed to know exactly where she was heading. The realization of that steeled his resolve. He touched a hand to his sword hilt and urged Gray on.

Several miles later he emerged from the woodland to find himself at the base of a large hill. Fiona was tethered nearby. There was no sign of Alianor. Leaving Gray beside the mare, Conan started up the hill. It was longer and somewhat higher than the one the abbey perched on but it had the same gently mounded effect, as though nature had intended it for climbing. Distantly he remembered the tales that nature had in fact had nothing to do with such places. Stories that they were built by ancient peoples for unknown purposes. But he discounted that, presuming the effort to achieve a mound of earth the same dimensions as a good-sized cathedral would have been beyond anyone's ability—or desire.

And yet, climbing the hill, he couldn't help but notice how symmetrical it was. The sides flowed smoothly upward, all at the same angle, to meet at a flattish top high enough to provide an unimpeded view for miles in every direction.

The top was bare except for a slim, white form standing at one edge, looking out toward the west. He stopped, uncertain what to do. He didn't want to frighten her but neither did he intend to conceal his presence. Protect her, he would. Deceive her was another matter entirely. That, of course, presuming he could have.

He must have made some sound—an indrawn breath, something. She turned suddenly.

"Who's there?"

The moon was behind her. In its shadows he would have been nothing more than a dark silhouette, vaguely human-shaped, threatening. Her hand went to her throat.

"Conan," he said quickly and stepped into the silver light.

Under other circumstances, her response would have been gratifying. She wasn't an easy woman to surprise but she was that now and more. Her lips parted soundlessly even as her eyes went wide.

"Conan?"

"I'm sorry if I frightened you."

It wasn't clear to him exactly which frightening he was apologizing for, this small one or the far greater transgression at the cottage. But his regret was tangible. Still, she did not move, simply staring at him as though not quite sure he was who he appeared to be.

"What are you doing here?" she asked finally.

"Following you."

Truth. He had decided on it. Anything else was just too complicated.

"Look," he went on, "I know I'm most likely the last person on earth you want to see right now and I don't blame you for it. My behavior was worse than abominable. But the fact is you're out here by yourself at night in a land where rebellion is brewing and someone may be trying to kill you. That just isn't smart."

"And being with you is?"

That stung but then it was meant to. He accepted the hurt and went through it. "Allowing me to protect you is."

"I see . . . And I suppose this protection means that I go wherever you think I should, do whatever you say. Is that it?"

"If I say yes, is there any chance you'd agree?"

"No."

"I didn't think so." He took a step closer to her. When she didn't move back, he risked another. "All it means is that I don't want you to die or be hurt. If you're up here to meet with someone, I'll find some rocks or something to hide behind and try to be as unobtrusive as possible but I'm not leaving."

"And what about anything you see or hear? You wouldn't hesitate to use that to your own purposes, would you?"

He was silent for a long moment. Honor had always seemed so simple, so absolutely basic. He'd never had to spend much time thinking about it. Slowly he said, "I seem to have developed conflicting loyalties." The admission cost him dearly. He had never faced such a situation before. Between Eleanor and Alianor, how would he choose? Queen or woman? Honor or love?

Alianor flinched. It was almost as though she had felt his pain. Softly she said, "I'm not here to meet anyone."

He frowned, not sure he understood. "Then why come?"

"I come here on this night every year."

"This night—?" He thought quickly. What date was it exactly? What significance could it have?

She crossed the distance between them until she stood directly in front of him. Moonlight washed her eyes silver. Her voice rode on the night, soft, elusive as a whispered breeze.

"It is Beltane."

Somewhere off in the woodland, an owl called.

Chapter 31

If he'd been at court, he would have known. Every member of the royal household from the lowliest stable hand to Eleanor herself would have been busy with preparations for May Day—Beltane, in the old tongue. Flowers would be gathered, garlands sewn, special foods prepared, new songs composed, every room aired out and freshened, and so on until the eve of May itself when the court would succumb to ribald revelry. The winter ended, spring in full flower, and summer beckoning, when better to set aside the ordinary bounds of self-control and let impulse rule?

But out here in the hinterland, he'd lost track of the date and never noticed May Day coming.

"That's why the townspeople had all the wood cut," he said, feeling foolish in hindsight. The bonfire had been built too quickly for happenstance. It hadn't been merely the supplies for their own hearths that went into the flames. They'd burned the sacred woods of Beltane to celebrate Alianor's vindication. The coincidence of the timing—Master Longueford's murder, her own desperate gamble, all coming on this day—rippled through him. He set it aside for later thought.

"It's still customary here to mark the day in the old ways," she said, with modest understatement, he thought.

"Including that you come to this place?

"That's more of a personal matter." She paused, looking up at him. Her face softened. He glimpsed forgiveness and something more—concern? Not for herself but for him. But why?

"Conan, there truly is no need for you to be here. I'm in no danger."

"You may believe that but I don't. I can't."

"The danger is more to you, if you stay."

His hand flexed round the sword hilt. "From what source?"

She was very pale in the moonlight. Her skin seemed washed clean of color save for the green luminescence of her eyes and the soft, ripe rose of her mouth. He watched her lips move. "Yourself."

"Myself? That makes no sense."

A cloud obscured the moon. The world seemed to waver around him, not quite there as it had been. A trick of the light, nothing more.

Though she was still standing close to him, her voice seemed to come from a greater distance. "You have a sense of the world, of what it is and how it works, of your own place in it. If you stay here, that may change."

A small chill ran down his spine. He ignored it. "I've seen more of the world than most men. I know it encompasses more than most people believe, but at the same time I've seen how shallow and foolish the superstitions are that plague men's minds."

"This is—different."

She believed what she was saying. He could see that. A wave of tenderness washed over him. For all her courage and her strength, she was not completely immune to the secret fears and whispers of the night. They had affected her as they seemed to everyone.

"I'll take the risk. I'm not leaving you alone."

A small smile lifted the corners of her mouth. "Of

course, there's a possibility that you may just be bored."

"Oh, no, not that, please."

She laughed. It was the loveliest and most joyful sound he had ever heard. The knowledge that he could still make her laugh, that she would still laugh with him, filled him with profound relief. Without thinking, he reached out and took her into his arms.

"I'm so sorry," he said gently, breathing in the fragrance of her hair.

For a moment she was stiff against him. But then her body relaxed and they flowed together as they had from the first moment ever he touched her. As though something in each of them recognized the other in a way that went beyond memory.

"So am I," she said and held him tightly.

The wind felt chill. He wrapped his cloak around her, gathering her into the warmth of his body, and led her over to a rock outcropping that offered some shelter. Together, they sat as the moonlight washed over the hilltop and clouds danced across the blaze of stars.

After a while, they talked. Or more correctly, Alianor did. Conan listened. She began without preamble but then the beginning had been made a fortnight ago in the Queen's Tower chamber.

"Matilda loved my mother dearly and I believe her love was returned. Gwyneth was beautiful, with golden hair and eyes the same color as mine, and she had a very sweet disposition. Whether she was really suited to the island and to what Matilda needed to teach her is another matter. I don't think Eleanor ever wondered whether or not Gwyneth really belonged there. She had vowed when she married Henry to give her firstborn daughter by him to Matilda and she kept that vow at all costs."

She paused, gathering her thoughts, and resumed

slowly. "I don't believe the vow was especially important to Matilda. Eleanor had asked her counsel in the
matter of getting free of Louis, and later marrying
Henry. Matilda gave it readily. She was worried about
who would follow her but she would never have demanded a child in payment. That was Eleanor's idea.
She didn't want it all to end, you see. She wanted there
to always be a Lady of the Lake and I think she liked
the idea that it would be her own blood continuing the
line.

"Of course," she admitted, "I could be wrong. There
may have been more involved in the whole business of
Louis and Henry—and in Henry becoming king—that
I don't know. Matilda was always circumspect about
such things. At any rate, Gwyneth grew up on the
island, taught by Matilda. In the natural course of
events, she would have taken her place. But she had little aptitude for the training. Matilda was in contact
with Eleanor and thinking about sending Gwyneth
back into the world, when events spiraled out of
control.

"In my mother's sixteenth year a young man came
to Glastonbury. He was passing through on his way to
the Holy Land where—as it happens—he would
shortly die. But first, he lay with Gwyneth and got her
with child—with me. He left and in due course I was
born. Matilda was as skilled a midwife as has ever
lived but she had no cure for what afflicted Gwyneth
after my birth. When I was scarcely a fortnight old, my
mother walked into the lake and drowned."

Conan's breath sucked in harshly. Her pain swept
over him, the old, rock-hard pain of abandonment and
failure. In an instant he knew it all—the blaming of
herself for her mother's death, the anger at Gwyneth
for what she had done, all a child's helpless fury and
fear crystallizing in the determination to do better, be

stronger, to survive where her mother had been destroyed.

His arms tightened around her. "You were a baby. There was nothing you could have done."

"Oh, I know that but there is some part of me that will always hold me responsible for what happened to her. I know it's wrong, even foolish, but I've never been able to root it out. The best I can do is live with it."

"And your father—nothing was heard of him before his death?"

Alianor shook her head. "I don't think he ever knew Gwyneth was with child. If he had, it's possible that he would have returned immediately."

His face must have revealed his thoughts. She smiled faintly. "No, it's not that I'm so naive. My father's name was François du Blois." She paused, waiting to see if he would put it together.

He did. It took a moment, mainly because disbelief clouded the way. But the pieces fell into place suddenly and he saw the whole of it. It helped that he had a good memory, and a passingly good education.

"François du Blois was the natural son of Eustace du Blois."

Alianor nodded. "Eustace, King Stephan's nephew and heir but for his choking on a fish bone, thereby clearing the way for Henry to take the throne instead."

Shock roared through Conan. The implications of what she was saying were unmistakable. Alianor of the Lake, erstwhile accused witch, was of royal blood through both her parents. In this age when bastardy was no sure bar to any crown, she stood in the direct line of succession both as Henry and Eleanor's granddaughter and as the granddaughter of Eustace du Blois. Within her were reconciled the two contending branches of the family spawned by the great William the Conqueror himself. Were the truth about her ever to become known, she would at once become both the greatest marriage prize and the surest path to civil war that England had ever known.

Still reeling from the discovery, his mind nonetheless leapt ahead. "Was François's coming here mere chance?"

"I don't know. It may have been or he may have heard some rumor and come to find out whatever he could. If that were the case, I suppose from his point of view nothing came of it. He would have died never knowing how very close he had been."

Close to the one woman who could have been the key to his family regaining the throne. Married to her, and with Henry's rule constantly threatened by dissension and disloyalty, François might have managed to topple the Plantagenets and take the crown for himself. Fate had decreed otherwise. Rather than a throne, he'd gained a forgotten grave in a foreign land and left behind a daughter he never knew.

The daughter who stood encircled in Conan's arms.

She trusted him. Flowing above and through the stunning discovery of who she really was came that shining thread of gold. Alianor trusted him. How could he think otherwise when she had just shown him the path to overthrow a dynasty?

Eleanor was old and besides, he knew her too well. If he had to, he could best her. Richard was away, too busy in the Holy Land to pay any attention to what was happening in the kingdom that should have been his greatest jewel. There was John Lackland to be sure, the surly youngest brother, hovering at the edges, but he had few followers.

Conan had many. He was admired and respected. He had wealth and power at his command. If he chose—

For a heady instant, the possibility tantalized. The

throne, the crown, the chance to set this realm on a new and far firmer foundation that would carry it proudly into the future, all lay within his grasp. Except first, he would have to destroy the land he loved. Rip it apart in the very civil war he was trying to prevent. Plunge it into the cauldron of death and despair. His path to the royal diadem would run red with blood.

He rejected the thought as quickly as it had appeared. He would never do such a thing. Whatever he gained as a result, he would lose himself.

Somehow, Eleanor must have known that when she sent him to Glastonbury.

He smiled a wry homage to the aged Queen and turned his attention back to her granddaughter. Alianor sighed tiredly. The events of the day and the trauma of revealing herself to him at last had left her exhausted. He drew his cloak over them both and settled her more comfortably in his arms.

They talked awhile longer, softly in the way of lovers. Despite all the questions he still wanted to ask her, he contented himself with murmured comfort and reassurance. She accepted both, the barriers down between them now and her heart gladly open to him. Silence came at intervals, stretching out, until finally there were no more words.

When, exactly, he fell asleep, Conan couldn't have said. His intention had been to keep watch while Alianor rested but his eyes grew heavy-lidded and though he fought to keep awake, the battle was lost eventually. He was vaguely aware that Alianor had already drifted off. She lay in his arms with complete trust, her breathing soft and regular.

He followed. Nothing stirred on the hilltop. Quiet descended on the woodland below. The world lay hushed.

Conan dreamed. He was standing on top of a hill

just before dawn. Whyever he was there and wherever he had come from, he felt peaceful and content. Looking out toward the horizon, he saw that the day promised to be fair. The scent of spring was in the air.

A horn sounded. He turned, eager, and smiled when he saw the huntsmen emerge suddenly from around the base of the hill. Their cloaks billowed out behind them. He caught the glint of their helmets and breastplates. Lean hounds raced before them, barking their excitement. He heard the men call out to each other, unable to catch the words but recognizing their pleasure in the day and in themselves. They were well mounted, their horses spirited. In moments they were disappearing down the track that led through the forest.

If he could have gone with them, he would have.

He turned and found Alianor watching him.

"Good morning."

And it was. He was there, standing on the hilltop in the gray light before dawn, in the new day, with the echoes of the huntsmen still sounding in his ears.

It wasn't a dream.

"What just happened?"

She shrugged, still watching him. "You tell me."

"I saw a group of men ride out. They appeared to be hunting."

"Surely that's a common enough sight."

"Indeed, but where did they come from? They were just suddenly there. And now that I think on it, they were dressed oddly. I didn't recognize their helmets and their armor looked different."

"You only caught a glimpse."

"No, more than that. I saw them clearly. I could hear their laughter. It was in my mind to join them."

She swallowed hard. He saw the muscles work in her throat. "I'm glad you didn't. Do you see that track down there?"

He followed the direction of her gaze. A narrow path, just wide enough for a horseman, led into the wood.

"The people hereabouts call that Arthur's Lane. Some believe that on Beltane, he and his knights ride out along it to hunt."

"Arthur?" His voice was thick with skepticism.

"So people say."

"You think I saw ghosts?"

"I think there are things in this land that cannot be explained. Perhaps what you saw was the earth's memory of something that happened here long ago. I do know that it is given to very few to see those riders and to the best of my knowledge, no one has ever heard them before."

But he had. Even as he doubted it, the memory was too strong. He had seen and heard men where there were none, or had not been for a very long time. Men riding to a hunt that was not of this world.

And he had wanted to go with them.

She had been right, then, to say that the danger was in himself.

The sun was rising in glory out of the east. In the distance he could see the hill above the town and the scarred abbey on it. The wind carried the ragged pealing of church bells.

He told himself they were only ringing for matins even as he knew they were not.

Chapter 32

Du Sully lay in a pool of blood, his skull crushed. He was in the small garderobe just off his office and had apparently been answering a call of nature when the event occurred.

But what event exactly?

Frowning down at the body, Conan tried to determine if it was possible the abbot had merely slipped off the wooden commode built into the side of the wall and struck his head as he fell. Perhaps he'd had a seizure of some kind, fainted, and fell.

He bent closer over the body, not touching but looking carefully. Sir Raymond also peered intently.

"What do you think?" Conan asked.

"Could have been a fall." The knight sounded doubtful.

"But his head would have had to twist on the way down to hit there on the side like that."

"Aye, it would have had to do that."

"On the other hand, if someone came in here suddenly, taking him by surprise, and he started to rise, the blow could have landed just like that."

As he spoke, Conan mimicked the action, lifting his arm, swinging it down to where the abbot would have been sitting.

"Especially if he'd turned his head toward whoever was entering," Sir Raymond said.

"To see who it was."

"He wouldn't have expected anyone coming in here."

No, Conan thought, he wouldn't have. Alone among the residents of the abbey, Du Sully had enjoyed a fair measure of privacy. He would have expected it to be respected. Certainly, the last place he would have thought an intruder might come was into his own garderobe.

"So," he said, straightening, "another murder."

Sir Raymond nodded. "It does seem that way. Mistress Alianor—"

"Was with me." And was now back in her cottage on the island. He knew that because she had told him she would be there. Trusting her, and knowing she trusted him, certainly made everything easier.

"Then who?" Sir Raymond asked. He was frowning.

"I have absolutely no idea but you'll admit he had more than his share of enemies."

"It could be anyone in the village."

There was a disturbance at the door to the garderobe. FitzWilliam pushed his way in. The sheriff looked pale and was sweating as though he had ridden hard, which Conan supposed he had.

"I thought you'd be on your way back to Bath," he said as FitzWilliam gaped at the body.

"I was—one of the monks caught up with me. My God—"

"He's dead."

The sheriff had been going down on his knees as though to determine that for himself, or perhaps even to try to render aid. He froze, pulling his hand back. "He is, isn't he?"

"Very. Getting the side of your skull smashed in generally does that."

"Mistress Alianor—"

"Is fine, thank you for asking."

FitzWilliam reddened. "I'm not suggesting for a moment that she had anything to do with this."

"Good. She was with me all night." That was mainly true. At least he could account for her whereabouts every moment.

The sheriff's mouth flapped just like a fish's. "She—"

"You heard me and woe betide the man who suggests otherwise. As to who killed Du Sully, I suggest you make a list of everyone in Glastonbury and start at the top."

FitzWilliam took on a dazed look as he contemplated doing that. "This has to stop, these killings. A town can't go on like this."

"I imagine it will stop fairly soon. Now if you'll excuse me, I have things to do." Conan stepped over the abbot's body and walked toward the door.

"Wait," FitzWilliam said. "You mean you're just leaving?"

"There isn't a great deal I can do here, is there? Besides, I'm sure you have it all under control."

In fact, Conan had no idea what, if anything, FitzWilliam would do but he also didn't care. The monk who had found Du Sully's body when the abbot failed to appear for matins was standing just outside the garderobe. He was an older man, hunched and pale, who looked as though he might be sick at any moment.

"You should sit down," Conan said to him, not unkindly. When the man merely stared, too dazed to respond, Conan pushed him gently onto a stool. He got down on his haunches so that he could look at him eye to eye. "Tell me again what happened."

Trained to obedience, the monk replied, "I came to find Father Abbot. The bells were ringing for matins and he wasn't in chapel." His eyes widened as though

it had suddenly occurred to him that he might be accused of an impropriety. "I would never have entered
the garderobe without permission but the door was
partly open and when I passed by, I caught a glimpse
of a—body. When I looked farther, I saw him lying—"
His voice broke. He shuddered and put his hands to
his face.

Conan rose. He patted the monk's shoulder, scant
comfort but he thought he had to do something. The
man would be all right, he supposed, but if he wasn't,
there was little to be done about it. As he turned, he
found Brother Wynn watching. The young sacristan
looked somber and deeply saddened.

"I will tend to Brother Francis," he said.

Conan nodded. He went out into the radiance of
midday. The sky was clear of any cloud, the air fragrant and soft. He started down the hill on foot, not-
ing as he did the small group of townspeople gathered
near the bottom. They seemed unwilling to come any
closer to the abbey. They made way for him without
speaking but he felt their eyes follow him on into the
town.

He'd left Gray at the inn stables. His intention was
to fetch the stallion and ride out to the island to tell
Alianor what had happened and enlist her help. Without it, he had no hope of solving this latest killing. Not
for a moment did he believe the timing of Abbot Du
Sully's death was a coincidence. It was a direct response to his attempt to convict her of witchcraft. The
only question was who had sought such effective
vengeance—a townsman or -woman whose loyalty to
Alianor went a shade too far, or someone driven to
commit murder for some other reason? The notion of
vengeance was easy to grasp but it sat uneasily on
Conan. Du Sully had been beaten, even humiliated by

Alianor. How much urge would the townspeople have
still had to kill him?

Yet dead he was and there was no denying it. Someone had crept into that garderobe, taken him by surprise, and smashed his skull in, leaving him to bleed to
death on the stone floor.

Mounted on Gray, he headed out along the road
that led over the bridge toward the lake. The normal
back-and-forth traffic of the busy town was lacking
this morning. People were huddled together in groups,
talking among themselves. He saw no one as he entered the fringe of trees just beyond the common fields
and continued along the track to the lake.

He was within a quarter mile of it when he saw the
shape lying across the road. Gray shied slightly as
Conan reined him in. He sat for a moment in the saddle, staring at the dark, crumpled bundle.

A body. Lying there right across the track.

Sweet heaven, was there no end to this?

Dismounting in a single, lithe motion, he quieted
Gray with a word and moved forward cautiously. The
body appeared to be male. He couldn't see the face but
the clothes suggested a farmer or some such, a com-
moner who was neither poor nor rich. And young, he
thought—judging by the breadth of the shoulders, well
set up, healthy.

Except for possibly being dead, of course.

He knelt and reached out to touch the man's shoulder. He meant to turn him as carefully as possible, get
a look at his face, try to determine what had happened. But he never had the chance.

The blow that struck his head came from behind. He
neither heard nor saw his assailant before blinding
pain exploded behind his eyes and hurtled him into
darkness.

* * *

Alianor stood at the window of the cottage looking out toward the lake. It would be evening soon and there was no sign of Conan. She drew her shawl more closely around her and sighed. Fiona was munching on oats under the shelter. She, at least, seemed content. So did Mirabelle, lying before the fire, well fed on fresh fish and cream.

Contentment was not what Alianor felt. She had assumed Conan would come to her long before this. Where was he? What could be keeping him? Surely he knew she would be consumed by curiosity. If she couldn't actually help, couldn't he spare a moment to at least let her know what was going on?

She moved away from the window but could find no occupation for herself. She wasn't hungry, tired, or thirsty. If she tried to work, sorting herbs or preparing medicines, she was certain she would only make mistakes. There was nothing she could do until Conan came except sit and wait, and she was singularly bad at both.

Swirling eddies of pain and the hard feel of ground beneath his face drew Conan back into the world. He lay unmoving for several minutes, trying to remember what had happened to him and get some sense of where he was.

He was outside. He could feel a slight breeze moving his clothes. He was lying directly on the ground, slightly moist from a recent shower. His head still felt as though it were going to come off, but he could hear movement around him and when he opened his eyes a crack, he could see.

Specifically, he saw an ant crawling over a lump of dirt directly in front of his nose. That ant, struggling up what must have seemed like a high hill to it and lumbering down the other side, fascinated him for the space of several heartbeats. He was utterly focused on it until it reached the other side and disappeared into a tiny channel leading down into the soil.

A horse neighed. Gray, somewhere very nearby. The urge to try to jump up and reach his horse was almost irresistible, the result of long years on battlefields where an unhorsed man was usually a dead man. But he resisted, knowing he'd never make it.

There were others close by him. He could make out the sound of someone drinking and another person walking back and forth, crunching small twigs under his boots. There were more, too, he thought, although he couldn't count them. He heard murmured voices, breathing, all the usual signs of humans that he rarely noticed except when he had to.

One of them was very young. He could hear that in the higher-pitched timber of his voice and the evident uncertainty.

"Think he's going to be all right then?"

"It was hardly more than a tap. He'll be fine."

The second voice was older, gruffer, casually assured. Conan frowned. Some tap.

"Maybe we should've just asked him to come along nicelike and he would have." The young one again.

"Oh, right you are there. Please, Baron Wyndham, won't you come with us outlaw rebels so we can all have a nice wee chat? Yes, indeed, that would have done the trick." A third man, not as old as the second, tired with a fine edge of anger and worry to him. Also possibly the leader. Leader of outlaw rebels. It seemed he had found Alianor's patient.

He took a breath, another, ignoring the pain, willing it away. His body responded. Strength flowed through him. In a breath he moved, coming up off the ground into a low crouch, whistling for Gray.

Foolishly they hadn't tethered the stallion. He broke

into a trot, exactly as he had been trained to do, and came directly between Conan and the men who were even then reaching for their weapons and cursing his sudden recovery.

His sword was missing but the knife he kept in his saddle was right where it was supposed to be. He had it in his hand and was mounting before they could fall on him. Still, they tried, he had to give them credit for that. Three, maybe four of them tried to bring him down. They might even have succeeded but for the sudden shouted order of the leader.

"Let him be! I need him alive."

Alive? Well, now that was interesting news. Still and all, he preferred to contemplate it from Gray's back. In the saddle, knife in hand, he surveyed the men who had brought him here.

There were more than he'd thought, at least two dozen, all held in check only by their leader's command. For the most part, they were seasoned men, strong, well armed, with the look of those to whom battle is no stranger. But there was also a boy, the young one he'd heard, who appeared pale and shocked by the sudden turn of events.

Conan addressed him. "What's your name, lad?"

The boy glanced at a tall, blond man nearby, as though looking for permission to answer. The man nodded almost imperceptibly.

"Jeremy, milord."

"You're the one who was lying in the road, the one I went to help."

Jeremy had the grace to look abashed. "Aye, milord, I was but I was only—"

"Helping to ambush me. Now that we're straight on all that, who would you be?" That question was flung at the blond man who stood, seemingly at his ease, eyeing him with what looked remarkably like amusement.

"Take a good look at him, lads," the man said. "That's the flower of Norman manhood before you. A warrior to the bone, proud as Lucifer, and not about to give an inch to anyone."

"I'm English, actually," Conan said, "but why quibble. What brings an Irishman to these parts?"

"A yearning to see the wider world?"

"Or a yearning to see what kind of mischief could be stirred up? I see you've been recently injured."

The man glanced down at his arm. "Aye, but healing nicely and that brings us to why you're here. If you'll get off that fine bit of horseflesh, I'd like a private word with you."

"And why would I want to listen?"

"Because it involves a certain young woman I've been hearing you seem fond of. She saved my life so I'm in her debt. I'd like to see that paid before it's too late."

"Too late—?"

"Get off the horse. For God's sake, man, if I'd wanted to kill you, you'd be stone cold by now."

He did have a point. Slowly Conan kicked his feet free of the stirrups and slid a leg over. He dismounted but didn't let go of Gray's reins or the knife.

"Fine, bring him along if you want." The man stalked off toward the trees. The others stayed behind.

Conan followed. When they were perhaps twenty yards from the encampment, the man stopped. He rubbed his right arm absently, as though to ease the lingering hurt.

"My name is Godwin, by the way. Godwin Haroldson."

Not Irish then but Saxon, or at least by family tradition. "Ancient names," Conan said, "with a proud lineage."

The man looked mildly surprised. "So you aren't totally ignorant then. Well, that's something. I came over to take a look around for myself, judge the lay of the land as it were. See what might be done."

"See if a little rebellion might go a long way?"

"Aye, something like that. Richard's a fool to stay gone so long."

"Richard is king."

Godwin shrugged. "I'll not debate that with you. There's no time. Look, a man in my position takes help where he can get it but that's not to say there aren't limits. The healer—Alianor, Lady of the Lake, whatever they call her—I believe she's in grave danger."

Conan's chest tightened. In the shadow of the oak trees, looking into the face of the man who recalled a lineage older than Alianor's own and possibly more dangerous, he asked the only question that mattered.

"From where?"

Quietly Godwin told him.

Chapter 33

She couldn't stand it anymore. The waiting was misery. Alianor gave up trying to drink the cup of herbal tea she had finally made for herself and went outside. It would be dark soon. She was deeply worried about Conan and the whole situation.

Gazing up at the night sky through the leafing trees, she tried to summon patience. She had told him she would be on the island, knowing he would regard that as a promise. It was one she intended to keep but sweet heaven, it was hard! To do nothing, to simply wait, ran so counter to her life and her nature that it was all but unbearable.

He had to come soon. He couldn't possibly leave her like this much longer. Any minute, she would hear Gray fording the lake, see horse and rider come out of the darkness. He would be there with her, to hold her and tell her all, and then—

She sighed deeply and turned to go back inside. But even as she did so, she heard a faint splash, followed by another. Hope surged through her. Grabbing the torch from beside the door, she ran down toward the lake.

In the gathering darkness, she could just make out the shape of a horse and rider. When both were a little more than halfway across, she called out.

"Conan, where have you been? I've been so worried."

There was no response. Surprised, she thought perhaps he hadn't heard her. A moment later the moon drifted out from behind a cloud and the first faint sense of unease stirred in her.

It wasn't Conan. The rider wasn't quite so tall or well built, and he didn't sit the saddle quite so easily. He had sent someone else.

She waited, silent now, until the horse emerged from the water. Lifting her torch, she stared into the face of her visitor.

"Brother Wynn?" What in God's name was the sacristan doing here? How had a monk of the abbey found the gall to venture onto her island?

He nodded politely as he dismounted. "Your pardon, lady. I'm sorry to come without warning. But his lordship, Baron Wyndham, sent me to fetch you. He's concerned about your safety."

"My safety? But why—?"

"I don't know exactly, he didn't say. But the abbot is dead and the baron is very worried about what will happen next. He asks that you come to the abbey."

"He's there?"

"Aye, he is. There are strange things happening, my lady. It would be best for you not to be alone."

"Why didn't Baron Wyndham send one of his own men?"

"They are busy searching for some rebel outlaw, mistress. Apparently, the baron believes this man may be planning to attack the abbey to claim the bodies found there. Please, it would be best to make haste."

Alianor hesitated. What he said was believable enough, if very alarming. She had told Conan she would stay on the island but if he himself was sending for her—

"I'll go," she said suddenly. "I just need to saddle Fiona."

Brother Wynn nodded gravely. "Allow me to do that for you, my lady. Perhaps you would like to bring some supplies, medicinal herbs and the like in case worse should come to worst."

Alianor agreed. She had to hope no such preparations would be needed but if the rebels actually attacked, there would be wounded to care for, if not worse. She directed Brother Wynn to where she kept Fiona's tack, then hurried inside to put together a basket. Barely a quarter hour after he arrived, Alianor and the sacristan left the island together.

The abbey appeared very quiet, wrapped in night. "The baron's men are hidden," Brother Wynn explained in a whisper. He helped Alianor dismount. "The sooner you are inside, the better, mistress."

Despite the warmth of her cloak, Alianor shivered. She was anxious to see Conan and hear from him that everything would be all right.

"This way," Brother Wynn said. He opened the scarred wooden door and stood aside for Alianor to enter. As soon as she did so, he closed the door behind them and slid the heavy iron bar into place.

She looked around, surprised to still see no one. "Where are—"

"In the chapel. The attack may be imminent. If you please, my lady—" He gestured toward the small, arched opening that led to the chapel. "You will be safest there."

Her own safety was not paramount in Alianor's mind but she did as he bid. Conan must be somewhere nearby, organizing his men. She didn't want him to be fretting about her.

"Will you tell the baron I'm here?" she asked as she glanced around the chapel. The remains found in the

grave were still in place before the altar but now they
had been joined by the body of the abbot. Du Sully lay
on a plain piece of wood draped with a cloth that
might have been taken from the refectory table. There
hadn't been time to make a coffin. Several tall white
candles stood in iron holders around his body but no
monks kept vigil.

"My brothers are exhausted," Brother Wynn said.
"And truthfully, they are also badly demoralized. I
hadn't the heart to ask anyone to stay here."

Alianor nodded. She supposed that made sense but
Conan had been careful to keep a guard on the remains ever since they were discovered. He was determined that they wouldn't be tampered with. Was the
crisis truly so grave that he hadn't been able to leave
even a single man-at-arms on watch?

The back of her neck prickled. She walked closer to
the bodies, putting some distance between herself and
Wynn. But the chapel was very small. She couldn't get
far from him.

"Where is the baron?" she asked.

"I told you, mistress, with his men." Torches set in
brackets around the walls flickered as a draft blew in
under the door. In their wavering light, the sacristan
smiled. "At least, I suppose he's with some of them. In
fact, I have no idea."

With deliberate calmness, Alianor set down her basket. "Then you lied."

"I've lied about a great many things but I assure
you, it's always been in a good cause."

"Which would be—?"

He drew himself erect, staring at her down the
length of the small aisle. "The freedom of this land and
the dignity of its people. The time is long passed when
we should have erased the Norman oppressor, thrown
him back into the sea, and reclaimed our heritage for

ourselves. Our failure to do that is merely the result of poor leadership but I can change that. I *will* change it."

Her chest was very tight but she managed to keep her voice steady. "Grandiose notions for a humble monk."

"Entering the clergy was useful. It took me places I needed to go and put me in contact with the right people. But it also provided me with ample opportunity to see for myself the damage foreign rule does to us. Over a century ago, the pope conspired with William the Bastard to put the Normans in control here. Church and crown alike are equally to blame, and both must be cleansed."

"You seem very well informed." She wasn't entirely flattering him. Wynn was clearly an educated man and his interpretation of the events surrounding the Normans coming to England was correct, so far as she knew.

"Mine is a very old family. Although our lands were stripped from us we retained our memories. I was raised on them."

Raised on hatred, from the sound of it. Generations of anger and humiliation handed down from parent to child, dripped like acid on the most impressionable souls. The thought made her stomach churn.

"What leader will do this cleansing," she asked. "You?"

His smile thinned. "I'm hardly that naive. Two years ago I became aware of the existence of an heir to the Anglo-Saxon dynasty in Ireland. I found a reason to visit there and meet with him. He is cautious but possibly willing to undertake the task. My challenge has been to convince him that the people are willing to support an uprising."

"Starting here in Glastonbury?"

"Where better? I hardly have to tell you what this place means to our ancient heritage."

Alianor did not reply directly. She wasn't about to tell him anything, not even to confirm his suspicions. "You killed them, didn't you?" Some part of her needed to hear him say it but she also wanted to keep him talking. Surely there was someone around, Conan's men, someone who would come along eventually.

"Not Brother Bertrand, although I admit it was his death that gave me the idea. Du Sully hated you. He didn't hesitate to grab hold of the idea that you were somehow responsible." Almost pleasantly, he added, "You know, you really ought to thank me for disposing of him. Despite that very clever trick you pulled, he wasn't ready to give up. He was quite mad on the subject of witches."

"What trick?" How much exactly did Wynn know about poisons and where could he have learned it?

"The paternoster peas, of course. Don't think for a moment that I fail to appreciate the daring of that. It really wasn't until then that I realized what a worthy adversary you are."

"It seems as though I can say the same. Do you mind my asking where you learned so much?" She was only distantly curious but she would ask him anything, do anything, to gain time. Someone had to come eventually. But time, she suspected, was very fleeting. Wynn hadn't brought her here to chat.

"My grandmother had some training," he said grudgingly, as though it wasn't the sort of thing he talked about very often. "Scattered bits and pieces, really, but she got me started. The rest I learned on my own in my travels."

"I suspect you're being modest. I still have no idea how you killed Brother Raspin and Master Longueford."

He looked pleased. "You really don't? Come now, you examined the merchant and the baron took a close enough look at Raspin. Surely you can guess."

"They were poisoned."

"That's obvious, you don't get any credit for that."

"I've eliminated dozens of possibilities because they wouldn't have worked quickly enough or some evidence of them would have remained."

"And you're left with—"

Alianor thought. She had some schooling in such matters but obviously not as much as Brother Wynn had acquired. Even so, she was hard-pressed to puzzle it out.

A possibility flitted through her mind. She caught hold of the tail end of it and followed where it led. "I've been thinking in terms of something those men ate or drank but that wouldn't necessarily be true, would it? Brother Raspin was working in the garden when he died. It was his usual job. You would have known when he'd be there and what he would be doing. Master Longueford was studying his accounts. There, too, you could have predicted what he would be handling."

"And therefore—"

"It was something they touched. A tool in Brother Raspin's case, a scroll or perhaps a pen in Master Longueford's. The poison entered through their skin, minimizing any chance of vomiting or diarrhea, but they showed no sign of pain either and all the poisons that act through the skin cause extreme suffering—"

She broke off, staring at him. He looked so very ordinary—a well-built, pleasant enough young man in the habit of a monk. The kind of person anyone would pass and either think nothing of or notice kindly. And yet—

"They were paralyzed," she said. "That's why their

faces showed no indication of what had happened to them. They couldn't cry out or move, or even alter their expressions."

"Very good," Brother Wynn said. "But you have to get it all. What specifically did it?"

She was heartsick. The truth of what had happened to those two men was even more terrible than she had thought. But their pain seemed to mean nothing to the sacristan.

"Monkshood," she said. "I won't comment on the obvious irony of your choice. The leaves and roots are extremely poisonous. Any contact with them can be deadly."

"Why didn't you find any traces on the skin?"

"You must have found a way to contain the poison with a thin liquid. By the time the bodies were found, it had disappeared."

He grinned and sketched her a courtly bow. "I congratulate you. For that matter, I congratulate myself. It took me years to develop a liquid that was deadly within minutes but dried away into the air in a very short time. I use a variety of monkshood found in the northern Italian provinces. For reasons unknown to me, it is even deadlier than its more common cousins."

"Is there any particular reason you set out to develop such a poison?"

He thought for a moment, apparently wanting to give her an honest answer. "The challenge amused me but I did consider that I might need it someday. You see, my plans have been developing for a very long time."

"To bring civil war back to England and hope that in all the resulting turmoil a dynasty will fall?"

"To offer my people a clear choice," he corrected, "between reclaiming their heritage or continuing to bow before a foreign oppressor. Henry was just a good enough king for people to tolerate him but he's dead now and his loathsome son wears the crown. When the people of Glastonbury rise up and burn this abbey, Godwin Haroldson will see the flame of his destiny. He will know that his time has come. Moreover, the French will know it. They will send men and money to support him. Before Richard even has a chance to get back here, it will all be over."

"Is this a dream or do you know for a fact that the French stand ready?"

He shook his head, as though saddened by her doubt. "My dear lady, do you honestly think I didn't look to the political realities? War is expensive. It requires both blood and gold. The French will supply the latter and pay for some of the former. We'll do the rest."

Bile rose in her throat. She swallowed hard and slipped a hand into her basket. Her cloak, falling open, concealed the movement. "I hesitate to ask but why exactly would the people of Glastonbury decide to burn the abbey?"

"When their beloved Lady of the Lake is found dead here, obviously killed by the monks in revenge for the death of their abbot, the townspeople won't hesitate. They've been longing to finish the place off for years. This will give them the perfect excuse."

There was only one door to the chapel and he stood between her and it. The windows were cut into the stone wall near the ceiling. She had no hope of reaching them.

Wynn saw her glance at them and sighed. "You would be wise to simply accept this. I can do it quickly and, I promise, virtually painlessly. I won't use the monkshood; I have no intention of that. There has to be blood, you see, to incite them properly. But you needn't suffer." He came toward her. From within the sleeve of his robe he withdrew a thin, gleaming stiletto. "The Italians are so clever, don't you think? One stab to the heart or the base of the neck with this, and it will be over. Think of how it would have felt if you'd gone to the stake or if the paternoster peas had been broken open inside you. For that matter, think of the toll of old age or childbirth if it were to ever come to that for you. There are so many terrible ways to die and this way is so easy."

Alianor backed away from him, holding her basket tightly. He was quite mad, she knew that now, but the knowledge did her no good. Time had run out. She gathered her breath—and her courage—and screamed.

"Conan!"

She hadn't really thought to call his name but it just came out. Tears threatened as a wave of longing ripped through her, riding side by side with terror. To never see him again, never feel his body against hers, never know the joy of simply being with him.

Life, always sweet, had never been more precious to her. She could not bear the thought of parting from it in service of a madman.

"That won't do you any good," Wynn said sternly. "I've barred the door and even if anyone hears you, which I doubt, they won't be able to get in."

"But you won't be able to escape either. You'll be caught and they'll kill you."

"What if they do? What I've set in motion won't be stopped. However, I should tell you there is a way out of here. I discovered it by accident when I was planning how to arrange for the bodies to be found." He gestured toward the ancient wooden log and the bones it enclosed. "There's an ancient crypt under this building with a passage to the outside. I will shortly use it to remove myself. Now enough of this. You grow wearisome."

"Wait! You're saying you actually found those bodies under this building?"

"I was clear on that, wasn't I? Stop trying to delay me. I—"

"They aren't Arthur and Guinevere. He is buried elsewhere and I have no idea what happened to her."

"Interesting that you're so certain about him. It confirms what I've suspected all along about you."

"Which is?"

"That you're the real thing. The genuine heir to the tradition of the Lady of the Lake. The latest link in the chain forged down through all the centuries. In a way, it's a shame to have to break it now, but there's really no alternative. The bodies will burn with you. No trace of them will be left. When Godwin Haroldson calls upon the people to rise, word will spread that he was healed by you. How long do you think it will be before the two tales become entwined—the body of Arthur found, restored to life by the magic that lingered here all this time exactly for that purpose? The King who was and will be returned to claim his rightful throne. It's irresistible."

"It's insane."

"Oh, I knew you'd say that eventually but it isn't worthy of you. My reason isn't in question. Yours is." From the pocket of his robe, he withdrew a small vial. "Do you really prefer the monkshood? If this touches you, you will feel intense pain, followed by cold and paralysis. You won't be able to move but you will be aware of everything. You will know as your breathing slowly stops as the muscles cease to work. You will be conscious to the very end and I assure you, it will be agonizing."

"Then I suppose I'd best avoid it," Alianor said. She felt cold already, struck through by terror, but she couldn't let that affect her. Matilda had schooled her to courage, warning that any woman embarked on their path in life would need it. She had never done so more than now.

Her hand snaked deeper into the basket, closing around a small stone container. With one finger, she flipped the lid open. In an instant she dropped the basket and flung the contents of the container at Wynn.

He screamed. Too late, his hands flew to his eyes to protect them. The lye had fallen just short, striking him across the bridge of the nose, but his vision was damaged at least temporarily.

Alianor ran. She darted around Wynn and raced for the door. Frantically she tried to raise the bar across it. Her fear strengthened her but the bar was very heavy. Struggling, she gasped for breath as she managed to get it halfway up.

Only halfway, not far enough to get the door open. Wynn blinked furiously. His face was covered with ugly red blotches, his mouth twisted in a snarl.

"Du Sully was right, you are a witch. But you'll die all the same." The stiletto gleamed in his hand. He raised it, aiming directly at Alianor's heart.

Something flew through the air behind him. Something very large and dark that struck him straight on and knocked him to the ground. For a moment Alianor had the stunning thought that a great bird had sailed into the chapel to do battle with her would-be killer. She seemed to hear the whish of mighty wings and see a flash of midnight dark plumage.

No, not plumage. Hair. Conan stood before her, attired in black as she had seen him on the hillside, his head gleaming in the torchlight, his sword singing a battle chant as it left the scabbard.

"Get back," he said to her and advanced on Wynn.

She stumbled against the wall even as the sacristan vaulted to his feet and came at Conan. The stiletto was back in his hand. Madness gleamed in his eyes. If he was going to die, he would not do it alone.

In his travels Wynn had apparently studied more than the fine art of poisoning. He managed to avoid Conan's first slash. Cautiously the two men maneuvered around each other. Wynn had the knife grasped for throwing but he still had to get closer to find an opening. Conan was determined not to give it. Or so Alianor thought. Minutes into the fight, she saw with horror that Conan seemed to have dropped his guard.

Wynn saw it, too. With a hideous grin, he took aim and hurled the knife straight and true, directly at the center of Conan's chest. Alianor cried out. In the shadows of the chapel, the air seemed to bend. One moment Conan was firmly in the path of the knife. The next he was not. The weapon whispered past him harmlessly, inches from flesh.

Wynn stared in disbelief. "I had you—"

The look on Conan's face made Alianor put her hand to her mouth. His skin was pulled taut, his eyes merciless. In an instant she knew this was a part of him she had never seen—the warlord, prince of battles. The man who would kill to protect what was his.

Quietly she said, "He murdered Brother Raspin and Master Longueford, as well as Du Sully."

"I know," Conan replied and brought the sword down.

The chapel door stood thrown open. The room was filled with Conan's men. Exclamations—and explanations—flew back and forth. Alianor heard little of them. She leaned against Conan's chest, keeping her eyes averted from what had been the mad sacristan, and simply waited for it all to be over. They would be able to leave soon, to go somewhere to be alone. She would be able then to truly convince herself he was all right, and she was, too.

Conan sighed deeply. She felt the mighty rise and fall of his chest against her cheek. Fingers curled beneath her chin. He lifted her head until she looked directly at him.

His face was his own again. The one she knew and cherished. The man of intelligence, gentleness, and joyful passion.

"Please don't misunderstand," her dear Conan said, "but there are times I really wish you were a quiet little woman who would stay where she was put."

Through the tears that were at last beginning to flow, she looked up at him. At the core of her vast love for this man lay the certainty of truth. "I'm never going to be that."

"It's all right," he said and oddly didn't sound as though he minded much. Ignoring his men who were busy looking the other way, he lifted her into his arms and carried her out into the star-streaked night.

Epilogue

 "Your obedient servant, Conan, Baron of Wyndham."

Eleanor lowered the parchment scroll on which the message was written. She gazed out the Tower window at the river beyond, but hardly saw the busy flow of barques, dories, and rafts, the surging traffic of the great city.

All in all, she was well pleased with the results of her decision to send the Baron of Wyndham to Glastonbury. Later in the day, after she had met with the various ministers who required her attention, she would pen a letter to his mother telling him of her satisfaction.

His report on the final denouement had been succinct—the abbot and sacristan dead, the rebel leader departed for parts unknown, the supposed bodies of King Arthur and his Guinevere secured. And, oh, yes, that last part—*Lady Alianor and I will be arriving in London soon and pray audience with you on a matter of a personal nature.*

The queen smiled. Sweet, blissful May—so fondly remembered from her own young womanhood—was the perfect month for all sorts of adventure. She missed her own daughters dreadfully and barely knew her granddaughters. Perhaps it was time to remedy that and any other things left undone through the long years. The past could never be recaptured but there was still the future to be seized. She was, after all, still shy of seventy.

She rolled the parchment and tucked it into her surcoate. A moment longer, she gazed out at the river, the vast, triumphant ribbon of empire leading down to the endless sea. Still staring at it, she clapped her hands, summoning servants. The day was young and there was so very much to be done.

Author's Note

This is a tale told in that realm where rumor, romance, speculation and the bite of slander engage to entertain us. Of all the mysteries of the Middle Ages, Eleanor herself is among the greatest. She was a woman who broke all the rules of her world not so much with impunity as with flair. She married two kings, gave birth to two more and spent a good deal of her life reigning supreme in her own kingdoms of Poitou and Aquitaine.

No other woman through all the centuries even to the present time commands the stage as Eleanor does. She inspired poets, helped to create the very form of romantic literature we enjoy today, and changed the fate of not one but two nations. And she lived to be eighty-two, despite at least ten pregnancies, one crusade, and numerous plots against her.

Was Eleanor a witch?

There is strong evidence that pre-Christian worship continued throughout Europe during these years and for several centuries thereafter. Knowledge the church tried to suppress—especially medical knowledge—was kept alive by the so-called cunny (cunning or wise) women. Particular places, e.g. the Langue d'Oc region that was Eleanor's domain, were said to shelter keepers of such knowledge, practitioners of the old ways.

Was the Queen one such? We know she took a notably pragmatic approach toward religion, viewing the clergy with suspicion and when necessary, challenging its members even including the Pope. She endowed several abbeys but these seemed intended primarily to serve as shelters for women in need. No writings of her own survive but those inspired by her are unabashedly worldly, sensual and bold. No hint of religious fervor is to be found in them.

What Eleanor knew—and what she believed—will never be known any more than will the truth of Glastonbury. Did the monks there really discover the tomb of Arthur and in doing so, firmly identify the ancient tor with Avalon? Or was theirs a contrivance, designed to raise funds for the abbey rebuilding and perhaps please a royal house tired of Welsh rebels claiming that Arthur would return to champion them?

For years, historians dismissed the Glastonbury find as a forgery. But in the early 1960s, a new archaeological dig determined that Glastonbury had indeed been an island in earlier times and that the monks had dug where they claimed, reaching a stratum of very early burials. Further, the cross they supposedly found uses Latin spelling and iconography of an archaic form prevalent five hundred years before the monk's discovery (at about the time historians agree Arthur lived) but not in use from that time to theirs.

In 1275, an earthquake destroyed the abbey. Several years later, Edward I ordered the re-interment of the royal bodies in a new tomb where they remained, a major pilgrimage site, until the destruction of the abbey during the reign of Henry VIII. Today, their where-abouts are unknown.

Avalon remains, as perhaps it always should, a mystery.

WE NEED YOUR HELP

To continue to bring you quality romance
that meets your personal expectations,
we at TOPAZ books want to hear from you.
Help us by filling out this questionnaire, and in exchange
we will give you a **free gift** as a token of our gratitude.

- Is this the first TOPAZ book you've purchased? (circle one)

    YES   NO

    The title and author of this book is: _____

- If this was not the first TOPAZ book you've purchased, how many have you bought in the past year?

    a: 0 - 5   b 6 - 10   c: more than 10   d: more than 20

- How many romances in total did you buy in the past year?

    a: 0 - 5   b: 6 - 10   c: more than 10   d: more than 20 _____

- How would you rate your overall satisfaction with this book?

    a: Excellent   b: Good   c: Fair   d: Poor

- What was the main reason you bought this book?

    a: It is a TOPAZ novel, and I know that TOPAZ stands
        for quality romance fiction
    b: I liked the cover
    c: The story-line intrigued me
    d: I love this author
    e: I really liked the setting
    f: I love the cover models
    g: Other: _____

- Where did you buy this TOPAZ novel?

    a: Bookstore   b: Airport   c: Warehouse Club
    d: Department Store   e: Supermarket   f: Drugstore
    g: Other: _____

- Did you pay the full cover price for this TOPAZ novel? (circle one)

    YES   NO

    If you did not, what price did you pay? _____

- Who are your favorite TOPAZ authors? (Please list)

- How did you first hear about TOPAZ books?

    a: I saw the books in a bookstore
    b: I saw the TOPAZ Man on TV or at a signing
    c: A friend told me about TOPAZ
    d: I saw an advertisement in_____magazine
    e: Other: _____

- What type of romance do you generally prefer?

    a: Historical   b: Contemporary
    c: Romantic Suspense   d: Paranormal (time travel,
        futuristic, vampires, ghosts, warlocks, etc.)
    d: Regency   e: Other: _____

- What historical settings do you prefer?

    a: England   b: Regency England   c: Scotland
    e: Ireland   f: America   g: Western Americana
    h: American Indian   i: Other: _____

- What type of story do you prefer?

  a: Very sexy   b: Sweet, less explicit
  c: Light and humorous d: More emotionally intense
  e: Dealing with darker issues f: Other

- What kind of covers do you prefer?

  a: Illustrating both hero and heroine b: Hero alone
  c: No people (art only)   d: Other_____

- What other genres do you like to read (circle all that apply)

Mystery	Medical Thrillers	Science Fiction
Suspense	Fantasy	Self-help
Classics	General Fiction	Legal Thrillers
Historical Fiction		

- Who is your favorite author, and why?_____

  _____

- What magazines do you like to read? (circle all that apply)

  a: *People*   b: *Time/Newsweek*
  c: *Entertainment Weekly* d: *Romantic Times*
  e: *Star*   f: *National Enquirer*
  g: *Cosmopolitan*   h: *Woman's Day*
  i: *Ladies' Home Journal* j: *Redbook*
  k: Other:_____

- In which region of the United States do you reside?

  a: Northeast b: Midatlantic c: South
  d: Midwest   e: Mountain f: Southwest
  g: Pacific Coast

- What is your age group/sex? a: Female b: Male

  a: under 18 b: 19-25 c: 26-30 d: 31-35 e: 56-60
  f: 41-45   g: 46-50 h: 51-55 i: 56-60 j: Over 60

- What is your marital status?

  a: Married b: Single c: No longer married

- What is your current level of education?

  a: High school   b: College Degree
  c: Graduate Degree d: Other: _____

- Do you receive the TOPAZ *Romantic Liaisons* newsletter, a quarterly newsletter with the latest information on Topaz books and authors?

  YES   NO

  If not, would you like to? YES   NO

  Fill in the address where you would like your free gift to be sent:

  Name:_____

  Address:_____

  City:_____Zip Code:_____

  You should receive your free gift in 6 to 8 weeks.
  Please send the completed survey to:

  Penguin USA•Mass Market
  Dept. TS
  375 Hudson St.
  New York, NY 10014